T0370437

My Oprah: Recreating the Legacy

Building a Community

HELEN J. COLLIER

authorHOUSE®

AuthorHouse™
1663 Liberty Drive
Bloomington, IN 47403
www.authorhouse.com
Phone: 833-262-8899

Published by AuthorHouse   05/22/2024

ISBN: 979-8-8230-2592-8 (sc)
ISBN: 979-8-8230-2593-5 (e)

Library of Congress Control Number: 2024908935

Print information available on the last page.

This book is printed on acid-free paper.

Sometimes, our most important deeds enhance the lives of people we will never meet or even know. Something you say or do at any critical moment may change the path of another human life forever. Great minds do not narrow their vision. They broaden theirs and others.

Helen J. Collier

Helencolliermeow.com

This book is a tribute to Oprah Winfrey.
My daughter challenged me to
write a book showing her favorite celebrity in the best possible light.
Which is as she sees her and has been written to honor her as One
Black Female American Pioneer of the 21st Century

I present this book to the American People as
the Holy Spirit has given it to me.

To Mrs. Verna Lynne Reese, thank you for your devotion to the final edition of this book!

In loving Memory
Of My Family

My sister Pearl Williams and sister-in-Law Mary Frances
Campell Mother Susie Pearl Adams-Green, Twin brother
Eugene Green &
My brothers Eugene and James Green
My Uncle Theodore Adams
&
Friends
Rev El Marie Mosley
Grace Cole
Clara Mae Bennett
Clara Frazier
Beatrice Foots
Associate Professor Jane C. Pennell, Southern
University of Edwardsville, Illinois

Contents

*G*od's Spirit in us moves us through this life, depending on our willingness to be led. I must acknowledge and be thankful for its presence in me to complete this challenge.

My mother, Susie Pearl Adams-Green loved my brother and me enough to carry us full term when it seemed as though she would burst at the seams. Thank you, Ma' Dear for the years you spent single-handedly making sure all your children survived their childhood. We all love you.

Eugene my twin brother pushed me out of the womb first so that he could get an extra fifteen minutes by himself while I slipped into an unforgiving world with no silver spoon in sight. I am now guided by his light and spirit as they guard the path of my journey through this life. Death has not taken him from me but given him to me as a gentle breeze warming my heart.

I remember one high school teacher telling us we would never amount to anything. She would be surprised to learn that we both finished college. Eugene went on to law school and served the city of Seattle as an attorney for fourteen years until his untimely death on December 30, 1998. My brother's spirit reminds me that when my faith is weak, I can always hit that tree standing ninety feet away if I keep my presence and stay focused. Also, I must never forget the plan. My Uncle Ted realized our potential and made college a reality in our lives, leading to a path of upward mobility.

On May 31, 2000, my mother was honored for thirty years of tireless work for the Children & Family Services department working with Children at risk, as you can see, the acorn does not fall too far from the tree. I have worked with children now for some Thirty plus years and with the Seattle King County Juvenile Detention Department over twenty-six of those years. It has been my pleasure to have helped change the path of many young people who felt the tree was too far away and the rock too small for them to throw such a long distance.

A very special thanks go out to my two co-workers, Tyrell Stewart, a creative writing teacher who guided the writing of this book, and Tanya Washington, who is responsible for the cover of my book. Richard W. Mohan critically read the manuscript for me.

To my dear friend Stephanie Owings Hatcher, a creative writing teacher, I salute you for your tireless efforts in keeping me focused while writing this book. You taught me how the spirit wanted this book written, again I thank you.

To the staff at Fed EX Kinko's in Fairview Heights, Ill, to staff Keri at Fed EX Kinko's in Federal, Washington, and to the East St. Louis Library thank you for your patience and help getting the copying I needed done for this book.

Staci Conley-Williams we traveled a long distance from the Arch dividing East St. Louis and St. Louis but we proved we could go the distance.

Margaret Campbell Duggins, Earnestine Blue, Rev Yvonne Gallaher, Bishop Marie Gallaher, Teresa Rhodes, Beatrice Foots, and Diane King thanks for your input and sense of direction.

Thanks to Beatrice Clark and her belief in my writings I have soared with the eagles. Thanks to the Renton Writer's Critic Group for many years of writing with fellow writers in Washington State. Thank you, Deborah, Brown you taught me how to create characters who are not afraid to speak, take a stand, and not give up.

Thanks to Professor Georgia McDade and the African American Alliance Association our public speaking was great fun.

To Deborah Jordan and Dale Golden thank you for seeing in me what I did not or could not see in myself. I have cared enough to dream and have taken the risk expecting nothing but God's grace in return.

Thank you for your unwavering belief in me. And for introducing me to editor Susan Seykato-Smith...

Thanks, Lee Davis the editor of the Regional Magazine who published many of my writings.

To Mrs. Ethel Mitchell, Lucille Perkins, and Mrs. Alexandria Ruth thank the three of you for your encouragement through the critical times in my life.

Thank you, Mr. Joe Greene, Mr. Hullet Gates, and all my co-workers at the Department of the Juvenile Detention Center for proving great things can be accomplished through prayer and the courage to take a stand.

Dr. Leslie Tregillus for your spirit of love and kindness you made a part of your medical treatment. Dr. David White thank you for your advice to look every day out of the window and see the sun shining even when it's raining.

Charlene Younge, it has been over twenty years now. Thank you for the care you have given my hair down through the years.

It was you Barbara Harrington my occupational Therapist who taught me how to hit the tree from one hundred feet away. You created that hundred-pound dummy for me to carry so I could return to work when some said it would be impossible.

To my sisters, Elsie Mister and Lavonda Dorsey thank you for always being around when I needed your support.

From you Attorney Judith Lonnquist I learned what it means to take risks even when the odds are against you.

Anthony Evans, thank you for teaching me the beauty of poetry. Had it not been for the dignity and respect given to me in your Court Room Judge Jim Rodger I would not have taken that task upon myself thank you and Attorney Val Carlsen, Fred Hyde, Guerry Hoddersen, and of course, Attorney Jared Karstetter for the support and help you have always given me. Attorney Andrew Carrington, I thank you for the years you have helped my family since the passing of my brother Attorney Eugene Green here in Seattle Washington.

I want to give special thanks to all my family members, friends, and supporters. Without your encouragement and support, I could not have completed this task, and want to thank each of you from the bottom of my heart.

Especially to my children Susie Brandley, Shenee Poe Johnnie Weslynn Duff, Cliffert Mylo Collier, and husband John W. Collier for supporting my writing.

Helen J. Collier

Introduction

At four o'clock in the evening, telephone ringers are turned off. Do not disturb signs are hung from the doorknobs of homes all over America. With remotes in hand to prevent accidental channel changes by spouses or TV-addicted children, those who love Oprah get ready for a relaxing evening in front of their television sets. It's time to visit with Oprah. Whether Oprah personifies every woman is a matter of opinion. That Oprah has changed the lives of thousands of both women and men is a fact. Her idea of giving and sharing has won her a special place in the hearts of many men, women, and even children all over the world.

Her visions are as broad as her arms are wide. Not everyone is a fan of Oprah but those who are not her fans must respect her determination and will to take care of her business. Through the years I have followed Oprah Winfrey's life from a distance, unlike my daughter Weslynn who loves her enough to keep up with her every chance she gets challenged me to write about her through the eyes of those who love her. When it comes to my passion for writing I am always open to a challenge I must admit, however, even my life, has been touched by this black woman who touched the lives of many people. It is not to speak of her perfections and not her flaws. We all have them. It is a human trait.

I often listen to my American friends, both men and women discuss Oprah's rise to fame and fortune. Many reasons are given for her success. Some are realistic, while others are from people who believe if they are not the ones receiving her gifts it gives them reason to invalidate the good, they don't see coming their way. As Dr. Martin Luther King Jr. understood no one is perfect but if the heart is right, it will define one's character. Not, withstanding while it is a fact that this is a male-dominated planet, the United States of America is one of the few countries on this planet where women have a voice that brings about change.

Too many of us women; however, have narrowed our visions to coincide with our present circumstances and have not bothered to realize how far we have come and how far we have to go. What you do to change the lives of others enhances or diminishes your own. To impact the lives of others may mean, changing how you feel about your life. What you give returns back to you whether it is negative or positive. It has to do, I believe, with your Karma returning to you.

Dear reader, the main character in my novel is a woman who believes in the ideals of Oprah Winfrey. Those ideals helped forge changes in the lives of not only the seven young ladies she is helping but also many others as well, even people she may never meet. She uses what she feels are Oprah's ideals to make others reach into their hearts, grab hold of their pain head-on, and not let that pain stop them from making their dreams a reality. Dr. Martin Luther King Jr. was a dreamer. His dreams I believe were of the same fabric as those of Oprah and the woman in this story, Mrs. Johnnie Bea. She carries the torch her father left in her care by giving her life to help enhance the lives of others. The legacy of those dreams, she hopes, will live long after she is gone.

Chapter One

Mrs. Johnnie Bea surveyed her front lawn when she pulled up in front of her home on Sixty-First Macklin Street in her old sky-blue 1993 Ford station wagon, the one her husband had bought brand new for her. She reached up and touched the edges of her gold-rimmed glasses as she sat looking at the depressing sight before her. The blackberry bushes her husband always cut and pruned when he was alive were now growing all over her yard. What had once been a beautiful lawn now lay overgrown with weeds. Her house needed a paint job. Her husband would have been on top of that quickly and in a hurry. She thought to herself.

Though she had not gone out back for quite some time she knew the beautiful garden they both adored lay as a field in ruins. Mrs. Johnnie Bea had promised herself every year since her husband's death she was going to have work done on the house and her lawn. Fifteen years later she just had not gotten around to it. On June 14th, she will have looked out on the earth for eighty years.

Seated there in her car tears filled her eyes as she thought about how good God had been to her. It seemed like only yesterday she buried Mr. Taylor, yet the time had gone by as fast as his untimely death. A heart attack took his life without warning at least there was none to her knowledge. Of course, there were her great step-grand-nephews Dwayne and Mylo she and Mr. Taylor had raised. Five and three when their parents, her husband's grand-nephew and his wife had been killed in an automobile accident. Under the care of her husband and her, they had flourished into fine young men she was proud of.

1

The fuss her great-grand nephews made over her she complained about but loved. Both had offered to have professional landscapers come in and take care of her overgrown lawn and course, the repairs she needed to be done to her house; a house they had grown up in. That had not happened because she always insisted, she had to be present to make sure the repairs were done the way she wanted them. And of course, she had never had the time, always working at 'The Safe Place' she started ten years before so that school children in her community could get fed before and after school. On the weekends she had to go down to the Village and set up the food stands to make sure the homeless people were fed, "after all," she thought to herself, "the meals they got during the week were not available on Saturday and Sunday. Everyone knows a body needs at least one hot meal a day.

It had been a hard day at 'The Safe Place,' she thought to herself remembering how the number of children coming had increased in the ten years since they first opened their doors. Too many children required help. She thought to herself.

What had become of mothers and fathers? Where were they and why did young children seem so much like miniature adults instead of children so soon?

The funding she had hoped for had been stalled. What business could she take care of if there was no money to buy food or clothing when the young ones came in ill-dressed and needed socks and shoes to put on their feet? It didn't matter that 'old man arthritis' was paining her joints from time to time or that she worried about dying and not having anyone to take her place. What would happen to the children needing the help of 'The Safe Place' if she died before she could bring together her young friends to teach them about carrying on her legacy?

Who would feed the homeless? Where would they find another woman foolish enough to spend long hours many days at a time out begging those with more than they would ever need to give where need was so critical?

A sudden sigh escaped Mrs. Johnnie Bea's lips as she hit herself on the back of the hand saying out loud:

"My Oprah, Mrs. Johnnie Bea, where is your faith? Hasn't God always been there when nothing looked like it was going to work out? And had she forgotten her song? 'He May Not Come When You Wanted Him but He Was Right On, Time.' Always he had been on time making a way out of no way; making some miracle out of what seemed to be a hardship. Yes, she knew as sure as she knew her Oprah was going to continue her legacy of making things better for others, a way would be made for her, she did not doubt that she reminded herself smiling.

Like she believed, Oprah had started with nothing but a dream, a prayer, a hope, and a lot of love in her heart. These were all they both had ever needed. Her smile widened across the wrinkles in her red pepper face as she thought about those times. Her long braids bound high on her head like ropes looked like a grey horn turned upside down. Her faith in God had sustained her when she and her mother were forced to move away from the only world she had known. As tragic as it was, for many years of her life she missed the long white cotton fields of Mississippi. Her hands moved down to finger the pearl earrings that adored her pierced earlobes. They were a gift from her father on her sixteenth birthday. So many memories were connected to them. She squeezed her earlobe as she thought of those long walks to school. They never hurt her. Her father had taught her that the mountain she was climbing had a blessing at the top, a blessing the white children riding the bus would never receive because their bus was filled with hate, and blessings never came from hate.

Mrs. Johnnie Bea's mind went back a few months before her father's tragic death. For too many years Mississippi and its Jim Crow laws had torn her people's lives asunder. Though many would die, the time had come for them to fight back against Jim Crow. Her father had talked to her about it. "It is the only way," he said, "America would awaken and release God's children from the bondage of Jim Crow's cruel claws. "The world," her father said, "beyond America has begun to see our people's suffering."

Talking to her about the struggle that he believed would change the South forever he told her he must join the fight for the right to vote. 'Not for himself,' he said 'but for the memory of his father and other black men generations before who had faced the sting of slavery. His fight for their civil rights was for his mother's memory and the memory of her mother and her mother's mother.'

Most of all he must join for her to have a better life he said holding her fingertips up to his light cheeks. "I want you to learn to fight for what you believe in knowing that even when it seems that all is lost the stand you take is what counts." He told her.

Mrs. Johnnie Bea remembered looking at her father with mixed emotions. After all, he did not have to go sit with friends and listen to them debate over what should be done as far as voting was concerned. Some wanted no part of anything to do with voter registration. They feared more for their safety and that of their families. Others wanted to get their weapons and start an all-out war. Many were after all college students who wanted to participate because they saw themselves never being able to vote because of Jim Crow laws. While Mrs. Johnnie Bea listened to her college friends, it was her father who in the end made the difference in her thinking.

When she returned home from one such gathering, she found her father seated in his den reading the evening paper he had published. Kissing him on his cheek she took a seat next to him. His long legs stretched out from his desk. He was a tall thick man not fat but muscular in a six foot two athletic frame. She and her mother who was but five feet three, were always looking up at him. Balding in the front his wavy straight black hair peppered with grey strains hugged his skull. Mrs. Johnnie Bea liked the way her father talked with those expressive hands of his. He had an infectious smile and a way of explaining things that drew people to him. She understood clearly what her friends meant when they said it was her father's genes they saw in her. Somewhat like a college professor lecturing, he pointed out facts to her. She sat glued to his every word. Her facial expressions showed as her father's words conveyed her emotions. She could tell he noticed her emotions surfacing as she began telling him of her concerns and that she did not want him risking his life for a cause that might get him killed. Slowly folding the paper in his lap her father turned to her taking her hands into his. "I must' he said join the fight for the right to vote, not for myself but,"

4

he said tightening his grip on the hands in his "for you and the other younger people out there looking to me for guidance. This fight is the legacy of our people that must not die."

The next evening, they stood in their living room, she, her mother, and her father. He was still dressed in a gray suit having just gotten off work from the newspaper business he ran. Her mother, a small chocolate-skinned woman with large beautiful marble eyes stood staring with a fearful look at her husband, her arms folded, she sobbed silently Mrs. Johnnie Bea's father paced the floor, trying to make them understand the importance of his decision to go forward and register. She, at the time, had thrown up her hands telling him,

"Papa, I don't care about those others, and I most certainly don't care about a legacy that might cost you your life." He had looked at her and shook his head.

"I might have to die," he said, walking over to her and taking her hands into his. "So that you can live a better life. Haven't I always taught you to fight for what you believe in," he said as he looked down into her eyes with endearment. "Those you stand against," he said, "may hate you but they have to respect your courage to fight the wrongs they forge against you."

Mrs. Johnnie Bea remembered pulling her hand away from his turning to her mother for support in not wanting him to risk his life for something she felt was as dangerous as fighting for the right to vote. Tears rolled down her mother's cheeks as she turned her back shaking her head as if to say there was nothing, she could do to stop him.

"Papa those white people will kill you!" Along with her outburst, her tears flowed with a gust.

"It is important to me as a man to become somebody instead of something to be stepped on and shamed into an 'IT' instead of a human being!" Mrs. Johnnie Bea remembered quivering at the sound of his raised voice. "I must be able to walk down the street with my head up looking any other man in the eyes, not shamed into moving out of the way, not being able to look at a white woman or child without the sting of a rope in waiting." His words stung like a bullet entering her heart.

"Look at the many hats you and your mother must wear to survive. How long can this last?" he asked shaking as tears rolled down his cheeks. Mrs. Johnnie Bea's eyes grew as she watched her father clutch a lamp in his hand and hurl it into their living room wall. She grabbed his tall thick body in her arms saying to him.

"I know Papa. I know."

It was not long after their heated discussion at home her family was called to meet with members of the community when one of the families in their neighborhood found their seven-year-old son missing and a few days later another family said their ten-year-old daughter had been missing for two days.

After the meeting that night she found her father seated on their back porch swing fanning with a part of the Sunday newspaper. The night was still. Nothing but the crickets could be heard rubbing their legs against each other. It sounded like they were sending messages in a code she could not decipher. Kissing her father on top of his head, she sat next to him.

They both knew the tension between the Negroes and the white Southerners in Karo, Mississippi, had intensified since the young Northern white people had come to help them get registered to vote. No one knew who the Klan would come for next. Now, it seemed even little children were not exempt. At a meeting about the whereabouts of the missing children, questions were asked if voting was worth the lives of so many dead already.

Mrs. Johnnie Bea had sighed knowing how heavy her father's heart was.

Thinking back it was hard to believe she could have easily worn a size six dress. Her parents always talked about how the genes of her mother's Indian grandfather had come out in her, giving her a reddish overtone accounting for the length of her thick black hair that reached way down her back when it was straightened. She and her mother had wrestled when it came time to comb it. Everyone thought that all that tight hair was so pretty once it was straightened. It would have been cut off had she had her way and not her father.

Mrs. Johnnie Bea sat there looking at her father knowing after the children came up missing it was not about what she wanted any longer. Taking his hand in hers she asked almost in whispers.

6

"Papa, how can Negroes not hate white people when they can so easily kill little children?" At the time she shook her head and looked up at what seemed to be a million stars shining down to light up the dark porch where they sat. "Nothing makes sense anymore Papa." She said moving his and her hand up to cover her heart. Her dream of going away to study aviation would be stalled. With so much happening, there was no way she could leave her parents alone. Her world had suddenly turned upside down.

The silence of the night seemed endless. Fireflies and mosquitoes pressed against tiny holes on the screen, keeping them out; Mrs. Johnnie Bea had sensed how desperate they were to get inside so they could suck fresh blood from their flesh.

"What good does it do us to hate?" her father had answered shaking his head. "Our sorrows have been with us always."

"Papa, what else can we do but hate?"

"Hate," he said as he continued to fan away at the hot night air with no breeze in sight "would cause us to lose not only our lives but our souls and the Glory of God."

"Papa, it makes no sense to me" Mrs. Johnnie Bea responded then stood up and walked to where the screen separated them from the screams of the mosquitoes needing to get to feast on their flesh the same as the Klan sought to feast on their lives.

The swish of the paper fanning her father could no longer be heard. His voice sounded strange in the darkness.

"My grandmother's mother was born a slave. Five of her children were sold as slaves before they were ten my grandmother told me." He gave out a long sigh and crossed his legs saying to Mrs. Johnnie Bea, "Just imagine in your mind you have given birth to a fine young handsome baby boy. Your breasts are swollen with milk. Nursing him fills your heart with joy. Three months to the day he is born in comes the master with a buyer. Paying no mind to the fact that you are nursing he pulls the baby from your breast telling the buyer he should give him fifty years of hard labor while ignoring your pleas not to sell the infant. He shows the baby off as though he is an animal he is about to sell. No one thinks of the man who fathered him but has no rights to him. The master states how strong and healthy the baby looks. He then tells the buyer his wife has grown tired of nursing, and since both your baby and his wife's baby were born relatively close, he will be using your milk for the baby born to his wife. Tell me daughter where would your love go once your baby is gone and you begin nursing the master's baby? "Mrs. Johnnie Bea's eyes grew large as she listened to her father's words.

"It most certainly will not go with a child. I know I will never see again on the face of this earth, Papa. I would grow to hate the very thought of conception." Mrs. Johnnie Bea remembered her father turning away from her as he folded his arms and looked out into the screened darkness.

"The master, with your baby screaming in his hands, looks around the shed then says to the buyer of the other female slave in the shed with you who sat also nursing a child, says he cannot sell that baby because it looks too weak and sickly. Tell me, daughter, what would your prayer be for the next child you gave birth to?"

"That it be born dead, Papa, not born sickly, not weak, but that it died as soon as it came out of my womb." Like waterfalls, tears fell from her father's eyes, as they fell from the eyes of Mrs. Johnnie Bea. Her shoulders shook as she screamed at her father.

"Your great-grandmother and the other women who had their children sold had to have hated white people for that Papa" Mrs. Johnnie Bea turned back to face her father as the full moon showed the tears streaming down her cheeks. Her father gathered her into his arms whispering

"Girl, what good would that do? Hate doesn't give you a bed to sleep on. Hate doesn't right the wrong done to you or stop the pain that wrong caused." He let her go. She watched him slap his arm with the newspaper he had been fanning with and guessed that at least one of the mosquitoes had somehow squeezed through the screened porch.

"Baby all hate does is cause you to do things that get you nowhere. Your Papa is looking for you to become someone,"

"Did I ever tell you," He said as if to lighten the dark mood of their conversation, "that Johnnie Bea was the name of your grandmother three times removed? It was given to her by the slave master, who saw her as nothing but his property. I gave that name to you with Ms. Behind Johnnie Bea to bring pride and honor to a name that meant nothing to the man who gave it in the first place. My grandmother's mother belonged to the master but her heart belonged to God, that's the difference between hating and giving your heart to God. She was an old woman before she heard someone say her name behind Mrs. But my mother told me her mother never gave her heart up to hating but to God. She kept it until she was past ninety." He walked a few steps and stretched his arms before coming over to place one around her shoulders.

"Papa, I don't want to hate, but white people...." Mrs. Johnnie Bea began to say as she placed her head on his chest and her arms around his waist.

"Daughter you are confusing behavior with color."

"No, Papa, I'm not about to like people who kill children." She said, releasing her hold on him while pulling away from the arm around her shoulder.

"What do you fear most about the young people who have come down to help us?" He asked, turning her to face him again.

"The fact that so many of them are white is what I fear. The white people living here become more like vicious animals than they already are when the people they call 'nigger lovers Yankees' come to town," Mrs. Johnnie Bea had answered, looking up at her father with tears in her eyes.

"What is it about the behavior of the white people who come to help us you dislike?"

"Papa there is nothing wrong with their behavior, like you said they have come to help us."

"So, it isn't about them as people," he said taking her hand and leading her from the porch into the kitchen after him.

"I hear you, Papa. This is about color. It's all about color. The white people's hate is against the color we are and nothing more."

"I wish I could say you are right and that it is only about our color. If that is so in a few generations our color will change. He said looking at his near-white hands and arms. I am afraid it is more than just about color."

"What Papa? Tell me what more is it than color?" Mrs. Johnnie Bea had asked as they came inside taking a seat at the kitchen table across from each other.

"It is much more sinister, daughter."

"Sinister! Papa how so?" Mrs. Johnnie Bea remembered asking, seeing that strange gaze on her father's face as he looked over at her, holding his head as if a migraine had suddenly stuck him. He looked at his yellow hands again, saying as if to someone other than her,

"When the white slave master's vile lust found him in the body of the female slave, he had to find a way to continue feeding his lust while keeping his white woman from the body of the male slave. Like the biblical David who sent his lover's husband to the front line to die because of his vain lust for the man's wife, so did the white slave master seek means of defiling his black male slave. He didn't want the desire for him to fill the heart of the white female as it had his for the black female slave. One has to have an erection to desire a woman. If they could freely desire each other where might that leave him if her desire shifted?"

In all his thoughts of superiority, he never could admit the weakness in him that drew him into the body of his black female property. If any inferior strain ever existed it was that which became evident as the color of the slaves changed." Mrs. Johnnie Bea had felt his pain as he looked again at his near-white skin. "With it came his desperate need to keep the white woman from the lust he took pleasure in, a part of history few historians are willing to include in their documentaries."

"I guess you are right because if he had truly believed in our bestial nature, we all would be as black as the day our first ancestors were dragged off the ship.

"It more than anything accounted for his need to create a cloth to hide behind to group kill and lynch after slavery was over. He could not afford to have her know the true nature of his lust daughter." Mrs. Johnnie Bea and her father sat a moment staring at each other as she digested his words.

"What you are saying then is that the pedestal he created to sit her upon was really to deceive her." Mrs. Johnnie Bea knew she had pushed the subject to give herself more time to spend with her father.

"Had she come to enjoy the same pleasures he took for granted American history would have been completely different. How tragic for the white woman and to think Papa how many black men were hung to justify that fear."

"When the excuse to destroy another human life grows in the mind the reason given could be as simple as the mole behind an ear, a spot on the lip, or the smell of one's breath. Though it is denied, man's need to destroy others of his species is about the nature of the human need and the diabolic thirst for violence. Man would never admit it of course, but true to his nature he is the most violent of all animals on earth in his thirst to kill and destroy. It is the beast that lives within his consciousness.

No man can escape the true nature of what he is. Our lynches and killings of not only adults but our children and babies as well are the result of what he was back then.

Those responsible for the destruction of our lives are not horrible aliens who have arrived on Earth from another planet out of space to kill as shown in the white man's movies. They are called the Klan, born on this earth. Everyday White Americans, doctors, lawyers, judges, and politicians. White men, women, and their children who are taught by them and live around us. Americans, who at any given moment become upset with us for any or no known reason given to us cover themselves in white sheets and become our faceless killers. Killers who are given the freedom to do so by white American leaders of our government.

"It may be subdued for generations but like a cloud moving in. It overtakes their diabolical minds. With thoughtful reasoning that the violence about to occur is a necessary evil for their survival, they set out with a vengeance. Once that reason is solidified in their minds they go after their prey without mercy or compassion. It is only Man who kills millions of his kind. No other animal on the face of the earth can commit such massive atrocities against its species. This violent nature lives within him as sure as the hate that lives within him to despise his limited existence on this earth. He has never learned that it is not about the salvation of one race it is about the survival of the human race.

"I am afraid," Mrs. Johnnie Bea, it is also about fear and the need to have some way to feed those fears." Her father had said taking her hands into his. There was an unsettling look in her father's eyes, now red from the tears he had shed. In that awful dead heat, a gentle breeze cooled the kitchen as it caressed the cheeks of Mrs. Johnnie Bea. Her father looked around as though he expected to see something or someone.

Mrs. Johnnie Bea got up walked over to the cupboard and pulled out her father's favorite coffee cup. The coffee brewing on the stove filled the room with its smell. She poured him a cup placing two sugars and three teaspoons of cream into his cup. Years later she would remember the recipe and make it her favorite way to drink her coffee.

"This Klan that groups to kill, the White Citizen Counsel that fixes laws to discriminate against those they cannot otherwise beat down, it's all about their fears Child."

"Fears? Papa, what is it that white people fear except doing what is right, fair, and honest?" Mrs. Johnnie Bea asked her father as she handed him his coffee.

"Remember when I first took you to visit your mother's relatives in Washington State and you saw all those evergreen trees? Remember telling me that since the evergreen tree stayed green all year long, it must be better than all the other trees?

"Yes, Papa, I remember, but as you recall, I was only ten at the time." Mrs. Johnnie Bea smiled at her father, saying to him, "You taught me that if the evergreen tree thought like I thought it would be like the people in America who think they are better than all others simply because their skin is white." "What would have happened if you had asked me if the evergreen killed off all the other trees? The old oak tree would never have stood at the river's edge, nor would the poor weeping willow have had a chance to live with its mild temperament, giving shade, would it? What if the eagle thought itself better than the dove or the sparrow or if the osprey that gets its food from the water thought itself better than the hawk that eats from the land?" "That is why you said to me, we have a God that knows better than humans and realizes that everyone is in the plan of the creator no matter what their race or color. I remember your sayings, Papa."

"Now tell me what are you to learn about the people who have come here to help us?" Mrs. Johnnie Bea could tell the coffee was too hot the way her father eased the cup to his lips waiting for her answer to his question.

"If I did not know that the white people were coming to help us I would look at them and hate them pure and simple," she said reaching into the cupboard and taking out another cup. "I would never want to get to know them because my hatred for their color would prevent that from ever happening," Mrs. Johnnie Bea says to her father with the cup in her hand.

Everything we do mimics the white race. They taught us everything we know if not by participation for sure by observation."

"Just like white people who teach their children to hate us that hate prevented their children from ever getting to know us. If we hurt them, we would not realize that like every tree and every bird, every human is as important as every other human." Mrs. Johnnie Bea said realizing again why her father eased the coffee cup away from his lips. Though the taste of the coffee was good. the hot liquid also burned her lips.

"Exactly," he said. "Every ant, toad, and seed is here on this earth for a purpose. When you kill and destroy their existence senselessly, who knows what distant consequence may come about." As the coffee cooled her father consumed every bit of it and licked his lips as if to say it had been prepared just right.

"You see when the slave master brought his human cargo over in chains, he gave them that which he valued the least." Her father tells her, as he moves toward the sink turning on the faucet to rinse and wash his empty cup.

"What was that?" Mrs. Johnnie Bea asked her father.

"His God and of course he threw in the bible since it also was of no real value in the success of his business of enslaving human labor. He never imagined we'd use what he considered useless to us to overcome the inflictions of his oppression on us. The Bible teaches us not to hate but to love our enemies." He leaned with his back against the sink. "My God, sometimes it is hard but that bible has been our salvation and we cannot give up on it because lost souls use their godless ways to use it as an excuse to destroy us. We are God's children and payday is coming.

Mind what I tell you, girl? Payday is coming just like it did ending slavery." So many white people died in that Civil War on both sides right along with us." He said shaking his head.

That Mississippi summer heat was unbearably hot in July. Tension filled the air because no one knew what time of night the Klan would come or how many lives would be lost. Mrs. Johnnie Bea listened to her father tell her that at best his life was temporary. "She must," he told her "Give love to those weak vessels that have only hate to sustain themselves."

"No matter how I die" he had said walking her up the stairs to her bedroom "You are going to love me as your father. It is how I live that will determine the legacy that lives on after me in you. I don't want you to be ashamed of your father's legacy." He stopped at the top of the stairs to take out his pipe and stuffed it with tobacco. When he lit it the smell of the tobacco filled the air with a woody scent she loved.

"You are your mother's and my only legacy Mrs. Johnnie Bea, your life must represent the lives of poor black women long dead now, who laid down their bodies in shame, forced to give up the children they gave birth to like any other animal the master owned. Their very identities erased like chalk on a blackboard."

"Papa, I don't know if I want to."

"You must know. Too many of our people are too ashamed to remember how our women were brought to this country in chains. Bred they were to birth children that would be sold like cattle, having no identity but that given by the white slave master who owned them. If their child were born female they too could be bred at any age with any male, even the master if he so desired. Living under those atrocities our women kept strong their spirit to love God. When I die the torch will be yours to carry no matter where you are. Our legacy must not die." With that he walked over and kissed her on top of her head hugged her then turned towards his and her mother's bedroom. She looked at her father's back feeling so helpless.

Mrs. Johnnie Bea didn't want to feel the tears swelling in her eyes but she could not push away the memory of what happened soon after that night. It returned to haunt her at the most unexpected moments. Sweat began to pour from her skin as her eyes clouded. She continued to reflect on that horror. It seemed to her it was the same sweat that poured from her body on that awful day so long ago in history. It was the saddest day of her life.

She knew she was running but her legs felt like rubber. The howling and crying still rang in her ears. She stopped dead in her tracks upon seeing all those people mostly white, staring up in that tree. There hung her father in that big old oak tree. In the distance a weeping willow stood, its limbs hung over like the body of her dead father. From out of the corner of her eyes she saw white people standing alongside an abandoned car allowing their children to throw rocks at that strange fruit that had suddenly appeared on the strongest of the oaks' branches. It was a fruit that ought not to have been there. Her mother never understood how she bore the pain of seeing her father's body hanged in that tree. How she could watch those white children throwing rocks at his body and the backs of her father's friends when they cut him down and not cry out. It was the poem he had given her written by him about his grandmother and about her mother's mother that carried her through that day and years later. It was a poem she never really understood until she sat in her home watching *"The Color Purple"* and a black woman who came out of a prison hole after seven years so scarred she would never again look as she had before those years destroyed her life. It was then that she realized what the poem meant. When she saw Oprah's character forced to ride with the white woman who was the source of her scarred life, was when she understood the true depth of endurance suffered by her female ancestors. Like a voice from the grave, the poem spoke to her. In her mind's eyes, she looked into the eyes of the character Oprah played as she listened to her heart chant the verses of the poem.

Two hundred years too late

Rape was my bond long before I was born.
Ghosts haunt me now.
Shadows lie at my feet
All colors, shapes, and sizes

From between my muddy legs, the babies came
Screaming and crying as they lay dying
In the hands of the white man's land.

Like the boils burning on the body of ole' Job
I felt the master's sperms churning deep in my
soul. My black body stretched, pulled, and
destroyed til it was void.
God poured into me a supernatural endurance
But for me, there was no insurance.
It was more than I could take
When for me they called it rape.
Two hundred years too late.

Years later she would again see the legacy of the poem and its meaning in the movie Brewster Place' when the character Oprah portrayed lost her home because of a wayward child, but her endurance prevailed. She was able to help a younger woman grab hold of her pain and move on to surrender to what she could not control while going forward to live again. The poem's words often came to her when she needed strength. Again and again, that voice from the grave came as a constant reminder of their hundreds of years in the wilderness trying to find a way out.

It was, however, one of the many writings left behind by her father that touched her heart the most. One that he must have written on behalf of his great-great-grandmother in a moment of outpouring writers often have. His quiet voice entered her heart. Mrs. Johnnie Bea closed her eyes to listen to the words in the piece she found among his belongings after his murder.

Remembering

'The ole' familiar breeze gently wrapped its breath around my neck caressing my right cheek as it whispered in my right ear. "Do you remember," it whispered, "when early in the morning before the crack of dawn the sound

of the master's whip woke you? Remember when the sweat of your brow was your only reward? As the sun set in God's heavens you stumbled back onto your bed of straw in the master's shack". Remember when only the sweat on your brow was your reward?"

Ole' breeze, you are gently awakening the memory of my other life. The one I had forgotten. I looked down at the check that would pay my waiting bills when that ole' breeze whispered in my right ear after brushing a stolen kiss on my left cheek.

"Remember when nothing you had was yours? The red soil was your bedroom and the night air sang to you its songs of a new day coming. While you could not see that day, you felt it coming as a welcome blessing for it was only with that knowing that you could go on."

I unfolded the newspaper lying on my lap. The headlines read KIDNAPPED CHILD. A sudden chill cut like a knife into my heart. It was the Ole' Breeze now cold as a winter's morn'

The sound of its roaring winds brought back to me the pain of that other life, the one I had forgotten. There were five all totaled. Three were my man's, at least I thought he was my man til the master came and gave his body to those others. Those babies were sold the same as mine.

Remember, your five babies were not kidnapped or stolen. Right before your eyes, all five sold down the river like cattle. Those who were my master's were the first to go.

Right into my soul, that cold wind blew. AND I BEGAN TO SHIVER. I tasted my blood as it flowed down into my lips as if it were a river. Yes, Ole' Breeze, you are blowing right into my soul. Your words are flowing

Your years, Ole' Breeze, are older than mine. Into my soul, your breath is flowing. That old breeze whispered again as it placed a kiss on my lips. You remember when I walked down to the river's edge to fetch a pail of water for my babies in that land I'll never see again? I was snatched like those others whose history sings my song, Ole' Breeze.

Who am I really, Ole' Breeze? Tell me, am I an African or an American wrapped in an African body, Ole' Breeze? A black can come from one hundred different countries. An African in America can be black or white. It has been so long, Ole' breeze and the terms for us continue to change from nigger, to that of ole' Negro. It is I, Ole' breeze, who must remember who

I am never changed. Only who others say I am keeps changing. Before I went to fetch that pail of water along the Nile River's edge, I was an African queen, free as a bee. I have been afraid to remember after that Ole' breeze until your cold, piercing air plugged me into the depth of despair, causing me to remember

Called a slave, I was less than human. I remember for many, I became a Negro, or was it a nigger from that to black from black to 'ole niggra. Ole' breeze I am not the minority they say I am. I am who I remember I am and that is a descendant of Kings and Queens and freemen as well as slaves. I am a part of the universe! Yes, Ole' Breeze, remind me! I am a part of the wind, the rain, Ole' Breeze I am one of the stars that not only shines at night but one of the heavenly bodies that have been shining for an eternity! Who I am has never changed. At this moment I am a human on this planet. Yet my Presence is as eternal as yours. Thanks, Ole' Breeze for reminding me that it is only when I forget to remember who I am that I become who others say I am.

As the voice of her father became still in her heart, Mrs. Johnnie Bea wiped away her last tear for she knew she would be fine because she never forgot who she was. Her Oprah was real to her not because she had so much money, but because she understood the mountain Oprah was still climbing. Oprah made her feel proud because she had character and she did the best she knew how to do. Not someone else's best but her own, in her way she took care of the business of moving the legacy of the black woman forward just as she did.

She felt in her heart the pain of her scars only she would ever know. Those scars could not make her hate. She had a soul to save and a father to make proud. She realized better than anyone she had grown to the twilight of her years. Old man arthritis had robbed her of her steady gait. Now she hobbled when she walked to keep the pain at bay.

At eighty her time was winding down. Her days seemed too long and her nights too short. The rest her body so desperately needed remained a whisper in the back of her mind. Taking a long deep breath Mrs. Johnnie Bea realized the time had come to pass on the torch. She needed others to carry on for her. People she trusted to treat those she helped sternly but with love and compassion.

Long ago the government had turned the homeless out to fend for themselves, mostly people whose minds had failed them and had at one time resided in mental hospitals where they received the help they needed. Now on the streets, all she was able to give to them was a little of God's food and a warm smile. There must be others who can love even the unlovable with all their problems. She must stir in other hearts the desire to carry on her legacy so that 'The Safe Place' and her Village can continue.

Her thoughts turned to all the young women who had become her family. They often came together and discussed what they thought should happen to make a difference in the community. When she called on them for help, they never hesitated. Day or night, they would be there. I have to get them together again. "Yes, I'll invite them to visit with me. They will understand when I tell them I'm cooking beans that there is something I want to share with them." She said aloud, looking across the street from her house at the red rooster weathervane that switched back and forth when the wind blew strong.

Mrs. Johnnie Bea smiled wide showing her gold-crowned denture eyetooth. She looked at the clock before turning off the switch in her car. It was just about four o'clock and Oprah would be making her appearance soon.

I best put on my pot of beans, Mrs. Johnnie Bea thought to herself. Just as she was about to step out of her car, she spied Big Tom, her male cat, darting across the street into the yard. His black coat had not a white spot on it. He resembled a panther with deep yellow eyes that made a lot of her friends nervous.

"That cat is getting too big," she thought to herself. "He looks as if he weighs twenty pounds." It occurred to her that she was going to have to stop feeding him so much. She had not seen him in a couple of days. He probably got babies strolled all over the neighborhood she continues to think to herself.

Looking out the corner of her eye Mrs. Johnnie Bea sees a young white boy with wild brown hair running behind a large black and brown dog. He didn't look familiar so she knew he must have been from the new housing development on the next block. In a flash, it came to her the boy and the dog were running towards her yard after Big Tom.

"She noticed the young white child looked to be about nine or ten as he and the dog got closer.

"Get it, get it" she heard the boy screaming at the young Rottweiler that was now in her yard coming up on Big Tom. At that point she knew for sure the boy was new in the neighborhood otherwise he would have known better. When the dog ran up on Big Tom, he growled showing his teeth as if ready to tear the cat apart. Big Tom arched his back as he backed up. As soon as the dog came close to him, Big Tom took an unexpected leap in the air on top of the dog's back. Its claws dug into the dog's head. Hair and soon blood was flying everywhere as the cat continued to claw the dog. Everything happened quickly. The dog began shaking its head in a wild effort to escape the claws buried inside its flesh. Big Tom flew off the dog his back still arched. Now with his feet on the ground as he moved away licking his paws lightening, fast he flew up a nearby tree. Not one hair of his black fur was missing. The boy sat on the ground with his yelping dog. Mrs. Johnnie hobbled into her house and came back with some gauze and ointment.

"Here take, this son. Put this on those deep gashes and wrap this gauze around his head. He is going to need to see the Vet now but you know if you had gotten your way, I would be the one holding my dead cat that you were going to have your dog kill." The boy put the ointment on the dog's head without answering.

"I've seen dogs and cats not bothering each other until someone like yourself comes along making them mean-spirited like you want your dog to be. Have you ever heard of Dr. Martin Luther King Jr. young man?

"No" the boy answered speaking for the first time as he reached up to take the gauze.

"I thought not. He and his teaching of nonviolence make a lot of sense when you begin to realize that when you bring violence, you better expect violence in return.

"You are sitting here now because your mind was set on hurting something that wasn't bothering you at all. Isn't that true?"

"Yeah," he said crying as hard as the dog was yelping.

"I teach Big Tom to be loving and kind just like you need to go home and teach your dog about love instead of how to kill things that are not even bothering it".

"Well, why did he try to hurt my dog if he's so loving?" the boy cried, wrapping the gauze around the dog's bloody head.

"Because you taught your dog to be mean-spirited, you put Big Tom's life in danger. Big Tom saw his life about to end, and he was protecting it. You are lucky the poor fellow still has his eyesight. If you had been teaching your dog to be loving, he wouldn't be all bloody and scratched up. Now you take him on home and teach him better manners." Mrs. Johnnie Bea told him as she took the unused ointment he gave back to her.

"Okay." He said slowly walking back from where he came.

Mrs. Johnnie Bea looked at the boy with his seriously wounded dog. She shook her head thinking to herself. If somebody doesn't teach him any better he will grow up becoming that same kind of man. Given a little power no telling what harm he will cause to innocent people.

A loud meow came from the tree just above her head. She stared up at Big Tom. He looked down at her, licking his paws, the two-inch claws on the end of them stretched out for her to see.

"He is not the first dog you have had to teach some manners. Is he Big Tom?" Big Tom meowed, darted down the tree, and ran into her backyard.

Looking at her watch, Mrs. Johnnie Bea turned and hobbled inside her house, but just before closing her front door behind her she hung the do not disturb sign outside on her door knob. It was time to visit with Oprah.

Chapter Two

>+<+>+O+<+>+<

$\mathcal{M}$ rs. Johnnie Bea glanced around the rooms of her home trying to decide where she would seat seven women. They all had gladly agreed to visit with her especially when she assured each one her navy beans would be on the menu. It wasn't that she did not have the room, she did. The funding for the food and the clothes she needed for the Village and 'The Safe Place' had been approved but the delivery service had mistakenly delivered every order to her home. She had to pack up all these boxes of goods she had prayed for and take them to The Safe Place for the children they were donated for.

Looking around at all the boxes, she thought to herself, that she had not gotten around to moving God's blessings.

Everywhere there were boxes of canned food to be stored in the village. She had told the fundraisers over and over again there was storage space in the Village to put the supplies, not to send them to her home as though she was the one in need. If she had even attempted to eat one-third of this food she would be larger than her eight-room house.

Seven of her friends were coming to visit and she needed to find space for them to sit. She could have rented a conference room but they were dear to her and she wanted them to feel at home. Their lives had melted into hers becoming like family. Elsie and Teresa's families had relocated up from Mississippi with Mrs. Johnnie Bea and her mother right after her father's hanging. His wish had been for her mother and her to leave Mississippi if anything happened to him. A promise he had made Mrs. Johnnie Bea promise she would keep. She sold his newspaper business after her father's death and left Mississippi. Along with Elsie and Teresa's family, Mississippi was replaced with Washington State and its evergreen trees. Elsie and Teresa had become a part of her family. They were as close as little sisters.

She married a man who had lived all his life in Seattle. She and her husband raised his two great nephews after their parents were killed in an auto accident; at the time, Dwayne was three, and Mylo was five. They came to Mrs. Johnnie Bea like children that come to mothers in the change of life when God feels the wisdom the elderly have to offer can be useful in young people's lives if they are willing to listen. She loved the two as though they were her sons. Mylo, the older of the two, stood six feet four inches tall and had worked as a police officer for nine of his thirty years. Chocolate-dark Mylo wore on his face a look of authority, especially when his dark, thick brows came together. Dwayne wore red dreads that hung around his caramel-brown face. They hung down to his shoulders. Five-nine in height, Dwayne succeeded in his career as a rapper, winning over many of his young supporters with songs that gave meaning and understanding to their lives. His engaging smile suggested Mrs. Johnnie Bea often told him, "too much mischief." For whatever reason, God had placed them in her hands to influence the direction of their lives so that when the time arrived, she could pass on the meaning of her father's legacy to them.

"Look at these bowls," she said to herself as she prepared for the ladies' arrival. "Which Salvation Army did I get these from?" Mrs. Johnnie Bea picked up the bowls and looked at their designs and sizes. They were all different, but they were not cracked or chipped, the ladies she thought would hardly notice after all her beans would be even better than ever. She planned to add just a bit more of her mother's secret to them. The beans had to soak overnight to bring tenderness to their taste. She always cut up small bits of smoked ham hocks to add flavor along with two tablespoons of brown sugar. Along with that, she added her mother's secret just a little honey and two cut-up sweet peppers. It made your lips pop just a little but the beans tasted wonderful.

Surveying her sewing room she thought more about seating arrangements. La-Joyce would have to sit on the sofa chair because her baby was due soon. She needed to be comfortable. Lord, she thought to herself the child looked as though she was carrying twins. Mrs. Johnnie Bea had planned to buy a long couch that would at least seat six people but the Goodwill did not have one.

She had to smile as she thought about the fine nephews she and her husband had raised. They never neglected her. She never let them know that most of the money they gave her went to supplying the needs of 'The Safe Place' and The Village where breakfast was served on Saturday and Sunday mornings. They had insisted she use the money to spend on herself. She always told them the money was helping to create her father's legacy. And it was doing just that, she thought, smiling to herself.

As Mrs. Johnnie Bea moved about her home preparing for her young ladies' visit, she thought about when she brought them all together for the first time at Elsie's Condo. Elsie, thin and tall, stood five-nine in her stocking feet. The small rimless glasses she wore hung down her neck were only worn when she had to read small print. Those glasses gave a meaningful look to her small face. Her silver-gray hair now hung down her back in long salt and pepper braids tied in one of many ribbons she chose depending on the color of her attire that day. Elsie was a serious-minded woman who went about her business with little humor to share.

In her younger days, Elsie had worn her hair cut short. Her dark brown complexion was still smooth giving her thin facial features a youthful look. Before going off to nursing school Elsie had performed modern dancing with a group of twenty-four women and men.

Though Mrs. Johnnie Bea prided herself on being a thorough cleaner, Elsie was meticulously clean and neat. Her cleaning reminded one of a nurse preparing for surgery, not a speck of dust anywhere. Mrs. Johnnie Bea guessed that thirty years in nursing had taught Elsie the true meaning of germs and what the wrong germs can do to the human body. Sometimes though, she felt Elsie went a bit overboard but what could she say? Elsie wanted to quit nursing and continue pursuing her dancing career, but Mrs. Johnnie Bea would not hear of her or Teresa dropping out of college for any reason.

It was enough that she had to forego aviation school after the murder of her father. She would go later she assured herself but after her mother became ill it became a moot subject. Elsie was not about to fight with Mrs. Johnnie Bea about something she was adamant about. She would stay on her leaving no tactic left unturned. After her fiancé was killed in the Vietnam War Elsie never married. Now a retired sixty-year-old nurse she lived in the condo next door to Teresa.

Teresa was five years older than Elsie. Coming to Washington from Mississippi as a teenager she had placed herself under the guidance of Mrs. Johnnie Bea many years before. Five-eight she ran track but liked academics better. When ribbons were fashionable Teresa's ponytails became the playground for boys' hands as they pulled the bows just to get a reaction from her. The freckles around her tan nose and cheeks drew even more attention than Mrs. Johnnie Bea or her parents liked. It did not help that her sandy red hair and hazel eyes had always caused the boys to glance her way more often than Mrs. Johnnie Bea thought good for her.

It was tough going for Teresa's parents and Mrs. Johnnie Bea keeping her away from the arrow of love long enough for her to finish her schooling. When Teresa thought working at Sears was the greatest event of her life after graduating high school, Mrs. Johnnie Bea assured her that working at Sears was the entry into other great works she was talented to do.

Teresa was sixty-five with thirty-five years of teaching elementary school students, math fundamentals to her credit. Though she and her late husband never had children, her love for children led her down a path that kept her guiding young lives. A task-focused person, Teresa's wisdom in sensing when things were not as they should be helped steer Mrs. Johnnie Bea away from people who would have often taken advantage of her goodness when they worked on projects helping those in need.

Mrs. Johnnie Bea stirred her beans and threw the sweet peppers her mother always used to season hers into the pot. She checked on her baking sweet potatoes. The stick that held her oven door shut had to be removed so she could look inside.

"Chili said she would be coming," Mrs. Johnnie Bea said, talking aloud to herself. "The child could do some hair, and that's why her shop was filled from the time she opened her doors until the time she closed in the evening," Mrs. Johnnie Bea said again aloud. At thirty she was as yellow as a sunny day and as tall as Elsie but built heavier with an athletic look from working out at the gym. She wore contacts in her slanted eyes that made her iris look slightly red much of the time. The red tint of her hair blended well with her smooth yellow skin tone. A southern-raised girl, Chili expressed her opinion without hesitation, sometimes without thinking about the feelings she hurt. Chili loved a good debate and did not hesitate to be the cause of serious debates. She guessed Chili's gift of gab went with all that hair-dressing she did.

Rosie, on the other hand, reminded her of her petite size six before the years added on the pounds, she found difficult to remove around her hips. With a light brown skin tone, Rosie looked like a young girl still in her teens, not a twenty-nine-year-old mother of five children. Her face held a hard, unfriendly stare that took away from the beauty she must once had before the scars of her life had taken their toll. There had been no steady man in her life through the caring of her children. Mrs. Johnnie Bea felt proud to have been a part of the turnaround Rosie had made in getting a handle on the depression that had taken over her life.

Walking back into the front room she thought to herself, that there was no way she was going to move that six-foot box standing in the middle of her living room floor. Mrs. Johnnie Bea figured it to be the new refrigerator that had been donated to The Village. There were too many homeless people on the city's streets. Money once allocated for their care had been shifted away leaving them at the mercy of elements outside of their control. She wondered what pay raises given to high-ranked government officials took those funds. The taxpayers sure got no reimbursements when those tax dollars were taken away.

The burden of caring for the mentally ill now on the street remains a problem someone has to confront. Mrs. Johnnie Bea said to herself as she leaned against the large box.

She was so glad those streets had not destroyed La-Joyce. Running away from one life trying to find another at sixteen, she ended up on the streets living under bridges, fighting for her survival. Now twenty, that niece-in-law of hers had married her nephew Mylo making him the best wife Mrs. Johnnie could have hoped for. Her dimpled smile was contagious. The large loop earrings she wore complimented her ebony soft skin tone. The round white rimmed eyeglasses she wore mostly on her nose could not hide her large brown beautiful eyes that seemed to take in all her surroundings. She had extra white teeth. At five feet five inches, she wore a size nine before her pregnancy.

"Susie," she said the name and smiled while moving a smaller box. The Forty-five-year-old wife and mother of two teenagers worked as a detention Officer in a Juvenile detention facility. Susie reminded her of her personality.

Susie worked with both girls and boys. She spoke directly and with the authority of someone used to taking charge. That caramel-skinned short woman had a way with the kids she liked. She was stern, but caring. The same five-three in height as herself, she and Susie met eye to eye not only in height but in their thinking as well. After lengthy conversations with Susie, she realized they held similar ideas about life. She met Susie while volunteering at the juvenile center. A no-nonsense kind of person she found her to be.

Susie could be thought of as confrontational the way police officers are stereotyped. If you did not understand the environment in which she worked and what it required of her you would think her cold and distant. Still, Susie's kindness and compassion for the children in her care were demonstrated by how they reached out to her to help them get their lives back on track.

If she needed advice about legal matters, it was Shenee, whom she called. They had met accidentally after Shenee' walked away from Nordstrom's store, leaving a package behind on the counter. As God would have it, Mrs. Johnnie Bea had stopped in to get a bottle of lotion. She said it was too costly, but she liked to keep her hands soft. Standing five feet five in her stocking feet, Shenee' was not average. No one would guess her African heritage by looking at her shoulder-length blonde hair that held curls at their ends that moved when she walked. Her Lauren-tinted glasses gave her the look of a model. Her attire was such that seeing her on the street made you think she had just stepped out of a Vogue magazine. Shenee' had unusual blue eyes that stared at you with a deep intensity. Always meticulously dressed, you had no doubt there was a silver spoon in her background.

Mrs. Johnnie Bea had in the past always been doubtful about lawyers and their greed for money over what she thought should have been the goals of their profession. This young lawyer; however, proved otherwise and the way she handled herself everyone in the group had to respect. Mrs. Johnnie Bea would enjoy this gathering she was sure of it.

She walked into her sewing and sitting room where they would be. Though poorly furnished the room was large and spacious. Pictures of her parents and her father's grandmother hung high on the wall in one corner. A picture of Teresa and Elsie as teenagers hung in the middle, with her two great nephews on the farther end. She and Mr. Taylor's picture hung there also. She remembered those strong dark arms. His thin mustached lips gripped a long black pipe. His dark brown eyes looked not at the camera but at Mrs. Johnnie Bea as she looked up into his." Remembering his kind, gentle, loving ways brought tears to her eyes.

"Bare walls indicated an empty home." Mrs. Johnnie Bea thought to herself, looking away from the picture and up at the large vacant space beside it. She reminded herself that those vacant spaces must be filled.

Excited about the women coming, Mrs. Johnnie Bea's thoughts turn to Shenee's and La-Joyce's first meeting with the other women in her circle.

When La-Joyce walked in and said hello, Chili wasted no time asking her what country she was from in Africa. It took a lot of explaining to get the women to understand that La-Joyce was also a black American. The explanation they received was that her parents were anthropologists. La-Joyce's accent developed, because, she told them she had lived in many foreign countries. Of course, they then wanted to know who her parents were and how they happened to be in other countries when enough bones were buried in America. La-Joyce had looked at them, taken a seat, and not said another word.

When thirty-six-year-old Shenee first met with Mrs. Johnnie Bea's black American girlfriends she was not welcomed. Everyone had arrived at Elsie's on time except Shenee'. When Elsie's doorbell rang, she left the room where the other women waited for the last guest. Elsie returned with Shenee' following her.

Mrs. Johnnie Bea laughed as she moved more boxes into a corner, still thinking about that first meeting.

When Shenee' walked into the room behind Elsie all conversation ceased. Shenee' of course, swung her blonde hair, smiled, said hello, and took a seat. Mrs. Johnnie Bea remembered that, except for La-Joyce, a discomforting, strange look suddenly appeared in the eyes of the rest of the women. Their body language sent out an even stronger message.

Mrs. Johnnie Bea smiled as she remembered saying to the other women, "Now, don't let her blonde hair fool you. Even with blue eyes, she has enough of our genes that says she is as black as the rest of us and a sister whose race is the same as ours."

"Do I have to undress so that you can see my entire body because the way you are looking at me, I feel like I'd better get up and run?" Was Shenee's response to their stares. This eased the tension Mrs. Johnnie Bea thought to herself as she continued to move boxes, smiling while thinking back to what Shenee told the women who sat staring at her.

"I guess I could pass. However, I decided I didn't want to be something I was not. Here is a picture of my husband and my children." Shenee' said, removing the photograph of her family from her wallet for them to see. Though I don't look it, I am a part of the same race as you, so you might as well say hello."

Chili had been the first to speak as she stood up to get a closer look.

'They are black, girls," Chili said, looking at the photograph Shenee handed her before passing it around.

"Can you dance?" Elsie asked, looking closely at her long, slender, smooth legs.

"What does she know about black music? I went to a Pop concert once and the white people there never moved. They didn't feel a thing," Rosie said after offering Shenee a glass of tea.

"What I want to know is what gave you the idea you were black. I feel as though I have walked in on the Imitation of Life you remember that movie don't you girls?" Susie asked getting a yes nod from the others.

"DNA," Shenee' answered, still smiling.

"Well, you can't fight science" Elsie replied. She lifted Shenee's hand so that she could inspect it. Mrs. Johnnie Bea's doubtful friend had laughed, shaking her head in disbelief.

"I guess you are right" Elsie," Teresa said, popping a high-blood-pressure pill in her mouth and then hurriedly swallowing a glass of water. "I can't see black anywhere on this child."

"She must have some of us in her girls. She doesn't have a problem speaking her mind." Mrs. Johnnie Bea recalled Chili saying, still fingering Shenee's hair to ensure the blonde hair was not fake.

"Oh no," La-Joyce said, jumping up from her seat on the sofa. Give her a break. She doesn't need us examining her like she is some alien from another planet."

"I guess you are right, La-Joyce. After all, she is not trying to pass for white, and white folks are for sure not trying to pass for black." Susie said, smiling over at Shenee.

Chili pulled on the sweatband around her head, which was the same color as the purple and white sweatsuit she wore.

"I'll accept her as our sister," Mrs. Johnnie Bea," Chili said because while she doesn't look like one of us, I like how she spoke up like black women are known to do."

"Intimidating women is what we are called." Susie said still smiling at Shenee'.

Mrs. Johnnie Bea would not have her in our group if she was not one of us. Too many of us have trouble with being proud of our race," Chili had said as they all stared at Shenee'.

"Welcome to our group sister but I swear one day people are going to ask what happened to the descendants of black slaves that once lived in this country when we all start looking like you!" Elsie exclaimed.

"They will say we were all absorbed by the sun," La-Joyce said, raising her hands to make her point.

"No, they will say the sperm absorbed us." Everyone looked at Chili. She, looked back at them as if to say don't you get it? Suddenly, laughter filled the room.

"I guess you are right." Susie agreed. She must have some pride about being black because she sure could pass. Still laughing, Susie added, to make matters worse, "Girlfriend, you even dress like a white girl with that green suit on." The laughter grew louder as Mrs. Johnnie Bea remembered the ladies shaking their heads as they looked at Shenee's attire. That white girl's suit has got to go. Susie spoke of the dark green tailored suit Shenee was wearing then.

"These are my work clothes. Should I have worn a sweatsuit?" Shenee' asked, looking at the sweat suits Chili, Rosie, and La-Joyce wore.

"Shenee' is an attorney and owns a law firm." Mrs. Johnnie Bea remembered telling them at the time.

"She must own more than one firm because she sure looks rich to me." Everyone turned in surprise at Rosie's sudden outspoken reply.

"The only way you can truly become a part of us is that you become an Oprah fan." Rosie told her I don't mean you have to like or dislike Oprah but Mrs. Johnnie Bea has indoctrinated all of us on what she believes her Oprah stands for."

"Trust me; I have already become acquainted with Mrs. Johnnie Bea's My Oprah and what she stands for as a black woman in America." A deep sigh could be heard from Mrs. Johnnie Bea as she placed her hands on her hips, allowing her mind to return to the present. She gazed about the sewing room. This time, they would be meeting at her home, and she needed to hurry and get things ready before they arrived. Mrs. Johnnie Bea hobbled over to start her next task.

Her attention was once again drawn to the picture of her parents. On the wall far to her left of them hung a picture of her grandmother. It reminded her of the poem and the legacy her father had left for her to fulfill. She must, she thought to herself find others to carry the torch.

Her Oprah was in the heart of these women they just have never had the opportunity to fill those shoes, shoes she had waiting for them. She began moving the boxes thinking she had much work to do and not much time in which to do it. Rosie managed to find a babysitter for her five children. While Bunkie her oldest child was mature enough to watch her younger brothers, according to state law at thirteen, she was not old enough.

Mrs. Johnnie Bea remembered some years ago when Rosie and all her children were seated in the welfare office. Seventeen was too young for any young girl to parent alone. Without a husband or someone helping it was a twenty-four-hour, seven-day-a-week full-time, thankless job. Mrs. Johnnie Bea had not been surprised to find Rosie and her youngsters living in filth.

"My Oprah", she said to herself we have come a long way doing for others. "With help, Rosie had become a fine, independent woman with a future ahead of her. Mrs. Johnnie Bea smiled as she thought of the miraculous transformation Rosie and her children had made. Children who probably would have grown up to be criminals and problems for society now wanted to be doctors and boxers, like Muhammad Ali. Bunkie, she thought, wanted to be a basketball player the way she was always playing basketball, even playing against boys. She was good at getting the ball in the basket. There was nothing wrong with that. "Anyways," she thought to herself, "those children will have a future and that was what was important."

Picking up the ringing phone, Mrs. Johnnie Bea listened to Chili inform her she would be coming after she closed up the beauty shop. One of the girls working for her had a late customer to finish, and Chili did not want to leave without closing herself. Hanging up the phone, Mrs. Johnnie Bea hurried to answer her front door, smiling as she stared down at Susie, who stood at the bottom of the front door steps.

"Mrs. Johnnie Bea, I tried to come up your steps, and that one started to crack. I'm afraid to step on it. Look it is nearly broken in two. You're going to have to have it fixed right away." Susie bent down and pushed on the step. The boards holding it up broke into with the weight of her hand. Susie quickly removed her hand from the wreckage.

"My goodness child, are you hurt?" Mrs. Johnnie Bea asked, moving down the steps towards her.

"No, I'm alright, Mrs. Johnnie Bea, but not only are your steps broken, but there are way too many weeds around your house. A snake could be hiding in them. We must do something about getting your yard cut."

"Oh, don't worry. I'm going to take care of all of that soon."

"Mrs. Johnnie Bea, you are always taking care of something or someone else it is time someone takes care of you. Look at these steps if I had put my weight on that step we would be going to the hospital right now. I better put a sign up letting the others know to come around back if they are not here already"

"My Oprah you are right. I am so glad the Lord saw fit not to let you take that step. You are the first. Come on round to the back door. You can make up a sign right quick letting the rest of the ladies know they will have to come to the back door." Mrs. Johnnie Bea said when she met Susie at the back door. The young detention officer pulled open the door smiling as she gave Mrs. Johnnie Bea a good solid hug.

They had become acquainted when Mrs. Johnnie Bea had been asked by her church to volunteer at the juvenile center where children were housed when they were picked up by the police for allegedly having committed a crime. Before meeting Susie, she had always thought only criminals went to jail. Susie had reminded her that until the courts find a person guilty their innocence is presumed until the judge says differently.

Mrs. Johnnie Bea knew of Susie long before meeting her, because all the children she talked with spoke so well of her. Her care of the kids was sometimes performed in a way that made her seem too compassionate to children, many thought of as criminals. Mrs. Johnnie Bea had to admit she was surprised people she thought of as guards had that kind of compassion in an environment where even a kind word was rarely permitted.

Mrs. Johnnie Bea said to her of the broken steps "I got to get them fixed before someone breaks their neck. Come on in here and get some of these beans, child. I fixed some special beans for my girls today." Susie hurried inside looking behind her to see Big Tom staring her way. Still, in her juvenile detention uniform, she caught hold of Mrs. Johnnie's hand saying more to herself than to anyone else, "That's a big cat!"

"He wouldn't hurt a flea unless it is hurting him." Mrs. Johnnie Bea assured her. Susie looked into the yellow eyes of Big Tom and moved quickly out of its way.

"How's my children doing down there in that jail?" Mrs. Johnnie Bea asked after Susie returned from placing the sign-out front.

"The children are fine, considering where they are." Before long there was a knock on the back door.

"Mrs. Johnnie Bea, that broken step is dangerous. You don't want to get sued, do you?" Mrs. Johnnie Bea smiled down at Shenee' as she watched her come up the back steps into her home.

"You want me to help you with that briefcase, Shenee'?" Susie asked, coming up behind Mrs. Johnnie Bea. Shenee made it up the stairs with the heavy-looking briefcase in her hand. Her favorite attorney stepped through the back door wearing a dark grey suit and matching heels. Giving her sound advice about those steps Susie had just missed falling into; Mrs. Johnnie Bea was glad Shenee' didn't see what nearly happened to Susie. She gave a silent thanks to the Lord that Susie had put that sign up before the other ladies coming made a bad step and hurt themselves. Giving Shenee' a hug when she walked in, Mrs. Johnnie Bea sighed saying to her, "I'm so glad you took time off for an old lady needing to see you, child. Come on in here my beans will be tender soon."

"Girlfriend you must have been tossing clients out left and right to get here on time," Susie said taking Shenee's briefcase and sitting it on top of a box nearby.

"I have other attorneys and clerks there to take over when I need to leave early, remember?" Mrs. Johnnie Bea and Susie looked at Shenee' as she gave them a classy smile causing them to break out in laughter while Mrs. Johnnie Bea waved them into her sewing room.

"Mrs. Johnnie Bea how many times haven't I told you if you don't hurry and get these front steps fixed someone is going to get hurt," Teresa said when Mrs. Johnnie Bea went to open the door after hearing voices and the sound of knocking at her back door. Both Teresa and Elsie were together so Mrs. Johnnie Bea figured they must have just come from the casino.

"Lord if it has to happen, let it be me. Teresa you are right, I'm going to see about getting someone out here first thing in the morning. Let me help you up Elsie so you won't hit those bad corns, come on in." Mrs. Johnnie Bea said reaching for Elsie's hand.

"Don't worry about winking at us Mrs. Johnnie Bea You just get ready to use some of this money Teresa and I won at the casino to get someone out here to fix those broken steps," Elsie said winking back as Mrs. Johnnie Bea who took the hand offered her.

"I made sure I didn't eat dinner because I know you were cooking those good old beans we grew up on," Elsie said walking into the kitchen with Teresa right behind her still mumbling something about broken steps.

"Amen, I'll not see a body go hungry if I can help it." Mrs. Johnnie Bea answered kissing the cheek Teresa offered her. Before the door shut Chili's smiling face lit up the doorway with Rosie right behind her. Speaking softly Rosie quietly followed the rest into the sewing room.

"Child didn't I just finish talking to you on the phone?" Mrs. Johnnie Bea asked Chili.

"Now you know Mrs. Johnnie Bea I'm about taking care of business," Chili said, coming through the door still in her beautician's sweat suit laughing as she gave Mrs. Johnnie Bea a big hug. "Isn't that what you taught me?" A big smile stretched the wrinkles in Mrs. Johnnie Bea's red-pepper face. Her fat cheeks spread as she grabbed Chili and Rosie, giving them the same hug she had given the others. Everyone filed into Mrs. Johnnie Bea's sewing room, pulling a chair after them.

"La-Joyce, you have a seat right down on this sofa chair so that baby can kick comfortably." Everyone laughed as La-Joyce eased what looked to be two babies inside her stomach down on the sofa.

"Where is Shenee'?" Chili asked. "Just like a lawyer, always late." "I have you know lawyers are not always late Shenee' said to Chili as the rest of the women walked into Mrs. Johnnie Bea's sewing room where she was already seated.

"Here is Mrs. Attorney in her tailored-made suit?" La-Joyce said.

"I want to know where that briefcase she always carries, looking like Perry Mason," Teresa said, smiling at Shenee as she placed her chair beside hers.

"It is right over there in the corner," Susie said. "Someone here might need a good lawyer who knows?" The room filled with laughter as Susie stood up and pointed over at the large briefcase still sitting on the box where she placed it. "I need to ask," Susie started, "are you sure one-sixteenth black blood makes you black?"

"Ten generations back and you're still black." Teresa said causing more laughter as she moved over so Shenee' could squeeze her chair in between hers and Susie's.

"Ten generations back let's see I do believe I read somewhere that J Edgar Hoover might have been black."

Elsie said joining the circle of women.

"Ten generations back, anyone could be black. Just think how many women are sweating for nine months hoping their dominant genes filter through," Shenee' said causing an uproar as more laughter filled the room.

"Girl talking about genes," Susie said. "Chili and I went to Fay's to get some films developed. A friend stopped me. She said she was with her son. We talked for a few minutes. A boy black as..."

"Oh, my Susie that boy was not her son Chili said giving Susie a serious stare.

"As me," La-Joyce said when Chili turned and looked over at her.

"He was blue-black, trust me," Chili said. "You are dark, but certainly not as dark as this child was. Now..."

"Let me tell this, Chili," Susie said, laughing as she pulled up her chair. Suddenly, my friend called to her son, asking him to look at the film that had been developed. Girl, I had to lead Chili out of the place. Her mouth hung open so wide. I was glad there were no flies around."

"Look, that woman was as white as Shenee' ain't no way a baby that black come out of her body with hair that bad." Chili insisted as the others laughed. "He had the nerve to call her mom just like she had spit him out."

Mrs. Johnnie Bea looked at La-Joyce, smiling. La-Joyce looked back at her and laughed, saying: "Chili, why do you always use a negative adjective to describe our natural hair? I'd like to know what constitutes good hair. Do you whip it to make it good? You do know good and bad denote behavior now, don't you?" La-Joyce asked, staring across the room at Chili, who stood doing arm stretches.

"I never do that, do I girls?"

"Yes, sister girl you do that all the time," Susie assured Chili.

"The same way you accused me of being African like it was a sin. And, by the way, parenting has nothing to do with giving birth." La-Joyce told Chili as she kicked her legs in the air while sitting as though doing her stretches."

"Now, La-Joyce, don't get to beefing with me. I am a beautician, hair is my passion, and what do you mean parenting has nothing to do with giving birth?"

"I mean, just because a woman carries a child for nine months, Chili," La-Joyce said, stretching her arms out to make her point. "Doesn't necessarily make her a mom. Those who care for the child and nourish him or her constitute a parent. Susie's friend was the mother of that black child. Whether she birthed him or not, it makes no difference. That is what's so terrible about Americans. Everything is based on race. No one believes that a white mother can love her black baby here in this country?"

"I'm getting better about white people, but I sure don't think a white mother can love a black baby in this country," Chili said, stopping her stretches as she reached into the tote bag she had beside her, smiling at the ladies looking up at her while she rubbed lip balm on her lips. "I can remember a time when I felt uncomfortable in the presence of white people. I guess I was afraid they would try and hurt me in some way for no reason. It was always their nature, you know." Chili said, then looked over at Mrs. Johnnie Bea, sighing.

"I know Mrs. Johnnie Bea," Chili said as Mrs. Johnnie Bea gave her a side glance. "It is bad to say, but Mrs. Johnnie Bea, you know, being from the South yourself, white people used to do some terrible things to black people in the name of inferiority. To this day, there are places where they still think of us as their niggers. You know they are not going to be taking up with no black nappy-headed babies. Come on now, you know I am telling the truth."

"What did they do to you? That was so terrible." La-Joyce uttered in an annoying voice.

"Who raised you, child, white people?" Susie asked, taking a seat on the sofa next to La-Joyce. She planted a kiss on her dimpled cheeks as Teresa explained her current concerns to them.

Too few of our young black children know the true history of their ancestors, Teresa pointed out, "so they ask questions like you are asking. Unlike Jewish children, who have been taught their history even from biblical times, our children have not been taught theirs.

You are one of ours. We need to repeat our history over and over again, just like the Jewish people do for their young people so that we don't forget it. We need to teach it so that it is heard and felt in our young people's hearts today."

"What can you teach us we don't already know?" La-Joyce asked. Teresa turned to La-Joyce saying, "It was just under 50 years ago, they made us drink out of water fountains that were old and nasty sitting right next to their water fountains they made sure were modern, clean, and well kept. We had to eat out of back rooms while they ate up front in nice clean restaurants."

"It made no sense when their men were sleeping in our mom's beds at night. My color did not come from no white woman." Chili said taking a seat on the floor and doing more push-ups.

"And neither did mine," Shenee' said, turning her lips up to indicate she agreed with what Chili said

"Why didn't you just build a modern restaurant and buy modern water fountains for yourselves?" La-Joyce asked, staring at Teresa as if it was the simplest thing to do.

"My Lord, child if we had done that the white folks would have burned the restaurant down before we got two boards nailed together not to mention they would have torn down the water foundation if they didn't poison the water first."

"What!" La-Joyce said as she and Rosie eyed each other laughing.

"Don't you know jealousy is worse than the grave?" Teresa said. They wanted us to eat in the back of their places to continue belittling us and because then they would get our money and the white folks' money as well."

"I can't believe that," La-Joyce said.

"I can't believe it either," Rosie said.

"I don't mean I don't believe it. I meant it is hard to believe." La-Joyce corrected herself after seeing the looks the others gave her and Rosie.

"Well, it's the truth! Not only is that true, they didn't want us to show up the truth of their lies about us being lazy." Elsie said, looking at La-Joyce, smiling as if to say don't you know that?

"You are not about to tell me they would have torn down an entire building if you had built a new one?" La-Joyce asked as if the idea of someone doing that would be ridiculous.

"Girlfriend, your folks kept you out of the United States for far too long. Those white people would have burned it down to the ground before the foundation was up, especially if it looked anyway better than their building. Sounds stupid, I know, but they were like that." Chili said, resting her arm on the back of her head.

The looks on Rosie's and La-Joyce's faces caused Teresa to speak further on the subject while examining the newspaper on the table before her. "Those white people let their dogs eat out of their plates, but we couldn't even eat in the same room with them."

"Now, how nasty is that? And get this; our grandmother's breast milk was good enough for their babies, but we could not drink where they drank. How white people in this country reason is too illogical to explain. I can't understand why so many of our people want to mimic them." Chili said

Looking up at the concerned look on Mrs. Johnnie Bea's and the rest of the women's faces, Chili added, "Now, Mrs. Johnnie Bea, I realize not all white people are the same. There are one or two that are nice enough to like. You have helped me a lot to see that." She said, pulling at the braids on Elsie's head.

"Chili, you have come a long way, but she is right La-Joyce," Susie said. "Many of us feel white women here in America are incapable of loving out of their race unless the children are biracial especially when it comes to black babies. Can you imagine me looking up at a white mother trying to find love in her face for a child black as me and I'm brown, think about if I were black?"

"First of all, they are afraid of how other white Americans and some black Americans will label them. Even babies they have who are bi-racial create problems for them that black women with bi-racial children do not face." Teresa said.

"I don't think, here in this country, race colorblindness has reached the point where even liberal whites don't blink in mixed company. You need to learn your real history, girlfriends, not white folks." Susie smiled at La-Joyce and Rosie then waved her hands in their face as if to say hello it was real.

"I may very well need to learn the real history of my people; however, you ladies need to know that while you are referring to yourselves as African Americans, you need to be more specific."

"What do you mean by that statement, La-Joyce? Be more specific, how?" Susie asked."

"I have met many African Americans who are not black people. Some are white people. Many are 19th-century Africans, Asians as well and white people who were born in Africa and came to America and became naturalized citizens. They are African Americans also. Now respond to that bit of information."

"But their ancestors were not enslaved in this country. That is the difference you know." Everyone turned again surprised to hear Rosie speak up.

"On that note, I think I will start passing out these bowls of beans to you ladies. Don't want you to get to talking so much you go home hungry.

"How many Americans are aware that there is a difference? It is not taught in school and it most certainly is not known by a third of the children who happen to believe they are quote-unquote African American. Thought I would throw that out there to give you ladies something to ponder over" said La-Joyce smiling back at them as she rubbed her swollen stomach and then waved her hands to make her point.

"Only Mrs. Johnnie Bea can answer to that," Chili said lying in the middle of the floor doing bicycle leg motions waiting for Mrs. Johnnie Bea's response. The rest of the women sat with their mouths open as if wondering how to respond to La-Joyce's last announcement.

"Back in the day when we were Negros everyone knew you were speaking of an oppressed group of people whose heritage stemmed from slavery. Now, we have been included with anyone who is a quote-unquote minority. I taught my boys Mylo and Dwayne when they decided it was cool, as they called it, to refer to themselves as Niggas. Don't, I told them hurt my father and his father and his father's father. The black man in this country with your history is already culturally deprived. The love he should have taught his woman and their siblings was stunted by his tragic history. Africa is a continent and there are many races born there. I lived in a world where I was born a Negro, now that name has been abandoned for one that does not define who I am. There is one thing that I do know without a doubt."

"What is that?" La-Joyce asked, penetrating the dark mood of those listening.

"I am God's child. The spirit of God tells me I am human and a part of his flock. That I do know. Since I was born in this country, I must consider myself at least an American citizen. It is true for me as well as it is for any white American. My parents never taught me to hurt or hate a thing God put on this earth unless it will harm me if I don't. Let me say it again: Mrs. Johnnie Bea has no hate in her heart, and she loves everyone." She passed out the last bowl of beans to Chili.

"Oh my goodness girls," Chile said. "She is not lying. We were out there feeding those homeless people. There was this one white woman who stood helping. Elizabeth! That's her name. She asked Mrs. Johnnie Bea to taste a spoon of the soup she had made. Mrs. Johnnie Bea didn't say a word she picked up the spoon the white woman had just eaten from and scooped a spoonful of soup sucking it down telling her how good it was."

"She did what?" Elsie asked setting her bowl down as she placed her hands over her lips staring over at Mrs. Johnnie Bea her glasses on her nose.

"Come on Mrs. Johnnie Bea now that's loving white folks a little too much," Elsie said taking a spoonful of her beans into her mouth.

Later, I asked Mrs. Johnnie Bea wasn't she afraid she might catch something eating behind her like that. Chili's contagious laughter caught on. The others covered their mouths trying to hide their laughter. Elsie stared at Mrs. Johnnie Bea having reached and placed her glasses on as she shook her head.

"I see nothing wrong with that," La-Joyce said, pushing her glasses up on her face looking serious as well.

"Neither did I," Mrs. Johnnie Bea said, speaking up. "My Oprah, child, I don't have time to worry about no disease I might catch when I got my soul to save." Elizabeth and I have worked together on weekend breakfasts for the past nine years. When her daughter's son was sick, she and I took to praying up at that hospital like two sisters; I told her, the Lord says where two gather in my name, I will abide. That child got up and went on back to school with no ill effects from that infection that threatened to take his life. In our quiet time, we sometimes visit and do needlework together many evenings after giving service to the homeless in the village. I have been meaning to bring her over to 'The Safe Place'. She is always talking about how she would like to see the children we help."

"That still does not mean you have to eat out of the same bowl with the same spoon she eats out of my goodness Mrs. Johnnie Bea, that's unhealthy." Elsie insisted.

"When people don't understand something, they fight against it. I took Chili with me to attend service at Elizabeth's church. Chili saw all those white faces, and I thought I would have to carry her out. One of the white women shook her hand, but she was so busy looking around that she didn't start shaking her hand until after the woman withdrew from shaking hands with her. I could tell she was uncomfortable; however, she managed to stay with me through the entire service." Chili placed her bowl of beans in her lap still seated on the floor as she listened to the conversation about her.

"I'm not judging you, Chili," Mrs. Johnnie Bea said, "Given your history, you are making great strides where white people are concerned. I know you have come a long way since you left Louisiana. And trust what I tell you, child, there are many whites to this day that are just like you, some even worse because they have never learned better and can cause harm you cannot." Mrs. Johnnie Bea stopped and rested a minute on one of the stacked boxes in a corner. "Don't think gaining a better understanding that all white people were not the same came easy for me. I looked for them to be mean and that is exactly what I found. Let me tell you, I used to be there too. I used to say the same thing to my father and he would tell me the same as I am telling you."

"What caused you to change Mrs. Johnnie Bea?" La-Joyce asked.

"Yeah, what made you feel differently when all that awful violence was going on around you?" Shenee' asked, looking over at Chili, who was giving her the evil eye.

Mrs. Johnnie Bea looked up at her parents' picture removed her glasses and shared the story of the night she and several freedom riders were on their way back home from a trip to another town in Mississippi one night.

"We were on our way back from Seal. That's another town in Mississippi close to where I was living with my parents at the time. The Klan men waved us down" Mrs. Johnnie Bea said to them as they gave her their attention. "We were blinded by the spotlights they flashed on our car. I don't think I have ever been so scared in my life. My knees shook so hard when they made us get out of the car. I couldn't stop them. That's the kind of fear that brings water running from your body you can't stop."

'Git out of the car niggers.' "One of them shouted. We go have us a hanging hare tonight. Katie the white girl riding with us grabbed my hand. She and I were in the back seat of the car.

'Look what we got here a nigger lovin' bitch in the back seat.' She refused to get out of the car when they told us to. Tears were falling from her eyes as we looked at the hate in the face of the white policemen calling her a nigger loving bitch with such venom you would have thought cobras were biting her.

"One of them grabbed her by her blonde hair and dragged her out screaming. She was a little girl and just nineteen years old at the time. I don't know what happened; either she didn't understand the history of the Klan in this country, or her privileged mind clicked in."

'I'll have your job. You, white cracker trash.' She screamed at them when the others began helping drag her out.

'Leave me the fuck alone, you dirty white bastards' "When she uttered those words, I started praying to the Lord to step in because I knew death was on us if he didn't do something.

"The one wearing the police uniform dragged her over by a tree and put a rope around her neck, telling her.

'We kill nigger lovin' trash like you little bitch. How would you like the feel of this rope around your neck stretched with your tongue hanging out? Then whose job will you have? They all laughed while we stood there wondering which one of us they would come for next.

"He and the others pulled her clothes off and fondled her body, saying,

'How many niggers you let touch you like this?' About that time, another carload of whites come up. I knew then we were going to die that night. One of the men got out and walked up to us looking over at Katie there on the ground with the rope around her neck and her clothes torn off.

'We cannot afford to have Mississippi gutted by Feds like they is in Alabama. Y'all knows that.' He said, his eyes still on Katie. He went over to where she lay sobbing on the ground, pulled her up by her arm, and slapped her so hard I felt it."

'If any of this gets back to them nigger loving Yankees up North, all these niggers will die. Do you understand me?' he screamed in her face.

"At last, I think she finally realized how deadly our situation was, especially when he pulled her into his face and said,

'Not only will these niggers die, but we will come kill their little nigger babies down to the last one. Do you understand what I mean' She nodded yes, sobbing so hard when he let her go, that she fell to the ground. Walking over to one of the men with us, he said to him.

'She will be dead before the next nightfall if I catch her riding with you niggers again, and I didn't need to tell you what will happen to the rest of you.' He walked off a few steps, then stopped turning around. He said to no one in particular.

'Tell that newspaper nigger I will be looking for him.'

"My heart stopped. I can't remember when it started beating again. I only remembered he would be looking for my father.

"I believe to this day the Lord brought those others up to where we were. That is the only reason why they didn't kill us. The terror I felt that night I don't know how to describe, except to say my heart pounded so loud in my chest I could not only hear it I could feel it in my throat choking me to death.

After that night, I moved to another level, a higher one than most, in knowing how to truly let God abide. Katie wanted to stay and keep fighting, but we knew better than she did what that White man said he meant." Mrs. Johnnie Bea said, tears streaming from her eyes.

"Mrs. Johnnie Bea, it had to be God hearing your prayer because that was a miracle. Louisiana is bad, but Mississippi's horrors are a thousand times worse." Chili said tearfully.

"Maybe she went back and told what they did to her, and that was why they hung your father," Rosie said.

"If she had gone back and told what they did to her that night, Elsie, Teresa, and I would not be seated in this room this evening," Mrs. Johnnie Bea said, shaking her head.

"That Cracker meant every word he said. Didn't he Teresa?" Elsie asked, looking over at Teresa, who sat across from her.

"They would have killed all the babies first, Elsie, then they would have killed us older children and Granny them last. Yes, Elsie, they meant every word. They probably have drowned a thousand Emmett Tills in that neck of the woods. She most certainly remained silent because after that happened to her, she had to know what Mrs. Johnnie Bea and the rest of us would face even if she were safe." Teresa said, shaking her head as she broke the silence.

"How can you not have love for someone who has seen their life at its end and still be willing to continue to carry the torch with you?" That's not about the color of one's skin but the character of one's heart. I thank my father for teaching me about the power of love for another human being. That young white girl wanted to stay and continue fighting even though she knew it could mean her life the next time around. Wouldn't you say she deserved to be loved?" Mrs. Johnnie Bea let her words soak in while she left the room to get the baked sweet potatoes.

"What did Mrs. Johnnie Bea put in these beans; they are so good they make your mouth pop," Susie said placing another spoonful in her mouth after taking a deep breath as did the others after listening to the details of Mrs. Johnnie Bea's near-tragic story.

"They are good." Shenee' said, getting an Amens from the rest of the group. Mrs. Johnnie Bea returned, hobbling over to each of her friends and offering each of the sweet potatoes she had baked in her oven.

"Mrs. Johnnie Bea, I'm glad you told us that because now I don't feel guilty for caring about some white people who I know care about me," La-Joyce said, giving Chili a menacing look.

"When a person says they believe in God," Mrs. Johnnie Bea said, "no matter what their race, faith or religious beliefs are they know that the power of God is mightier than man's weak need to kill because of the hate that feeds his fears. My slave ancestors must have realized sometimes God gives man power to see how he will use that power."

"Mrs. Johnnie Bea, I don't mean to change the subject, but I need to ask you what happened to those china dishes Mylo and I bought you just last month?" Mrs. Johnnie Bea paused before placing her potato on her plate, then answered.

"Child, I got them packed away to save until I can get a real china cabinet to place them in."

"What about eating out of them?" La-Joyce asked,

"Now, child, those nice bowels are for guests."

"What are we, Mrs. Johnnie Bea? I'm just asking, not trying to be smart or anything." La-Joyce clarified, pushing her glasses up on her nose as very large dimples grew out of the smile starting on her face.

"Now La-Joyce, you know Mrs. Johnnie Bea has them for her special guests," Elsie said, answering La-Joyce's question.

"What are we?" Shenee' asked, dropping her spoon in her bowl, and making a loud clanging sound.

"Why, family." Mrs. Johnnie Bea said, raising her hands in the air. "You young ladies are my family, and my family do not care about silly things such as what they eat out of. They're just glad to be a part of my family." The ladies' smiles indicated they were happy to be included as a family member.

"You can go on with what you were telling us, Mrs. Johnnie Bea, now that La-Joyce and Shenee' know that the bowls they are eating out of make them a part of our family."

La-Joyce licked her tongue at Chili, who placed her spoon in her empty bowl, looking up at Mrs. Johnnie Bea.

"If a man is true in his belief in the God he worships, he will find no need to kill his enemy he will leave them for God to deal with. Who but the creator can best revenge my sorrows? So I say, 'Yes, I pray for my enemies too,' if you call them that. I call them lost souls searching for something they cannot find. That is why hate exists. I see hate as fear needing something to feed on. My father taught me that."

"Mrs. Johnnie Bea, I'm still not getting your point," La-Joyce said, tossing her head at the mean stares she was receiving from the others in the room.

"I have friends who are Muslim, La-Joyce. If we go to their service and they ask that I cover my hair, how does that hurt me? It is their faith that I have respected just as I expect respect for my own. I am out there helping those filled with hate find some love to put in their hearts so that they can live better lives. If revenge by violence was the answer, why hasn't it produced what it sat out to do? It cannot. Once you take a life that life will never return on this earth, what is worse, the atonement for that life will be felt not only by you but by all of humanity."

"Mrs. Johnnie Bea, may I ask you something?" Everyone looked again in surprise to hear Rosie join in on the conversation. Mrs. Johnnie Bea appeared surprised, asking her: "What is it, child? Speak about it, and I will answer if I can."

"Mrs. Johnnie Bea, you put Kevin and Jerry out of The Safe Place for calling each other 'nigga' last week. I wondered about that because black rappers all over the country use the word 'nigga' in their lyrics, not to mention how many black people I know respond to each other by calling their friends and themselves 'nigga.'"

"Come on, Rosie, by now, you should understand what that word meant to our people. Too many died because they were thought of as niggers." Teresa said, a stern, look on her face.

"What do you mean?" Rosie asked.

"Emmett Till, child," Teresa said.

"What about Emmett Till, and who the heck is he? I heard Teresa mention him just a little while ago." Rosie asked.

"We need a history class up in here, for real," Chili said, holding her knees together as she sat on the floor shaking her head.

"Child," Teresa continued, "he was a young fourteen-year-old black male child whose body was mutilated after he was hung and then thrown into the river by white men who said he whistled at a white woman."

"She's kidding, of course. Mrs. Johnnie Bea, tell me she's making up some horrible joke." La-Joyce shouted looking as though she had been told some insane made-up tale."

"That is incredible, that happened to him because he whistled at a white woman. No sane person would kill anyone for a reason that stupid." Rosie said shaking her head along with La-Joyce.

"Child," Mrs. Johnnie Bea said looking at La-Joyce and Rosie. "It was Emmett Till the nigger that was hung, mutilated, and drowned by those white men. In the minds of the white community who thought his crime fit the punishment, Emmett Till was not a child just a nigger. The four little black girls were not murdered in that church by those white people when it was bombed it was four little niggers. White folks had no love for those they coined niggers no matter how young or old they were. They had been brainwashed into thinking only they were human. Their insanity was far-reaching." Mrs. Johnnie Bea said.

"My goodness you mean I have to tell my child this is the history of our people." La-Joyce sat back, rubbing her stomach harder. He will think all white people are horrible." La-Joyce said.

"Mine will too," Rosie said frowning.

"So what? They are." Chili said staring at both Rosie and La-Joyce. Mrs. Johnnie Bea looked away from the women seated in her sewing room with her. Her eyes wandered up to the picture of her father and mother.

"Like I have been telling you, child, before you know who you are, you must understand your history. When you know and understand it as it was lived by your ancestors, there are some things you never say or do out of respect for yourself and those who lived that history knowing what they went through." Teresa said, also speaking to Rosie's question.

"As broken and abused as it may be, one's history has to be taught and understood early, especially by those it belongs to. Because we live still with those who would rather not speak on that horrid past, our written history is not made available to us wholesale." Teresa looked away from the women as if seeing something they could not see.

"Our ancestors came to this country in chains but the real chains came much later after our so-called freedom was given to us. The chains in our minds are so deeply entrenched to this day we live with them daily and don't even know it. It is the same with white folks who have no clue about the shame their past leaves as their legacy. A shameful past even they no longer want to claim."

"There are no chains around my mind," Rosie said.

"Mine either," La-Joyce said, waving her hand in the air.

"What are you trying to tell us we don't already know?"

"Me," Susie said, "I worry about Shaharra. She's a beautiful girl, my daughter, but she is dark-skinned. There is no way she will find a husband in our race here in this country."

"That's not true Susie, Mylo is as dark as I am. He is always telling me how beautiful I look to him." La-Joyce said

"He's one in a million," Chili said her head down as she stood touching her toes.

"La-Joyce, Mylo got Mrs. Johnnie Bea's teachings you can thank God for that," Teresa said

"Susie you are right about what's happening around here because I went to a wedding not so long ago and every, I mean every black man there was with a white woman including the woman my friend's son was marrying. Now I don't have a problem with mixing the races but that was a bit much."

"Well, how many black men were there? One or two?" La-Joyce asked.

"Twenty-five, La-Joyce; I made it a point to count," Teresa said, looking at the women seated in the room.

"Maybe they were pulling themselves up by their boot strips, who knows?" Chili said, sucking her jaws inward.

"That is all well and good, but when there is no soul on the bottom of that boot, what good is the strip?"

"Elsie, you are a crazy woman," Teresa said.

"Now, you girls might as well tell it like it is. Those brothers don't want to turn over in bed every morning and see black." Chili said causing the others to look at her with widened eyes.

"It's true, bad enough he has to see black in the mirror daily when he looks at himself. At least when he turns over and sees white, he can dream. Now don't look at me like that, sisters you know it's like that." Chili said as she bent over, reached for her tote bag taking out a large comb. You hate cause Chili is telling you the truth about those brothers," Chili pulled out some of her hair, bending over, saying to them as she combed through it.

"When that brother gets up every morning crying ouch, ouch, ouch while combing his nappy hair he is saying to himself, black may be beautiful," Chili stopped combing her hair looked up at the others, and said in a baritone voice, "but white is gorgeous and I don't want" Chili continued as she began to comb her hair again as if with effort "no child of mine coming into this world black as me with hair this nappy." Chili dropped the comb back in her tote bag and stood up looking at the women with a big smile on her face.

Rosie, who was usually quiet and detached, bent over laughing. Before long she was on the floor doubled up fetal style laughing as hard as she could.

Elsie who was usually serious and matter-of-fact about everything could not conceal the laughter that surged from her lips, lips that had been shut tight a moment before.

The others began to laugh. Soon everyone was holding their stomachs trying to stop the laughter that had become contagious. Teresa finally got up and began to pass out tissues to the others after taking one for herself.

"Chili you have a ruthless tongue in that month of yours," Teresa said shaking her head as she continued to laugh while wiping her eyes.

"Chili you need a good cussing out," Susie said, as she reached for a tissue finding it impossible to stop laughing.

"I'll second that!" Shenee' said shaking her head as she laughed along with the other women.

"Self-hate is a mother. My two brothers are the same way that's why I know. Oh, that reminds me I have to call my mother and see if their house was damaged by the storm."

"Mrs. Johnnie Bea go ahead and give these girls some of your history cause, they sure don't want to hear the truth I'm telling them."

"Chili, go on in there and use my phone to call. I remember how terrible those storms can be coming through the South this time of year. Elsie, show her where that phone is," Mrs. Johnnie Bea said, still laughing at Chili's outlandish remarks.

"Tell her she needs to use that axe to split the storm next time," Elsie said, placing her hands on her hips after she rose from her seated position.

"Elsie, that's old black folklore. You can't use an axe to split a storm." La-Joyce said laughing.

"It may be called old black folklore these days but back then it worked. My mother said the lightning would not strike your house with that axe stuck in a stump or directly in the ground. She would look and see which way the storm was coming and down that axe had business in that stomp or the ground. We never had our house struck by lightning and no other house that used that axe was struck. Why I can't say but it works." Rosie and Susie looked at Elsie and then each other lowered their heads as if suppressing laughter.

"You young kids nowadays think nothing is for real unless it comes through the white man's lips. I remember my mother telling me when she got snake bit once her mother took a live chicken split it into, pressing it against her leg to draw the poison out." Susie shared.

"And if someone comes down with the sore throat," Mrs. Johnnie Bea said hobbling over to retrieve a large towel from a rack nearby, "you'd go outside and get hog waste put it in a pan, and cook it until it was good and hot place it around their neck. The next day it was as if they never had the sore throat."

"If the smell didn't kill you, you should be over the sore throat and any other illness you had," Lajoyce said laughing along with the others.

"Mrs. Johnnie Bea, you are not serious, are you?" La-Joyce asked, pinching her nose.

"That Cow Susie Tea made out of cow waste was good for pneumonia, and that old flux weed prepared saved many baby's lives back then."

"Cow Susie Tea? Why did they have to give it my name?" Susie asked, laughing along with Rosie and La-Joyce as they pointed at her. "Nothing worked like a good dirt dabber's nest soaked in coal oil for a badly cut foot. Make a good mud pack and tie it around that foot. In a few days, it would be as good as new." Teresa said smiling as she looked at the shocked woman staring at her.

"Mrs. Johnnie Bea, where were the doctors?" Rosie asked. Mrs. Johnnie Bea, Teresa, chili, and Elsie looked at each other."

"Like I said, Mrs. Johnnie Bea, these women come up on backs they don't know nothing about," Chili said, following Elsie out to where the phone was.

"Child, there were no doctors for us. The few we had worked themselves to death going from house to house. Blacks were not allowed in hospitals. If a white doctor saw you, it would have been in a shed. Maybe after you sat there all day, he might come by. If he knew your family he'd ask about their health and what he could do for you. A person he took no interest in might be dying and he would never look their way. If you took pity for them and begged him they might be seen."

"What Mrs. Johnnie Bea is saying," Teresa said, turning to give her attention to Rose, Susie, Shenee' and La-Joyce after Chili and Elsie left the room. "Is that we became a people who learned how to survive. We found plants and made our medicines. We learned to treat our illnesses as best we could. Some of it you might turn your nose up at but those remedies work for us. We, as the old folks used to say, 'Made a way out of no way' That is why you are here today laughing when you should be proud."

"You are right Teresa." Susie said looking at La-Joyce, Shenee', and Rosie. We should be proud. But we have been taught by white people and misled by black people to make fun of things we feel make us look bad in the faces of whites and our people who believe nothing unless white folks say it is so."

"Children don't you know that when freedom came," Mrs. Johnnie Bea said taking Susie's hand in hers, "our people soon came to realize it wasn't freedom at all but a worse kind of hell we found ourselves in thirteen years later. Time enough for the white southerners to form their plan of revenge for the Civil War they lost."

"I guess our forefathers were not treated very well huh?" La-Joyce said to Mrs. Johnnie Bea.

"Well, La-Joyce, imagine, if you can, that you've been freed, or so you think. You and your family are traveling by horse and wagon, trying to find lodging. Your black skin gives you away, so no matter where you go, even though you are free, no white person you have to deal with treats you as though you are free. Hooded Klansmen stop you and slaughter your father and all your brothers. If you hide well, you might escape that slaughter, but nowhere can you find a place to sleep because your black skin will not allow you lodging in any establishment owned or operated by whites. Only the back doors to white homes have a welcome mat for you."

"Dog, that's something," Rosie said, placing her hand under her chin as the others leaned closer to hear Mrs. Johnnie Bea.

"Let's make that boot strip even tighter. Say you, by some strange miracle, get a piece of land. You work that land every back-breaking day until your crop blossoms. You tell your family we won't starve this year. Before putting up your plow, you notice a white man eyeing your progress suspiciously. You eye him back, hating that feeling that has come over you. You dismiss it and go in to be with your family. After all, you are a free man now able to pull yourself up by your boot straps.

The next morning, you get up just at dawn, go out to inspect your boot strip, and find that your entire field has been plowed under. A year's work has gone down the drain because of someone's cruel act of white jealousy.

If that is not bad enough the white man you know is responsible comes to your house the next day. You know he can take up with any female in that house with no laws in the country to stop him."

"Even the man?" Mrs. Johnnie Bea "He could take the man too?" La-Joyce asked, removing her glasses.

"La-Joyce don't be ridiculous," Susie said.

"Susie, it's not ridiculous. Back then, even the man was whipped to the ground." Shenee' said, looking at Susie as her teeth bit into her lips.

"Yes, daughter, even the man." Mrs. Johnnie Bea said. The man's wife, his daughters, even his sons if he so desired one or all. Who would the man complain to if he did, the Klan, the White Citizen Counsel? You might find your entire family dead one night. Child the one chain you soon realize you can never free yourself is your black skin.

"As long as your skin is black and the white man sees that it is black you know you are doomed to live in a country that could use it to justify its oppression against you as a human in this country."

"Mrs. Johnnie Bea many people believe not everyone black person fought to end Jim Crow oppression.

You are right, Teresa. There were lots of black people who believed it was the right of the whites to treat us as inferiors. They wanted the colored and white, water fountains to remain if that was what the whites wanted as long as they didn't harm them. Those of us who fought against the Jim Crow system also fought against our people who thought that way as well,"

"Why would you have to fight with your people over something wrong for them as well?" Rosie asked.

"Because they lived in fear of a change, they were not sure would come about for their good having lived under Jim Crow's laws for nearly one hundred years," Elsie said.

"And because they had seen too many killed trying to fight back," Teresa said, folding her arms as she looked up at the picture of Mrs. Johnnie Bea's father.

"Today, there are many people who do not understand that kind of poison nor do they understand why they should not want to call themselves something that is a total humiliation to their forefathers who fought to be more than a nigga' to anyone. Why because they never lived it. Having no deep-rooted culture it is just another word to them."

"I say nigga' all the time," Rosie said as she looked at the others and then covered her mouth as they stared back at her.

"You say it because you have never been taught and don't understand your history in the way you should, Rosie," Teresa said to her.

"Mrs. Johnnie Bea, Elsie and I, and even Chili lived in an environment where that word was the instrument of pain and death in so many black people's lives.

"Back in the day, our ancestors felt the pain of the slave being given the name nigger. Like horses and the cows, the nigger was a part of the master's livestock." Teresa said as she continued to speak for Mrs. Johnnie Bea, who tearfully looked at the pictures of her parents and grandmother.

"I lived in the house with my grandmother until I was ten she died right about the time of Mrs. Johnnie's father's hanging. I know because we had not come up here yet. Had we, Elsie?" Teresa asked Elsie as she walked back into the room.

Upon hearing about Mrs. Johnnie Bea's father's hanging, the rest of the women in the room looked over at Mrs. Johnnie Bea with shocked looks on their faces. Each sat their bowls down, seeing tears slowly ease down Mrs. Johnnie's face as she gazed up at her father's picture.

"No, Teresa, we had not. Your granny died right before we had to leave Mississippi," Elsie answered.

"If the master wanted to take the life of a baby calf, my granny told me, it would be done. If the master wanted to punish a nigger that was pregnant, he could beat or even kill that female nigger and the baby inside of her. It did not matter that she might not be physically able to work; it was his right to kill or beat what was no longer his property, the nigger. Long after she was not his property, he still was given the right to violate her any way he wanted by the laws in this country."

"Even after the Civil War? A War Harriet Tubman and other blacks fought to end slavery?" Rosie asked.

Girls, all of you looked at 'The Color Purple,' which was real life for us in Mississippi." Teresa said to those listening to her with their mouths open.

"No wonder Mrs. Johnnie Bea is so into the part Oprah plays," Chili said.

"Yes, it means more to her than we will ever understand," Susie said.

"Mylo and I will have to talk about this," La-Joyce said to no one in particular. I will tell my son his history early.

"If you don't teach him, he will call himself a 'nigger' just like the rest of our young people do because our history has been so diluted that they don't know they are giving the white world an easy out by diluting its meaning."

"Mrs. Johnnie Bea, these beans are so good," Elsie said, taking a spoonful of the beans from her bowl and putting it into her mouth as she continued talking to the others.

"When those freedom riders were killed, it was the white nigger lovers and the black niggers being killed just like Mrs. Johnnie Bea was telling you. Strange Fruit, as sung by Billie Holiday, was the way of life for niggers after slavery. Jim Crow Laws were a way of life for us when I was growing up. That meant a nigger had no rights to his life and could be hung by the neck until death, without it being thought wrong by white people in this country years before we began to fight back and after." Elsie said then taking another spoon of beans into her mouth.

"My Lord, what kind of people were they?" Rosie asked, sitting her bowl on the table next to where she was seated, her eyes never leaving Elsie's lips.

"The 'Strange Fruit' that Billie Holiday sings about in her song is riding by trees seeing black folks hanging in them dead."

"Strange Fruit, I never heard of that song. Who is Billie Holiday? Was she back in the day, too?" La-Joyce asked.

"Billie Holiday must have been the person singing Strange Fruit like Elsie said," Rosie said.

"Come on, Rosie, you and La-Joyce cannot be that ignorant. Mrs. Johnnie Bea was not kidding when she said that Billie Holiday was riding by and saw dead black men hanging in trees, wasn't no white ones hanging there." Elsie said, shaking her head and then closing her mouth firmly, indicating her annoyance.

"Lesson to be learned," Mrs. Johnnie Bea said. "If a man calls me a fool and I know I am not a fool, I am not going to name myself fool and tell him he cannot call me what I do not believe I am yet I use it to address me. I already know that no matter how I fool myself, we both know what a fool is, especially the ones who coined it. Nigger is the animal the white master enslaved on his plantation. You have seen pictures of how his back looked. To him so is the Nigga; you just can't see his scars because he doesn't know they are there. He doesn't know you can't try to take a letter out and make it mean something else when it sounds the same. My ancestors and the people in my day fought for respect and dignity. I asked my young nephews when they started calling themselves niggas.

"Why would we call ourselves a name that is a constant reminder of the atrocities inflicted upon our ancestors? A name so disgraceful white Americans don't like to be reminded that they coined the term? And what it meant to their history." Mrs. Johnnie Bea said, having gained the ladies' full attention in the room.

"Now that I am learning, I guess I have a lot to teach my children about our history," Rosie said, smiling at the others.

"There are nights I wake up in my sleep hearing those little white children's voices singing,

'Die nigger, die nigger die' some more while they threw stones at my dead father's body and upon the backs of those rescuing his body from being further mutilated."

"I will never say that word again or allow my children to use it, Mrs. Johnnie Bea. I promise." Rosie said, shaking her head as she looked around the room.

"Explain to me what endearment such as that could have for me unless I am still mentally chained to the enslavement of my past or have no understanding than to give my blessings to the type of behavior that places chains around me I cannot see. My heart still feels pain for poor Emmett Till, the freedom riders, and all those unnamed soldiers who died being called niggers and nigger lovers, just as the Jewish people must still feel pain at the senseless death of so many of their people in

Germany. God would not permit me to entertain such a word in my vocabulary."

"I never had anyone explain our history to me so thoroughly yet in so few words. I have never been taught to think or understand what you are sharing and teaching us," Rosie said.

"Neither have I," La-Joyce said, pulling her large pregnant body up from the sofa where Mrs. Johnnie Bea had instructed her to sit. La-Joyce walked over to Mrs. Johnnie Bea and planted a kiss on both her cheeks.

Mrs. Johnnie Bea smiled up at La-Joyce, saying, "I don't judge our children for their lack of understanding because so many have had no one to teach them better. They destroy themselves for reasons they don't understand. It is a self-fulfilling prophecy; he who does not know his history does not know himself and endures death while living. I tell my children they cannot come into the Safe Place disrespecting who they are. They will be welcome back tomorrow but I will teach them their history no one bothered to tell them. There is no one else to teach them better than me who lived it."

"I now understand why Mrs. Johnnie Bea sent them home," Rosie said, smiling as she nodded.

"Mrs. Johnnie Bea those white people are going to burn in hell for all the wrong they have done aren't they."

"Well, Rosie. I can't say that. The father is such a forgiving God. Who knows but that on their dying lips, they ask for forgiveness. Would it be wrong that it be granted them?"

"I don't know. It just doesn't seem right somehow." Rosie said.

"When this civilization is long gone, and others coming after it, they may think of it as barbaric, and the things that we feel are important, not important at all. Who knows? All we can do is to do what we believe God wants us to do and leave their fate in his hands.

"Well!" Chili said, looking at La-Joyce and Rosie.

"Well, what!" La-Joyce answered, realizing Chili was also speaking to her.

"Well, do you understand what Mrs. Johnnie Bea has been trying to get you to understand, girlfriends?"

"Of course, I understand now, Chili. Thank you very much." Pushing her glasses higher on her nose, La-Joyce frowned at Chili and received a kiss on her cheek.

"We scream for acceptance and respect yet we have not yet learned that we must acquire self-respect in our actions." Mrs. Johnnie Bea said, still wiping the tears from her eyes.

"Every time a racial issue raises its ugly head, we as Americans smother it under self-denial while the rest of the world looks on feeling shame for us. Americans hurriedly tried to stitch up that shame after Rodney King's beating that turned into a racial monster, opening up wounds and behaviors thought to have died long ago. O'Jay's trial should have been just another one of thousands of such trials taking place in this country. Instead, that trial tore open old wounds again, splitting the country along racial lines. Again and again, we tell ourselves we are over the past, yet every day, we grind away at our inability to respect ourselves and each other because of that very past."

"Heaven, help us? How do we get past it? That is what I want to know. How can we cure the infection and become healthy?" Shenee' asked.

"That's what I need to know too," La-Joyce stated, staring into Mrs. Johnnie Bea's eyes. "Mylo and I were so hurt when the news media chose to point out every negative activity going on by black people after Hurricane Katrina as if someone cared who went into those flooded stores when babies were dying on that bridge and in that dome, many such horrors they neglected to report. Reporting that those in that terrifying condition were refugees. White people can't help themselves. They are still enslaved to past thinking.

Mylo said that every thirty seconds of news coverage that depicted negative behavior committed by blacks after Hurricane Katrina is engraved in the hearts of every person looking at that footage. It tells them they are not to take what was happening to those persons seriously, or even that they deserve the horrors that were happening to them. He believes it is done purposely. I wanted to say to him that there were others besides blacks in that awful ordeal but the focus of attention remains a serious black problem."

"The white news media chose to call those victims refugees instead of Americans. After four hundred years, we are labeled referring to us as non-Americans. This is coming from the white news media that has become the eyes and ears of all America." Elsie said.

"They forget their ancestors were immigrants coming to this country from England and Ireland.

"The news media is not knowingly being mean. They are simply giving white people the news they believe they want to hear. On 911 it was happening to the majority of white Americans. They were not going to talk about all the crime going on in New York at that time. White Americans would have felt it too insensitive to air such as that in a national crisis." Susie said as her gum popped twice.

"Where black suffering is concerned, few white Americans identify even when it is as serious as it was with Hurricane Katrina," Elsie said, looking down at the seated women.

"As Susie says, the people writing for those papers and providing news coverage are whites and blacks writing what they believe white Americans want to read and believe."

"When I see white people acting racist, I put them in check," Rosie said, narrowing her eyes.

"Not me," Teresa said. As intelligent as white people claim to be, there is no way they are unaware when they are being cruel to other people."

"I'm sure they had crime going on in New York after 911, but rightly so, it would have been cruel, to repeatedly broadcast such as that after that devastation like they did in the case of Hurricane Katrina."

"Not unless you had no feelings for those having suffered that devastation," La-Joyce said taking her glasses from her teary eyes.

"You know," Shenee' said, "I am proud to say that many Americans white and black cared and did what they could, but it needs to be so that it is an automatic thought in the American heart about every American."

The others echoed yes and agreed with Shenee and La-Joyce.

"Mrs. Johnnie Bea, how do we change this hateful trend?" Chili asked having returned from her call, now seated on the floor fingers pressed against her temples.

Mrs. Johnnie Bea walked over looking at her father's picture hearing her father's voice as he told her

"We must reach up and pick up the torch left by those who have gone before us," Mrs. Johnnie Bea said to the women hoping for answers "We must carry it with respect for ourselves explaining it to them that don't know or understand its meaning.

"There are four groups of Americans living in this country. We need to acknowledge and find respect in our hearts for each."

"Okay Mrs. Johnnie Bea, don't keep us in suspense." Susie urged.

"There are the Native people first before the Europeans. It has been said that they traded with black people who it is said came here centuries before Columbus. There are the English who later came to America on the Mayflower. Then there are the black Americans who are here because of American slavery. Africans were brought to America and forced to endure chattel slavery so that white southern landowners would not have to pay wages to white southern farmers. You see, their history is not clear to the white southern young people either." "Those people were being cheated by the very people who taught them to hate us," Rosie said.

"You are right, Rosie; as long as the landowners who could buy slaves didn't have to pay the white southern farm laborers for their labor, he benefited by having his attention focused on hating us so he didn't have to worry about giving them fair pay for labor they had taken from them when they brought us here," Elsie said kicking her shoes off as she rubbed down her long legs.

"After the slave master cheated them out of their jobs all they got in return was their white skin and their hatred for people who were no more responsible for taking their jobs than they were for losing them," La-Joyce said shaking her head as she looked down at her hands.

"And the next group," Chili said smiling in agreement at La-Joyce's statement.

"Some immigrants came to this country in free form to find a better way of life. This group includes Africans whose ancestors were never enslaved in this country and white immigrants who came over from all over the world long after slavery ended and were taught Jim Crow behavior by the white Americans living here after slavery ended.

"The Africans are sometimes more racist than the whites who live here aren't they Elsie," Teresa said more than asked.

"Yes, they are. Had they come over under our similar circumstances they would have sympathized with us after running to escape their past oppression instead of using the fact that they had never been slaves as an excuse to join the cruel behavior of the white people already here." Elsie answered. They never realized white people didn't welcome them. Black people fought saying that if white immigrants were allowed in this country black immigrants should also be allowed to come here."

"We as a race of people have to admit our heritage makes our history different from even those immigrants whose color is the same as ours so that when we face our concerns, those concerns are given the respect they deserve." Mrs. Johnnie Bea said reflecting on the writings she found after her father's death. She then said to her friends,

"Without a clear understanding of one's history, you become who someone else says you are. We must understand being placed under the label of 'minority' does not give us history or define our culture. It simply includes us with groups of people who are not white. It causes us not to have a definite cultural heritage, unlike other races that are quite aware of their cultural heritage and how it formed the people that they are.

You must remember Africa is a continent. It is not a country. Black people from many different countries in Africa were enslaved together. Since they came from many different languages and dialects, it took centuries for any form of language to develop a culture if you can call what we have a true culture."

Turning on the secondhand television next to her, Mrs. Johnnie Bea said to the women as she stuck a tape inside her VCR player, "Until we all see ourselves as Americans no matter what our race, gender, or ethnic background, we will always be divided among ourselves."

The picture was unclear but they could see the freedom riders seated on the ground, while the black nonviolence trainer talked to them about the dangers of this venture they were about to undertake.

"Mrs. Johnnie Bea you've got to buy a new television," Teresa said putting on her glasses to see the dim faded-out picture.

"I was just thinking the same thing," Mrs. Johnnie Bea said. She could see that the picture was not clear at all. Most of the people looked like they had sun rays in their eyes. Even the color of their clothes is hard to distinguish." Susie said.

"Mrs. Johnnie Bea this television must be at least forty years old. I'm going to talk to Mylo and see about getting you a better one."

"I have one at the salon better than this one she can have," Chili said placing glasses on her eyes to see better.

"Now, don't you two, worry about buying me a thing. I'm not at home enough to care about this old television except to sit and watch Oprah and these old eyes know how she looks."

Susie stood up, walked over, and hugged Mrs. Johnnie Bea saying to her, "Mrs. Johnnie Bea, Oprah has probably changed her looks twenty times since you were able to see her clearly on this television. We are buying you a new one even if we have to chip in to get it." An outburst of laughter filled the room at Susie's words.

"Just sit your bottom down now 'cause, I know you ladies' eyes are better than mine and I want you to take a look at what I am about to show you. Come on Susie, plant another kiss right here." Mrs. Johnnie Bea said also laughing as she pointed a finger at the cheek Susie had not kissed. Susie planted the kiss just where Mrs. Johnnie Bea asked and took her seat.

They looked from the scene of the freedom riders to see the car the three civil rights men were driving being pulled from the river that had been driven by the three freedom riders. Another scene showed police dragging black and white folks out of restaurants by police officers in cities around the country. Finally, the film ended.

"Mrs. Johnnie Bea, you don't have to worry we are certainly not going to accept that kind of treatment today. I guarantee you that." La-Joyce said shaking her head.

"She's right Mrs. Johnnie Bea that was back in the day not today," Rosie said holding up two fingers indicating the peace sign.

"This is history and it is relevant today if you listen," Susie said reprimanding both La-Joyce and Rosie for interrupting Mrs. Johnnie Bea.

Mrs. Johnnie Bea turned to them saying: "These young people became the conscious of America during that time. While most white

Americans didn't care that we were being murdered in this country without a thought from the general public, many white Americans did care about what happened especially to young white demonstrators who came down to help us."

"Chile living in our home the young white students said to us that their parents had taught them about a different America than the one they were seeing down in Mississippi. The freedom Riders both white and black that came to help were unprepared and shocked at what they saw. They didn't say 'Oh that is too bad for them'. They knew they had been taught to believe a different truth about their country. What they were seeing certainly was not it.

They took action by risking their lives. We were shocked to see what some whites thought about the pains of others and not just about the privileges of whites gaining at the expense of another race. Their minds were set on making this country stand for what they believed it was supposed to stand for."

"What is that some more hating white folks?" Chili asked getting hard stares from the rest.

"I can never say I hated all white folks," Chili said stretching her arms up skyward seeing the looks she was getting. The rest of the group turned from Chili back to listen to Mrs. Johnnie Bea.

"On many a night, the white freedom riders who had come to fight for our freedom stayed in my parent's home as I told you before. I listened to my mother praying for theirs and our safety from the evil that lurked beyond our doors, evil so deadly it would kill its kind if they violated the codes that evil held so dear."

"That poor white girl out there with you must have peed a thousand times before they took that rope from around her neck. I know I would have." Rosie said shaking her head as she looked at the others holding her arms around herself.

"Despite that evil, they refused to be sold a bill of goods they knew were wrong. Whether they were heard or not they stood against the wrong they witnessed and then experienced firsthand."

"I truly needed," said La-Joyce, "to hear you say that Mrs. Johnnie

Bea. The way the telling of our history was going at first, I was beginning to feel that all whites should be hated."

"Now, Mrs. Johnnie Bea don't forget," Teresa said moving a box aside so she could get her chair better placed, "there were also those young white people who started to change the world and soon became money chasers and ended up following the same path as their parents."

"You are right however we must never forget the white people who either lost their lives or risked them fighting our fight Teresa. Some changes give no reason to nullify what good has occurred. Don't you forget?" Mrs. Johnnie Bea said hobbling around collecting empty bowls.

"Mrs. Johnnie Bea set yourself down, we can take our bowls into the kitchen and wash them," exclaimed Susie, standing up again and planting kisses on both sides of Mrs. Johnnie Bea's cheeks this time confiscating bowls from her.

"Lord, I don't know what I am going to do with that young lady. She is always giving orders." Mrs. Johnnie Bea said taking her seat again as she felt her cheeks and smiled.

"Yes, but I worked in the school system. Lots of racism still exists among whites in that system especially stereotyping black kids. The social consciousness you are talking about is just about gone now and like I said most have become money chasers and are no better than their parents. They were supposed to teach them to be better people by being more aware of the wrongs going on around them."

"It is still good to know, however, that not all white people participate in racist behavior and were a part of stopping it," La-Joyce said, kicking her shoes off.

"Come on La-Joyce, grow up. Didn't you hear Mrs. Johnnie Bea tell us we would not have had The Rodney King crisis and that ridiculous O'Jay trial if things had changed in this country?" Chili said, stretching her right leg as far to her left side as it would go. She added, "Wonder how those jurors are living now?"

"I have to admit Chili is right. It shocked me how white people carried on." Teresa said handing her bowl to Susie.

"Teresa it wasn't just white people it was black people as well so we all still feel the chains of our horrible past right?" La-Joyce said her hands up in the air.

"Why should you care? As dark as you are no one would look at you and think white," Chili said to La-Joyce staring hard at her.

"My Oprah, Chili that was not a nice statement to make to your sister," Mrs. Johnnie Bea said, "You know you all are my children."

"La-Joyce I apologize but I'm just saying why should she care so much about white people."

"Well, I do care. Just as Mrs. Johnnie Bea, I have white people in my life I think a lot of, even if you don't."

Chili shrugged her shoulders saying to La-Joyce, "Are you sure they like you as well as you love them? Chili asked as she began rubbing lip balm on her lips smacking them together. The other women laughed at the two and shook their heads. Then adding "We do know how white people can pretend."

"Go on Mrs. Johnnie Bea at least you have their attention," Susie said laughing along with the rest.

"She sure has mine," Rosie said turning back to listen to Mrs. Johnnie Bea.

"We were the wretched of the earth down there in the South and I guess you could say all over America, but when people both white and black, saw through the television what was happening in the South, they came. Many, as I said, were just college students coming by the busload to right a wrong and destroy the evil beast of Jim Crow living there."

"I remember my mother telling me once that a white housewife from somewhere in Michigan was so taken by what she saw she left her family and went down to help. She never returned home because she was killed by the Klan. Like La-Joyce says Chili, I have to admire her courage especially when it cost her, her life, and the lives she left behind Rosie said.

"Thank you Rosie I have to agree also," Shenee' said.

"I believe what Dr. King said about there being a moral order that reaches higher than man's changing laws. As you can see by how they have changed since the Civil Rights Movement. We all know how the white man's laws change going back and forth like the wind. God's laws are, as Dr. King says, 'eternal.' No man can dispute or defy God's code of conduct without sowing the seed to reap the dreaded consequences." "Hallelujah!" Elsie said.

"Amen and hallelujah again!" Teresa said smiling over at Elsie. "As Kirk Franklin says, "Let's have some church up in here," Susie said clapping her hands as she smiled along with the others.

Rosie threw up her hands and began to clap them. La-Joyce joined in as she began to laugh along with Shenee', Chili, and Susie. The room was beginning to feel warm again.

"Those warriors should not have fought in vain. Mrs. Johnnie Bea continued, "We must recreate the legacy they left with us. They dreamed of a day when equality would be a reality for all Americans. Their lives are living testimonies of the actions they took to see that those dreams come true. It is what my father taught me to believe in, there should be a burning need in all of us to stand and fight for right when you see wrong before you. Mrs. Rosa Parks and others like her were an example of just what it means to carry the torch I want you girls to reach for." Mrs. Johnnie Bea told them.

"Is that how you want us to carry the torch, Mrs. Johnnie Bea?" La-Joyce asked taking her glasses off and wiping them on the edge of her shirt.

"How does that saying go? Mrs. Johnnie Bea If you don't stand for something you will fall for anything." Teresa said getting a nod of agreement from the others.

It is the right of every human person. We all long to live a decent life. There may be those out there like yourselves who never had anyone to tell them what they are doing is wrong. They need someone like my girls to show them the pain they have placed in someone's life that doesn't need to be there. I want you ladies to go out in the community and find some good that can be done to save one human life. Give back to humanity like those young and old people did fighting non-violently to right the wrongs of some of their ancestors. I want your promise that each one of you will help to recreate Dr. King's Dream and the legacy of those who have gone on before us, leaving us with the task of carrying the torch to make that legacy a reality and a part of all Americans' lives."

"Mrs. Johnnie Bea I feel like I have just been born again," Rosie said smiling as she looked around at the other women saying. "I will teach my children our history the right way so that they know it and can pass it on to their children in detail like you are telling it to us, even if it is missing from the history books or schools that reject them."

"As horrible as it is Rosie, and La-Joyce it is our history, a history that makes us who we are and we need to be telling it to our children so they understand it right," Chili said looking over at La-Joyce with a smug grin on her face.

"Meaning?" La-Joyce asked throwing both hands up in the air. "It means that if we don't recognize white people who placed their lives at risk to do what is right, we teach blanket hatred like white people taught. White people who died fighting the cause speak to the fact that color is not what was evil but the sick minds of those people who acted with evil spirits."

"That's coming out of your mouth Chili. I cannot believe what I am hearing hallelujah," Susie said smiling over at Chili.

As we all know white people who are racist live all over America." La-Joyce said waving her hand at Chili.

"Amen," Teresa said adding, "Because I know white people who are not from the South but their ways would sit them front row center stage in the Jim Crow world of thinking."

"You got that right," replied Shenee', "and I know black people who shame us by their actions of racism against other blacks because of self-hate."

"Amens" sang out in the room from the lips of the ladies in agreement.

"Me," said Mrs. Johnnie Bea" Course' I can't fix everything but what I can do, I do. I see suffering and though I can't end it I do know that the one way to help people live better is to give them good healthy food or teach them to give it to someone who doesn't have any. My Oprah and I, help in our way and let others help in theirs. It is the only way to carry the torch and keep the legacy my father talked about alive."

"I want to be a part of that legacy. Learning in-depth about my history from a person with first-hand knowledge who has inspired me," La-Joyce said sighing as Chili helped her up from the sofa. "Mrs.

Johnnie Bea I am going to take Mylo some of these beans," La-Joyce said wobbling her heavy body from the sewing room into the kitchen with her empty bowl in her hand.

"That is why I invited you here to talk about tonight. The legacy my father spoke of and the Dream of Dr. King are the same girls."

"Mrs. Johnnie Bea those were the best beans I've eaten, better even than the ones you brought with you when you came knocking on my door to help me change the course of my life. Something I could not have done without you. I will do whatever you want me to do," Shenee' said rising as she stretched out her arms yarning.

"So will I," Susie said putting the shoes on her feet she had slipped out of.

"Of course, you know I will," said Chili.

"Me too," Rosie said, hugging Mrs. Johnnie Bea after she stood with the others getting ready to leave.

"How is Oprah doing these days?" Chili asked licking her spoon as she swallowed down the last of her beans.

"My Oprah's doing just fine, thank you ma'am. Glad you brought that up 'cause I was just thinking about her. That child has enough money to be thinking only of her own needs, yet she helps where she sees a need. It doesn't matter if that need is or is not what I think it should be. It is a need she sees. I need not bother with stopping her show but create one of my own."

"I don't know Mrs. Johnnie Bea," Rosie said looking hard at her, some people say"

"Say what child that they don't like my Oprah because she is not what they think she should be. What perfect person do you know in this world? What they should be doing is reflecting on their own lives and the imperfections that exist there." Mrs. Johnnie Bea said smiling at all the ladies as she hobbled around the room retrieving the plates of sweet potato peelings, her gold tooth flashing. Of course, Oprah is not perfect but neither are any of us. Listen to us tonight with all our different views. Does that make us unlikable? No. We all have a job to do in this world helping others and we should be about that not using precious time to down trot my Oprah."

"That reminds me Mrs. Johnnie Bea may I have that tray I asked you about when you called me about coming over." Shenee' said turning toward the door of Mrs. Johnnie Bea's sewing room. "I have to be in court at 7:30 to meet with a client before trial tomorrow morning. So, you need to tell me what you want me to do? Now I can't be Oprah for you. It's like asking me to be God."

"No, it's not Shenee' Mrs. Johnnie Bea is not asking you to step into Oprah's shoes. Oprah works on a large scale Mrs. Johnnie Bea wants us to be there for someone who can't be there for themselves, Isn't that right Mrs. Johnnie Bea?" Susie asked, stretching her legs, indicating a need for movement.

"Susie," Teresa said standing herself, "I think Mrs. Johnnie Bea wants us to see what she sees in us so we can learn what she already knows. But you know you cannot do what you don't understand my granny always said."

"I don't know about all that, Teresa. Mrs. Johnnie Bea, I don't think anyone but your Oprah can equal you in doing. Susie said yarning. "It's like walking in the shoes of The Fisherman. You saw that movie with Anthony Quinn. He played a priest who became a pope."

"Oprah is no pope but she does know how to treat a friend the same as Mrs. Johnnie Bea does," Rosie said.

"No one, but Oprah and Mrs. Johnnie Bea would take the crap they take from unappreciative haters who don't see freebies coming their way," Elsie said, mulling around the room as they prepared to leave.

"Think about what I have told you. How you start is you find someone in need and help that one person. You will be amazed at the happiness that person will feel knowing there is one person out there compassionate enough to see their need and do something to help them learn how to solve one of their problems. You then go and find people in your community who have not given. You ask them to help someone in need. That is how villages are created and legacies are born. As you're doing all this, remember someone somewhere is going to find something to take away from your goodness by speaking about some sin they believe you have committed. If you let that stop you, you might as well not do a good thing to start with.

Folks having nothing better to do than to find fault in your goodness will make a point of devaluing your efforts. Poor souls have not found the light in their own lives. Most importantly you must remember, that we all have something we don't like to be reminded of, but by the same token we have done good deeds we need reminding of."

"She's right girls. People will do that." Susie said. "When I'm trying to help some kid, someone will come and tell me the kid doesn't deserve the help they deserve whatever punishment they are getting. I don't even listen I go right along and do what I got to do and pray for that poor soul who is thinking that way. Isn't that right Mrs. Johnnie Bea?"

"Susie is right. You cannot let that stop your work. There is a purpose in creating legacies that last. Dr King is an example of that. Many people hated him because he stood for what he believed was right. No one said he was perfect but he sure had character and he stood for what he believed was right. That is how he won in the end.

"There are many people I know who have fallen short on their journey in life but their hearts are good and that is what I look to see not that they have lived perfect lives. I have not met that person yet. Let me go out back and get that tray I promised to give you the other day Shenee'." Mrs. Johnnie Bea said as she hobbled into the next room.

"Thanks, Mrs. Johnnie Bea, I need it for that formal affair I'm having at home next weekend.

"I'm sure Shenee will be able to find plenty of people in her neighborhood to help because there is no one there in need," Chili said as Mrs. Johnnie Bea left the room. If they are, they are hiding it." Chili laughed as she continued to count her up-and-down sit-ups. Laughter filled the room coming from the others. All were aware of the exclusive area where Shenee' lived.

"Your neighborhood could be as nice as mine if the blacks in this city would demand more out of the black politicians they vote into office." Sudden tension filled the room at Shenee's response to Chili was heard.

"What is it our black mayor and the other black politicians here should be doing that Colgate's white mayor is doing?" Chili asked, turning towards Shenee'.

"Come on now, Chili, don't come with an attitude. You put the plate of food on the table now eat out of it." Susie said, placing her hands on her chin and puffing up her lips, having just walked back into the room from the kitchen. "What were you saying about those black politicians we put into office Shenee'?" Susie asked, her gum popping one two three.

"Those you have voted into office lately will never become anything but local politicians because they don't know what it means to play with the high contenders on the political scene."

"What?' Chili said ending her exercises and rising like the others.

"I drove my four -by-four here this evening because I did not want my Benz broken down by what... I can't call them ditches but are more like deep holes in your streets. It's worse than riding on an airplane in harsh turbulence." Shenee' said staring over at Chili who now stood facing her.

"Tell the truth and shame the devil," Susie said, looking at both Chili and Shenee saying "Hallelujah."

"Amen," Teresa said echoing Elsie.

"Back in the day, as you like to say, when the white people burned down that Oklahoma City it was due to jealousy and envy of how beautiful the black city was kept and the people were living like the white man who plowed under the black farmer's field Mrs. Johnnie Bea was telling us about. Today you have the white mayors sighing with pity as to how black people continue to vote into office the kind of leaders who make sure that they get the highest taxes and the worst rates from the utility companies with trash lining the ditch-filled streets while providing nothing to help them improve the conditions of their lives or the city.

When the government sends in millions of dollars to help with the cost of those high utility bills no one benefits but the politicians and their families, oh and their friends."

"We better go and see what condition our mayor's street is in." Elsie said, folding her arms as she continued to listen to Shenee' tell them why their city's conditions were not improving."

"I bet you are not having these discussions with your black husband." Chili said, looking hard at Shenee'

"Now Chili, I told you don't come with an attitude. Shenee' is telling us the truth whether we want to hear it or not. You know as well as I do that there are so many holes in the streets here in Shilow, every election it is on the top of the list of unfulfilled promises." Susie said laughing along with the other women while the sound of her gum popping filled the room at their agreement."

"Not to mention the weeds and vacant rundown houses on every corner in town," Susie said shaking her head.

"And yes we do put those same people back in office every year to treat us the same way as before," Teresa said.

"You are right Teresa. She is surely telling the truth about those holes and high taxes." Elsie said shaking her head.

"I'll Amen that," Rosie said.

"As for my black husband, it was he who told me it is a pity that the black people in Shilow cannot demand from their mayor what the people here in Colgate demand from our mayor and get it.

"And what is that?" Chili asked her arms folded as she stared over at Shenee'.

"You and I both know that if the mayor in Colgate treated his voters like the mayor in Shilow treats his after he was voted in, they would be out in numbers asking for his resignation."

"What?!" Chili said a look of disbelief on her face as she looked up from her tote.

"We look at what is going on in Shilow," Shenee' said no longer looking at Chili as she lifted her briefcase "saying to ourselves that mayor could never become governor because he doesn't even have a clue as to how to make improvements in a city as small as Shilow. How in the world could he possibly manage an entire state let alone a country? It's a pity I tell you." Shenee' said facing Chili.

"I have been asking myself where are the black men hiding who could properly run your city?" Many of us blacks flee cities like Shilow to get the same good treatment we feel the whites are receiving."

"Tell the truth and shame the devil child," Elsie said her arms on her slender hips as usual.

"Mrs. Johnnie Bea I'd better go because Chili is going to cause me to get to cussing up in here and I don't want to disrespect the one person I dearly love." Shenee' said as Mrs. Johnnie Bea hobbled back into the room with the tray for her.

"What you are saying may be true," Chili said, a serious tone now in her voice. "But I do know that we blacks in Shilow neither appreciate driving over holes and ditches nor do we appreciate having the highest utility rates in the state. But you must understand we can't vote for good leadership when only bad leaders run for office. That should make sense to those who would condemn our choice of leadership. You tell those people running us down to send in good people willing to make promises and keep them. We will not care whether they are green we will vote them into office," Chili said throwing a kiss Shenee's way.

"Chili you're too much." Shenee' replied.

"I may be, but I do know my people, and while you are speaking the truth about our situation as far as leadership is concerned here in Shilow. I'm here to tell you yes we want better, better just has not come our way yet. When it does, we will be ready to receive it just like the white people in Colgate." Chili said as she picked up the tote bag beside her.

"Amen," they all said in unison.

"I've got to go to Mrs. Johnnie Bea but I will be watching Oprah more often. I'd like to learn what you see in her and what I need to do to keep the legacy going even if it means taking to the streets here in Shilow to see that we get the treatment Colgate is receiving, especially with the money that comes from the government." Chili said no longer smiling.

"It's all good Chili 'cause we know what Shenee' has said is true. But like you said, if good leadership comes to Shilow, we will welcome it," Susie said. The gum in her mouth again went pop, pop, as they all began to walk from the sewing room. Screams and what sounded like a door falling, causing the women to stop talking and look at each other.

"That's La-Joyce isn't she in the kitchen?" Chili shouted, running along with the others towards the kitchen where La-Joyce had gone.

"La-Joyce what is the matter?" Mrs. Johnnie Bea said rushing into the kitchen towards her. It's that cat. I swear it looks like a panther or something. It rubbed up against my legs and liked to have scared me to death!" La-Joyce said seated upon Mrs. Johnnie Bea's kitchen table holding her stomach with one hand on Elsie's arm.

"Oh, child I thought you were about to have that baby you screamed so loud. You know Big Tom is harmless." Mrs. Johnnie Bea said picking up the cat and rubbing his head.

"That thing's father is a lynx," La-Joyce said staring down at Big Tom. "Didn't Mylo tell you that Mrs. Johnnie Bea? Look at its' paws I don't want him touching me" La-Joyce said holding on to Elsie while Mrs. Johnnie Bea continued to rub Big Tom while kissing him on his head as he purred.

"You were screaming so loud I thought you had dropped that baby," Teresa said, staring at La-Joyce as she picked up Mrs. Johnnie Bea's oven door that had fallen. The stick that had held it up lay on the floor next to La-Joyce.

"I almost dropped it when I felt that strange hair on my leg and looked down into those big yellow eyes staring up at me."

"Girl, you got your sweatpants rolled up that's why he rubbed up against your legs. He does us like that all the time if our legs are exposed." Elsie said.

"Don't you ladies look at me like I'm nuts," La-Joyce said placing her feet on the chair in front of her.

"Calm down La-Joyce we don't want Dwayne coming over here jumping on us thinking we let the cat attack you," Chili said as laughter filled the room causing, the tension to ease up.

"That is a big cat, Mrs. Johnnie Bea. I would have run myself if I saw it out somewhere." Chili said moving away from the purring cat as she leaned over to pick up the stick that Mrs. Johnnie Bea used to hold up her oven door.

"She is a big one," Susie said looking with caution at the large black Cat staring back at her and Chili as they worked to get the stick back in place so the door to the oven would stay shut.

"It's a tom cat. Nothing wrong with you ladies but fear of the unknown Mrs. Johnnie Bea said rubbing the cat as she looked around the kitchen at the women staring at Big Tom. Just because you haven't taken the time to make friends with Big Tom you have already decided he is something to fear. Now, Elsie and Teresa, I know you ladies are not afraid of Big Tom?" Mrs. Johnnie Bea said still stroking her cat.

"Of course not," Teresa said rubbing the cat on its head. "But you need to put him outside until the other ladies leave, they don't know Big Tom like we do."

"It's a shame the way people love to draw conclusions about other lives without having a bit of facts. Come on Big Tom, I'll let you outside until these ladies leave." Mrs. Johnnie Bea said walking towards the front door with her cat.

"Big Tom! That is definitely a good name for an animal that big." Shenee' said looking with the others at the cat in Mrs. Johnnie Bea's arms.

"He should be renamed 'Giant Tom'. If anyone comes up on him in the dark is in for a heart attack for real." Everyone laughed at Chili's joke including Teresa, Elsie, and even Shenee'.

"We are here all the time so, of course, Elsie and I aren't afraid of Big Tom that old pussy cat won't hurt a soul but most people shy away from him because of his size Teresa said rubbing Big Tom as Mrs. Johnnie Bea passed her.

"You can't prove that by me and I wouldn't make him mad. I've seen him whip grown dogs. He even blinded a couple. Those yellow eyes get to staring up at you there is no telling what you are in for." Elsie said grabbing a hold of Big Tom's tail causing him to give out a loud meow. La-Joyce, Shenee, Susie, and Chili jumped quickly away from Mrs. Johnnie Bea and Big Tom as Elsie laughed letting go of the tail.

Rosie stepped back as Mrs. Johnnie Bea passed her with Big Tom saying to her "Mrs. Johnnie Bea am I supposed to help out at The Safe Place in the morning while you take care of some business downtown?" "Yes, child, I have to be downtown to meet with the foundation people at 7:00 in the morning. Let me step outside and cut on that light so you girls can see as you are going out."

"Mrs. Johnnie Bea you can't go out that way; You got to go out the back door don't you remember," Susie screamed as Mrs. Johnnie Bea stepped outside the front door with the cat in her arms. A loud crash could be heard.

Chapter Three

A river of tears flowed from the eyes of Mrs. Johnnie Bea's friends as they attempted to pull her out from between the steps she had fallen into. The steps that were not broken would not budge. Mrs. Johnnie Bea was short but stout so it was hard to pull her out from where she was wedged in. The stout wood would not allow her large butt to come back through. Her groans made it apparent that something had been broken.

"Shenee' get on that cell phone and call the medics tell them to come in a hurry. Oh, my Lord Mrs. Johnnie Bea I warned you over and over about that broken step. Just hold tight we'll get you out." Teresa told her attempting to pull the boards loose.

"I'm calling Dwayne and Mylo. They are strong enough to free those boards loose." La-Joyce said.

"Somebody bring something to knock these boards apart so we can get Mrs. Johnnie Bea from between these steps!" Teresa screamed. Susie and Rosie attempted to pull the broken steps but they were nailed down to stronger boards that would not budge. The cat jumped from Mrs. Johnnie Bea's arms as soon as she fell.

"I've broken something. Every time I try to put my weight on my legs, they give way and it hurts terribly." Mrs. Johnnie Bea said.

"Don't pass out Mrs. Johnnie Bea. We are going to get you out of there." Chili said running around back.

Night was beginning to fall making it hard to tell exactly how to get her out from between the broken steps.

"Move away so that I can cut them," Chili said coming from around the back of Mrs. Johnnie Bea's yard.

"Chili what are you going to do with that axe?" Elsie asked, looking up from where she was bent over trying to get Mrs. Johnnie Bea free from between the boards that held her.

"I'm going to cut those boards away so we can get Mrs. Johnnie Bea free."

"Chili don't you make a mistake and cut Mrs. Johnnie Bea with that axe," Elsie said shielding Mrs. Johnnie Bea with her body.

"Chili you sure you know what you are doing? Perhaps we should wait for the Medics to get here" Shenee said placing her hands over her eyes as Chili raised the axe to begin cutting the boards.

"Who knows when that will be in this neighborhood? Move out of the way La-Joyce I sure don't want to hit you, girl."

"I don't want you to hit me either," Susie said moving back with La-Joyce.

Chili gave the boards a hard lick. On the second blow, the boards split apart allowing Elsie, Teresa, Shenee' and Susie to lift Mrs. Johnnie out from between the steps.

"Go around back La-Joyce into the house from that side door. I need a blanket to keep Mrs. Johnnie Bea warm. We don't want her to go into shock. Elsie said gently laying Mrs. Johnnie Bea on the grass.

"Elsie I am not going around back dark as it is and let Big Tom jump on me. Like I told you that cat's daddy is a lynx. Have you seen those claws on his paws?

"I'll go get the blanket," Chili said. If Big Tom jumps on me he is going to have this axe to deal with" Chili said.

"Lord now don't go killing my poor old cat Chili."

"Mrs. Johnnie Bea your cat will be killing himself if he runs up against this axe in my hand," Chili answered raising the axe over her shoulder as she started towards the dark backyard.

"Susie go around back with that child. Big Tom will not jump on anyone unless they mess with him. Now hurry up and return before she goes into shock" Elsie said kneeling beside Mrs. Johnnie Bea.

When the medics arrived, everyone began answering their questions at once.

"Girls, everyone cannot talk at the same time," Teresa said over the raised voices. Why don't we let Elsie tell them what is going on since she is the nurse." It became quiet. The medics knelt beside Mrs. Johnnie Bea and questioned Elsie as to what happened to her.

"My Oprah," Mrs. Johnnie Bea said through clutched teeth as she tried not to scream out in pain when they attempted to move her to the gurney to be transported to the hospital "What will become of my children and those poor homeless souls with me down like this?"

"My Oprah indeed Mrs. Johnnie Bea," Elsie said wiping her own eyes with a handkerchief she retrieved out of her dress pocket, "if you haven't taught us anything about taking care of business, I don't know who has. Wasn't it you who just pleaded with us to recreate the legacy your father died for? Isn't that what you said your Oprah was about?"

"Yes, you did" the others echoed in agreement with Elsie.

"Just get better and let us take care of everything you have been doing until you come out of that hospital," Teresa said her hands pressed inside Mrs. Johnnie Bea's hand as she and Elsie got into the ambulance with her. Mrs. Johnnie Bea smiled as she looked up at the teary-eyed ladies looking down at her.

"Lord it is in your hands, my faith is in you and these ladies here. I trust they will see through the eyes you have given me and carry the torch my father gave to me." Her eyes closed as the medication from the needle injected into her arm took effect.

Chapter Four

>──┤◆>─◆─<◆├──<

*O*nce the word was out that Mrs. Johnnie Bea had been hospitalized her semi-private was changed to a private suite. Friends came to see her from near and far. So many flowers arrived that Mrs. Johnnie Bea complained she felt like she was attending her funeral. She however never let on how proud she was about the fuss being made over her. Elizabeth brought in her church friends spending half the day. The Asian and Muslim ladies she worked alongside on Sunday feeding the homeless people came in to see her. Even her Native American and Spanish-speaking friends who sometimes volunteered at The Safe Place came in.

One evening after Mrs. Johnnie Bea had been in the hospital for about three weeks the nurse came in and told her "a little creepy thing called a man" was outside wanting to see her. Mrs. Johnnie Bea beckoned for them to let him in. Not able to recognize him she put on her glasses to see her guest better. Still not able to recognize him, she took her glasses off and slowly placed them on again.

At first, she still did not know who the little fellow was. He stood five feet Mrs. Johnnie knew because he was shorter than her. His foot-long white beard matched the crop of white wooly hair on his head. He smelled like someone had sprayed him with Lysol after giving him a good cleaning because he looked nothing like the filthy little critter begging for three servings of food before everyone else was fed.

Most of the women refused to serve until he was out of sight he looked and smelled so bad. Now having been scrubbed he stood before her sparkling clean. Someone had given him a scrub suit to put on. He looked like some doctor about to go into surgery. As Mrs. Johnnie Bea's eyes grew in recognition, she leaned closer so she could see him better.

"My Oprah, Lord if it's not Little Willie." Come on over here man and tell me what you have to say for yourself." Not waiting for him to answer Mrs. Johnnie Bea continued her questioning.

"For Christ's sake, how did you get down here?" Mrs. Johnnie Bea asked the little homeless fellow who was always first in line to get her Saturday and Sunday morning meals.

"Tell you the truth Mrs. Johnnie Bea I walked." "You walked twenty miles, Willie?"

"Seemed more like forty but I wanted to see you." He began to scratch his head. "I had no idea them nurses would make me bathe. That big old ugly yellow sister just grabbed me by my collar, yes she did. Looking just like a wrestler. Come asking me who I was looking for. When I gave her your name, she said I had to bathe first. I tried to turn around and go back out but that old rascal had the security cop grab me by the collar and pull me into a shower room. They told him to tell me I wasn't getting out until I bathed. 'Coming in here stinking up her place'. I had no other choice but to wash that stuff that fool poured on me after ripping off my clothes. It made so many suds I had to scrub for an hour trying to get rid of all those bubbles it caused. Fat fool don't understand I need that dirt to protect me when I'm out there in that cold," he said again scratching his head.

Mrs. Johnnie Bea shook her head laughing as she thought again about how hard it was to get the women to issue out food to him smelling like he did. He had not bathed since she had known him. For five years he always stood first in line to be fed. Little Willie was one of the reasons she and Elizabeth had hit it off so well. Elizabeth had taken off her three five-carat diamonds and served Little Willie never letting on to her or him he smelled any different than anyone else coming to be fed.

"Little Willie I sure am glad to see you. And you sure look nice. It is good to know you were thinking about Mrs. Johnnie Bea. I'm going to give you a bus ticket so you can get back to the shelter in the village. Twenty miles is too far for you to walk. When you get there tell Betsy I said to let you stay inside the shelter. No, on the other hand, I'll call her. I don't want you sleeping outside all cleaned up."

"I don't know what they did with my clothes. Gave me these hospital rags."

"Go down to the Sally House and get you some clothes more to your liking Little Willie you know they will give them to you free of charge," Mrs. Johnnie Bea said looking at the blue hospital scrubs he had been given.

"I'm going to do just that. Mrs. Johnnie Bea, you always give me such good advice. You know them women you sent to take your place don't take time to spend a minute talking to a body. They wear their long white aprons and have their heads tied up giving out food without saying a word to a body."

"Who are these women?" Mrs. Johnnie Bea asked.

"That white woman named Shenee,' sounds like that is what she said her name is, told me I could not get any more than two servings because other people had to eat. I told her Mrs. Johnnie Bea always gives me three."

"Where was Elizabeth?" Mrs. Johnnie Bea asked still looking at him amazed at his present appearance.

"That's what I asked. They told me she was Head of Operations whatever that is. Seems like they got some money to set up a blood pressure and a mental health screening hut."

"They did get it going. Good for them. Have you had your blood pressure checked now that it's got started, Little Willie?" Mrs. Johnnie asked him as he took a seat beside her bed.

"They told us we had to have had a bath within two days before we could come into that hut they got set up." Little Willie and Mrs. Johnnie Bea looked at each other sarcastically.

Finally, she said "Willie you go on in there tomorrow and get your blood pressure checked. Elizabeth and I worked hard to get the foundation funding to pay for that program. Your health is as important as any other American's, in this country don't forget that."

"Yes ma'am. I guess I should since you worked so hard to have it there for us. Anyway, that fancy white gal told me she was making sure everything gets done like you would want it is what I was told."

"Little Willie she is not white she is one of our own. Black, if not in color, her genes say she is one of us.

"Huh," Little Willie said scratching his head as he thought about what she told him. "You could have fooled me."

That one named Chili told me I had to wait til all the others were fed then come back for thirds. 'Where is Mrs. Johnnie Bea' I asked her. That's when they told me you were in here."

"Did you go back after everyone was served, Willie"?

"They had twice as many people coming because they had slices of apple pie. Mrs. Johnnie Bea, folks was coming I know had to live somewhere else 'sides the streets. There were too many of them. When they heard that they would be getting not only beans but chicken and pie as well the whole village showed up. They didn't finish up until way after four o'clock ain't no way I could stand that long. When those two left a pregnant girl came you remember the one that was with your nephew that day in the Village. She and a short peanut colored woman started to serve."

"You must mean La-Joyce my nephew's wife and Susie my girl that works for the juvenile center, Little Willie."

"Yeah must have been them any ways I stayed around, finally, Teresa and Elsie came but by then I had got my third helping."

"My Oprah Little Willie I'm glad you came up to see about poor Mrs. Johnnie Bea. I broke my hip because I didn't take care of business like I should have. Opportunities came and went and I overlooked them now I'm paying dearly for it. I feel proud you cared enough to come see about me." Little Willie got up from his seat and scratched his head.

"I'm glad you are no worse off Mrs. Johnnie Bea, of course, I will be glad when you come back. Those women are too sassy. Now what good is two servings when you have grown accustomed to getting three?"

"Head on back Little Willie before it gets dark." As she said it Mrs. Johnnie Bea had to smile as she reminded herself that Little Willie lived on the streets, and slept under bridges at night if not on the doorsteps of someone's establishment.

"Here take this bus token and catch that bus out front back to the village," Mrs. Johnnie Bea said giving Little Willie one of the bus tokens she always carried in her purse just for such emergencies.

"I'll talk to them the next time they come see me. Course, I can't promise they will do no better they got in their minds on how they want to do and if they are feeding as many folks as you say are coming, there just might not be enough."

"Yeah, I had better go so I can get my shoes that they made me leave outside the door. Somebody might take off with them. I've had them going on for ten years now. They feel like home to me."

Little Willie then walked towards the door; stopping he turned around.

"Mrs. Johnnie Bea, I get to tell the others I saw you and you are coming back to us okay."

"Yes Willie, you tell them for me that Mrs. Johnnie Bea is alright and she will be back when this old hip gets well." Little Willie smiled showing the few ill-kept teeth in his mouth then turned and walked out the door saying more to himself than her

"I had better hurry and git my shoes fore' someone walks off with them."

Mrs. Johnnie Bea shook her head and smiled as she dimmed the lights sliding under her covers while thinking to herself My Oprah her father's legacy was well on its way.

Chapter Five

Mrs. Johnnie Bea smiled in happiness with the rest of the audience as she sat up in one of the large lounge chairs next to her bed watching a rerun of Oprah. Maybe she thought to herself that if enough black people looked at television enough to see Oprah helping this black woman pay off her bills, they would know that she did help her own people. It was good the things she did few people knew. Mrs. Johnnie Bea thought to herself.

That show made her think of her present condition and what she would be doing to help the children at The Safe Place if she had not had that accident. Sitting up in this hospital was not something she wanted in her life not when the children and the homeless needed her. The girls could not do everything, she thought to herself, after all, they had their jobs and families to care for.

It was nearly a month since Mrs. Johnnie Bea had been hospitalized. She should have been out but when trying to help another patient she was visiting, who had fallen out of bed; she had re-injured her hip prolonging her stay. The doctor had just informed her how well her hip was healing and that soon she would be ready to be moved to the rehab center to learn how to walk again. Of course, she informed him she had not forgotten how to walk and all she needed was the Lord to give her, her strength back, then walking would be the least of her worries.

Suddenly she heard a code blue call over the intercom. Thinking someone was in serious condition she said a quick prayer. Light from the corridor shone inside her room as her door opened. Several people entered. The stool she used to elevate her feet fell over.

"Pee Wee you are so clumsy. You knocked over the stool. You want those nurses to come in here and run us out," Bunkie said, smiling as she hurried the children behind her inside the room looking over at Mrs. Johnnie Bea who was seated in the lounge chair in her room. Mrs. Johnnie Bea reached to turn on the light with the remote lying on her bed. She looked behind Bunkie and Pee Wee to see about twenty more young faces echoing each other saying "Hey Mrs. Johnnie Bea."

"I'm sorry," Pee Wee said, moving up beside Bunkie showing his bucky beaver-looking teeth that stood out over his lips like white ivory. He pushed his thick horn-rim glasses upon his face which made him look like a nerd. It took a lot of persuading to convince Pee Wee it was all right to be smart.

He was hard-pressed when told he had to choose new friends if he wanted to make something of himself. Teresa was happy to report that by the time she had finished with him, Rosie's oldest son, had not only made new friends but he had changed schools as well.

Mrs. Johnnie Bea quickly grabbed her glasses. She looked at the group of children. The three brothers from the Moss family, Donyea eight, Jontay six, and Damon four, all three stood smiling at her. "What," Mrs. Johnnie Bea thought, "was Bunkie thinking, those boys had so much energy she had to put playing equipment outside so they could run and get rid of their excess energy. Little Rodney had come. A chubby little fellow who was always asking questions she had no answers for. She assured him one day he would become a preacher or a lawyer if he didn't question himself to death first. Even five -year-old little John Brown stood in the room smiling at her. Seeing Mrs. Johnnie Bea, he ran up to where she was seated.

"Mrs. Johnnie Bea my mother's taking me to Six Flags." Mrs. Johnnie Bea smiled down at him asking

"Will you carry me with you?'

"No!" he quickly answered.

"Why not?" Mrs. Johnnie Bea asked.

"You too heavy," Laughter filled the room as children filed in one right after the other running up to give Mrs. Johnnie Bea a kiss or a hug. After the last child entered the room, Shaharra Susie's seventeen-year-old daughter came through the door to Mrs. Johnnie Bea's relief.

"Aren't you children supposed to be in school," Mrs. Johnnie Bea asked from her chair the shock showing on her face at seeing the group of children that frequented 'The Safe Place'. There they stood surrounding her, smiling. She knew after work little John's mother always came up to The Safe Place to pick him up. She would be worried sick if he came up missing

"Mrs. Johnnie Bea we are out of school it is way after four o'clock," Bunkie said.

"Isn't that Oprah you are watching?" Jamecea Sunshine asked Mrs. Johnnie Bea smiled as she pointed at Oprah on the TV screen.

"Why yes," Mrs. Johnnie Bea said smiling over at the seven-year-old girl everyone nicknamed Jamecea Sunshine because of the high yellow texture of her skin tone and because she smiled all the time.

"Mrs. Johnnie Bea we miss your beans. Those women just cannot cook beans as good as you," Bunkie said.

"For real," the others echoed.

Mrs. Johnnie Bea smiled at Bunkie's compliment noticing how much she looked like her mother Rosie. Bunkie had grown into a beautiful young teenager, without the worn-out look her mother wore when she first met her. She had not noticed before how pretty a young girl Bunkie was becoming. She was developing fast just turning thirteen. Not at all quiet like her mother. Bunkie was a lot like little Rodney. She could talk your head off if you didn't stop her long enough to get your work done. Of course," thought Mrs. Johnnie Bea to herself," some folks said it was because of the cow milk babies got instead of breast milk from their mothers."

Shaharra stood smiling down at her, her chocolate face lit up like a Christmas tree. Mrs. Johnnie Bea remembered Susie's worry about her daughter and thought to herself it was needless. Shaharra was a blackberry beauty if she ever saw one. Wearing her green and white basketball suit Mrs. Johnnie Bea thought perhaps she had just got out of practice. A big girl even for seventeen, Shaharra wore her hair in a ponytail. Mrs. Johnnie Bea looked down at her thick strong dark legs that looked as though they were accustomed to lots of running. Tiny pearl earrings adored her earlobes much like the one she wore. Walking over to the lounge chair next to Mrs. Johnnie Bea's bed after giving her a sound kiss on the jaw Shaharra took a seat beside her.

"You children sit down on the floor in front of me so I can look at you." Mrs. Johnnie Bea said smiling.

"I am not sitting my behind on that filthy floor," Bunkie said looking down at the tile on the hospital floor.

"Does filthy mean nasty and dirty or does filthy mean the most beautiful thing in the world?" Mrs. Johnnie Bea asked Bunkie still smiling. Bunk was about to answer Mrs. Johnnie Bea when Shaharra rose halfway out of her seat. A frown replaced Shaharra's smile. Staring hard at Bunkie she said.

"Girl, what did Mrs. Johnnie Bea tell you to do? You don't give her lip you ask how high and how fast get your butt on that floor like she told you now!" Her finger pointed to the floor. Everyone sat down including Bunkie. Mrs. Johnnie Bea listening to the authority in Shaharra's voice knew without a doubt what capable hands the children were in.

"Mrs. Johnnie Bea, I didn't mean to be sassy I just didn't want to get my new uniform dirty," Bunkie said as tears filled her eyes. Mrs. Johnnie Bea looked at Shaharra and shook her head.

"Don't look at me like that Mrs. Johnnie Bea. That's how I was raised. When my parents said move, they meant right then and for sure don't question them. And Momma doesn't accept any back talk unless you are ready to take her on, something even my dad doesn't want to do. I don't know what they are teaching her down at that jail but we don't want any part of it." Shaharra said her smile returning as she looked at Mrs. Johnnie Bea.

"Oh, Mrs. Johnnie Bea you are on it. Boy did they diss you Bunkie?" Pee Wee said laughing.

Pee Wee, Rosie's oldest son came up and gave her a sound kiss on the cheek causing the rest of the children to follow suit to receive more kisses from the most important person in the world for most of them., "My goodness," she thought to herself "he has grown taller than Bunkie and at twelve already had fuzz growing around his mouth. Five years ago, he could not reach the top of her dinner table. "Now look at him."

"Bunkie look over there and get those two blankets out of the drawer and spread them out so you and the children can sit on them."

"Yes ma'am," Bunkie said looking first at Shaharra as if to see if it was okay for her to do what Mrs. Johnnie Bea asked her to do.

"Get them and be quick about it," Shaharra said giving Mrs. Johnnie Bea a big smile seeing the startled look on her face. "Mrs. Johnnie Bea they talked me into bringing them up here," Shaharra said after Bunkie got the blankets as she was told. A big grin spread on Mrs. Johnnie Bea's face as she shook her head while watching Bunkie shake the blankets open with Pee Wee's help.

"They said if I didn't bring them, they were going to find their way here on their own. Plus, I wanted to see you too." Mrs. Johnnie Bea looked around at the rainbow of races in the room. When all the children raised their hands waving it was truly a rainbow. Children there to see her, she thought to herself. Her eyes widen seeing the Asian twins, Lee and Lung there with the group. They came sometimes to play after school when their parents worked late. Her eyes misted looking over at Amur the Ethiopian boy. She first learned about him after hearing the children laugh at how they played tricks on him and had him do things they would not dare do because they knew they would get them in trouble. She had to sit them down asking them how they would feel if they came to his country and the children there played dirty tricks that got them in trouble. She made them realize how they not only disrespected themselves but the country they lived in. Of course, it got them thinking when she added that God looked down on their every deed and when the deed was unbecoming God was not pleased. Amur was happy to play safe games at The Safe Place which made him a part of the group not an instrument of cruel pranks by the American children he played with.

"We miss you," Pee Wee said bringing Mrs. Johnnie Bea's thoughts back to the group at large as he wiped tears from his eyes as did the rest of the children moving in close so they could feel the comforter that covered Mrs. Johnnie Bea in the big lounge chair she preferred instead of the wheelchair they had first brought in for her.

"I miss you too. But I don't understand how they let this many children in here."

"Lucky for us there was a code blue called and they ran into the room where the light was flashing and we ran in here. I was home washing dishes when I heard Momma tell some lady on the phone your room number. I hope we can get back alright I didn't realize how many children I had with me The bus driver didn't want to let all of us on the bus." Shaharra said smiling.

"Pee Wee pass me the telephone. I don't want you kids having trouble getting back to the Safe Place after coming to see me. You know your mother and the other ladies will be worried about you".

Mrs. Johnnie Bea ignored Bunkie's pleading look not to call and dialed The Safe Place. "Hello, hey Joe, let me speak to Elsie. Look, the children are here with me. No, no, don't worry and for Christ's sake don't let their parents punish them. This is a one-time visit. I will be home before long. Have Joe bring the bus and come pick them up. There are too many for the van. I know he has to make his rounds. They will be alright here with me until he comes. They look so pretty in their new outfits. You were right about me not worrying; you ladies are creating a legacy that will be in place long after I'm gone. No, I don't mean I'm about to die child. I got plenty of work yet to do." Mrs. Johnnie Bea said smiling as she hung up the telephone.

"You know I had to call because they would be having a fit not knowing where the kids were. And Shaharra even with you these are too many children to be responsible for on the streets." Mrs. Johnnie Bea said placing the telephone receiver inside its cradle.

"If we didn't know it, we know now," Pee Wee said.

"What do you mean you know it now?" Mrs. Johnnie Bea asked. "Since you have been in the hospital Mrs. Johnnie Bea things have kinda changed around 'The Safe Place'," Bunkie said hunching her shoulders.

"What things?" Mrs. Johnnie Bea asked staring at Bunkie.

"Nothing to worry about Mrs. Johnnie Bea these kids have been put in check that is all," Shaharra said crossing her legs as she examined her nails.

"Mrs. Susie is what she makes us call her now," Bunkie said "insists that we must have structure in our lives. She said we have been working you to death picking up behind us."

"We can't run through the rooms and play like we used to when you were taking care of us," little Blue Moon the seven-year-old Native American boy who had been coming to The Safe Place since he was three said.

"Like I told you Momma don't be playing around. She wants no-nonsense. Shaharra said interrupting Bunkie and then giving her the evil eye that shut her up.

"Ms. Elsie makes us wash our hands before and after we eat and after we are done we have to brush our teeth," said Henry, the ten-year-old sandy-haired white youngster she liked to call Henry Fonda. He looked so much like Henry Fonda must have looked when he was ten, Mrs. Johnnie Bea thought smiling over at the young white boy.

"We can't go out to play until our lessons are done because Ms. Teresa says an empty head is worse than an empty stomach and makes for a fool and she is not going to have us grow up being fools therefore we have to study one hour unless we have homework then we have to study until the homework is finished.

Mom, Ms. La-Joyce, Mrs. Susie, Ms. Elsie, Mrs. Chili, Mrs. Teresa, and Mrs. Shenee' each come to The Safe Place and spend a couple of hours helping with homework. I hate homework but I love it when Chili and Pricilla come to do our hair," Bunkie said shaking her red ribbon-tied hair back and forth.

Mrs. Johnnie Bea felt something wonderful filling up in her heart. Her girls were recreating her father's legacy, moving it up levels she in her humble way never thought of.

"If we don't finish our studies," Pee Wee began, "we are not allowed to play any games or watch television."

"And they make us watch the Animal Channel, Discovery Channel, and the Walt Disney movies only after they view them first to make sure the movies are appropriate," Moe, one of Rosie's ten-year-old twins said. Mrs. Johnnie Bea. Knew those words must have come from Teresa.

"Mrs. Johnnie Bea you know how I love my rap music. Mom took my CDs and listened to every one of them. The ones that had the words 'nigga', 'hoe', or 'bitch' she broke in half right in my face. I tried to explain to her the lyrics didn't mean anything and that when black people said the word nigger it was a sign of endearment but she insists that what you listen to is what you will become and she was not living in the house with no hoes, or bitches or niggers or niggas."

"Then Mrs. Johnnie Bea," Pee Wee said, throwing up his hand to express his feelings of anxiety, "she screams out to us that the word nigger died in the sixties with Jim Crow if it didn't for some people it sure as hell did for her and her children. Mrs. Johnnie Bea she told me as she was smashing my ten-dollar CD, she knew I loved to listen to, she wanted her children to grow up to become doctors and lawyers not fools or something coined by the white man to debase."

"She was really on a roll Mrs. Johnnie Bea," Joe, Rosie's other twin said. "She had got to screaming saying that is why we have our children out killing one another because they don't know their history."

"Joe is telling you the word Mrs. Johnnie Bea," Bunkie said taking over. "She said if I had forgotten about them big cock roaches and rats we use to live with. If I start allowing males to call me 'bitches' or 'hoes' living with rats and roaches is exactly where I will end up. After that Pee Wee broke his CDs himself."

"He did?" Mrs. Johnnie Bea said sounding surprised.

"Mom asked me if she was my bitch. I knew she was referring to my CDs so I just broke them all up and went into the front room and turned on the History Channel, figured that would make her happy.

Mrs. Johnnie Bea's eyes stretched. She could hear Oprah's voice in the background and was wondering if their spirits were connected.

"Now, down at The Safe Place Mom and them guys even got all the girls penny loafers. You see how we are dressed in these uniforms. "Mrs. Shenee' ordered these uniforms for us to wear. She says it makes us look special. Not like poor kids at all. I don't like wearing the same thing all the time. But I have to say people treat us differently. Some of my friends who have plenty even ask if they can wear a uniform."

"The kids no longer refer to us as 'those 'Safe Place kids' but now we are 'the kids from 'The Safe Place' Bunkie said smiling.

"Just look at these white and red ribbons matching our red pleated skirts. Who would have thought how you dress would make that much of a difference?" Bunkie said smiling up at Mrs. Johnnie Bea after retaking her seat on the blanket beside the other children.

"Is it a good thing Bunkie?" Mrs. Johnnie Bea asked.

"Now Mrs. Johnnie Bea how is that a good thing? You never made us dress alike," Pee Wee said grinning up at her.

Ms. Teresa told Shenee not to buy the boys dress pants because they played too rough outside and would come back to The Safe Place every day with their clothes all torn up so Shenee' got blue jeans and tan sweaters." Shaharra said looking with Mrs. Johnnie Bea down at the blue jeans and tan shirts the boy wore.

"Mrs. Johnnie Bea my daddy says we look like princesses in our uniform." Mrs. Johnnie Bea looked over at Jamecea noticing her older sister Joharri standing behind her. They both looked like bean poles. Their mother was a stay-at-home mom with four children. She made sure they got the blessings of good home training. Their father was the family's sole provider. Her two younger brothers, John and Jerrell ages nine and ten seated behind Pee Wee smiling in their blue jeans and tan sweaters that had 'The Safe Place' written across the front. 'The Safe Place' was written on the white blouses the girls wore.

"First of all, you all look so pretty, and just look at my boys so well-groomed you all look like you belong to somebody rich. Second, when you do not have to think about what clothes you are going to wear to school, you have more time for your studies."

"I forgot to tell you about Inventory," Bunkie said smacking her lips.

"Inventory?" Mrs. Johnnie Bea said as though questioning what the word meant.

"All the shoes are on shelves with their size labeled. Mrs. Shenee sends all the children's clothes out to the cleaners to be cleaned at the end of the week. Our uniforms are also labeled in size and type of clothing so Momma says you don't have to look so hard to find things. It causes, she says, for better organization and it helps get us to school on time."

"My God those girls are wonderful. I should have had them at The Safe Place years ago." Mrs. Johnnie said as she listened to the update she was getting about changes going on there.

"Mrs. Shenee' says when you get back we will all look like the girls and boys you wanted us to be," Jamecea Sunshine said, sticking her forefinger in her mouth after speaking.

"My Lord baby, she is right." Mrs. Johnnie Bea said smiling back at Jamecea Sunshine.

"La-Joyce fired your bookkeeper and took over the job of keeping your books in order herself," Pee Wee said smiling as if he had told some big dark secret.

"Yes, she did. She said that woman was skimming off the top whatever that means," Shaharra said holding her manicured nail up in the air.

"Well, I do say," Mrs. Johnnie Bea replied.

Mrs. Johnnie Bea, we have to clean and help mop the rec room. We must, Mrs. La-Joyce told us help with the dishes and put up our clothes that we take off there. It is not okay for us to rank on each other or say bad things to hurt another kid's feelings."

"Twice a day Mrs. Susie wants us to say something kind about another person," Moe said with a frown on his face.

"You kids don't like The Safe Place anymore?"

"It is okay but it is not like it was when you were there taking care of us, Pee Wee said, while the rest of the group echoed yeah we want you and your beans back." Mrs. Johnnie Bea smiled but did not say a word still listening to Oprah in the background as she gave thanks while praising the Lord for their unexpected but beautiful visit. She looked down again at the many different hand colors all of them held together and smiled.

"Mrs. Johnnie Bea, before they come for us, may I ask you something?" Pee Wee said.

"Of course, child what is it?"

"What is social consciousness?"

"It means to be aware of what is going on in your community and the rest of the world for that matter Pee Wee. Why do you want to know?" Mrs. Johnnie Bea asked him?

"My Mom and her friends made all the children look at this old movie from back in the day about a lot of college students seated on the ground while this man talks to them about non-violence. They told us the people in the movie had social consciousness because they did not pretend they did not see a bad thing and what was best was that they attempted to do something to change the bad thing they saw. When they found out black people in the South were forbidden to vote, they saw this as a bad thing and stood up against a very bad system in this country that allowed it to exist back in that time.

"Yeah, Mrs. Johnnie Bea," Bunkie said. "They told all of us that it is important that we learn social consciousness about what is going on in the world around us. Learning is not all about making money Mrs. Susie said."

"Those freedom riders stepped out of their comfort zone and risked their lives to help bring about a change for something they saw as wrong," Pee Wee said, again taking over the conversation. "Ms. Teresa said people should never forget them or any of the other people who during that period risked their lives because they helped change the course of American History.

"They had social consciousness," Jameaca Sunshine said surprising everyone as Mrs. Johnnie Bea's eyes beamed with joy. She was so pleased with how the children were coming along that she could hardly contain herself. My Oprah, she thought what a blessing thank God they were learning so much that will help them in life.

"Pee Wee you were listening. I thought you told me it was a bunch of garbage and you were not even listening," Bunkie said to her brother.

"Well, they said we got to keep Mrs. Johnnie Bea's legacy going and the only way to do that is to learn early about our history and what is going on in the world. Doing good, instead of always thinking of evil makes God happy and helps make you a better person." Pee Wee proudly stated sticking out his chest as his last words were spoken.

Mrs. Johnnie Bea felt a small hand touching hers she looked in between the children and realized it was Jameaca Sunshine trying to squeeze in to get to her.

"Jameaca Sunshine come on up here and give me a hug looking like the sun shining every day."

"Jameaca Sunshine don't hurt her. We don't want Mrs. Johnnie Bea to re-injure herself again on account of one of us. Momma and them will be mad," Shaharra said moving forward to pull her back.

"Don't you worry about me Shaharra let that baby come to me. Jamaeca Sunshine weighed about forty pounds soaking wet and looked like Peter Pan. Mrs. Johnnie Bea thought to herself giving the child a sound peck on her cheek.

"The police came down to 'The Safe Place' Mrs. Johnnie Bea. It was seven of them the same as my age," said Jameaca Sunshine showing seven fingers. Mrs. Johnnie Bea released her hold on Jamaeca Sunshine her eyes now focused back on Shaharra then Bunkie and Pee Wee.

"Mylo came and brought some officers from the precinct with him to The Safe Place," Shaharra quickly responded.

"They lost their guns. I looked inside their holsters but they were empty," little Moe said.

"Dwayne and Mylo said they had to keep an eye on us for you while you were in the hospital Mrs. Johnnie Bea," Bunkie said.

"Yeah, Mylo told us he had a responsibility to help out with us because you were always there for him. Dwayne has been coming too." A smile replaced the look of concern on Mrs. Johnnie Bea's face. When the kids said, her nephews were coming by.

"We sat together and ate popcorn while Mylo explained to us about how when he was ten years old a friend of his was killed by a police officer. He said a police officer who watched the neighborhood had the boy selling drugs. His mother worked a long way from home. When another policeman shot and killed her son, Mrs. Johnnie Bea told her who was responsible. The officer, Mylo said, pretended he was unaware that the kid was doing anything like that."

'Most of us kids knew what was happening and blamed him for Benny's death,' Pee Wee told Mrs. Johnnie Bea, repeating what Mylo had told them at 'The Safe Place'. "He said it is the policeman's job to keep our communities safe. They are sent where crime is taking place and it is their job to stop the crime from happening if at all possible. Sometimes their lives were at risk but they had to act anyway. He became a police officer he told us because he wanted to prove a black officer can be seen as a decent guy too."

"He said we can help him by not playing hooky from school. Saying no to drugs and listening to our parents when they are advising us about life." Henry said, hopping up and down on his knees as if he had said something big.

"Mylo told us in this decade alone more than 25,000 black males have died on the streets being murdered by another black youth and there has not been any serious public outrage by our black or white leaders the way it had been when race matters between whites and blacks become public knowledge," Moe said as the rest of the kids began shaking their heads up and down indicating it had been said.

Your nephew Dwayne is down with the serious rap sounds Mrs. Johnnie Bea" Shaharra smiled as Mrs. Johnnie Bea gave her a knowing look.

"Shaharra." Mrs. Johnnie Bea said giving her a stern look.

"I'll be eighteen next year old enough to date whomever I choose. Mrs. Johnnie Bea. Why can't I be in your family like La-Joyce? Stunned by Shaharra's announcement Mrs. Johnnie Bea was just about to comment when another question was asked her.

"Is it true Mrs. Johnnie Bea that sometimes kids as young as ten years old come out and kill another kid or they are the victims of crime themselves? Can you imagine a nine-year-old with a gun? He might aim it at anybody," Bunkie said turning Mrs. Johnnie Bea's attention away from Shaharra and her announcement.

"No grown-up should allow that many kids to die and not do something about it Mrs. Johnnie Bea should they?" Shaharra placed her finger up to her lips to quiet the children as their voices grew loud.

"No child, but it looks as though we are living in the end of times with how the world has run amuck."

"I wanted a gun so I could shoot somebody until Mylo told us every black man killed by another black man kills generations of babies that might have been born to cure a disease or build a different kind of stop light maybe even help people live longer." He said that loss affects mankind all over the world whether we realize it or not." Pee Wee did the peace sign as he ended.

Mrs. Johnnie felt as though she was sitting in school learning about life from the minds of college professors.

"He told us there has been no black public outrage since the Black Panthers were killed by police officers like himself who couldn't see that the actions of the Panthers were an attempt to keep the importance of who we were as a people alive," Moe said, after raising his hand to be heard and of course mimicking his brother's peace sign.

"He also said, had they not used a violent approach, he believed much of what they tried to do for the children in their poverty-stricken communities would have been successful," Henry said smiling at Jameaca Sunshine.

"Don't tell me you were listening to Henry?" Bunkie said to Henry, who was so pleased with the knowledge he had learned, that they all began clapping.

"Dwayne came in while Mylo was talking to us Mrs. Johnnie Bea he had his rappers with him. They were filthy," Bunkie said, her eyes lightening up, as did Shaharra's.

"As in what?" Mrs. Johnnie Bea asked with a raised brow and a knowing smile on her lips as she and Bunkie looked at each other."

"As in nice-looking Mrs. Johnnie Bea but you know I am too young to court," Bunkie said, looking over at Shaharra to make sure the older girl was not upset by her conversation. "At least that is what Mrs. Teresa calls going out with boys," Bunkie said looking back at Mrs. Johnnie Bea smiling.

"Mrs. Johnnie Bea, I asked Dwayne how he got interested in rapping. Didn't I Pee Wee?" Moe asked his brother.

"Yes, and Mrs. Johnnie Bea he said you were the cause of him liking music. He said when he was growing up you used to have them listen to all kinds of music and then they had to tell you who the artist was and what type of music was being played."

"Mrs. Johnnie Bea, who was Dr. Watts?" Tina a little native girl asked, speaking for the first time.

"Dr Watts? Where did you hear that name?"

"We heard it from Dwayne. He said when you taught him about Dr. Watts he knew he would be a singer because he had learned something about his history he had never known before." Pee Wee said.

"But he left with his friends before he explained who Dr. Watts was and what it had to do with our history," she said.

"Well, children years ago most of our people didn't know how to read or write."

"Why?" The children asked in unison.

"Because there were laws that forbid slaves and former slaves to read the King's English or even write it."

"Why would someone not want you to learn," Tina asked her eyes growing wide with interest.

"Fear baby, fear that you might prove them wrong about your humanity. Now let me tell you about Doctor Watts and its meaning, you ask so many questions you make Mrs. Johnnie Bea forget the first question you asked." Mrs. Johnnie Bea said smiling down at the children she was so glad to see.

"The few of our people who did know how to read would sing the lines of a song out loud to the rest of the people. Because they could not read themselves, they would simply repeat after the person who could read by listening and repeating the lyrics they learned the words of the songs. That is how a lot of our songs were born.

Mylo and Dwayne were surprised to know that there was a time when it was against the law for black people to be caught reading or writing and that the person teaching them could be killed for teaching them. The great-great-grandchildren of slaves now take lightly going to school when their forefathers were killed trying to learn the basic elements of reading and writing," Tears filled Mrs. Johnnie Bea's eyes as she began to explain to the children how it was even before her time.

"We fought too long and hard and for so much and to now see all of that thrown away breaks Mrs. Johnnie Bea's heart children. Lives were lost and stolen because of an evil system that starved the life out of us. Now our children are lost having nothing to do but look at the white television that teaches them to act and behave like Al Capone, a white man who wouldn't let them shine his shoes. Talking about drive-by shootings as if they couldn't see what that kind of behavior got him, a common criminal who died of a brain disease he brought on himself with his wicked ways."

"She's talking about the colors of the clothing to indicate their hood right Mrs. Johnnie Bea?" Pee Wee asked.

"Yes, our poor children are wearing the white man's rags that tell everyone they have taken on a new god. A god that teaches them if the white man doesn't kill them or hang them, they must kill themselves. My Lord, where did we go wrong back then?" Mrs. Johnnie Bea's voice became evoked with sadness.

"Mrs. Johnnie Bea," Pee Wee said, "Dwayne said you were always saying to them that we black people are becoming so much more like white people you see no sense in our complaining, and as soon as we can get our skin as white as theirs there would be nothing to complain about. Did you say that?"

Before Mrs. Johnnie Bea could answer Little Rodney spoke up. "He said you were right in a lot of ways because it is hard for us to be under the rule of another race and not take on their ways, The one thing he was sure we have retained over the three hundred years of our transplant that started in chains has been our music." Little Rodney said grinning at the other children on the blanket beside him.

"That is why he loves hip hop music. Trust me; music for us is like water is to what...?" Pee Wee asked turning to his sister.

"Fish stupid, fish as in water. You know." Bunkie answered with her arms folded in front of her.

"Bunkie," Mrs. Johnnie Bea said in a raised voice leaning over from where she was seated staring at Bunkie.

"I apologize for using disrespectful language to you just because you asked a stupid question Pee Wee," Bunkie said throwing up her hands.

"Bunkie," Mrs. Johnnie Bea's voice was lower but a bit sterner. Shaharra also stared down at Bunkie. Bunkie grabbed Pee Wee and kissed him on his head. He moved away wiping his head saying,

"I don't want no girls kissing on me. That is nasty."

"That will change soon enough, boy. Your sister remembers what I've been teaching you and her about how we must treat one another." Mrs. Johnnie Bea said smiling once again.

"Just like your yard Mrs. Johnnie Bea it looks so different."

"Pee Wee what are you talking about." It was Teresa standing in the doorway. Mrs. Johnnie Bea I better get these children home their parents are already calling about their whereabouts. Go kiss Mrs. Johnnie Bea so that we can all go. When Bunkie cut her eyes in Pee Wee's direction he ran over and kissed Mrs. Johnnie Bea on the cheek whispering to her that she needed to "hurry home."

Just about the time the last child came up to give Mrs. Johnnie Bea a hug the nurse entered the room staring at the little uneven heads smacking Mrs. Johnnie Bea on the cheeks and then scrambling from the room as Teresa hurried them out of the door followed by Shaharra.

The Oprah show was long gone by the time the children left but Mrs. Johnnie Bea could still hear Oprah in the background as she felt her uplifted spirit lingering. Smiling her thoughts on the many different hand colors she had never paid attention to before.

Chapter Six

>—I—◆—O—◆—I—<

Mrs. Johnnie Bea looked around the room in the rehab center that had been her home for nearly a month after leaving the hospital. She could walk better now though she still needed her cane to help her get around. She would be leaving the hospital the next day. Elsie and Teresa had come together to see her the night before. They were like sisters she had never had. Not long after they arrived the rest of the girls came in making a fuss over her. With all her heart she loved each one of them.

"Now Mrs. Johnnie Bea I need to know what instructions the doctor has for you?" Elsie asked looking around the room as though she was re-familiarizing herself with her former employment.

"How were you treated Mrs. Johnnie Bea," said Shenee, "Malpractice suits are common these days?"

"He didn't repair the wrong hip did he," Chili asked kissing Mrs. Johnnie Bea on the cheek after her inquiry.

"Mrs. Johnnie Bea is coming home tomorrow now leave her alone," Susie said, popping her gum in between every other word.

"Susie you are killing me popping that gum," Teresa said pretending she was also chewing gum.

"I'm so glad I don't work with a lot of females they are too picky about the small stuff," Susie said taking the gum from her mouth and placing it in one of the napkins on Mrs. Johnnie Bea's food cart. "Now does that make you happy young lady?"

"I'm old enough to be at least your older sister so don't get sassy girl, Teresa replied speaking to her with a stern voice." Everyone laughed as they all started talking at once.

"Too many questions girls, I have twenty more years of living so I can answer them all if I can just get out of here."

"We love you so much we want to know everything," Mrs. Johnnie Bea," Rosie said looking at her a little teary-eyed.

"You girls have made me proud the way you have taken care of the children and the homeless people while I've been stuck in here. Chili looked at her watch. "Girls it's past three. The children are on their way home. We had better get going."

"I guess we had better," Teresa said, reaching for her purse.

Mrs. Johnnie Bea waited until the last of the seven women waved goodbye before allowing her tears to flow down her cheeks. She was happy about so many things. The small clinic she and Elizabeth had gotten funded for now provides blood pressure testing and primary care for homeless people. Many had even registered at drug and alcohol centers from the referral center the girls had gotten going while she was away.

She picked up the soft pink blanket thinking to herself, how God even amid the storm could bring comfort, understanding, and a binding friendship. Since she could remember, Mrs. Johnnie Bea had always been up before the rooster crowed at six. Breakfast finished by six thirty with unfinished business on her mind; Mrs. Johnnie Bea was on her way out the door by seven. This challenge God had sat before her had been hard for her to handle. She had always pushed herself to keep going otherwise she had time on her hands and extra time meant thinking too far back in time.

Scars roped around her heart that no one saw pulling at her heartstrings taking her back to Mississippi and her father hanging in a tree causing depression to sit in. She accepted the fact that putting off having that step fixed was her fault. A month in the hospital had been hard enough after that it was another month in the rehabilitation center, which, to Mrs. Johnnie Bea was nothing more than a nursing home where old people went to die. While she was old, she thought to herself she surely wasn't dead yet.

She also knew sometimes God in his gracious mercy has a bigger plan than the human eye can see. Had God not moved her out of the picture, the legacy she had wanted would never have materialized to the level it now has. She would have never developed a lasting friendship with at least one visitor had she not been the victim of the broken step.

Remembering when she first arrived Mrs. Johnnie Bea thought about how loneliness had begun sucking at her thoughts three days after she entered the hospital sending her on a downhill spiral.

The door to her room had opened and the smiling face of a gray-haired stately woman whom she said always reminded her of Eleanor Roosevelt popped her head inside asking Mrs. Johnnie Bea if she minded a little company. Mrs. Johnnie Bea sat up in bed waving Elizabeth in.

"Do I mind some company child I'm about to go crazy laying up here in this bed with no one to talk to." Mrs. Johnnie Bea knew that Elizabeth lived in a world where white rich people isolated themselves from the poor to escape the fate pronounced on the less fortunate. Elizabeth had challenged herself in more ways than one. She had shown Mrs. Johnnie Bea there were always two sides to every story. She watched as Elizabeth removed her white gloves exposing the large four-diamond five-carat rings two for each hand the largest on each ring finger the smaller five carats she wore on her small fingers.

Elizabeth never however wore them to the Village while she and Mrs. Johnnie Bea served the homeless. That she might be able to afford anything more than the average American was never mentioned to those they helped.

Elizabeth, a kind-hearted, spirited person never wanted to offend those they helped. From the first time, Mrs. Johnnie Bea remembered inviting her to help out in the Village Elizabeth had shown she was up to the challenge and could meet in it on all levels.

Becoming lasting friends, Mrs. Johnnie Bea and Elizabeth worked side by side to invent ways to improve the conditions of those poor lives in the Village. Off to fundraisers and benefits, they recreated a resource center so that those they helped had other places to go for help they could not receive in the village.

When Mrs. Johnnie and Elizabeth visited each other, the chauffeur brought Elizabeth and came to pick up Mrs. Johnnie Bea on her occasional visits to Elizabeth's home. It was on one of those occasions she informed Elizabeth she needed to get home so she could stop by Sears before it closed. Elizabeth asked if it would be alright if she accompanied her. Now looking at the purple dress Elizabeth wore Mrs. Johnnie Bea realized it came from the Sears store. She had a blue one just like it hanging in her closet. She knew Elizabeth could have bought Sears three times over but she had come to know her as a modest woman. Taking her time Elizabeth removed her white hat turning with a grin she looked at Mrs. Johnnie Bea and kicked off the white heels that matched the hat. In her stocking feet, she modeled for Mrs. Johnnie Bea the $12.00 purple dress that had four large pockets trimmed in white lace down the front. Both women laughed until they cried hugging each other like long-lost sisters. The dress was nothing special to anyone else but it meant something to the two of them.

Playing bridge with her lady friends she told Mrs. Johnnie Bea had not given her the lasting fulfillment working with her at the Village had, just as shopping at Sears with a new friend and sharing their purchase had meant. This she shared with Mrs. Johnnie Bea in the hospital where they sat together praying when her grandson was so ill. Having her there at that critical time meant more than Mrs. Johnnie Bea would ever know she told her after her grandson's recovery. Little did she know that her visits to the hospital meant more to Mrs. Johnnie Bea than she could imagine.

It seems after Mrs. Johnnie Bea became hospitalized Teresa, Elsie and the others allowed Elizabeth to instruct them as to how she and Mrs. Johnnie Bea took care of feeding the homeless people, Elizabeth informed Mrs. Johnnie Bea during their earlier visits, in turn, she had listened to them explain the ends and outs of the operation of 'The Safe Place.' Together they had modernized what had been a makeshift storefront into a respectful center for homeless people who before lacked the medical options offered them now.

Elizabeth came to visit with Mrs. Johnnie Bea every day at the hospital and during her stay at the rehab center in the Nursing Home. Quick to tell the therapist when she saw stress in Mrs. Johnnie Bea's face relieving her of the burden of having to go through more physical punishment than her body was ready for.

"I thought it would be nice for us to share these grapes," Elizabeth said during one of her daily visits with Mrs. Johnnie Bea. The lounge chair next to Mrs. Johnnie Bea's bed was where Elizabeth came promptly every day right before Mrs. Johnnie Bea had to attend therapy. Afterward, they snacked together on whatever Elizabeth brought with her. Sometimes they hardly spoke a word while each stitched thread through embroidery Elizabeth brought in. Mrs. Johnnie Bea's face showed a wide grin as the depression disappeared going God knows where. During one of their conversations, Mrs. Johnnie Bea asked Elizabeth if it was not time for Oprah.

"I think it is," Elizabeth said "You know Mrs. Johnnie Bea Elizabeth continued to say as she reached for the remote control "With so many children needing help here in the States it is a wonder Oprah doesn't start a home for wayward children right here."

"Now Elizabeth," Mrs. Johnnie Bea said taking a sip of water from the glass at her bedside. "Wouldn't it be a shame, to have Oprah do everything for everyone? It would then leave nothing for you, me, or others like us, especially those of us wanting to do good. I know I am not going to South Africa. If Oprah had taken it upon herself to take care of the homeless down at the Village or provide for the children at 'The Safe Place' you and I would have never had the privilege of becoming friends. Oprah needs to help where she sees a need and we need to help where we see a need don't you think?"

"Why you know Mrs. Johnnie Bea I never looked at the matter in those terms. Now that I have, I believe you are correct." Without another word the two allowed Oprah to entertain them for the next hour.

One morning Mrs. Johnnie Bea awoke to find uniformed policemen standing in her room along with Elizabeth's daughter and grandson.

"Megan, what are you doing here?" Elizabeth asked as she opened her eyes staring at the people who had entered the room.

"Mother there is an all-point bulletin out for you. We thought perhaps you had been kidnapped after the maid told us you had not made it home since early yesterday when I called to check on you."

"It took a minute for Mrs. Johnnie Bea first to get over the shock of the policemen in her room and what Elizabeth's daughter was saying to register in her mind. Elizabeth had fallen asleep, moments before Mrs. Johnnie Bea. Neither had said very much so busy were they with their embroidery."

"My Lord Mrs. Johnnie Bea I do believe I fell asleep right here in this chair."

"Child, I believe both of us nodded off about the same time."

"Grandmother you're past eighty it's not good that you burn your candle at both ends like Mother says you are doing."

"I'm not a day over seventy-two I'll have you to know," Elizabeth said quickly correcting her grandson as she stood to her feet brushing off the dress she had slept in.

"Mother," said the young teenager Mrs. Johnnie Bea recognized as Elizabeth's grandson. He walked over to where Mrs. Johnnie Bea lay. Taking her hand into his he looked down at her with deep sea-green eyes that seemed to penetrate hers. I remember you. You were with my grandmother at the hospital praying for my recovery every day when I was so ill. Now here you lie. Mother," Elizabeth's son asked as he turned to face Elizabeth's daughter standing behind him, "wasn't I ten the year I became so ill?"

"Yes, four years ago I believe it was. She has been such a dear to all of us even when my brother Paul decided he should explore the world and learn how others live it was you Mrs. Johnnie Bea who assisted Mother in getting him to return home."

"I am proud to have grandmother here with you," Elizabeth's grandson said turning back to face and then recapturing Mrs. Johnnie Bea's hands. I will pray that your recovery be a speedy one, Mrs. Johnnie Bea."

"Thank you, son I need all the praying I can get." Mrs. Johnnie Bea said pulling herself up better in bed.

"No problems to report. Mrs. Dante stayed over with a friend in the hospital." It was the police officer reporting in Mrs. Johnnie Bea assumed as he got the nod of clearance from Elizabeth's daughter.

"I shall never forget your warm words of encouragement during my son's illness. Mrs. Johnnie Bea," Megan said moving up beside her son also staring down at her. "Mother told me how you slipped and broke your hip."

"Now Mother you know we don't mind you spending time with Mrs. Johnnie Bea," Megan said turning to face her mother. She is your dear friend however we would like to know that you are safe."

"Mother, you know we don't mind you spending time with Mrs. Johnnie Bea," Elizabeth said mimicking her daughter. Why Mrs. Johnnie Bea you'd think I was a child being reprimanded. I can visit who I want, when I want, and stay as long as I want." Elizabeth said to her daughter. Mrs. Johnnie Bea smiled but said nothing.

"Mother we were terrified that something awful might have happened to you." It was then Mrs. Johnnie Bea noticed the distressful looks on the faces of both her daughter and grandson.

Suddenly the door swung open. In walked Elizabeth's son. He rushed over and examined Elizabeth as though she might have been damaged in some way

"Mother you must let Megan or me know when you are going to be away from home like this. We simply want to know you are safe." Elizabeth brushed off the comment with a wave of her hand.

"Stop your fussing boy Mrs. Johnnie Bea and I fell asleep talking. Of course, you will recall it is the same advice I gave you when you decided to take off worrying your father and me half to death."

"Now, Mother I believe that was different." Her son said walking over to take Mrs. Johnnie Bea's hand as he kissed her on her cheek. Mrs. Johnnie Bea smiled still saying nothing.

"It was no different at all. Now take me home so that I can freshen up. If it is alright with you Mrs. Johnnie Bea I will return as usual after all, I do believe I am still an adult."

Mrs. Johnnie Bea nodded her head a quick yes smiling without a word uttered from her lips. Elizabeth took her time putting on the hat she always wore on her visits with Mrs. Johnnie Bea. She then slipped on her white gloves, walked over, gave Mrs. Johnnie Bea a pat on the hands smiled, whispered to her "I will see you later," then, with a wave of her hand signaled to her family to follow her out. Mrs. Johnnie Bea shook her head thinking as she picked up the embroidery needle she had been using. She could have stuck herself with that big needle that had slipped from her hand when she fell asleep.

It was not long after that incident Mrs. Johnnie Bea noticed the treatment, she received from the staff vastly improved. Now it seemed there was someone always peeping in on her whereas before she had to use the call button for any kind of assistance. Elizabeth sat with her on one of her visits when the evening nurse entered the room

"Is there anything you need?" the black nurse asked looking not at Mrs. Johnnie Bea but Elizabeth. Mrs. Johnnie Bea frowned. She knew it was hard getting the colored nurse to come in on time to give her, her meds let alone ask if there was something her guest needed. Of course, discovering one of your patients is a friend to a rich celebrity did help some. She also figured it had to do with the young chauffeur who now came up and sat in the lobby to wait until Elizabeth was ready to return home. Not to mention the thought that she might have been kidnapped gave her more media coverage, she told Mrs. Johnnie Bea than she had allowed in all her life. Elizabeth's overnight stay brought to bear intrusions they had not been faced with before.

"Why would you ask me if I needed something? I do believe Mrs. Johnnie Bea here is the patient" Elizabeth said to the nurse a frown forming on her face. Mrs. Johnnie Bea watched the nurse turn to her as if seeing her for the first time.

"Is there something you need?" she asked as though she'd just been reprimanded.

"It seems to me I could use another lounge chair like the one my friend here has so that I can get out of this bed."

"Yes, ma'am," she said turning to leave.

"Elizabeth continued her stitching. She said out loud but as if to herself."

"We were visiting Nairobi Africa one year. My husband, grandson, granddaughter, and I walked into a restaurant and took a seat waiting to be served. At the time the waiter was waiting on two blacks we later learned were Americans. The waiters quickly abandoned their orders and hurried to our table.

The American blacks sat with stunned looks on their faces. My husband told the waiter that he must return and finish their order. We were in no hurry and could wait our turn. Kathy our granddaughter only six at the time looked at her grandfather saying,

'The waiter left those people to serve us first because we are special like Mother says we are. Why didn't you let him serve us?' My husband rubbed her head telling her.

'We don't want to be special that way Kathy.'

'Why grandfather? Isn't it important to be special?' She asked him.

'They did not come to our table because they thought of us as special. They came out of fear that their jobs might somehow be in jeopardy if we were kept waiting. They despise all Americans especially whites whom they feel think they are special in a superior way just because our skin is white. When a person's actions stem from fear, and not respect for the person they have encountered they don't see them as special nor do they respect them.' The Black Americans knew they had been slighted for an unfair reason. In that sense they are special. Just as we would have been had we been first to come in.'

"My husband told my granddaughter." "Never take advantage of your privilege unless it is earned."

"The young nurse came in just to look closer at a person she feels deserves better than one of her own. What else could I conclude? Mrs. Johnnie Bea, I don't need vanity I need a good friend such as yourself." Each continued their work on the embroidery allowing no more conversation until the lounge chair was brought into the room. Elizabeth laid aside the pink blanket she had been working on to help Mrs. Johnnie Bea get comfortable in it.

"My Oprah," she thought to herself "God is a good." Careful not to drop the pink blanket Elizabeth had finished crocheting and given to her, Mrs. Johnnie Bea decided to spread the blanket across her bed. She would carry it out to the car so as not to drop or leave it behind.

So deep in her thoughts was Mrs. Johnnie Bea she didn't see her last two visitors who turned up that evening at the hospital to see her until they grabbed her around the waist and whispered her name. She jumped feeling hands around her.

"Hello, Mrs. Johnnie Bea." She was more surprised this time at seeing Bunkie and Pee Wee than she was the first time.

Hearing Bunkie's voice Mrs. Johnnie Bea dropped on her bed with her mouth open. Bunkie ran over and threw herself into Mrs. Johnnie Bea's arms weeping.

"What's the matter, child? What has happened?"

"Mrs. Johnnie Bea Bunkie had to go to jail." Pee Wee said in a rush to get the words out. "Yes, she did. The police came to the school and took her to jail. They were going to put the cuffs on her but the teachers said it was not necessary and they did not want the other children to see her in handcuffs like a common criminal especially since she was one of their honor students."

"What did you do child?" Before Bunkie could answer Pee Wee answered Mrs. Johnnie Bea's question for her.

"She knocked a white girl out at school. I told Bunkie not to be playing with those silly white girls. I told her to come play hoop with me but since she has started wearing those silly skirts, she wants to hang out with the girls... white girls at that."

"Mrs. Johnnie Bea I thought they were my friends," Bunkie said still crying in Mrs. Johnnie Bea's arms. Pee Wee begins dancing and punching like a boxer does when he is beginning to fight his opponent. Left, right left. He hit the air with his punches. "Mrs. Johnnie Bea, she hit that girl so hard I thought she had knocked me out." Pee Wee said staggering backward.

"Mrs. Johnnie Bea, they said I can't go to that school anymore I have to go to an alternative school."

"Momma told them Bunkie was not going to an alternative school where all the children cussed and learned how to use drugs and gang bang. She talked to La-Joyce and she said La-Joyce said she would home teach Bunkie."

"Bunkie I still don't know why you did what you did". Large tears gathered in Bunkie's eyes as she dropped to the floor beside the bed where Mrs. Johnnie Bea sat, now crying out of control. "Pee Wee what happened?" Mrs. Johnnie Bea asked the dancing child.

"Well, after I told Bunkie to come hoop with me, that one white girl, it was three of them together. Well, that one told Bunkie she 'couldn't play with no black niggers.'

"Mrs. Johnnie Bea, I saw it coming, I looked at Bunkie's hand 'cause I know how she is when she gets mad. Her fists gets tight which means she is getting ready to hit something. She told the girl she didn't want to play with no white bitch either and gave her a left hook right in the face." Pee Wee said as he swung as though he was connecting with an opponent. "Mrs. Johnnie Bea that white girl fell on that ground like an apple falling from a tree. She was down for the count!"

"Bunkie you used that awful word to make you lower your standards to hers?" Mrs. Johnnie Bea asked holding Bunkie's face up to hers.

"Mrs. Johnnie Bea I didn't mean to, I thought she was my friend. The other girls and I had gotten along fine until she came. I know now she didn't like my being with Terri and Carol. I could tell because she would say things like why black kids don't play with other black kids. Or she would say black kids can't learn like us. Do you believe Mrs. Johnnie Bea, she asked me why [my] brother was so black and I was so brown?' Her brothers she said 'are the same color as her.' Bunkie said mimicking the voice of the girl she had injured. "I should have knocked her out then."

"You don't have to knock her out on account of her calling me black. I'm good with my blackness" Pee Wee said patting himself on the chest while shaking his head back and forth. "Momma already told me when I get my manhood girls are going to be falling all over this black cat. Black ones, white ones, brown ones, yellow ones, red ones, even purple ones I ain't even tripping 'cause see I'm a handsome fine young black male. Just like a blackberry, I cling to every vine." Pee Wee's long white teeth stood out as he grinned at Mrs. Johnnie Bea and Bunkie.

"Hush your mouth boy." Mrs. Johnnie Bea said laughing at him as she shook her head at his statement.

"I told Bunkie to drop those white girls."

"Mrs. Johnnie Bea he kicks it with white boys so what is he talking about," Bunkie said laying her head on Mrs. Johnnie Bea's shoulder as she settled down beside her on the side of her bed.

"See Mrs. Johnnie Bea" Pee Wee said as he started to dance and boxing in the air again "I know what's real. If those white boys are cool with me then I'm cool with them but if they want to feel the funk, come on let's get down with it. That's what it is about. I ain't gonna kick it with nobody like what Bunkie kicks it with. They got color on the brain thinking they are all that. And about that nigger calling, Mamma has already made us look at that movie Armistead where all those black people were jumping off that old ship so nobody could make them into niggers and slaves. I walk away when my homies start that old my nigga talk. And I already learned that those drive-bys ain't original. Way back in the day, a white cat named Al Capone came out with that before Elliott Nest nailed his a..., I mean nailed him." Pee Wee said placing his hand over his mouth laughing when he saw Mrs. Johnnie Bea's brows rise.

"I know what you were about to say," Bunkie said drying her eyes.

"I know what I was about to say, nothing! You have been jumping on me cause your daddy is teaching you how to box. Mamma already told me when I become a man all of that is going to cease, 'cause I'm going to knock you out, sister. That's if, if you don't go to jail for life first," Pee Wee said his voice stuttering somewhat as he hit the air fast and hard.

Bunkie rose from the bed where she was seated beside Mrs. Johnnie Bea with a clutched fist, she stared hard at her brother saying in a sharply raised voice

"Don't talk about it be about it!" Mrs. Johnnie Bea's eyes grew large in alarm as she slid down to the edge of the bed, Picking up the cane stick she used for walking she said to them.

"You children are not talking about fighting up in here are you?" the stick now raised above her head.

"No, no Mrs. Johnnie Bea we cool like that," said Pee Wee quickly. "It's expected of Bunkie to challenge my challenge if she wants respect in the hood. I called her out. I can't talk about what I'm going to do I have to be about it. You see." Pee Wee clutched his right hand with Bunkie's left hand they pulled into each other and patted the other on the back moving away in laughter.

"This younger generation is too much for me." Mrs. Johnnie Bea said laying the stick aside. "Children what is all this fighting talk I'm going to talk with your mother"

"Please don't Mrs. Johnnie Bea Pee Wee and I were just playing Momma is crazy we don't want no beating coming from her."

"Does your mother know you two are here with me?" Mrs. Johnnie Bea asked standing with the help of her cane.

"Yes, she knows. I begged her to let me come tell you," Bunkie said following Mrs. Johnnie Bea over to the large lounge chair she settled down in.

"Momma said Bunkie used to be your flower now she has turned into nothing but a weed out there fighting in the streets with common trash. You're going to jail for life, yeah, you are," Pee Wee said laughing as he tried to do the Ali shuffle while throwing his punches."

"Momma said my life had taken a turn for the worse because I was stupid. I should have walked away from that white girl and realized she was stupid. Now I might have to go to jail for a long time."

"Your mother is right about that. Not that you are stupid because we all make mistakes. She is right that you should have walked away from the girl and her friends if they also felt that way. You can't change people's feelings by beating up on them. Like my father always told me it doesn't take away the pain you feel to have to hurt someone. It simply creates more problems.

"What should I have done?" Mrs. Johnnie Bea.

"You should have told the child you didn't play with black niggers either."

"Mrs. Johnnie Bea" Pee Wee said stopping in the middle of a punch. "That wouldn't have done no good."

"What do you mean it wouldn't have done no good boy?" Mrs. Johnnie Bea asked about to chastise Pee Wee.

All that white girl would have told Bunkie was she was the nigger she was talking about."

"Well, Pee Wee Bunkie should have then told the child since she had referred to her as a black nigger and she knew she was not talking about her they should ask the teacher what a black nigger was."

"Oh, Mrs. Johnnie Bea" Pee Wee said laughing. Then the white girl would have been in trouble with the teacher for real, Right?"

"Exactly! When you don't understand how to solve your problems in the right way you create more problems for yourself. Physical violence simply added to your problem as you must realize from your visit to the juvenile center Bunkie"

"Oh boy do I realize that now. I am not going to hit another person unless, of course, they hit me first. I've learned from Mrs. Susie, Mrs. Shenee, Mrs. Teresa, Mrs. Elsie, Mrs. Chile, Mrs. La-Joyce and of course, you Mrs. Johnnie Bea that there are different ways to handle your problems"

"Good, as for you being a weed, I don't know anything about that. You are still my flower. You just need Mrs. Johnnie Bea to get back home so she can water and fertilize you and bring out all the good things about you," Mrs. Johnnie Bea said kissing Bunkie on the cheek.

"I might be going to jail for the rest of my life when I go back to court. Will you still love me?" Bunkie asked smiling as Mrs. Johnnie Bea held her close.

"Of course, I will still love you. I don't think a judge will send a thirteen-year-old girl away to jail for the rest of her life for fighting especially if it is her very first fight but he could place you under restrictions. What she said to you was wrong but so was how you responded."

"How else was she going to respond Mrs. Johnnie Bea? All her teachers are white. Telling them was not going to help Bunkie they ain't gonna say it but they probably think she's a nigger too." Another punch in the air followed another and another."

"Pee Wee stand still one minute. I'll be home tomorrow. We will talk more about it then. In the meantime, both of you have parents and adults in your lives you can talk to. Pee Wee you save that hitting for the ring and make sure you are getting paid. Do I need to call someone to get you two safely home?"

"No Bunkie's Dad's picking us up. I'm going with Bunkie and him out to the gym so I can throw a few punches to show him how good I am." Pee Wee said shuffling back and forth as he threw wild punches in the air.

"Bunkie might go to jail forever if she doesn't beat her case."

"Pee Wee you shouldn't say such a thing. You have got your sister crying again.

"Mrs. Shenee' came to court with me. The judge would have let me out sooner but Mom insisted I needed to spend the weekend in jail to learn what jail is all about. Mrs. Johnnie Bea, I cried so hard Mrs. Susie had to come up to what they call the holding room and quiet me down." "I'd like to go up there just to see what it is like being locked up." Pee Wee said throwing more punches in the air. Those cats ain't ready for Pee Wee that's for sure." Pee Wee continued to jab the air with hard lefts and rights as he danced around the room.

"You don't want to go to jail, trust me Pee Wee. They have tiny rooms with a toilet and a sink right where you sleep and if you have a roommate, they get to see you go to the bathroom. You have to ask to be let out of your room and asked to go back in. If you act out at all they will keep you in the room for two or three days.

"What! I don't need to ask anyone if I can come out of my room. Hey, that ain't for me," Pee Wee said taking a seat in the lounge chair where Elizabeth always sat.

"Many of the kids in there have no real homes. Some are doing things girls shouldn't even think about doing until they are grown. Others think robbing and stealing is fun. I am not like that and I don't want to be around kids that think cussing their parents out is cool. Mrs. Johnnie Bea." Bunkie said looking seriously at her as she lay across her bed. "Some of those kid's parents are in jail themselves. One girl said both her parents were clickers. You know crack addicts Mrs. Johnnie Bea." Bunkie said when Mrs. Johnnie Bea looked sideways at her.

"Me, I'm going to be an airline pilot just like the Bessie Coleman."

Bunkie's words jolted Mrs. Johnnie Bea's memory back too many years when she desired to become another Bessie Coleman."

"What made you decide to become an airline pilot of all things?" Mrs. Johnnie Bea asked pulling the stray hair that had fallen in Bunkie's face back.

"When I was in the fifth grade, I had to do my first book report on a famous African American remember. I asked you what famous black American you most liked when you were growing up. You told me about Bessie Coleman. Momma took me to the library to get the book. I got an A on that report and ever since then I have wanted to be an airline pilot."

Mrs. Johnnie Bea asked herself if the Lord might have been giving her the desires of her heart even after so many years had passed. She pressed Bunkie's hands in a way that indicated pride in the choice she had made.

"Gee Bunkie, all this time I thought you were going to be a boxer like me." Pee Wee said staring at his sister. "No," Bunkie said as she pulled back the stray hair to retie her ponytail. "I want to be someone famous like Bessie Coleman. She makes me feel proud to be a Black American female doing something most people don't think about especially girls. Carol and I have decided we both want to be pilots."

"Is that why you are always with that white girl?"

"She is my friend Pee Wee. At least she was my friend until that other girl who hates black people came around."

"Now wait a minute, said Mrs. Johnnie Bea, we have not decided that your friend Carol (that dark-haired thin girl) who always comes to see you at 'The Safe Place' has the same feelings the girl that made that cruel racial remark to you does." Mrs. Johnnie Bea said brushing the pleats back into place on Bunkie's plaid skirt.

"I don't know Mrs. Johnnie Bea, but even if she decides not to be my friend I am still going to become an airline pilot," Bunkie said staring seriously at Mrs. Johnnie Bea and Pee Wee.

"Well, at least you are not a crack smoker. I hate crack smokers," said Pee Wee his eyes focused out the window of Mrs. Johnnie Bea's room. "I'm sure glad Mom doesn't do no crack 'cause crack is whack. I have seen what it can do. Make a woman do almost anything. She's like nothing." Pee Wee said in a serious tone for the first time. He turned to Mrs. Johnnie Bea, tears in his eyes saying to her as he knelt beside her in the lounge chair where she sat laying his head in her lap. "Mrs. Johnnie Bea thanks for helping us before Momma turned to stuff like that."

"We would be just like those kids Bunkie is talking about if you didn't help us all the time. Momma tells us that over and over.

'If it don't' be for Mrs. Johnnie Bea, Teresa, and Elsie we would be in hell right now.' Pee Wee said moving Mrs. Johnnie Bea's cane out of the hand she had just picked up laying it beside her. He then took her hands and placed them in each of his lifting them to his cheeks looking up at her he said

"Mrs. Johnnie Bea these are grandma's hands. You remember how you were always coming by with your pot of beans. Boy were those beans good! Before you came around my stomach was always growling. I stopped feeling hungry all the time because I knew you were coming by with some food for us. When Momma was mad and wanted to whip us. You would talk her out of it and then stick a piece of peppermint in our mouths and tell us we had better behave if we didn't want a beating. I love these grandma's hands."

"Move over boy," Bunkie said to her brother taking Mrs. Johnnie Bea's hands away from him and laying them on her cheeks. "Mrs. Johnnie Bea your Oprah must be happy to have you love her. I know I am." Mrs. Johnnie Bea smiled as she forced tears back that had smartened her eyes. "Come kneel beside me. Let's pray for each other. God hears our prayers. Just as he heard the prayers of our ancestors, long years before it was thought they would live to get us here. That same God hears us now and will forever more. Come now let us pray even for the young child that called you out of your name."

"No Mrs. Johnnie Bea why would we pray for her?" Pee Wee asked. "Because those that have done wrong are the ones who need God the most." Mrs. Johnnie Bea said pulling them closer to her and kissing the forehead of each child she pulled closer to her.

"Not one child has come through my body yet I have so many to love."

Chapter Seven

La-Joyce eased out of her Subaru she had just parked in front of Ms. Johnnie Bea's home. Though standing was difficult since she had entered her last month of pregnancy, La-Joyce had to stand for a moment and shook her head as she smiled while looking at the job the contractors and landscapers had done on the house and yard she stood in.

"What a miracle," was all she could say as her eyes took in the change in Mrs. Johnnie's yard. The new sea blue siding was a lighter blue than the old paint job that had robbed Mrs. Johnnie Bea's home of its beauty for so many years. An arrangement of colorful annual perennials fully bloomed and adored the edges of the house. Whoever takes care of her yard will have to watch out for those beautiful creeping Jennies they grow fast but whoever planted them knew their bright golden yellow would do wonders surrounding her new white porch. She knew Mrs. Johnnie Bea would love the new wood-bleached swing placed on the far left deck of her front porch as well as the one on her back deck.

The house had sat on this corner lot for nearly forty years. Since Mr. Taylor, Mrs. Johnnie Bea's husband died fifteen years ago, the house had taken on a deathly look as if it wanted to pass away too. No one dared insult Ms. Johnnie by telling her that her house looked as though it was at death's door. That would mean a long tongue-lashing.

Now as La-Joyce stood viewing the transformation before her she could not believe her eyes. Manicured deep green grass covered the once desolate yard like a carpet complementing the flagstone blue and white pathway that was caressed by multi-colored pansies following it up to the steps and around the side of the yard. A center pot filled with mini pink and red geraniums stood in the middle of the yard. Thick ferns had been planted along the pathway with sweet woodruffs. Blue and purple myrtle smiled out at her alongside creeping yellow buttercups. Rose bushes not yet in bloom stood waiting for their summer yield at the base of the yard just to the side. Burgundy Ajugas mixed with dark green foliage enriched the oval picture window they stood beneath. Everything about the outside of Mrs. Johnnie Bea's home had been transformed to look like a picture out of a Lady's Home Journal magazine. La-Joyce was thrilled as she took in the spectacular beauty before her.

After leaving Mrs. Johnnie Bea the night before, the women had been chauffeured by limousine to the Ritz, Colgate's finest hotel. In the stateroom at the Ritz, they had dinner with Elizabeth going over all the accomplishments they would have to explain to Mrs. Johnnie Bea when she returned to take over The Safe Place and the Village.

What if she did not like the changes they had made? These questions they pondered over? Elizabeth eased that worry. After visiting with Mrs. Johnnie Bea every day for the last eight weeks she had been feeding her information as to those changes and what they involved. Mrs. Johnnie Bea talked freely about what should or should not be happening. Elizabeth made sure if their changes were such that Mrs. Johnnie Bea seemed pleased, they were incorporated into the new system they worked out to improve the quality of service given to both 'The Safe Place' and The Village. If the changes were of such a nature that though they were practical they took away the human element in working personally with her clientele the answer was no. One such change that would have made less work for everyone was to have prepackaged lunches for the people to pick up from a tray one person would simply hand them out so that less time was spent serving. Mrs. Johnnie Bea rejected this idea because it removed the human element of personal service to the people she helped. It would prevent her from actually seeing them and knowing which of their needs was not being met. They agreed that if Mrs. Johnnie Bea indicated that the changes desired to be implemented were thought to be unacceptable to her it was erased from the plan.

Elizabeth greeted Elsie and the rest as they walked in. When they entered the stateroom where waiters and waitresses stood waiting to serve them. They stopped and looked at each other.

"I believe we have been walking in the Shoes of the fisherman," Teresa said to the others as they stood together realizing their mentor and friend would be with them again soon.

"Maybe fisher person," Shenee' said tears flowing down her cheeks. "We have simply tried on the shoes of a great warrior," Elizabeth said completing her statement by adding, "A woman that makes women proud to be females in a world controlled by men."

"Amen, they all echoed. Elizabeth encouraged them to be seated as she dried her eyes.

"How did she ever do all the things we have come together to get done? I would never dream of taking on such an undertaking alone," Chili' said using the table napkin to catch the tears leaking from her eyes.

"My children have become students respected in our community because Mrs. Johnnie Bea saw beneath the ugliness of our poverty and helped us to overcome it. Now I may one day have children that will become important in the role they play in society." Rosie said not attempting to stop the tears sliding down her cheeks.

"Shenee' and I worked side by side scrubbing and cleaning children as tired and consuming as it was, we loved every minute of it. She may live among the rich and famous but she is a down with it, sister." Chili said smiling through teary eyes.

"That is the best compliment I have heard someone give in a long time coming from Chili," Susie said. "Sisters in these two months we have become what it is Mrs. Johnnie Bea sees in her Oprah, working to help those in need for a friend who has always worked to help us as well as others. Her work became our work. Like she believes Oprah does, we found a way to give back to our community a task set before us because of an accident. It was as if all that has happened was predestined." Susie said to the others.

"Now let's pray over this food and enjoy each other while we eat. Tomorrow we will be giving our gift of love to our beloved mentor."

Chapter Eight

❧⋆❀⋆❧

Everyone has a dream they want to be fulfilled Mrs. Johnnie Bea was no exception. She, Teresa, and Elsie had a habit of gazing at the Ladies" Home Journal. There was a picture inside the home journal that Mrs. Johnnie Bea always returned to. Viewing it from time to time she had torn out the two pages of what she wanted her home to look like one day. While house-sitting for Mrs. Johnnie Bea, Elsie, and Teresa had confiscated the hidden treasures and shared her friend's dream with the rest of those Mrs. Johnnie Bea felt were a part of her family. With her away for two months they went about taking care of her house the same way she had always taken care of them. La-Joyce stood looking at their accomplishment smiling.

The front door opened as La-Joyce turned to pull a tree plant out of her car. Turning around with the plant in her arms, she laughed when she heard Chili's voice from behind. Three other faces appeared in the doorway smiling at her.

"What are you doing La-Joyce? Let me help you with that. We don't have very long before Mrs. Johnnie Bea arrives. Everyone is here except Susie Chili said. "She has not gotten off work yet." La-Joyce turned handing the large leafed plant to Chili.

"Lord I can smell those beans way out here," La-Joyce said.

"Come on in baby. We are all in here waiting." Elsie called out as she stood draped in a red bibbed apron, a large wooden spoon in her hand. Long grey and black braids hanging down her back were tied with a red band the same color as her apron.

Shenee' appeared in the doorway. Her ash blonde hair swayed with her movement as she walked towards La-Joyce and gave her a warm embrace.

"Hi, Shenee'" La-Joyce said, "you always wear the best-smelling perfume girlfriend how is your law firm coming along?"

"Just fine, I hired two new lawyers there is so much work. I needed them now that I have to look after Mrs. Johnnie Bea's affairs. Look at your hair La-Joyce it is lovely. Chili you put a hurting on that head. La-Joyce you look gorgeous. Isn't that your word Chili?" Shenee's joking asking, as she touched the twisted braids adoring La-Joyce's dark checks. Both La-Joyce and Chili chuckled realizing what Shenee' was referring to.

"Yes, like she hasn't put a hurting on all of our hair when she can make time for us in her busy schedule," Elsie said walking with Shenee' and La-Joyce back into the house.

"Where did this sign come from?" La-Joyce asked slipping off her shoes at the door as she picked up a sign that read, 'Take Off Your Shoes at The Door.'

"Girl as soon as the people finished laying down that five-thousand-dollar white carpet in this front room, Elsie had me drive her to the sign store and stood there until it was completed," Chili told the others.

"I told her she might offend somebody. She said the only person who was going to be offended was her foot if someone attempted to put their dirty shoes on Mrs. Johnnie Bea's white carpet."

"Did you tell Chili that Elsie or is she making it up?" La-Joyce asked laughing.

"I sure did. These Negros are not coming in here messing up Mrs. Johnnie Bea's white carpet."

"Now Elsie, Negroes are not the only race of people Mrs. Johnnie Bea allows in her home." Shenee' said shaking her head as the others nodded in agreement.

"I mean them too," Elsie said putting her hands on her hips as if daring anyone to make another comment.

"She did allow me to buy some house slippers." Chili said as she added "But look at Elsie standing here stomp barefoot."

"Chili now that is southern, I have never heard of anyone calling a person with no shoes on stomp barefoot." Shenee' said

"Neither have I," said La-Joyce.

Girl I'm a southern woman here in the north on a mission. Yes, stomp barefoot is southern but what else can you call that but stomp barefoot with those corns standing out like ears on a coon's back." Everyone looked at Elsie's toes and laughed.

"Now that is racist Chili come on you know better," Teresa said as she shook her head, laughing all the while.

"I'm sorry I sure did not mean to be making racial remarks but my Lord, look girls." Laughter filled the room as the women gathered around to examine Elsie's bare feet.

"My toes feel good walking on this soft carpet and these corns need some air I don't know what you're talking about. You know the Chinese take off their shoes before entering their house," Elsie said. Why, I don't know but I'm told it's a habit they can't break."

"I thought it was the Japanese," Shenee' said.

"Shush your mouth girl! Back in the day black folks used to walk bare feet everywhere they went when they didn't have any shoes," Teresa' said causing everyone to laugh even harder.

"You two see how we've put a hurting on this house to bring it back to life, Elsie said standing at the stove stirring the beans, a large red apron covering the tan summer dress she wore. I don't know how on earth we found the time to organize remodeling Mrs. Johnnie Bea's house with all the work we had to do at The Safe Place and in The Village.

Shenee's smile broadens as she walks with La-Joyce into the living room. Her pink turtle neck showed from the top of the gray sweatshirt that matched the grey sweatpants she wore.

"Here are the pictures. How close have we come? La-Joyce, does this house look gorgeous or what? We outdid ourselves ladies if I must say so myself," Chili said, looking with La-Joyce at the pictures dressed the same as Shenee' except her turtle neck was lavender. Teresa wore an apron much like Elsie's except that it was yellow like the yellow band she wore matching her multi-colored sun dress. Their hair was styled the same, with long grey and black braids hanging down Teresa's back as well as Elsie's.

"Mylo and Dwayne were by here earlier. They said 'The Safe Place' looked so different they didn't recognize it."

"How is that husband of yours La-Joyce?" asked Teresa.

"Myylo and Dwayne are at the hospital now getting ready to bring Mrs. Johnnie Bea home."

"They will be here before you know it," La-Joyce said

Come on in here girl. The kitchen has been completely remodeled with new white pine wood cabinets. We finally purchased the eight-foot pine wood dining room table, Mrs. Johnnie Bea always dreamed about owning," Elsie smiled as she showed off the table.

"Mrs. Johnnie Bea will not believe her eyes. We better hope her heart can stand the shock." Shenee' added "Look this is the same kitchen island that is in the picture. They match the pine kitchen cabinets giving her much more storage space. Yes, they did get it right."

"I was told it would be the same model when I ordered it. I'm glad you placed it in the center of the newly tiled kitchen floor where her older smaller table used to sit. I did a good job matching the window blinds, didn't I? Did you destroy those old washed-out curtains she kept saying she was going to replace?" La-Joyce asked.

"What did you do with that broken down stove she refused to get rid of Chili?"

"I took it to the graveyard so that it could be buried."

"Leave it to Chili to come up with a smart answer," Teresa said.

"Yes, I did. Did you notice those steps outside are they wonderful or what?!" Chili asked no one in particular. Mrs. Johnnie Bea will not have to worry about falling with those steel steps and railings on the side of her steps. They also added a ramp she can use until she can walk up the steps." "Girls she will never recognize this as her home trust me," La-Joyce said.

"I had to circle twice before I got it right. The front yard looks like something out of a Home and Garden magazine. Who's going to take care of those beautiful flower beds you and Teresa had planted."

"Elsie and I will tend them. We love to see them grow and caring for them will be a blessing. Something we don't mind doing for Mrs. Johnnie Bea since the yard at our townhouses is tended by landscape professionals. My Oprah, won't Mrs. Johnnie Bea be happy," She, smiling with the other women.

"Everybody calls Mrs. Johnnie Bea. Mrs. Johnnie Bea no matter how old or young they are. Did the name just stick over the years?" Shenee' asked Teresa.

"Elsie, how did Mrs. Johnnie Bea come about that name? We've called her that as long as I can remember."

"Teresa, don't you remember, Mrs. Johnnie Bea was named Ms. Johnnie Bea by Mr. Green, her father?"

"I do remember Mrs. Green telling my mother that when her husband saw how wide opened Mrs. Johnnie Bea's eyes were at birth, he immediately named Ms. Johnnie Bea after his great-grandmother who was always called Johnnie Bea according to Mrs. Green, Mr. Green said their daughter was going to be just like his great grandmother. He wanted her name spoken with respect. It is written on her birth certificate that same way," Elsie explained to them.

I've known Mrs. Johnnie Bea as long as I can remember and she will tell you that quick and in a hurry. It is not by chance that her name is what it is. She has always been one to speak her mind even as a child. If Mrs. Johnnie Bea didn't think it was right Mrs. Green always said her daughter was bound to speak on it. She questioned Mr. and Mrs. Green about everything." Elsie told the others shaking her head as she recalled Mrs. Johnnie Bea's earlier life.

"Mrs. Green said Mrs. Johnnie Bea had been shocking her since she came out of the womb with her eyes wide open looking around."

"Was she born with a veil over her face?" Chili asked.

"I can't say if she was born with a veil but I do believe that woman was born with a questioning spirit. The Lord made her that way. At the time we lived in Mississippi, my mother said white folk looked at her strangely because even as a little girl she would walk up to them asking questions they had no answers for.

I was only ten when we moved here. How much older is Mrs. Johnnie Bea than we are Elsie?" Teresa asked.

"She's ten years your senior and five years older than me. We have always been her little sisters ever since I can remember."

"More like her little children I would say," Elsie said.

"Mrs. Johnnie Bea was always getting in trouble speaking on matters children had no business speaking on. Like the time she overheard her parents talking about how the preacher was going to get in trouble if he didn't stop making advances at those young women at church with him being a married man.

When the preacher came to tell them Mrs. Johnnie Bea had questioned him about this behavior, both Mr. and Mrs. Green stood listening to their words spoken about the preacher exactly as they had said them," Mrs. Green told us. They could not deny it had been said. After Mr. Green set him straight of course she was asked, she told me, why she took it upon herself to get into grown folks' business. She said she told her parents she liked the preacher and she told him so he would not get into trouble."

"You know when Elsie and I were coming up you could not get into grown folk's conversations. I overheard Mrs. Green and my mother laughing and talking. Mrs. Green was telling my mother about how Mrs. Johnnie Bea took a seat beside her in her sewing room when she was about eight years old. She thought Mrs. Johnnie Bea wanted to learn how to sew but she had other things on her mind. She said she sat down as politely as she could and told her God was a girl, not a boy. She said she told Mrs. Johnnie Bea God was neither male nor female. Mrs. Johnnie Bea then asked why the preacher says *he* when he speaks of God. She told Mrs. Johnnie Bea that the preacher was referring to him as the father and his son Jesus Christ. Mrs. Johnnie Bea, she said then wanted to know 'why God could not be the mother?' Mrs. Green said she answered that by telling Mrs. Johnnie Bea God was a spirit, not flesh and blood the way she was thinking.

She said 'No Momma God is all that is good and people are not always good, are they?' Mrs. Green said Mrs. Johnnie Bea's hands went up in the air a big smile covered her face. She said she was so surprised by her daughter's summation she grabbed Mrs. Johnnie Bea knowing in her heart God had given her a special child.

"Listening to many of their conversations, I learned that Mrs. Johnnie Bea was known to question the teachers, the preacher, the doctor, or anyone who had something going on Mrs. Johnnie Bea was curious about. She never avoids work or what she calls duty. It was always in her to do for others. She had to go by to see how Mrs. So and So was doing or making the bullies leave the little kids alone. Back in the day down in Mississippi, we went to country one-room schools for blacks only so everyone practically knew everyone else. Even in school, the teachers used to say Mrs. Johnnie Bea was the one child they 'believed would do something to make the race proud.'

"Our families got deep into the voting registration movement, Teresa said. Many of the families housed the young white and black students coming to Mississippi. Mr. Green was lynched for not only trying to register to vote but mostly for housing those white and Negro freedom riders. My mother said not long after the white freedom riders came down and their parents allowed them to live in their homes Mr. Green registered to vote. It was common knowledge that he befriended the white freedom riders.

He didn't come home one night. The next morning, they found him dead hanging from a tree not far from his newspaper office. White children were throwing rocks at his body. Mrs. Green tried to keep Mrs. Johnnie Bea from seeing it but we all saw. I'll never forget that day as long as I live."

"And I thought I had a reason to hate," Chili said.

"Three families left and moved here, Elsie's family, my family, and Mrs. Green came with Mrs. Johnnie Bea. My father got us out of there because the whites were burning houses and dragging people out of their homes at night burning and killing them at will. There was no one to stop them. It was like living in a war-torn country and through no fault of your own you realized you have become the victim to be destroyed," Teresa said as the room became quiet.

Which reminds me La-Joyce, Mrs. Johnnie Bea called and asked me last night to call and find out when you are due to deliver that baby, she said she doesn't intend to be in no hospital then. I was to call her back this morning before she saw her doctor. She is going to wonder if I have lost my mind." Elsie said quickly changing the subject. "And by the way, I can never get over how those large hoops you wear in your ears make you look like a little girl instead of a soon-to-be mother. The expressions on the faces of the women softened as they turned their attention to La-Joyce and her pregnancy.

"Any day now Elsie, can't you tell? I look like a swollen elephant. Who's cooking?" she asked sniffing the air."

"I got Mrs. Johnnie Bea's navy beans going on. I'm the only one who can get those beans seasoned the way Mrs. Johnnie Bea cooks them," Elsie said. Girls when we were coming up beans were always cheap and filling," she added as they examined the changes that had been made to Mrs. Johnnie Bea's home.

Chapter Nine

><!+>-<0>-<+!><

"Elie I'd like to take another look at those pictures from the Ladies Home Journal to see if we got the exact design for the living room that is shown in the picture," La-Joyce said reaching for the papers that had been folded and creased so many times it looked like discarded trash.

"My goodness, it looks the same. That purple velvet couch has a reddish overtone. Who found the marble tables? And that chandelier, I can't believe we did it. She is going to be in shock for days walking around in this dream home."

"Well let me tell you something it's going to be hard enough as it is to keep Ms. Johnnie Bea from buying plastic," Chili said.

"Why would she need to buy plastic," La-Joyce asked.

"Girl, you don't know nothing about southern black people living back in the day. She's going to be covering up everything we got her." "I know that's right Chili," Elsie said you know when black folk get nice stuff, the first thing they say is 'Chile' I'm going to buy me some plastic to keep my new furniture clean." The room filled with laughter as Elsie went on to say,

"That means, don't sit on my couch until I got some plastic covering it."

"Girls," Chili said still laughing, "my mother used to have that plastic on her couch, and in the summertime down south in Louisiana, it got so hot that plastic would stick on your legs if you had shorts on. When you tried to get up the plastic would rise with you as if to ask are you were going somewhere." Laughter filled the room as they all rubbed their hands over the soft velvet sofa. "Momma didn't ever have to worry about me sitting on that couch because I knew once it grabbed hold of me it wasn't letting go," Chili said laughing at her joke along with everyone else.

"I hope she likes everything," La-Joyce said her hand suddenly holding her stomach as if trying to still her moving baby.

"Of course, she is going to like it," Elsie said smiling her arms folded with a large spoon in one hand.

"My goodness," said La-Joyce slowly making her way into the sewing room. "Sister Girls, what have you done?"

"This looks nothing like the room we sat in two months ago. You girls have replaced that old house with this mansion."

"What do you mean you, we including you, worked our butts off to make this miracle happen," Shenee' said, looking around with La-Joyce at the newly remodeled room. They walked around the sewing room where they had visited with Mrs. Johnnie Bea the night of her fall. A soft pink velvet long sectional couch under a furry white carpet sat behind a marble coffee table with two smaller marble tables on each side. Chili led La-Joyce to a large oak China cabinet that stood where all Mrs. Johnnie Bea's fine china and crystals had been placed for viewing. Across from the wall where pictures of Mrs. Johnnie Bea's family stood, a 60-inch black LCD TV had been fitted onto a wall. Pictures of Mrs. Johnnie Bea's favorite people adore the opposite wall, of course, her parents, and grandmother. Teresa and Elsie as children Mrs. Johnnie Bea's husband with Dwayne and Mylo when they were just boys were still in place on the wall. The women stood amazed at the new additions of not only themselves but many dignitaries they knew.

Yes, you guessed it, her Oprah was the largest. She stood in the middle surrounded by all Mrs. Johnnie Bea's other favorite people. Of course, a picture of Mahalia Jackson and Mrs. Johnnie Bea hung side by side they looked so much alike that it seemed only right that they be placed together.

"Alice Walker, I never hear of her anymore. Is she still writing? Teresa asked gazing at her picture on the wall."

"After she wrote The Color Purple," Shenee' said moving her hand over the frame of a picture. "There was such a ruckus among our men that she began writing in Greek to avoid further problems, remember?" Shenee' said.

"That 'Temple of My Familiar' was a little too far out for me" Elsie replied.

"You think Whoopi and Oprah will play the parts in that book if it becomes a movie?" La-Joyce asked looking with Elsie at the pictures of Whoopi Goldberg hanging not far from Walker.

"Whoopi, Chili I swear you remind me of her the way you are always making people laugh and giving those answers that always get hot conversations going," Rosie said.

"Well, I guess I'm like Teresa about Mother Teresa," Chili replied. I'm in good company. She's a cool sister. I'm flattered."

"And trust me, that Walker is coming back with something we all can understand. I've read some of her earlier books that were great so I am sure of that," Chili said Writers are like that. Susie placed her beside Maya Angelo. Teresa said still looking at Alice Walker's picture. "She is in good company girls, good company."

There is the legendary Toni Morrison.

"Her stories are too way out to understand too," Chili said.

"Yes, they are, but her message is so profound." Shenee' said staring at the picture of Morrison with the others.

"Truly I can see why Mrs. Johnnie Bea would think of her as a remarkable woman."

"That Maya Angelou and her 'Phenomenal woman', and Still I Rise', yes Alice is in good company. Shenee' said smiling as she allowed her fingers to caress the pictures on the wall before her.

"Look there is Dr. King, alongside Mahatma Gandhi, Sister Teresa, Eleanor Roosevelt, and Rosa Parks," La-Joyce said calling out faces she knew.

"Susie outdid herself. Mrs. Johnnie sure will like these pictures."

"I see she's got her friend Ms. Adams up there gathering dust," Chili said.

"That's right," Susie said entering the room wearing her uniform with juvenile detention written on the front. Everyone turned to welcome Susie as they continued to inspect her contribution to the surprise waiting for Mrs. Johnnie Bea. "These pictures are of people Mrs. Johnnie Bea admires, not you or me."

"Here enters our police officer. Are you out there giving out tickets to poor drivers driving one mile over the speed limit," Chili asked laughing.

"Have you racially profiled our people this morning," asked La-Joyce still walking around looking at the pictures on the wall.

"How many poor souls do you have spread eagle on the ground like animals, especially if they are black," Teresa said smiling along with the other women as she walked over to hug Susie. Susie smiled walking in like she was the officer of the day.

"Look at her," Chili said "She has that look on her face that the officers get when they are demanding respect."

"If it's not for us giving tickets to those poor souls out there driving one hundred miles an hour over the speed limit you would be in the hospital or dead. Let us not mention those poor souls Teresa is talking about who would like to take control of the situation and take our guns putting us on the ground," Susie said returning Teresa's embrace.

"Girl we are just kidding. After all Susie Mylo is out there on the streets so believe me I know what you are talking about as worried as I am for him," La-Joyce said smiling as Susie walked over and rubbed her enlarged stomach.

"Oh, no ladies not only do you think like that, many people think like you think. They hate us not realizing that it is us who enable them to walk the streets without fear. It is us who make sure they are safe in their homes. Without me and others like me keeping young juveniles from breaking out of jail to rob your homes you would still be complaining. If law enforcers didn't ticket there would be no safe driving as little as it is already. As for racial profiling yes, I'm not going to lie it does happen. There are some police out there racially profiling, other police hate to partner with them because they know they are power-tripping but that is not the majority. Most are trying to do their job without getting hurt or killed."

"Susie is sticking up for her officers," Elsie said folding her arms while looking over at her smiling.

"I am Elsie but let me say this. It is all about attitude. When the police stop you, it is usually for something minor. But criminals, trust me they know having a policeman stop them means they are about to be caught," Susie said smiling at the women staring at her. "But the average person stopped by the police if their attitude is respectful the officer will usually be respectful as well. When you come with attitude the entire situation changes from minor to major sometimes in a matter of seconds. What could have at first been a warning or a small issue easy to handle becomes serious and dangerous for you if the officer feels your attitude is threatening in any way to his or the public's safety."

"Do I hear you admitting that cops do wrong at least some of the time?" Chili asked doing sit-ups on the carpeted floor.

"Yes, Chili after you've seen a certain clientele committing criminal acts over and over you tend to act too quickly or prejudge wrong sometimes, we have to work on that. Our reports must not allude to racial profiling. The restrictions on our activities are much more scrutinized now than ever. Those cops that got away with that have too many cameras and body cameras on them and now cameras in the community."

"What do you mean by that?" asked Elsie.

"She means they have to be on the job even when they are off" Shenee' said looking over at Susie.

"She's right. We cannot be taken to jail for any reason even if it is a mistake without calling our job and telling them we have committed a possible crime. We have to then go before a board and explain the reason and wait until the board decides if we were involved in any criminal activity. If someone in this room was smoking an illegal drug, we need to remove ourselves because if they are caught up just being present could become serious for us job-wise. Like I said we are on the job even when we are off."

"That is a correct assessment of your profession Susie," Shenee', said raising the glass of orange juice she placed up to her lips. "I know because I've had to represent a few having similar cases."

"Yes, it is Shenee'. And for your information, Chili, Yolanda Adams is not gathering dust. I heard what you said as I walked through the door," Susie said looking over at Chili as she stuck her gum out knowing how Chili hated to hear it pop.

When Mrs. Johnnie Bea gave me her CD to play for my girls after I complained to her about not having worked directly in the girls' units, I thought she was nuts. Those girls, I told her like nothing but rap and hip hop. She insisted I take it any way you know how Mrs. Johnnie Bea is. For some reason, I started playing the CD because I like Yolanda Adam's songs.

After I got the girls to bed one night, they called out to me. When it is at the end of your shift you don't want any drama so I quickly asked if they wanted their lights out indicating that was all they would be getting. Instead, they asked me if I would play my Yolanda Adams CD for them before leaving. I said 'What?', thinking to myself what is this? Then they started asking me to play certain songs of hers and put them on repeat like I did the ones I liked. So, you know they had been listening, right?"

"One evening I told them I wanted them to write about something they wanted that was most important to them. While they wrote I played Yolanda and Donnie McClurkin's song 'I Believe I Can Fly.' The next day this little white girl mixed with Asian came up and gave me a letter thanking me for caring about them. I was so touched by it that I couldn't speak for a minute and you know that is not me. Yes, Yolanda and McClurkin's words touched those girls. Words I continued to play for them day after day. They became my flowers. I didn't have to worry about fights and did not allow them to argue because they knew Flowers didn't talk badly about each other. Flowers, I told them look so pretty even people who would do bad things don't do it around flowers."

"Flowers!" Elsie asked.

"Yes, one night I had a guest speaker come in he brought each girl a rose. I knew not one of those twelve girls had ever received such a gift. After that, I always called them my flowers." Susie said smiling.

"All I have to do is play Yolanda and everyone mellows out. Mrs. Johnnie Bea knows her people. So yes, Yolanda is most definitely one of the family."

"Why did Susie place these pictures of Condoleezza Rice and Clarence Thomas on the wall?" La-Joyce asked tracing the outline of Condoleezza's face on the picture frame of her.

135

"What have you got against Rice and Thomas, girlfriend?" asked Susie turning her attention to La-Joyce.

"I never said I had anything against them I simply asked a question," La-Joyce replied defending the question she had asked.

"I see, you saw Elsie's sign," said Chili looking down at Susie's stocking feet.

"You know I did. That's Elsie. We have to accept her for her ways and love her right on."

"Tell them, Susie. You should have been Mrs. Johnnie Bea's daughter as much as you are like her." Elsie said smiling at Susie's swift comeback. Of course, they all knew Susie was not a woman at a loss for words.

"Let's get back to La-Joyce's question," Susie said turning to Chili saying, "Chili, I know you have not forgotten that tonguelashing Pricilla got when she confronted Mrs. Johnnie Bea about the people she thought weren't worth black consideration?"

"You know I haven't," Chili said, "It was the day you and Teresa, came into the shop with Mrs. Johnnie Bea to get your hair done. I had long since finished beauty school and was just opening my shop. Only two women working for me back then Pricilla was one of them. That Pricilla is something. She can wake up some hair but she made a mistake taking on Ms. Johnnie Bea when it came to Oprah."

"You tried to tell the poor sister but she wouldn't give her mouth a break," Teresa said shaking her head, something that caused the other women to laugh."

"What happened?" asked La-Joyce?"

It was right at four o'clock. I was thinking to myself. I am glad Mrs. Johnnie Bea won't miss Oprah. I already told her she could watch it there at the shop while I was doing her hair. Pricilla was talking to her customer when I turned the channel to Oprah."

'Turn that heifer off I can't stand her', Pricilla said grabbing the TV's remote control from me. I saw Susie's and Teresa's months fly open."

"She cursed Oprah in front of Mrs. Johnnie Bea?" Elsie asked raising her hands high in the air.

"Yes, she did", Susie said moving to look closer at the pictures of Mahalia and Ms. Johnnie Bea. "I think Mrs. Johnnie Bea would have

let Pricilla have her attitude but Pricilla called Oprah out of her name."
"No, Susie, Pricilla's first and last mistake was opening her mouth to
speak on a woman Mrs. Johnnie Bea felt she knew nothing about except
what those scandal papers write," Teresa said looking at Elsie while
giving her that questioning look.

"She's talking about the tabloids," Shenee' said.

"Yes, I am. They will find dirt and print it not even considering the
person it hurts," Teresa said.

"Teresa that is what they get paid to do. If people didn't want to read
dirt the paper would not sell let's get real. They say my gracious they did
that I wouldn't do that even if the reader knows they have done worse
they are just not important enough to become a tabloid subject. What
we hate to admit is that people like dirt. It is bad things about people
they get off on not the good otherwise there would be no tabloid news
selling. Am I right or not?" Susie asked. All heads nodded in agreement.

"You're right; nothing raises a brow like dirt. Good may go unnoticed
but never the bad." Teresa said sighing.

"Susie did you and Teresa notice Ms. Johnnie Bea's expression
change when she picked up that remote," Chili asked. "I thought we
were going to have to take her out of there on a stretcher."

"I never thought Ms. Johnnie Bea was going to be taken anywhere I
thought we might have to take that gal out of there because Ms. Johnnie
Bea had started looking more like Mahalia and less like herself," Teresa
said smiling.

"Do you remember after Pricilla called Oprah a heifer? She looked
at Ms. Johnnie Bea and asked her

'Why are you looking at me like that? Oprah isn't down here giving
you anything. You don't look like a white woman, do you?'

Pricilla said as if it was something Mrs. Johnnie Bea might not be
aware of."

"No, she didn't!" Both Shenee' and La-Joyce screamed as they stared
at Susie.

"Yes, she did. Standing there putting a perm in her customer's hair,"
Susie said "Told Mrs. Johnnie Bea 'Oprah isn't black she just looks
black.'

"Did you hear me tell Pricilla to shut up and just do her customer's hair Susie," Chili asked.

"Not before Ms. Johnnie Bea asked her what color was Oprah if she wasn't black?"

"I have to admit Pricilla didn't back down one bit at first," Susie said.

"Oprah is white inside she just looks black on the outside," she said right to Mrs. Johnnie Bea's face, and like all white people she thinks she has the answer to everybody's business like she is God or somebody." Mrs. Johnnie Bea looked at Pricilla. She didn't even act like what Pricilla said bothered her so if you didn't know how much Mrs. Johnnie Bea thought of Oprah you would have just thought she was an older lady giving a younger woman advice."

"What did she say to her Susie," La-Joyce asked.

"She was upset ladies. I know when Mrs. Johnnie Bea gets upset."
"When is that?" La-Joyce asked.

"When you can hear that southern accent coming through her voice as she told Pricilla

'Nobody trying to better themselves should be looked down on.' And as for white,' she said

'I guess you could say black people who mimic whites that are learned are acting like white people with an education because chile' black folks who can't spell cat act just like white people only those white people they act like can't spell cat either.'"

"It was all I could do to keep from bursting out with an Amen sister," Susie said. But I didn't want to miss the teaching that sister was about to get."

'There are no other people we can act like but the people who taught us their ways.' Mrs. Johnnie Bea told her. 'We've had three centuries to learn how to do nothing but mimic white ways and since the people we are mimicking are all white, I guess we all got a little Willie Lynch in us 'cause the only difference between us and white folk in this country is color and we are getting rid of that quick and in a hurry.'"

"No, she didn't tell her that. Lord Jesus Mrs. Johnnie Bea was mad." Elsie said

"She then had the nerve to ask Ms. Johnnie Bea who the hell was Willie Lynch. That's when Mrs. Johnnie Bea told her Willie Lynch was who white people made many of us into. Ultimately here in this country, white people set the tone. We all follow their lead good or bad. It is how the world sees all of us living here in this country. Now those words got them going." Teresa said

"Yes, Teresa," Susie said "It was then she told Mrs. Johnnie Bea that the next thing she would be telling her is that she was a Condoleezza Rice fan."

"Girl, Ms. Johnnie Bea got up out of Chili's chair walked over to her stared her dead in the face, and said to her

'Why wouldn't I be a Condoleezza fan after all Condoleezza Rice proved beyond a doubt that the lies white folks have been telling everybody about us being inferior to them when it comes to learning was just what it is, a big fat lie.'

"The poor child asked her,"

'What lie? Condoleezza Rice hasn't proved we are anything.' Teresa told them Pricilla said to Mrs. Johnnie Bea.

"'The lie that we are inferior and are not equal to whites when it comes to learning.' Mrs. Johnnie Bea then told her," Susie said.

"I had to admit I was proud of Mrs. Johnnie Bea myself when I heard her say that because I know white people who still think that, they try to say we don't measure up to them when it comes to learning like God gave them the only brains."

"I sure wish they would use their superior brain to do some good instead of destroying everything in sight." Teresa said."

"I know that's the truth," Elsie replied.

'She doesn't know any more than anyone else I know.' Pricilla insisted Susie went on to say.

"Mrs. Johnnie Bea took a seat on the stool next to her looked up at her and said,

'I have not seen many minds as brilliant as Condoleezza Rice's, white or black. There are white Harvard College professors who could profit from the knowledge little brilliant Condoleezza has and could teach them."

"Pricilla pushed the issue by asking her what was so brilliant about Rice," Teresa said laughing 'My Oprah chile,' Mrs. Johnnie Bea said, 'How many languages can you speak?' Susie raised her hands in the air as she shared Mrs. Johnnie's next words to her.

"I could see that Native American heritage coming out in Mrs. Johnnie Bea when her face began to turn red.

'Are you a concert pianist? If so, what music do you play? How many countries can you go into and talk with kings, Presidents even heads of state and get the kind of respect that Chile' gets? My Oprah,' Let's get real now?'

'Rice was nothing but Bush's flunky,' Pricilla quickly replied taking her customer to the bowl to wash her hair." Teresa informed the ladies.

"I nearly croaked,", when Mrs. Johnnie Bea told her, Susie said 'Every one of us is flunky to something if no more than the cigarettes we are addicted to.' The cigarette hanging out of Pricilla's mouth fell to the floor didn't it Chili?" Susie asked laughing as Chili shook her head laughing.

"I'm glad it wasn't lit because if it had been Chili it would have burned a hole right through your carpet," Teresa added laughing as she shook her head in agreement.

"I'm glad too," Chili said laughing along with the others.

"Oh my Lord, she didn't hit on her addiction did she?" Shenee' asked laughing while shaking her head saying?

"Somebody should have told Pricilla not to mess with Mrs. Johnnie Bea's Oprah."

"Mrs. Johnnie Bea then said to her," 'Child' is like me saying Malcolm X did nothing to impact the civil rights movement because I like Dr. King better. We got to stop hating on each other and see what we got good going on. We got to stop using our music and our minds to hurt our people.'

'What do you mean by hurting our people?' "Pricilla asked still not shutting up," Susie said.

'It is a pity when I take my people in to get help at the welfare office and folk their color give them more grief than white folks who sympathize more with their suffering than those who look like them and know their suffering or should know it. So no, when I see one of my people doing better, I am happy for them and me because I know their climb up to the top of the mountain did not come just from being white and privileged.'

"Mrs. Johnnie Bea was teaching all of us up in that room that day," Susie said.

'What do you have against Hip Hop?' Pricilla wanted to know. Chili told them.

'Why nothing at all. My nephew who is like my son sings hip-hop and rap. But I've taught him how sad it would be for a poor black female slave to sit and listen to their people who come after slavery referring to her shameful misery in terms of bitches and hoes. Her tragic body was used and destroyed by a system that bred her like an animal. Freedom was like God's promised land to those who never knew what it felt like to be free. Centuries later after all their struggles our female ancestors endured so that one day their children would see freedom. Now to have our young black males allow this white Willie Lynch system to make our music and violent living further demean her tragic history.'

"Now that is deep. I swear in all my life I have never looked at it that way." Shenee' said getting a yes nod from Rosie who stood aloft as she too listened and learned.

"Neither did I," Elsie said "But you know if you look at it, the disrespect some young rappers have for our females is a form of the Willie Lynch teachings. One would have to understand our history to know how it works." Elsie shook her head walking out of the room to look at the pot of beans she had cooking.

"To top it off she asked Ms. Johnnie Bea what good she has to say about Clarence Thomas' black ass?' I went to say something to her because at that point I knew she had overstepped her boundaries. No one disrespects Mrs. Johnnie Bea using curse words." Chili said but Ms. Johnnie Bea's hand went up and I knew she was about to handle that little sister right."

"And believe me she did," Susie said.

"What did Mrs. Johnnie Bea tell her?" Shenee' asked.

"Susie, tell us please," La-Joyce and Rosie asked looking pleadingly at her.

'That is just what I mean.' Mrs. Johnnie Bea said to her. 'What do you think Thomas had to endure from Negros like you with a little color staining your cheeks calling him black baboons, ugly and big nose? Any cruel self-oppressing name that indicated you didn't like what he looked like since it was what the original Africans who first came to America looked like. And believe me, in your Willie Lynch minds you never stop to think that you wanted yourselves to look like the people who enslaved us to work free for them and took away our identity while using our female bodies to make that color we love so well. Wouldn't you have to say chile' that in most of our Willie lynch minds white must still be more beautiful than black? All the time you are calling anyone acting white, you have been programmed to believe any American whose ancestors were slaves in America is better the whiter they look than the darker blacks with big lips and broad noses looking like our ancestors looked when they were dragged off the slave ships in chains. You never stop to think of the horrors the black female underwent to make that white-looking skin you love so well. As for Thomas, it took white people looking beyond Thomas' color and African features to see that he had a mind and because of his African features, he could be used against his kind because to them no matter how light you were if you were not pure white you were cold black as far as they were concerned. They were able to use his mind for their benefit. We can't blame Thomas or them for our undoings having been brainwashed into belittling our dark color while worshiping their white color against our own.

'Shirley Chisholm was another black sister who had a brilliant mind.' "Mrs. Johnnie Bea said, now on a roll," Susie said, 'But because she did not look like Lena Horne, not taking anything from Lena's greatness, Shirley could not gain the true respect of her black brothers and sisters who could have pushed her higher and given her the real respect she desired had she had Lena's white features. I believe she was a little too dark and African-looking for them to even think about her representing them as anything but a servant. Young lady, you need to reexamine your deficiencies before bad-mouthing another black person trying to do better, especially my Oprah.'

"She didn't stop there," Susie said, "Girls she told her,"

'While I don't know Oprah personally and probably will never know her. I know she comes from a humble beginning just like me. A little black girl that nobody thought much of until the Lord blessed her with the spirit of our ancestors Harriett Tubman and Sojourner Truth. Their spirits surely live in her from what I can see. God elevated her life through their spirit that lives in us as females on this earth.

"Chili didn't that child ask Mrs. Johnnie Bea what had Oprah ever given her?" Teresa asked.

"She sure did. Mrs. Johnnie Bea told her."

'No, Oprah has not given me one red cent but through her giving to others I realized that giving is what I can also do. Daughter, it doesn't take a lot of money to care about others all you need is a giving spirit and a loving heart that wins over those who might need someone caring enough to understand that life at its worst is important because whether we know it or not even the unlovable belongs to God."

"Is that when she won Pricilla over, Chili?" Asked Shenee'

"No girlfriend She won her over when she reminded her that she had a little of Oprah in her too."

"What did you just say Susie" Elsie asked as Shenee' La-Joyce and Rosie looked at her too stunned to speak.

"Yes, we all looked at Ms. Johnnie Bea wondering what would come out of her mouth next. Smiling, she walked over and told Pricilla she had overheard her customer say, she could not give her but half the money for her hair because she had to buy school supplies for her kids, and Pricilla told her not to worry about it God would bless both of them when their children made something good out of their lives. 'You are not rich.' "She told her" 'But your heart is in the right place because first you had compassion for a mother with children in need and you put yourself in her place but most importantly you believe God will make things right. That is as it should be. When those beautiful girls lost their lives in the basement of that church in Montgomery, becoming a part of the horrors that occurred when we finally gained the courage to stand up and fight, wouldn't it have been wonderful if the church had thought the way you think and made every church a pivot point of learning for all black children? Instead, we relied on the very institutions that had oppressed us in the first place to do the job of getting and keeping our children on track something that was the farthest thing on their minds.'

'In what ways' Pricilla asked Mrs. Johnnie, Susie said touching the picture of Mrs. Johnnie hanging on the wall.

'The poverty programs and Head Start programs for the poor started by the government,' she told Pricilla," 'Were simply weak treaties waiting to be broken. Our churches should have put in place at that critical time back in the 60s and 70s, an avenue that fostered preparation for our preschool children poor as well as the wealthy. That way before they became corrupted into gang life as a means of survival our children would have received a head start into that arena we were striving for. Had that happened they would not be in the streets killing themselves every day like they are doing now.'

'It fills my heart with love to hear that you understood the need to help young minds have the tools to assure they become the college students the Negro College funds are designed for. It breaks my heart to see how many of our young minds have gone to waste because our struggle has been always so focused on helping those who already have.' She told Pricilla. "I got closer so that I would not miss one word," Susie said

"Well, what else did she say?" Rosie asked. Susie walked over to Rosie saying as she took her hands into hers.

"Rosie, she said really to all of us there that white institutional racism against our people burned deep into our hearts, so deep we forgot our responsibility to the young looking to us for guidance and protection when they marched with us in the streets." The room got quiet when Pricilla said looking as though she was near tears.

'Mrs. Johnnie Bea every day I see women out there struggling to be both parents. I see men doing the same thing when their women leave them with children they are not prepared to raise or trying to make it on a poor income struggling single-handedly the same battle we took on against the white man. I am with you on one thing.'

'And that is?' Mrs. Johnnie Bea asked her.

'Help can come from anywhere but some things you have to do for yourselves. There was never a plan to ensure our children would survive the movement and move into the mainstream under the umbrella of those who started it. All we got for our efforts is a Negro College fund designed for children whose parents were able to help them through twelve years of making it with the help of the Nego College funds when there was no help for the children who had no way of getting out of grade school without help to receive those funds.'

'You are right baby' Mrs. Johnnie Bea told her finally taking a seat in Chili's chair again. 'We should have had our Head Start programs in those church basements instead of relying on the white man's broken treaties to last forever, especially when we already knew from the Native American history and our history of the many broken promises made to us.

It's young people like you who will change things around and make a difference for our children in this country.'

"Girl, Pricilla had the biggest smile growing on her face. All she needed to know was that she too was making a difference in someone's life no matter how small it still mattered. Mrs. Johnnie Bea ended by telling her,

'Pricilla when Mother Earth spun out of the spirit of God, the spirit didn't say let there be sameness, but differences. Everyone wants you to look like them, and act like they act; if not, there is something wrong with you. You gotta have small feet or unslanted eyes. You must be white or bright; your nose has to be fixed a certain way to suit whoever has the most to say. Without differences, there can be no learning, growth, or life on this earth.'

She told all of us, she did not care if Condoleezza or Thomas' thoughts differed from hers. A part of her learning, she said was to respect those differences so that she could learn how to live right herself. And if their actions were done to hurt someone the mark is on their lives, not hers.'

Mrs. Johnnie Bea told her that they all needed to learn from each other. Seeing the smile light on Pricilla's face she gave her a big hug saying of course, 'My Oprah girl, you need to come over and have some of my beans while we talk together.'

"Every day after that, girls," Chili told them Pricilla turns that TV set to Oprah at four o'clock. She never again had a bad word to say about her. Now when Ms. Johnnie Bea comes into the shop Pricilla meets her at the door with a hug."

"I know why I love that woman how does she win people over like that?" La-Joyce asked placing her hand under her chin as she shook it.

"Now La-Joyce do you see why Condoleezza Rice and Clarence Thomas are up there and of course Anita Hill's picture is also up there because 'Anita is a woman,' Mrs. Johnnie Bea says 'who dared to stand up.' No matter what the outcome, she stood. What Mrs. Johnnie Bea believes is that if Clarence Thomas a man of our race has deeds that hurt our people as has many others, it will unearth itself as the universe declares. His deeds will become crystal clear for all to see. No one can ask more than that. Mrs. Johnnie Bea reminded me of this once during a discussion about him.

La-Joyce touched her neatly braided hair as a wide smile spread across her smooth velvet black face adorned by large hoops swinging from her earlobes. As she continued to walk around naming the faces of the pictures such as James Baldwin, and Richard Wright, other voices could be heard trying to figure out the names of some of the dignitaries Susie had placed on the wall surrounding Oprah and Mrs. Johnnie Bea's family.

Chapter Ten

>―┼┼―◦―┼┼―<

"Rosie, don't sit over there behind those curtains like you are not a part of us. You have given to the world five beautiful children we all love. Come on; tell us how you met Mrs. Johnnie Bea," Shenee' said to her. A shy smile appeared on Rosie's face as she stood by the patio doors half hiding behind drawn curtains. Her hair had been tightly braided with white beads hanging from the ends

"No, I was not hiding I was looking out at the children playing in the backyard. They love Mrs. Johnnie Bea so we just could not keep them away from her homecoming celebration. I notice Elizabeth is still outside fussing over those flowers. I told her to come be with us but she insisted she wanted to be in the yard upon Mrs. Johnnie Bea's arrival."

"Come girl, the kids are fine especially with Little Willie out there watching over them," Teresa said. She was the one person Rosie felt the closest to out of the group of women. That got her moving away from the window. Her smile grew as she walked into the room to be with the other ladies.

"Tell us how you met Mrs. Johnnie Bea's child it's nothing to be ashamed of. We have all needed her in our lives."

Rosie took a seat beside Teresa. Looking around the room at the women there. Tears filled her eyes as she dared to empty her pain. Rosie began to talk.

"All of you have been great to me. All I can say is that once upon a time my life was so different. The most popular girl in school, I was what you called 'tight' my body was my greatest asset. I was built. Size thirty- six, twenty- two, thirty- six with smooth tan skin sweet as a peach in the summertime time I was told. Old and young men wanted me. Boys were at my locker, at my door, following me everywhere. Girls were jealous because I could get their boyfriend just by smiling his way. I was all that and more. My mother tried to tell me that beauty comes and goes and not to allow what I was being told to go to my head. I got caught up and the babies didn't stop coming until my tubes were tied. I learned too late that what people see as physical ugliness can sometimes be a blessing because boys find you uninteresting leaving you alone to develop without the strain of too early maturing if you know what I mean."

"Trust me, we know," Teresa said giving her a reassuring hug her arm across her shoulders.

"I understand now what happened to me. Mrs. Johnnie Bea explained to me, that a girl needs to give her body time to mature and her mind a chance to gain wisdom. When a girl is older and mature, she told me, she is better able to understand life. It is then that the proper man will be wise enough to see her inner beauty, unlike young boys who are guided by a head with a brain smaller than a pea." Rosie joined with the laughter of the other women.

"Now that's coming straight from Mrs. Johnnie Bea!" said Teresa releasing Rosie's hand as she relaxed on the couch now caught up in the part of her life she was about to share with the other women.

"When Mrs. Johnnie Bea knocked on my door that evening," Rosie told them, "I was home locked in my bedroom. My children, the oldest seven at the time had been running through the house back and forth. Sometimes I would scream out of my bedroom for them to stop. Bunkie was the oldest and it was her responsibility to make them behave. She and Pee Wee my oldest son would fight over who controlled whom. He was after all only ten months younger than her. Moe and Joe were twins and just two years under Pee Wee. My baby Buster was only ten months old and still in diapers. I heard them running through the house tearing up things. I just didn't care. Most of the time I had my head under the covers wishing they would all die." Silence filled the room as Rosie began to share with her friends the wounds that scarred her life. "I had just gotten off work. There was no food in the house. All my money had been spent every month to pay rent, utility bills, and bus fare so I could get back and forth to work. I had just a couple of days ago been down to the welfare office begging for some help so I could at least get enough money for the books my son Pee Wee said he needed for school. Mrs. Johnnie Bea was seated next to me as I was telling her and another woman my problems with having to pay for school supplies.

I had all the children with me because I had no one to babysit, not that anyone would take care of five young kids. My neighbors thought of me as a community disgrace. They laughed and talked about me while their children laughed and talked about my children. Even the local church was forbidden to me. I guess the members thought themselves too good to be seated beside Rosie and her "brags" as they called my kids. I know how they were treated at school but I honestly could not do any better. My kids went into foster care having my next child." Tears began to flow down her cheek. The room grew quiet as the ladies listened.

"You don't have to share if it is too hard Rosie. You don't have to," Teresa said, as she placed her arms around Rosie's shoulders.

"She is right Rosie that season is over for you. You don't have to recall it we will understand" Elsie said. "Sharing the heartbreak of having to parent your children when you were so young is hard. You don't have to talk about it." Susie echoed the rest.

"We understand," said Chili. "I know how hard it is when you live from pillar to post."

"They are right. You are one of us now." Shenee' said wiping away a fallen tear with the handkerchief she pulled from her pocket.

"As I said," continued Rosie. "It seemed I was always falling trying to get back up. When Mrs. Johnnie Bea came knocking on my door one evening, I was ready to leave this world forever. The kids kept banging on my bedroom door telling me some old lady was out in front of the door. I thought it might be my caseworker coming to hassle me about something. I got up in a hurry thinking to myself what could they be trying to take away from me now?"

"There, stood Mrs. Johnnie Bea with a big pot in her hands. She didn't wait for me to invite her in. She pushed past me after handing me the pot of what turned out to be beans. I sat them on my clustered table to the joy of my children. She asked:

"Are your children hungry?" By the time I realized she was the woman I had been talking to in the welfare office, the kids were gathered around that big pot waiting to fill their hungry bellies. We moved the clutter from the table. She helped me wash some plates out and dished out those beans for my kids. I could say nothing. I don't remember what we talked about. I was so relieved to see my kids full. My house was filthy but Mrs. Johnnie Bea didn't seem to mind. Rats and roaches ran everywhere, dirty clothes all over the floor. My kids climbed up on her lap and talked to her as if she were their grandmother or a close relative.

It was nice because they didn't know my mother. When she discovered I was pregnant with my second child and the first only six months, my mother packed my belongings and sat them out on the streets, cussed me out, and told me she didn't need any tramp for a daughter. Of course, I found housing and another man to make another baby. After the third one, I began to realize that was all I would ever be. A broken-down female man comes by to drop their load in and leave.

Though I did know the fathers of all my children what good was it when they denied fathering them once I was pregnant? Like my mother said, my life was shot. I would never amount to anything but something for a man to drain himself in when his wife wasn't feeling well at home. I had my tubes tied after the fifth child but by then it was too late because I felt smothered.

"Depression sat in and I couldn't let go of it. I didn't remember what it was like to be happy. At no time was I happy with my children seeing them as mistakes in my life that had crippled me. I began to hate so deeply that I could not rise above it.

The evening Mrs. Johnnie Bea came knocking on my door changed my life forever. After my children were full of those beans Mrs. Johnnie Bea asked them if they wanted the big bowl of ice cream and villa wafers, she had left at a friend's house. They all jumped up screaming yes running to the door ready to go. I hesitated. After all, I didn't know Mrs. Johnnie Bea that well, not to mention I had to go to work the next morning. The kids had to go to school.

"Oh, we won't be long," Mrs. Johnnie Bea told me hurrying the kids out of the door. We all piled in her station wagon. That is when I first met Teresa."

"We call her Mother Teresa down at 'The Safe Place' don't we Teresa?" Elsie said. Everyone laughed.

"It's an honor to be named after that lady." Teresa said adding, "Children come from all over the neighborhood to get help with needs their parents cannot provide. You know Mrs. Johnnie Bea will look at something, see it is not right, and say we can make it better. That is why when she sat listening to Rosie in that welfare office she came back to 'The Safe Place' and said to me. 'Teresa, there is a young child with five small babies that need help. I don't want to bring them directly to 'The Safe Place' I'd like to bring her to you first to build a little trust and let God's love flow,' Teresa informed the others while smiling over at Rosie.

"When Teresa opened the door," Rosie said. "I was ashamed to bring my children in everything was so clean and pretty. We were ushered into the dining room by Mrs. Johnnie Bea. The kids started running towards the table. Mrs. Johnnie Bea stepped in and said to Teresa

'Girl, take those kids in and let them wash up I have something special for Rosie. You come on with me' Mrs. Johnnie Bea said and we walked into another part of her home. All I could do was open my mouth and wish it was me who lived there.

'You go on in there, child. You look so tired and beat. No one going to hurt you here. If you want to step into the tub or shower or just sample some of that nice lotion. Smell it child it smells good. There are robes. That belongs to my friend Teresa you met at the door like me she doesn't have any biological children of her own. It does seem kind of lonesome with no children to share all that goodness she has laid up in her heart. I hope you don't mind helping me out. She'd love having you and these kids for the company even for a few days.'

"I didn't know what to think. But I knew I had been thinking seriously about killing myself and my children just an hour ago. The bathroom looked to me as though I had walked into a dream world. Mirrors lined the walls with rainbow-colored butterflies seated on yellow flowers covering the toweled walls. There was warm soapy water bubbling out of the jazzy bathtub. I dropped those drab clothes and slid into that tub thinking I would duck under that water and drown myself."

"I wonder how Mrs. Johnnie Bea and Oprah would have handled that?" Chili asked crossing her legs as she rested her hands behind her head.

"Oh my" Shenee' and La-Joyce echoed in unison.

"I don't know about Mrs. Johnnie Bea and Oprah but I knew the Lord was working in this miracle because when I saw those babies. Teresa said tearfully. "All I wanted to do was help make life better for them."

"Me," Rosie shook her head "I was at the bottom of the barrel when Mrs. Johnnie Bea brought me to Teresa's home. Tell them, Teresa."

"I mean no offense Rosie" Teresa said "but girlfriend you looked beat down by the world. I kept thinking to myself, now where are those pro-lifers when we need them? Is this what they mean by every child deserves to live? The kid's clothes were way too big and because Rosie didn't have laundry mat money the clothes were dirty and smelled awful I was too busy getting those kids bathed to think about what Rosie might be doing. Mrs. Johnnie Bea already had clean clothes for them. I left Rosie up to the Lord and put my faith in the word. If you are doing good as Mrs. Johnnie Bea always says, good will follow you. Now I have five children I didn't have to labor for just love."

"You are correct in your assessment. Mrs. Johnnie Bea would never worry about the things she does because she realizes it does take a village to raise a child. Mrs. Johnnie Bea and Oprah create villages," Elsie said.

"My children and I became a part of that village," Rosie said. "Was I afraid there might be something I needed to worry about? You must remember I worried every day since the first time I found out I was pregnant at age fifteen. Since then every decision I made was the wrong decision. No one came to help me. The boys and men in my life used me and then left me with unwanted children they cared nothing about. Each one of them now has to pay child support. That is money I never thought would come to me."

"All four of the men pay child support?" La-Joyce asked as more of a question than a statement. Rosie's story suddenly caught a new interest for everyone.

"Yes, they must pay." Shenee' said "You know how Mrs. Johnnie Bea is. When she is on a row you must paddle the boat along with her. Rosie knew her children's fathers. DNA tests were done and every one of the men now pays child support. Three of them after discovering they were the biological fathers of Rosie's children became interested in the children's lives, only the twins' father never asked to have a relationship with them. Oh well, he still has to pay.

"The well they filled has come back to haunt their paycheck every payday. When they bedded Rosie, it was all about them and the pleasure they took in using her body. It never occurred to them children are God's gifts to this world that are not to be abused or forgotten once they are conceived, especially by the people God honors with the privilege of using their bodies to ensure they get here," Shenee said a smug grin spread across her lips as she crossed her shapely legs smiling with her mouth shut as her eyebrows rose.

"Go on girlfriend, my Oprah, how Mrs. Johnnie Bea has influenced you," Chili said.

"Listen to Ms. Thang. Repeating Mrs. Johnnie Bea's words exactly. Elsie said, giving Shenee' a hug.

"When I came out of that bathroom, I could hear Pee Wee asking Teresa. 'Do you think I really got good hair?' The other women looked at Teresa and laughed.

"Girl that Pee Wee is something else. I told him, yes boy I just have to find it. I was brushing up a storm on that head wasn't I Rosie?"

Everyone laughed including Rosie.

"I found my daughter Bunkie the oldest of my children curled up under a blue and pink canopy bed my ten-month-old in her arms. Buster was not going to sleep with anyone but her. She's more like his mother than me. After looking in to see that the boys were giggling under the covers of a big king-size bed, I went back and got in the bed with my daughter and my baby, thinking I must have already killed myself and my kids and now we were in heaven.

The next day, I went to work, hating to return to the house I had been living in. Teresa looked after my three babies assuring me I could stay with her until I got a better place. Mrs. Johnnie Bea took the oldest to school and picked them up. I never thought so many people cared for me. They just kept coming out from where I don't know." Tears fell from Rosie's eyes as her memories surfaced.

"You know how Mrs. Johnnie Bea does her thing," Teresa said. "She doesn't care about color. She will ask you for help. I lingered in the background while she told those pro-life white women 'Five babies come into this world needing help.'

"Teresa, some of those women are not white. They are Jewish," Elsie said to Teresa.

"Well, they look white to me. I can't tell the difference. There is nothing about them that distinguishes them from other white women. But whatever they are, they are all good, caring women, Elsie. That's all I'm saying."

"Those babies needed them. Mrs. Johnnie Bea told them. She told them they needed to ensure not only that babies live but also have a quality life. I couldn't believe she did that."

"Mrs. Johnnie Bea taught me the same lesson."

"I used to think the same way as Chili about white folks until Mrs. Johnnie Bea showed me the error of my thinking when she told me, 'Rosie, I live in a village, and everyone in the village is responsible for raising the children in our village, and love doing their part. There is bad in everything in this world our job is to find the good that is also there.'

I thank God for Elsie and Teresa. They gave me a heads-up on what not to do when Mrs. Johnnie Bea gave me the job at 'The Safe Place'. It paid two dollars an hour more than the fast-food restaurant that barely kept me and my children alive. Soon I had Child Support help."

"I thought you were going to school?" Shenee' said an alarmed look on her face.

"I work at The Safe Place Shenee' while I am going to school. Mrs. Johnnie Bea allows me to work there while I attend dental school. I've already got my GED," Rosie answered.

Teresa interceded saying, "We told her whatever she did if she wanted to keep working at 'The Safe Place,' she better learn to hold in any feeling she had that was negative about the kids. Don't say anything negative about or to them because Mrs. Johnnie Bea will hear about it, usually from them."

Mylo took me up there to work with the kids before we married. We fed them breakfast and later returned to ensure they got dinner in the evenings. Some who did not have a warm place in the winter also slept there. It is a twenty-four-hour facility that works around the clock helping kids survive," La-Joyce said.

"Yes, we changed that entire place so Mrs. Johnnie Bea won't have to work so hard when she returns. I am proud of how all of you pitched in and helped," Elsie said. She added. "There is a sign outside our gate that says Safe Place for Kids. No one has ever tampered with the sign or the kids we serve."

"Shenee' those uniforms for the kids are incredible. They changed how people view them and 'The Safe Place.' Young lady, I am glad now we didn't shun you because you looked so white."

"I am too, really, Shenee. I wanted to let it be a reason to kick you to the curb, but it would have been the worst thing that could have happened as much goodness as you have inside of you," Chili said. The rest echoed their agreement.

"That is the one place where I've seen Mrs. Johnnie Bea work without taking lunch or a break," Teresa said.

"You are right, Teresa because a white girl no more than Bunkie's age came into 'The Safe Place'. I wondered why because you could tell she was well taken care of. She went into the bathroom. She came out smelling like she had been smoking marijuana. Mrs. Johnnie Bea stopped her on the way out the door and searched her backpack. She found a small bag of it that the child had stored inside. Mrs. Johnnie Bea put her in her station wagon and took her down on First Street to the crack house, didn't she, Teresa?"

"Yes, she did, Rosie, showed her what her life would be like in just six months," Teresa said.

"I don't know what she told the girl," Rosie said, "but every day she came to 'The Safe Place for Kids' and dumped her bag for Mrs. Johnnie

Bea's inspection and she never smelled like marijuana ever again in The Safe Place. That's when I realized how many kids had learned to respect 'The Safe Place.' Many coming to The Safe Place don't require help; they come because they love the healthy safe environment. There were games and social gatherings that were safe for the kids so their parents don't mind them coming."

"The Safe Place is Mrs. Johnnie Bea's heart," Elsie said. We warned Rosie whatever she did, do not talk badly about the kids or their parents. If she did, she would find herself back at that fast food job quick and in a hurry. The kids know Mrs. Johnnie Bea's rules and must abide by them. Those that don't get put in check by those that do without delay. We've seen Mrs. Johnnie Bea fire women one hour after they started work for talking bad about the kids. She says 'The kids come to 'The Safe Place' to find love, not hate and a putdown.'"

"One day Mrs. Johnnie Bea came in and overheard one of the female employees steady screaming at a kid about how nasty and filthy he smelled. Mrs. Johnnie Bea called me into her office and told me to pay the woman for the time she had worked because she had to go."

"Why?" the woman asked confronting Mrs. Johnnie Bea about firing her so soon after she had been hired. Mrs. Johnnie Bea told her she had to love kids to work for her. The woman said she did love kids. Mrs. Johnnie Bea told her not the way she wanted them loved. The woman shook her head and walked off in a huff."

"I bet not before she took her money," Chili said.

"I paid her as she walked out the door," Elsie said folding her arms together.

"I learned what Teresa and Elsie meant about Mrs. Johnnie Bea's standards for her employees when I overheard one of the kids sobbing in Mrs. Johnnie Bea's arms," Rosie said. Amy a female employee who worked the evening shift had informed him his mother was in a crack house sucking in a man's behind. He was crying so hard Mrs. Johnnie Bea had a hard time calming him down so he could tell her what had happened.

He finally calmed down and told Mrs. Johnnie Bea how nasty sucking a man's behind was and that he could never forgive his mother for doing that. He was only six years old. He pleaded with her to tell Amy not to tell his friends." Looks of shock filled the faces of the women when Rosie told them what had occurred.

"I looked at Mrs. Johnnie Bea she looked at me we wiped tears from our eyes," Rosie said. "When the woman came on that evening Mrs. Johnnie Bea called her in her office while I was there. She asked her who put God's britches on her, giving her the right to tell that six-year-old child about his mother's behavior in a crack house, that she must have been in there doing something herself. The woman looked at Mrs. Johnnie but didn't answer. Mrs. Johnnie Bea said to her.

'If it don't be for a stroke of luck there goes me or you. It could be our children hearing that about us,' she told her.

'And because of your cruel actions, I'm going to have to put off some important work I had planned to spend time trying to help the child work through this crisis you have made for him.'

"The woman looked at Mrs. Johnnie Bea with a frown on her face, saying, 'I made no crisis for him, his mother did.' That's when Mrs. Johnnie Bea told her to pick up her check from her mail slot because she could not have an employee working for her who didn't love kids and didn't even know they didn't love them."

"Trust me, if you say something around her kids you don't know which one is listening or when it will get back to Mrs. Johnnie Bea but trust me somehow it will get back," Teresa said.

"We all learned that when they found a way to get up to that hospital, Susie said.

"I walked in just as Pee Wee was about to spill the beans about the transformation of the yard. I had a good talk with him on the way home," Teresa told them shaking her head.

"I know you are right because my older kids wanted to know why the twins did not have a father wanting to be a part of their lives. Mrs. Johnnie Bea told them that the twins did have father figures. The next day, Dwayne and Mylo came over and told everyone that the twins belonged to them and that if anyone asked, they could tell them they were their fathers.

"Of course, Pee Wee was upset because the twins had two dads and he had only one."

"You know, I heard her tell those young men these are yours. Teach them to do right, and someday, when you need them, they will teach you about love," Teresa said, laughing. You know she can pull a rabbit out of a hat now."

"She can do that" the rest repeated.

"I am now in school to get my license to be a dental assistant. I'll always help out at The Safe Place, but I will also have a profession to go along with that because Mrs. Johnnie Bea taught me about Oprah." "I can hear her now telling me how Oprah started as a poor child with nothing more than a talent God gave her. 'She used her talent' Mrs. Johnnie Bea told me at a time I needed to hear it. 'God blessed her with more talents just like he will give [me]' she told me. She used those talents and God gave her still more. She said all I had to do was to thank God for the blessings I had already been given. My children Mrs. Johnnie Bea assured me were God's blessings to me. I just had to see my children as blessings and center my love around them. She said all I needed was someone to see my bootstrap and lift it so I could see it too. I have a safe daycare I trust to care for the kids while I work when they are not at 'The Safe Place'. The money their fathers contribute towards their support enables me to buy things for them I could never afford before."

"Are you comfortable with your children's relationship with their fathers?" Susie asked, rubbing lotion up and down her arms and pouring some into Chili's outstretched hands.

"I must admit at first I was against them seeing the children at all."

"Tell me about it, if they haven't been interested up until now tell them to keep stepping," Chili said holding her hands out so that Susie could pour the lotion into them.

"No, Mrs. Johnnie Bea said that would be mean-spirited, and she wasn't having it. If the fathers wanted to be part of their children's lives, it would be wrong to stop that because I was angry at the fathers. Whatever our disagreement was, the children had no part in that."

"Mrs. Johnnie Bea knew the special relationship between fathers and their children. She was a father's child herself. She probably was thinking that if her father and mother had decided to separate it would have been a tragedy for her mother to use her as a weapon to punish her father because of her anger."

"I never looked at it like that," Chili said "But since you put it like that," she said rubbing the lotion Susie had given her on her legs, "My sons' father would be devastated and so would my sons. They would never forgive me if I did that and they later learned I could have allowed them to see him but out of spite, I took away their right to a relationship with him. The money I may or may not get could never take the place of their relationship especially since now they know him.

Mrs. Johnnie Bea told you right it would be like sticking a knife in their chest because you feel a knife in yours." Chile said.

"Yeah, you know, she embarrassed me by saying there are always two sides to every story, and most people don't get to hear but one side. Whoever has their ear tells their story, and that usually is the only story the child ever hears.

"I am blessed. Every day, I am free of more and more of the bitterness in my heart. My mother and I have formed a relationship. I teach my children to help where they can so that those less fortunate than us can feel the love of Mrs. Johnnie Bea and Oprah."

"What about men"? Have you gotten over your hurt when it comes to relationships" Chili asked while the other women eyed her causing her to eye them back smiling.

"I'm twenty-nine years old. That is too young to say I never think about having a relationship but I am careful. Even though I know I will never have any more children, those I have are more than most men can love. Someday, I will learn to trust enough to love again in a different season, but not this season. I am not ready yet. Right now, I'm still learning to enjoy and love the blessings of spring; summer with its hot weather will come soon enough."

"Talking about seasons, let's go outside and check on Elizabeth out there in that sun all this time," Elsie said, walking toward the door leading to the patio. They looked out on the large, enclosed, spacious patio deck. Elizabeth sat talking with the two Muslim women and Little Willie, stood looking out the screened porch at the playing children in the backyard.

Let them enjoy that patio Chili is about to tell us how she and Mrs. Johnnie Bea became connected. Her sewing room will be better let's go back in there."

Chapter Eleven

"Chili I am so glad you hooked me up, as the kids from The Safe Place like to say when you have done something they like," La-Joyce said. "This way I won't look so wild and wooly."

"When did you say you deliver?" Teresa asked La-Joyce taking a pad of paper in hand.

"Any time now, But, my due date is tomorrow. I'm so excited."

"Chili, you know you're in the big times now, going all over the world doing hair," Elsie said, walking through the door carrying the large spoon she had just finished stirring in her pots. What you can do with hair is amazing."

"Did I tell you girls some African king wants me to come over and do his wife's hair?" Chili said holding a piece sign up into the air."

"Chili you are something else, girl. You have been everywhere." La-Joyce said responding to her announcement.

"Well, it was exciting to be asked," Chili replied, seeing the excitement in the others' faces.

"You think that African was for real?" Susie asked.

"We'll find out if and when he sends the money sister," Chili said smiling.

"Girls I am proud to say Mrs. Johnnie Bea helped me get my grove on. She taught me never to forget where I come from like I ever could."
"We are not about forgetting where we came from or not wanting to go further. That is the catch. Ms. Johnnie Bea would put a sister in her place when she tried to put another sister down for doing something to better herself."

"You got that right, Rosie," Teresa said. Come on, girls, relax. She is not in for a while. That woman will always be like a big sister to me. When her husband's brother's son and his wife lost their lives in that car accident, Mrs. Johnnie Bea and Mr. Taylor took Mylo and Dwayne in parenting them as if they were their own.

"Mr. Taylor, Mrs. Johnnie Bea told me," Teresa shared, couldn't have kids. He had some kind of mumps go down on him. Mrs. Johnnie Bea said he told her before they married in case, she wanted to call it off. Mrs. Johnnie Bea said she told him There are children already in the world we'll find some that don't have a family and love them.' All the fifty-some years they were married he loved him some Mrs. Johnnie Bea. Let her run him and the house but she was good to him. Like Oprah, she has her ways about her that draw people to her" Teresa said as if in deep thought.

"That's sort of how she won me over," Chili said. "Give us the word, girl," said La-Joyce. The ladies wandered back into the kitchen and took seats around the island, commenting on the good smells coming from the pots cooking on the stove Elsie was standing over.

"Like she didn't help all of us get our groove on."

Elsie and I were more like little sisters to Mrs. Johnnie Bea back in the days when taking care of business was what black women had to do" Teresa said.

"Elsie would never have become a nurse and I would never have gotten into teaching had Mrs. Johnnie Bea not been the big sister we needed to keep us focused."

"Dancing all over the country, I surely was not thinking about putting my hands on a sick person," Elsie said. All I knew was that Mrs. Johnnie Bea was always up to something. When we were kids coming up it was Mrs. Johnnie Bea who exposed the preacher. It was Mrs. Johnnie Bea who wouldn't let the bad teachers get away with lying about how they treated us. That woman got herself in a lot of trouble looking after us when she should have been looking the other way. After her mother became bedridden, she felt it was her duty to give up her plans to become an airplane pilot and focus her attention on taking care of her.

Becoming another Bessie Coleman was no longer a dream that would become a reality for her."

"If that woman had had her way the world would have known a short black female pilot looking like Mahalia Jackson. Instead, she has lived to make others' dreams come true" Elsie said. "Telling me I was not afraid of looking at dead bodies. If there was a car accident or someone got hurt while she and Teresa were going the other way I would be running to see if I could help. She always said I would end up in a hospital nursing someone back to health. Me, I thought I would be touring the world dancing the night away." Elsie said looking down at legs that could at one time stretch skyward effortlessly.

"I know you're right," Chili said, running her hands over the smooth, neat rows of braids on La-Joyce's head. "I was standing on the corner, having just finished doing my girlfriend's hair, a cigarette hanging from my lips, laughing and talking about her man and her problems, when Mrs. Johnnie Bea drove up. I was finishing up and had tucked the ten dollars my friend offered me inside my bra, thinking about the diapers my boys needed.

"You know she comes up to you, talking about 'My Oprah you can sho' do some hair child come do mine I got business to take care of. I grinned 'cause you know I love Mrs. Johnnie Bea she is so good to everybody. She said her hair was showing out and she needed a hook-up so she could get her grove on. I jumped in her car thinking another ten dollars would get the diapers plus some milk. We came over here to her house." Looking around Chili said, "It sure doesn't look the same does it, girlfriend." Everyone laughed.

"She's going to be surprised girls this place looks like a showcase compared to how it was before we delivered it from death's door. Anyway, as I was saying or about to say we went over to her house, and of course, we ate navy beans while I did her hair. Four hours later when I finished, she handed me fifty dollars. I told her 'No Mrs. Johnnie Bea I can't take that much money from you, you good people. It would be like taking money from my mother or something."

'My Oprah chile,' you ain't got no business sense,' she told me.

'God gave you a talent. He aimed for you to get paid for the service you do. I've seen some of the heads you do. Those sisters are ready for the world when you finish with them. All you need to do is get your license and you will have it going on' she said to me.

"Now Mrs. Johnnie Bea you know I can't afford no beauty culture school with two babies to feed. I'm a stay-at-home mom. My sideline braiding hair supplements what Tank brings home," I said to her.

'My Oprah Chili, all you need is a daycare to keep those babies while you're in school,' she told me.

"Mrs. Johnnie Bea, let's get real. Who do you think is going to pay for beauty and cultured school? Do you know how much daycare costs these days? Tank and I don't have that kind of money."

'Come go with me tomorrow morning we will go see what we can do.'

"Mrs. Johnnie Bea, I can't... I said, thinking I could never do what she asked me."

'I don't know, ole' can't. All I know is my friend, I'm going to give it a try anyhow.' Mrs. Johnnie Bea said to me.

"Mrs. Johnnie Bea, I tried to tell her. Then she stood up, girls. You all know I'm tall. Mrs. Johnnie Bea was looking up at me with all those thick, long grey braids circling her head while she shook her finger in my face. I felt intimidated to tell you the truth." Laughter filled the room.

'You know I don't take anybody with me kicking and screaming if they don't want to go. I thought you said Tank was laid off. It is Tank and your children that will profit from my help,' she told me.' Chili said.

"Of course, the next morning, I was at her house bright and early. She took me to Sony's hair salon."

"Isn't that the shop you took over there a year ago?" Teresa asked.

"Yes, Teresa. Mrs. Johnnie Bea took me over there and asked the girl doing braids what she would charge for a braid job like she had. I nearly peed on myself when she said it would have cost Mrs. Johnnie Bea two hundred and fifty dollars. When we walked out of there Mrs. Johnnie Bea had that smug look on her face. We got back in the car and she took me downtown to Lerner's beauty school. When we got in there, she asked the owner if I could enroll in her school. Now mind you I'm thinking to myself, I don't need no school to do hair. Hair is like therapy for me. I do hair because it keeps me sane. You feel me." They all laughed in agreement.

"Anyway, the woman asked Mrs. Johnnie Bea what kind of income I had. Mrs. Johnnie Bea told her I did not have any income and wouldn't have any until I completed beauty school. I'm standing there listening to their conversation, thinking Mrs. Johnnie Bea has lost her mind. I looked at that sister with those big diamonds covering her fingers. That black woman had class and money to go with it. That dress she had on must have come from that tight shop on the hill where Shenee' here shops."

"She's talking about Fine Wear. Yes, I shop there. So what? Where I shop makes me no more or less than the rest of you. Anyway, Chili could shop there too if she wasn't so cheap." Everyone looked at Chile and laughed shaking their heads in agreement then turned back to listen to what she was telling them.

"I thought to myself at the time, this woman is not going to let me in her school."

"I like to help sisters," she said, her Shore Line weave hanging down her back as she gave me an up-and-down look.

"Like you was nobody special she wanted to know, huh? You know how sisters look at each other right Chili" Susie said pop, po her gum sounded.

"You know it, girl, and as I said, she kept giving me a look down, saying to Mrs. Johnnie Bea,

'I like to help sisters but my business is making money not providing the city welfare. Maybe you can get some financial aid or see about grants. There are grants out there. They won't be happening until next year of course. Bring her back then to see me' she said still giving me the look down.

"Now you know I had a few choice words to say to her but it was Ms. Johnnie Bea's heat. She was taking it so I didn't lose my cool in front of her."

"My Oprah Lerner, next year this chile' will be making more money than you. Come on Chili we will be back to get you enrolled." 'She'll be making more money than me, when and how?' Mrs. Lerner said looking me up and down still being sarcastic.

'If she can handle my school she just might. I will see you when you bring Ms. Chili back Mrs. Johnnie Bea and make sure you bring some of that Oprah money with you. Oh, in a cashier's check of course. I do take that kind of money. Nothing personal but wasn't it you who taught me I need to be about business.' Mrs. Johnnie Bea smiled but did not say another word. I followed her out of the door shaking my head and thinking this was not about to happen, not in this world.

When we got outside, I turned to Mrs. Johnnie Bea and told her, "Look, Mrs. Johnnie Bea, I got a criminal record. Even if I finished school, I couldn't get a job working for anybody. Once they scoped that, they would fire me anyway," I told her.

'My Oprah chile' everybody got something to keep them from taking care of business, especially if they don't want to take care of business in the first place. If no one will hire you, go into business for yourself. Nobody I know of hasn't got some hole they had to deliver themselves from if it's nothing but gossiping too much about other people trying to make it.' She drove us downtown to Dover and Cleveland, that big exclusive area where all the business people hang out."

"Are you talking about those big High-rise buildings they just put up on Twentieth and Lander?" Elsie asked. Mrs. Johnnie Bea has some good white women friends down there, right, Teresa?"

"Shenee' isn't that where your firm is located," Teresa asked responding to Elsie's comment.

"Yes, Shenee' answered."

"That's precisely what I'm talking about. We entered this office that I thought looked as large as my apartment. They had furniture in there, which must have come from somewhere in England. This skinny, blonde white girl asked us to be seated. It wasn't a minute before she came back, ushering us into a room larger than the one we came out of. Elizabeth was there with three white women who looked to be in their fifties and sixties in this big colossal office playing Bridge."

"How did you know it was Bridge?" Shenee' said.'

"What white women with the kind of money they had play anything but bridge? They surely weren't playing bid whist," Elsie said.

"I know that's right I can't see no white women playing bid whist not holding up on Dover and Cleveland," Susie said.

"Shenee' why are you giving us the evil eye you ain't white. You just look white girlfriend," Chili said smiling back at her.

"Oh my God, do I have to go through this again?"

"She's right girls. Don't hate on her, Susie said. "When her father's sperm raced up and caught her mother's egg God said let Shenee' be. Let's get real she is a sister like the rest of us."

"Thank you, Susie, go on, Chili, we're listening, Shenee' said.

"What surprised me more than anything was how they treated Ms. Johnnie Bea said Chili."

"What do you mean, how they treated Mrs. Johnnie Bea," Susie asked, sitting next to La-Joyce, smiling as she laid her head on La-Joyce's stomach as though feeling for the baby's heartbeat."

"Immediately one of them pulled her up a seat at the table where they were seated. I thought Mrs. Lerner had some filthy diamonds on her hands, Elizabeth sat at the head of the table with rocks on her fingers that made my eyes grow like watermelons when I looked at them. She must have had five carats on all four! I mean diamonds, five carats a piece."

"We've seen them, Chili," Susie said, peeping out the window at Elizabeth.

She asked Mrs. Johnnie Bea what she had planned for their next project. They had the little white girl from the front office bring in another cushioned chair so I wouldn't look so stupid standing behind them, I guess. They continued playing Bridge while they talked.

"Mrs. Johnnie Bea told them we were there because she needed a sponsor to send me to beauty culture school and she knew they had the resources. Now I sat there too stunned to speak. There is no way in hell I would be up in no white women's faces asking for nothing. I hated white people. Girlfriends I'm a southern-born black woman who came up as a little girl when white people still killed blacks at the drop of a hat in my little town. My parents taught me how to survive in that environment and I carried it beyond there."

"Aren't you a mite young Chili seems to me all that was over by the time you were born?"

"You Negroes don't know nothing about the South right now. I witnessed people's houses being burned to the ground. Ain't nothing changed but the rent girlfriends."

"Chili you are something else," La-Joyce said shaking her head.

When Mrs. Johnnie Bea told us about her father, I thought to myself. Now, ain't this something? White people lynched my grandfather. I did not want anything from a white person ever. Of course, Mrs. Johnnie Bea did not know this. My mouth flew up as I watched all four of those white women reach for their purses."

'We are pro-lifers, Johnnie Bea.' They said to Mrs. Johnnie Bea not looking my way at all. 'We help children. It is what you said we needed to do if we were advocating for the right of a child to be born. Correct Johnnie Bea?'

"Now first of all you know we all call Mrs. Johnnie Bea Mrs. Johnnie Bea, not Johnnie Bea like she is some black servant. I was about to go off big time. Mrs. Johnnie Bea didn't change a beat. She told them I had two small children they wouldn't have to send to prison if they helped me become a beautician so that I earn the money to provide for them."

"What did they say," La-Joyce asked feeling her enlarged stomach after Susie moved her head.

"They all opened their purses at once. Elizabeth who I didn't know at the time was seated at the head of the table said Johnnie Bea you don't have to give us an explanation as to why you need the money. She pulled out a long desk drawer and took out this huge checkbook, wrote out a check, and gave it to Mrs. Johnnie Bea. The other three insisted on contributing to my cause. We walked out of there with over fifty thousand dollars. I wanted to pee so badly, but I couldn't embarrass Mrs. Johnnie Bea so I held it in, my stomach about to burst. When we got outside, I ran over to this fancy restaurant and asked to use their lady's room. When I came out, I still couldn't get over her asking."

"I never knew Elizabeth ever called Mrs. Johnnie Bea any different than what we call her," Susie said.

"I told her Mrs. Johnnie Bea was her complete name while we were serving free lunches to the homeless," Elsie said. "I knew she just didn't know and it was best that I inform her so no one else would negatively tell her something she was unaware of. Elsie smiled saying "Go on Chili I was simply clarifying.

"The woman didn't ask how much she needed?" Susie asked straightening out her detention officer's uniform.

"No, they didn't, and girls, those checks more than covered my expenses, plus they provided daycare for the next nine months. Some of it would even help me open my shop when I finished school. At the time I was in the frame of mind that if it came from white hands, I did not want it."

"I don't see why not," Teresa said shaking her head.

"Neither do I, as many hundred years as our ancestors worked free," Susie said, sticking a piece of gum in her mouth.

"Makes no sense to me," Elsie said" adding to their comments as she ran her hand over the nice smooth range countertop oven that required no stick to keep it closed.

"When I got back inside the car, I turned to Mrs. Johnnie Bea and said to her. I can't accept money from those white women; I can't accept money from no white person. I hate white people. You people up here always talking about Martin Luther King Jr. I have uncles and cousins who are dead and will never be found fighting against Jim Crow, which still exists in some parts of the South to this day. Mrs. Johnnie Bea looked at me and said,'

'And so have I, chile. My father was lynched for no reason other than he went to sign up to vote. Now what? My Oprah Chile' you still kicking and screaming. If you want to continue accepting ten dollars for doing hair instead of two hundred and fifty, I'm on that too. Me, I'm about building villages. I'll find someone else needing help. And let you fight your hate by yourself." She reached over and opened the door for me. It didn't take me but a second to get some sense. I closed the car door telling her that I would be paying that money back as soon as I got on my feet. She said that was precisely what she expected me to say. That way we will be able to help someone else just the way my Oprah does.'

"I guess she knew what I was thinking because she came right out and pointed me out when she said.

'I know you think I must be working as a maid or a housekeeper for one of those white women. Do you think I come begging? She asked. I tried to interrupt her and say it was okay but she stopped me.

'My Oprah child, let me finish. I met those women at a conference when black women and white women came together to find out what we had in common and if we could work together to make a difference. They knew their men had made a mess and we knew ours were not doing anything to clean it up. It would be up to us as women to do that if we could get passed our differences. And since the mule and the forty acres weren't coming, we had to devise another plan. We explained to them we wanted to improve the quality of life for our kids and their families. They wanted to improve the lines of communication between women, in general, to get past that bad blood we had between us. They said they were willing to try it.'

'Elizabeth stood up,' Mrs. Johnnie Bea told me and spoke.

'I know I come from privilege, but I'm going to ask you sisters the same question the young white girl asked Malcolm X back in the 60s. What can I do to help? If the answer is nothing, I will return to my Bridge parties and my mansion on the hill and allow you people to handle your problems.' Mrs. Johnnie Bea was laughing by then as she told me that she looked at Elizabeth and said perhaps you have not learned but even the privilege, meaning those with money are not exempt from the pains and suffering of this world.

"I would hate it to be said you had to call me in the middle of the night trying to locate your child because he or she has run out trying to find him or herself in the streets. Heaven, forbid I receive a call asking for help because you cannot understand why your daughter prefers the wooly head of a black boy instead of that darling white pumpkin you wanted her to love.

This is about all of us ladies. We must save our children, our communities, our cities, and even our state.' She said she told them. She said after she spoke another white woman that had reached in her purse in the office was in the group of about forty white and black women stood up and said she was about Senator Hilary Clinton's message creating a village. It takes a village to raise a child, not one person struggling. Mrs. Johnnie Bea said she looked at those women and said to her 'Thank you I quite agree with you.'

"That was when Ms. Johnnie Bea said she asked how many women attended church regularly. She said all forty raised their hands. 'Why?' She said she asked them. Of course, their answers were basically that they believed in God and they attended church to serve him. She said then she told them to go home take off all their fine jewelry and expensive clothes, and on the next Sunday meet her down on the twelfth and Blanchard with some plain clothing so they could help her service God by feeding some poor needy families if they truly believed in service the way Christ believed in service. She said she didn't think one would show up but to her shock, five of the twenty white women showed up and two black women from the group came. She gave them some gloves and big white aprons. They worked all day feeding women, men, and children. When they finished, she told them she would meet them back at the conference hall where they first met in two days."

"Did they show up?" Shenee' asked.

"Shenee' let her tell it. Trust me she can do a better job if you don't interrupt" La-Joyce said.

"It's the lawyer in her." Susie said as she smiled at Shenee' who frowned but ceased in her questioning.

"Ms. Johnnie Bea said not only did they come but asked when they could come again. One of the women said she had not slept so soundly in years. They were all elated at the service they had rendered, the people they would never otherwise have met, and the friendship that developed between them. She said that is how they became friends and ever since then they have been building villages tearing down stereotypes, and taking charge of their own lives since they had started taking care of business Oprah-style by helping others to live better."

"Ms. Johnnie Bea said it has been fun working with those women she now considers friends and girlfriends she made sure to emphasize the white women as friends as well as some of the black sisters she met at that conference. She said they just have a ball out there making it possible for kids to go to school safely and wear decent clothes and wouldn't you know it, she said it was that very privileged woman Elizabeth who called her in the middle of the night. Her son left home calling back to tell her he was leaving to find a name in hip-hop. Mrs. Johnnie Bea said she got her nephew Mylo to get the word out. Lo and behold, it turned out to be the white kid Dwayne had brought home with him, telling her he had nowhere to stay. Mrs. Johnnie Bea said they had the music going so loud some evenings she had to shut her door to keep from going deaf."

"My dear brother-in-law," La-Joyce said smiling.

"Yeah, La-Joyce, you are in the family. Elsie said.

"He was only fifteen. Mrs. Johnnie Bea said running like you were running La-Joyce trying to find himself. His privileged parents did not understand his need to be with people he felt were like him. And of course, these people were black youths out to make a name for themselves too. Your brother-in-law was one such youth. That son was their only son and all the money in the world wasn't important enough to lose him. Mrs. Johnnie Bea said she helped them come to terms with what present-day racism looked like and how to support their son in something she felt would be temporary at best which was what happened she said."

"My Oprah, don't tell me what God can't do!" Susie said smiling as the others laughed realizing she was mimicking Ms. Johnnie Bea's words for her Oprah.

"You are right Susie," Chili said because, with the money those white women gave Ms. Johnnie Bea, I was able to finish school and send my children to daycare, and when Mrs. Lerner decided she liked my abilities well enough to send me to Atlanta Georgia to compete in a hair braiding contest I had money enough from Mrs. Johnnie Bea's friends to get my cousin to come and take care of the kids while Tank worked. I won of course."

"I never doubted I would," Chili said as her fingers pressed the rolls of braids adoring Susie's head.

"Hmmm, listen at that arrogance," Elsie said, moving so Chili could take a seat on the couch beside her.

"No, Mrs. Johnnie Bea says it's the Oprah in me coming out. You first have to believe in yourself. After that, it's all about taking care of business. I have two shops. Tank, the boys, and I have traveled to two countries. I now train sisters of all races to do hair. I'm able to do that because someone believed in me and taught me to believe in myself. I no longer say when things are going well that something bad is going to happen or this can't last long. I now say, 'If Oprah can take care of her business I sure as hell can take care of mine.' Oh, excuse me, Mrs. Johnnie Bea. I know you don't allow cursing in your house even when you are not here." Chili said speaking as if Mrs. Johnnie Bea was there listening.

"Chili you said you have a criminal record. What was that all about?" Shenee' asked."

"Now here goes lawyer Shenee' grudging up a client," Susie said giving her gum a few fast pops.

"Well, I simply asked because being an attorney, I might be able to get your charges purged if it happened when you were a teenager.

"She is right there," Susie said. "Some kids come through detention, mostly white kids that have later had their files purged."

"That is right you do work with girls now don't you Susie," Chili said

"My Oprah, yes!" answered Susie. I never thought I would but I am working with them and it is an experience I will always be thankful for." "I was seventeen when I got in trouble with the law. I was pregnant with my first child. Tank and I had just got married. He was also seventeen at the time. We had just moved up here from Louisiana. Now back in the day, I was what you call a country I mean a real country.

We had just moved into the Central area. I never will forget it. Tank had just gotten a job. We had spent all our money moving up here. Tank hadn't gotten a paycheck so we were seriously broke.

One day I was standing on my doorstep talking to one of my so-called friends about how I wish I had some Chinese food but I had to wait until Tank got paid before that could happen. Hot Pepper, my downstairs neighbor was seated on the steps listening to our conversation. She offered to give me money for the Chinese food if I would deliver a package down the street for her. She said she was busy and had been waiting for her boyfriend to come home so he could deliver it for her but he was taking too long.

"Why couldn't she take it herself?" Shenee' asked.

"She said she was waiting on an important call and couldn't take the time to go. May, the girl I was talking to at the time smiled and said Hot Pepper pays good girl you should go to work for her making deliveries. Stupid, I didn't have sense enough to ask questions as to what I would be delivering and instead said I didn't have anything better to do sure I would walk the package down the street. When I returned, she gave me a hundred-dollar bill and told me I could make more if I was willing to work," The women looked at each other in shock then back at Chili.

"Now don't look at me like that I know a fool is born every day."

"You're, right honey but let me tell you," Susie said. "I have been in this business far too long. A mule is born every day. They come into the facility all the time. Women like May and Hot Pepper are on the prowl for young naive youngsters who are in need. That is how a mule is born."

"What's a mule," La-Joyce asked.

"Girl a mule is a young teenager used by adults to sell, deliver, or buy drugs. They know teenagers will not get as much time or even if they do the mule is someone they don't care about and can find another one if they lose that mule. Both women worked you. May probably knew you were new in town and gave Hot Pepper heads up that they could mule you."

"From the South too! No offense meant Chili but they knew they had a sucker." Elsie said jumping up stating she needed to go check on her pot of beans.

"You got it. A big sucker at that. I was so happy to get the money and not have to do nothing but knock on a door delivering a package that I didn't think."

"Did you share this with Tank?" Shenee' asked.

"Not until much later. There was a food bank close to where we lived so when we had food. He thought that was where it came from. He didn't find out until I was arrested. That's really where I first met Susie."

"Susie you never mentioned a word. Elsie said as the others echoed her words."

"You right I didn't. I was not supposed to tell her business. If I see a kid from detention on the street, I don't acknowledge them unless they acknowledge me first. It is a part of confidentiality." La-Joyce since you are about to deliver, we will allow you to stretch your feet out on Mrs. Johnnie Bea's new velvet sofa." Elsie said as La-Joyce lowered her feet to the floor when she saw Elsie looking her way."

"Attorney girlfriend Shenee knows that," Susie said, helping La-Joyce put her feet up on the sofa.

"She's right. Shenee' said. It is a part of confidentiality.'"

"This child was as bad as Bunkie when she came into detention. They were both scared to death." Susie, said laughing at my co-workers where she was housed, said she cried daily."

Chili laughed, too, as she listened to herself being talked about. "She had a good Probation Officer. Some of them are not worth salt on a wound but hers was one of the best they have down there. She talked to the judge on her behalf. You must remember you were to deliver in about how long Chili?"

"Four months," Chili said shaking her head.

"She could have gotten at least two years but, after her probation officer talked to the judge and then to the prosecuting attorney who was a decent woman whose aim was not to make a name for herself sending kids up if she didn't have to. She would listen and if it was possible to meet the child's needs. She did. You won't find many prosecutors that think like Tracy. And for a white woman dealing with a black child, she is alright for a white woman."

"I know, I know," Susie said as both La-Joyce and Shenee' gave her the evil eye. "Like Mrs. Johnnie Bea says it's something that has grown up in you. You have to constantly work to replace it with positive thoughts. Making racist remarks comes from much more than people think. But I have encountered some bad experiences dealing with white women who lied and used me the same way May and Hot Pepper used Chili, any way Tracy is not like that. She had integrity, principles, and a sense of justice she would not compromise. If the child kept coming when she socked it to them everyone knew that was what was needed. Let me taste those beans, Elsie. Put some in a bowl for me. Susie asked her removing her gum as she placed it in a napkin.

"Susie's right about that prosecutor. She didn't come at me like I was black trash she could discount. I only got two months. I don't know how much time May and Hot Pepper got or if they got any. Ms. Tool, my probation officer helped make sure I was out before my baby was born." Chili said looking at La-Joyce and her swollen stomach. I got counseling and help to understand what had happened to me. They even made me go to drug and alcohol treatment for a month so that I had a clear understanding of drugs, their effect on the body, and why I was in such serious trouble. Tank stood by me."

"Believe me Susie you don't have to come from another country to get caught up by someone thinking you are a sucker who doesn't know what's going on in the neighborhood."

"Or be like my daughter Bunkie and not think of the consequences before you act," Rosie said.

"Rosie, Bunkie is only thirteen she acted on impulse but she is learning how to work through problems without violence. Don't be so hard on your child Rosie. Her mother, I hope is teaching her better." Susie said looking hard at her.

"What happened with May and Hot Pepper?" Elsie asked coming in from seeing about her bean still cooking in the kitchen.

"In and out of jail, I guess. At least the last I heard they were in." Chili said reaching for the bowl of beans Elsie offered her.

"Susie, you have worked with children for how long?" Teresa asked.

"Over fifteen years," Susie answered after finishing her mouth filled with beans. "There is a story behind every day but I meet each challenge head-on. You have to remember I came up with five brothers and six sisters so even though I never lived in the South I do know what poverty looks like and how society can treat you when you are a poor child living in an urban city."

"Surely you haven't been in jail Susie?" Chili asked.

"Now Chili you know I know how to meet sarcasm with sarcasm but I know you are harmless and just want to know my business since you have told yours."

"To tell you the truth Susie your life is a little interesting in that Mrs. Johnnie Bea was telling us about you long before we met you. You are somewhat of a celebrity to us. We first met you remember at the prayer vigil you had for the kids in juvenile." Teresa said smiling at her as she took a spoon filled with beans into her mouth.

"You can start by telling us what prompted you to have a prayer vigil for those kids down there at the youth center in the first place.

Chapter Twelve

>–!–‹♦›–⊙–‹♦›–!–‹

"*I* saw Mrs. Johnnie Bea for the first time one evening when she came to volunteer with the chaplain program. I had never spoken with her. There was a radio transmission telling me to get down to Qui unit on the double. Soon after the emergency code was called and I ran down the stairs skipping steps as I went. I knew who it was and what was about to happen. I raced into the room where about ten of my co-workers stood with gloves on ready for the takedown."

"A young boy stood over in a corner with his shirt off daring anyone to come near him. My co-workers had gloved up ready to do physical force if I could not defuse him with non-violence. I had been working with this kid for two months but sometimes when a kid loses control it is hard to get them calmed down enough to focus on what you are saying to them. I walked over, put my arms around him, and told him to come with me. I did not want him to get hurt or for him to hurt someone."

'Oh, shit,' he said, 'I was hoping they would not send for you.' I smiled at him. He allowed me to move him into his room without having physical force used on him. My heart was pumping because it could have turned out much differently. We talked about his problem and worked it out."

"Sandy, the supervisor who had called me down, was standing nearby with Mrs. Johnnie Bea who somehow had not gotten asked to leave during the code. She must have overheard Sandy tell me 'Girl what took you so long you know you are the only one that kid will listen to. Another minute and I would have had to give the orders to have him physically restrained.' If staff had, had to use physical force on him, he could have been hurt or one of the staff could have been hurt because

178

he was a fighter. We never use mace or weapons to stop violence only physical force or the ability to convince without force. It is always best to defuse without force." She walked over and stood gazing at Mrs. Johnnie Bea's picture.

"I didn't know her until a bet was made that a kid, we had on lockdown was going to run her out of his unit."

"You mean he was out in the area where the chaplains are?" La-Joyce asked rising from where she was lying on the sofa.

"Of course not. Someone said she had asked to see him. Instead of the staff telling her he was on lockdown, he told her to go down and see if she could get him to stop screaming. Someone said 'I think we've got another Jesus freak in the building. Want to bet she'll get run out of that hall.'"

"Susie, I never knew you gambled. Of course, Elise and I go to the casino and play the slots once in a while ourselves," Teresa said.

"No, I am no gambler, but it was a joke they were playing on Mrs. Johnnie Bea because they felt the chaplains were simply do-gooders who babied the little criminals and sometimes got in the way of them doing their jobs."

"How do you feel about the kids?" Chili asked waving a stick of gum at Susie.

"That is the problem. I sympathize with the kids much more than my co-workers feel is good for them or me. I am not the only staff that is sympathetic with a kid's situation but I am what they call extreme in that I will fight for better treatment overall."

"I read in the paper where the juvenile jail was going to be placed under different management?" Teresa asked a stern look replacing the smile.

"Wait a minute we have too many questions and not enough answers for me," La-Joyce complained lowering her feet to the carpeted floor.

"What do you mean?" Susie asked turning her attention away from Teresa to hear at La-Joyce.

"You said there was a bet concerning Mrs. Johnnie Bea. What was it and how did it turn out?"

"Yes, I would like to know too" Rosie commented.

"So would I." Shenee' said.

"Oh, someone said 'I bet you fifty dollars she comes running out of that unit,' meaning Mrs. Johnnie Bea of course. Someone else said 'We have to have someone bet for her and since she is a Jesus freak like you Susie maybe you will be willing to put up for her.' Someone else said she was short like me so that was reason enough to lose fifty dollars.

"Jesus Freak! What in the heck is a Jesus Freak?"

"She loves the Lord and his son Jesus Christ La-Joyce. Finish telling us Susie at this rate we will never hear the rest.' Teresa said.

"I won five hundred dollars. First, bet I have ever made."

"Well?!" Chili said looking hard at Susie.

"Well, what!" Susie replied staring across the room at Chili.

"Susie, what did Mrs. Johnnie Bea do that caused you to win the money?" Elsie asked standing in the arched entrance of the dining room with the wooden spoon in her hand.

Susie laughed sticking her tongue out at Chili.

"Well?!" Chili said as they all gazed at Susie.

"She defused the kid so well we were able to call the nurse down to give him his medics. He didn't say another curse word even after she was gone. I think the staff was glad to give up that money just to have peace in the building. I could not have done that with that kid. You know I asked her how she got him quieted down? Mrs. Johnnie Bea never gave up her secret. Telling me she learned it from me. I had to laugh at that. You know they had the nerve not to want to pay me. I told them they had better cough up my money or trouble was coming."

"Did you get it?" Rosie asked laughing herself.

"Both my kids got nice winter coats that year."

"Girl, do you know how many of those kids come through 'The Safe Place'? He was probably one of them," Elsie said turning to go back into the kitchen.

"Now for my question Susie. Isn't it true your department is now under the leadership of the Adult Department? Lord if I don't need another blood pressure pill." Teresa said feeling her head as laughter filled the room.

"Yes Teresa, like I explained to Mrs. Johnnie Bea, before going to that system our goal had always been to get the kids to understand how their behavior contributed to the trouble they were in. Mrs. Johnnie Bea and I agreed that a lot of kids just did not know how to handle anger and frustration without becoming violent. We worked to help them understand how to get what they wanted without having to resort to violence. It's called counseling in problem-solving. When a kid starts acting out problem-solving techniques usually work. We'd ask the child what he or she wants and how best to get it. Sometimes supervisors would spend up to a half hour talking to a kid or getting into his head and find out what has caused his loss of control. The kid, the staff, and the supervisor would work out a plan to help the kid learn how to utilize ways to better work towards getting their needs met."

"What happens now?"

"Teresa, once the Adult system took over, problem-solving was replaced with immediate consequences. New staff coming in were no longer trained to solve problem techniques like we were. We became more physical after the adult system took over. Many more staff are getting hurt than ever before. I doubt if most know what non-violent defusing means now. Dorm confinements and long periods of isolated confinement became the norm."

"Someone should have insisted that not happen," Elsie said.

"Now who was going to do that after the commissioner had given orders that it should be that way?" Teresa asked. Elsie shook her head but did not answer.

"There was a time when our kids were given three free calls a week. A special free phone was placed outside our work area for that purpose. It was understood that a large percentage of the kids that came in were from poor families and could not afford the expense of collect calls to their parents.

Soon after we went into the new building, it was decided that parents should pay for the calls the children were making to them. The money would be used to bring in programs and help with the needs of the kids through the recreation department.

At first lots of programs were brought in soon those programs were cut from the recreation department. We kept wondering if they were going to go back to allowing the kids to have free calls once the programs were eliminated but that never happened."

"And of course, they kept taking the money for the phone calls billed to the parents, right?" Shenee asked.

"We never knew where the money went," Susie said pausing as if thinking." We just knew it was gone.

"Elizabeth what did you and Mrs. Johnnie Bea have issues with as outside observers?" Elsie asked.

"When we talked to the kids some of them complained that they were being farmed out to halls where kids had staff only to have to return to halls without staff, knowing the kids who were in halls with staff were getting the best treatment. We wanted to see that change." Elizabeth said as she rocked back and forth in Mrs. Johnnie Bea's new rocker.

"What's up with that Susie?" Teresa asked staring her way.

"For the kids in halls without staff, it was like visiting a friend with parents then having to go home where there was no direct adult supervision to attend to your needs. Worse was that those kids knew some kids did have the staff to fulfill their needs, just not them."

"Such as?" Elsie asked.

"Yeah" added the others "such as?"

"A kid with a supervising staff on duty all the time may forget to take a shower before going into his dorm. He can call out to the staff informing him or her of the needed shower and possibly get it."

"I get it," Elsie said. The kid going back to the hall without a staff member has no one to call out to, like the kid in the hall with a staff member in place."

"That's right because the post staff can't allow the youth to come out and shower or find articles he or she might need because their job is to monitor many different units not just one in case they are needed for backup. Sometimes the kids push the call button because they want to go to a hall where there is a staff that will program them, other times the staff would be dealing with issues that force them to leave the kids they are to program in those halls waiting to be picked up. The kids that are in the halls with staff, even if they are gone knowing that eventually they will return. It's all about the numbers."

"Now that makes no sense to me," La-Joyce said.

"It made no sense to us," Elizabeth said still rocking back and forth. That's something I do not understand. All of the kids should be getting the same treatment unless they act in a way that causes them to forfeit equal treatment," Shenee' said, her hand on her cheek as though her attorney's mind was at work.

"Mrs. Johnnie Bea came to the casino and told Elsie and me she needed our help."

"We got right up and asked her what she needed us to do. We knew it would be interesting, to say the least." Teresa said smiling as she told them about their part in the prayer vigil."

"That's right those slots will always be around. We left our car and drove with Mrs. Johnnie Bea to where the march was to take place after she told us it looked like there might be a poor turnout." Elsie said smiling too.

"We could see the distressed look on Susie's face. It showed disappointment in the turnout because Mrs. Johnnie Bea told us lots of churches had been invited. Not one minister came with his congregation. Even the NAACP Mrs. Johnnie Bea told us had been invited. I think one or two people belonging to that organization came but there were no identifiable posters or signs that indicated they were a part of this important event."

"We were marching and praying for kids that were in trouble and at the greatest risk. They had already fallen through the cracks and we needed to bring attention to that fact," Elsie said.

"I wish Mrs. Johnnie Bea had informed me. I would have liked to have joined that march," Chili said, "because I understand what it means to have someone caring enough to walk and pray for you. That is truly caring about the kids."

"We would have marched had we known, right La-Joyce," Shenee' said.

"My baby and I would have been right there marching," La-Joyce said rubbing her stomach.

"When I saw Mrs. Johnnie Bea walk over and whisper in Susie's ear then hug her. I wanted to do the same because the look on her face when she looked around at the crowd, which was less than thirty people told me she was hurt because she expected more people to care especially people who say they care," Teresa said, taking Susie's hands and kissing them and her on the cheek as they continued to discuss the prayer vigil.

"Girl this was about kids nobody misses or cares about. Criminals don't deserve love unless they get it at home from people who believe they are worth loving." Susie said taking the lemonade offered to her.

"I know what you mean Chili," Teresa said. "I worked with children for years, if their parents didn't have the money to invest in their education, they were left behind those with parents who were financially able to support their education."

Placing her lemonade on the table in front of her, Teresa said, placing her hands on her hips while standing by the screen door,

"Every year kids bring home a list of items not covered by the school district. These items can reach hundreds of dollars depending on what school it is and what they are expecting the parents to come up with. Heaven forbid if your child is from a poor family that cannot afford even twenty dollars taken from their income."

"It is like Mrs. Johnnie Bea explained to me. 'If the Negro College fund, had been the Negro Preschool fund guiding young lives through high school there would be a growing need for college scholarships because more black children would have been prepped early enough to receive the scholarships needed to attend college.' Rose said smiling at the children waving at her.

"The way it is now, poor black children like I was, have to prove they are smart enough without early help. It's like teaching Spanish to a twelfth grader versus a first grader."

"You are so right Chili but a lot of the kids even poor white children coming through our system have so many other issues that needed attending to. If there had been funds to meet those needs early my job would have been a lot easier and more Black American children would have been going to college instead of jail." Susie reached her hands out to catch the block of gum Elsie threw at her.

"You are right Teresa," Elsie said "not to mention the fact that many of the parents of poor children are uneducated themselves and lack the skills or knowledge to help their children with their studies. That is another reason our kids think it is fun to kill each other. They have no one to guide their lives early enough to help them understand how they are hurting themselves."

"You got that right because if we had thought about it while we were marching for our kids to go to white schools, we would have marched to make sure they got what school was supposed to offer them in learning. If that had happened Susie would not have had to be out in the rain and cold having a prayer vigil because our kids would not have been there in the first place. Were you stressing Susie because you wanted the same interest in kids at risk?" Elsie asked.

"Mrs. Johnnie Bea must have seen the big crocodile tears in my eyes because she pushed a tissue in my hand and whispered, 'Where two come together in my name I will abide.' Go forward she said and pray daughter. My fellow vigil prayer warriors who had met with me for months smiled and nodded.

"Girls, after Susie prayed," Teresa said, "we started our march to the adult jail with signs that read 'If you don't help us now, what will become of us later.' The two tall gentlemen carried a sign that read. Don't forget the power of prayer

Shaharra worked hard creating those posters Mrs. Johnnie Bea told us."

"Your daughter made the posters?"

"Yes, she loves doing the artwork but she and her brother complained about what they thought was a long walk that people weren't interested in."

"I was pleased to see several members from the Radical Women's group come and walk in the prayer vigil with us. People walking on the street saw our signs and walked along with us. It turned out beautiful." Teresa said as she walked over and peeped out the window as though looking for someone.

"Teresa and I had made our sign which read 'pray for our children not for more prisons.' holding our signs we marched to the adult detention jail." "The missionary sister in Susie's group prayed as we stood with our raised signs. It was one of the most beautiful sights you ever want to see. We marched back to where we started. Susie thanked everyone and we all went home."

"Later that evening, my doorbell rang." Susie said, "My son Eugene Jr. and my daughter Shaharra ran to the door to see who it was. I think it was Eugene Jr. I heard him say hi Mrs. Johnnie Bea, what do you have in that pot?" There is no shame in that boy. He hadn't met her once but acted as if he had known her for years. Now, girls, you know what she had in that pot, don't you?"

They all laughed, yelling as loud as their voice would carry:

"Beans!"

"That's right a big pot of beans. I hadn't cooked for the kids and they had walked too. Where Mrs. Johnnie Bea conjured up those beans God only knows?"

'Child, are you the one who drew those signs for your mother?' Mrs. Johnnie Bea asked Shaharra as she walked into the house.

"Yes, Ma'am," Shaharra answered her reaching for those beans.

'You should pursue a career in some form of art because your signs depicting the problems youth face today that many of the marchers carried showed great talent.' Shaharra placed the pot in her brother's hands walked over placed a kiss on Mrs. Johnnie Bea's cheek thanking her then followed her brother into the kitchen."

"It was Shaharra who designed the pictures on the walls at The Safe Place," Elsie said smiling over at Susie.

"Now," Susie said. "Shaharra is stuck with choices, whether basketball or art designing will become a career for her."

"Thanks, Mrs. Johnnie Bea for walking with us." As we walked into the living room, I told her, her words had saved the day for me. When I looked around and saw how few people responded I was devastated. I thought surely, we would have all the churches involved."

'Child when God sends you on a mission, angels surround you. Even when the hill turns into a mountain you will pass safely over.' Mrs. Johnnie Bea said her eye tooth gleaming as she spoke to me.

"We sat on the sofa. I was so glad to see her."

"The people who marched with us in that prayer vigil, I know God will bless Mrs. Johnnie Bea. "I was blessed that they came to help me." Mrs. Johnnie Bea smiled and said, 'Those people out there had to love you and what you were doing to stand with you like they did. The children that took part in that prayer vigil, did you see them skipping and begging to be given signs? Their honest participation stole my heart because they were not even a part of the march originally, they saw us marching read our signs, and asked to march for their peers they knew were locked behind bars.'

"But Mrs. Johnnie Bea, the showing was so poor. I thought..."

"You thought because it was for children that would spark great interest. God didn't want a show baby."

"Mrs. Johnnie Bea I..., she didn't let me finish of course you know how she is."

'My Oprah child no one there came for show. They came to abide in God's work sat in your heart.' "I was crying in the bowl of beans Shaharra sat in front of me."

'I know the Catholic Church was represented' Mrs. Johnnie Bea said 'because the sisters were there. I remember one of the ladies who came down to work with the kids.

We talked during the march. She and the other catholic lady who had worked with you to bring the prayer vigil about told me how hard you all had worked planning this event. The man with the bullhorn that kept everyone off the curb told me you were so dedicated it moved him to want to take part.

The two tall gentlemen held that long banner as though they were saints of God, Child. When I spoke with one of them later, he told me he worked with you and knew the power of your mission. The children who walked and prayed with us came off the street like little soldiers going to war. Some of the young men were the catholic college fraternity brothers Susie. Children walking and praying for other children, praise the Lord!'

'There was a white man I saw carrying his infant son upon his shoulder with two little ones by his side. What a joyous site. The great missionary who prayed at the end had such an effect, that I thought for a minute we might have church right there on the prison grounds.'

"Mrs. Johnnie Bea, I told her finally able to laugh. That wasn't a prison it was a jail where people are brought before they go to prison if they went at all."

'Can they get out when they want to?' She asked me. 'Do they have to first ask for their basic needs to be met just like children under the supervision of parents who may or may not be given them what they want?'

"Girlfriend you were getting that tongue-lashing Mrs. Johnnie Bea loves to give," Elsie said.

The rest of the women nodded in agreement intense in their listening.

"I didn't say anything I just listened."

'I don't know what else prison is if it's not that' she told me. We were out there praying to our father to give our children back to us. We know we failed to create a village for them to learn, grow, and become all they could be. They failed because the village turned into a desert with no water so weeds grew up around them and overtook their lives. We want the Lord to remove those weeds so that prison will not become the only home they have to look forward to. The spirit of God abides in what you are doing. You just wait and believe. Let your thoughts not be troubled. You stood on God's love. Now wait and see the miracle in Jesus Christ our savior. It is coming.' She said rising to leave.

"I love you, Mrs. Johnnie Bea. That walk was too long for you but you walked it."

"I know you have heard of the poem Footprints?' "Mrs., Johnnie Bea said smiling then hugged me as she stood up to go. I felt a weight lift off my shoulders and peace entered my heart because I knew a miracle was coming."

"When Mrs. Johnnie Bea got to the door, she called Jr. and Shaharra. 'How you like my beans?' She asked them.

'We loved them,' they told her.

'Wash my pot and give it back to me because I have some more kids to feed.' I said now you know Mrs. Johnnie Bea is something else.

"Listening to her I realized this was how Jesus would want our prayer vigil to be. We talked while they washed that pot. When she left,

I thanked God for her strength. The children complained it was a long walk but Mrs. Johnnie Bea hobbled every step of the way.

"I didn't see her for a couple of weeks after that. One day she stopped me in the hallway at work and asked if I had a minute to talk with her. We stepped into one of the vacant units.

'Do you remember when I came and asked you about that smell coming out of the area in the back halls?' She asked me.

"Yes, I remember I told her."

'You wouldn't say what it was.' She said cornering me.

"Mrs. Johnnie Bea," I told her they were already on to me about speaking out about how the treatment of the kids in terms of punishment. Now since we moved under the adult system compared to when we were a juvenile department, the mindset is all about adult criminal law enforcement. They already know I will not sit still and let them continue any inhumane treatment of these kids. But I still have to be very careful.

'Susie', she said looking me straight in the face. Something is going on in here that the Lord doesn't like. And we mean to do something about it.'

"We!" I said wondering to myself how many others knew.

'One of the chaplains I come here with took me down to that back area.' "Mrs. Johnnie Bea said her eyes still dead on me." 'She said the smell reminded her of a morgue.'

"That's right Susie," Elizabeth said who had been sitting quietly listening to the women talk.

"Mrs. Johnnie Bea and I had been taken there by one of the other Chaplains. I was horrified not only by the smell but the condition of the place where kids were being kept."

"I wanted to cry because I knew the area," Susie said. "Many other staff had also complained about those conditions but those complaints had gone on deaf ears. I would have been in big trouble if someone had heard me talking to Mrs. Johnnie Bea about the conditions she spoke of."

"Mrs. Johnnie Bea and I went down and talked to one of the boys that had been housed down there," Elizabeth told them. We listened to him tell us about how terrible the smell was and how it was so bad one girl coming in for the first time demanded to be moved or she would freak out. He insisted that there was a boy also a newly admitted youth begging to be placed somewhere else because the stench was so terrible. He was refused. He wanted to know if it was right that the girl and not the boy was allowed to move because it stunk so bad he had to hide his head under a blanket to keep from gagging."

"We were stunned by what the child was telling us." There was a quiet moment as they listened to Elizabeth.

"You know Mrs. Johnnie Bea. she found a way to get us in there. We smelled it before we arrived. How could anyone keep children in inhumane conditions such as this? I thought to myself. How can the administrators allow this, is what we wanted to know." Elizabeth told them.

"I was embarrassed when Mrs. Johnnie Bea came to me about it," Susie told them "But we as staff had done all we could do. Mrs. Johnnie Bea had asked a question I knew I had no answer for."

"The administrators at the top were not people who listened to any advice. They simply gave orders whether they made sense or not. Unless it became a public issue, they did not want to hear it; especially not from me. There was too much I already let them know I knew was wrong. It was not the route to take if you had a desire to move up into management. The saying among us who had to deal with them was that the Mafia had a way of getting you if you didn't play by their rules. You had to tell on too many of their managers and they were not hearing anything bad about them. Of course, Mrs. Johnnie Bea had no way of knowing this."

"Why was the kid put down there in the first place?" La-Joyce asked taking her glasses off and wiping them with the edge of her maternity top.

"The kid told us," Elizabeth said 'It would do him no good to make waves because being there was his punishment for acting out.'

"Elizabeth please tell us what did you find when you and Mrs. Johnnie Bea went to the area?" Shenee' asked an alarming look on her face as well as the other women listening to Elizabeth and Susie. Elizabeth fanned her diamond-ringed fingers in the air as if hating the reflection of where her mind had to take her.

"Feces, blood, and urine stood all over the floor and walls." She told them. There was no staff in the unit where he was housed. The ones in the area said it stunk too bad to even open the door. The child we were told had been locked down for months because he was a flooder. His water had been turned off. He was playing in his waste that stood not only on the toilet stool but all over the floor walls, even outside his door.

Mrs. Johnnie Bea got a copy of the pictures a supervisor had taken. He said he had taken it to management so that they could see it. The nurse from the health clinic stated, we were told, it was the most horrifying condition she had ever witnessed, but still nothing had been done to change those conditions."

Susie let the tears fall down her cheeks. "When he first was taken down there," she told them "He wasn't doing that but then he was there for so long not being able to flush his toilet. He asked to have his toilet flushed at first, but his door could not be opened without the Supervisor being present nor could his water be turned on. If they got busy it just had to wait. He would be standing there begging for water.

When some of us came on duty and he said he hadn't gotten water we would call for staff to come over for backup and we would get water for him but you had to be very careful because body waste was on him and the floor. My co-worker was a twenty-year veteran. He said he was used to the smell from the war. I was gagging coming out of there.

We saw feces all over his body Mrs. Johnnie Bea and me. Even his teeth were smeared with it." Elizabeth said shaking her head. "We were on our way to the papers to leak what we had discovered."

"I told Mrs. Johnnie Bea if they gave that information to the press first of all they didn't know how it would be used. More than likely innocent staff would become scapegoats for those who were responsible. Second, I had an e-mail sent to the top official and was told to take the information to the very people who were allowing it to take place. I also warned her that if she told this soon every volunteer allowed in the building would have their cards pulled and no one would be allowed back in."

"What did Mrs. Johnnie Bea say?" Chili asked, shaking her head along with the other women.

"If that happens, we will not be able to find the next problem because we wouldn't be here. Elizabeth told us she knew some people in the criminal justice system who might be able to help."

"I don't know Mrs. Johnnie Bea," I told her. "We have good staff that would be better if they had good leadership who realized we are working with children, not adults. But if it will help, I will become a part of that committee."

"How can you keep a child from having water?" Chili asked.

"I understand the boy's water had to be turned off to keep him from flooding the place. There however should have always been a staff available to turn it on when he needed to use the toilet or needed water to drink." Shenee' said.

"You are right," replied Teresa. No waste should have been left in his toilet for him to play in."

"Mrs. Johnnie Bea, calling out to the post staff when they have other duties was not going to help," I told her. When the memo came out that we had to call the supervisors before the water could be turned on created another problem because when the supervisors were too busy doing other things to come down the waste was not flushed. The kid already had mental issues not being addressed.

I know this to be true because the staff whose hall he was in said he exhibited some weird behavior that concerned her. Already a little touched, not being able to have his toilet flushed just sent him further over the edge than he already was. Like I already told you even health officials working in our facility talked about the horrible conditions but no one was ready to do what was necessary to stop what was going on."

"Some months later I saw Mrs. Johnnie Bea coming down the corridor. I was seated in a post. I smiled and told her the miracle we wanted had taken place. Of course, she wanted to know what I was referring to."

"From the committee, we formed," I told her, "a letter was written and sent to the judges concerning the conditions and that the isolation policy needed to be changed. I got a call from one of the attorneys working with us telling me that the director of our department had handed in his resignation after our letter had been sent to the judges.

The letter had been signed by three influential leaders in the community who were a part of the committee."

"Susie." Elizabeth said, "Mrs. Johnnie Bea, all the professionals on that committee, and of course, I was proud of your courage in working with those attorneys and social service directors to bring attention to a horrible problem in your department." Elizabeth said. "That place was spotless the next time we came in."

"Susie, what happened to the youth housed there?"

"He was sent to a long-term institution Elizabeth."

A few minutes after Mrs. Johnnie Bea and I finished our conversation she came rushing back over and told me she had heard that I was no longer a Charge staff. I smiled and told her that a couple of days after the letter had been written I came to work and was called into a separate room and given notification that the position I held had been eliminated."

"What do you mean eliminated," Teresa asked a frown on her face.

"Just like that! With no prior notice that it was to happen?" Shenee asked as she spread her hands to gesture.

"Mrs. Johnnie Bea never shared that or I would have."

"I know what you would have done Elizabeth but I made Mrs. Johnnie Bea give me her word she wouldn't say anything.

I had just walked into the building, before I could clock in one of my co-workers pulled me to the side and told me that the Mafia had taken me out. I could not imagine what he was talking about. Soon after two administrators from our department pulled me into a room and asked me to read the letter lying on the table."

"What did you say?"

"After reading that my position as charge staff had been eliminated, I knew why and what had happened. I had already been warned but I could not let the mafia know. It would have hurt too many innocent staff. The two administrators probably never knew about the letter sent to the Judge. They were simply messengers. It was nothing I was surprised about. I had no reason to be angry with them. They admitted being as unaware as I was.

Not one supervisor had been advised that this was going to take place. The strangest part was that neither our union attorney nor the president had received prior notice that this was taking place."

"How did they find out you were a part of that committee Susie?" Rosie asked pointing her finger in Susie's direction.

"First," Elizabeth said to the others. "She had already complained, making her suspect number one. Second someone on the committee probably mentioned her name as the one who leaked the problem. Of course, we know they should have been called on the carpet for allowing this to happen, and the fact that Susie was on the committee that put together the letter to the Judges to make the department heads change the isolation policy meant that she had to be punished. I wish she had allowed us to go directly to the media. She would still have her position and we would have gotten the isolation policy changed anyway."

"What reasons did they give to justify this deletion?" asked Elsie. "Budget cuts."

"How many major positions like yours were also cut?" Shenee' asked. "Why, if they were going to cut positions was it not negotiated with union? That doesn't appear to be legal."

"Legal is what management says legal is. I hated that the six other charge staff had to lose their positions because of something they had nothing to do with. When I talked to the attorney for our union at the time, he didn't lie; he told me that it took a lot longer than a day to take away a position that had been a part of staffing for the juvenile department for over fifteen years, way before the adult system took over. He said it should have had to go before the council for approval. And that is after a long timely debate."

'We have got to do something about that.' Mrs. Johnnie Bea told me. I said, "Mrs. Johnnie Bea we won our miracle."

'Won our miracle how?' She asked.

"Now they can't isolate kids in units for months without relief. I knew they knew I was the one who informed the criminal justice attorneys and the public defender's supervisor about those conditions. In doing so I knew there would be consequences for me. Now, did I want my co-workers to suffer because of what I was a part of? No. Did I want to lose my pay and my position? No. But like you said about our Oprah Mrs. Johnnie Bea, when you see what you know in your heart is wrong you have to fight back no matter what the consequences are.

When God gave me that charge position many of my co-workers didn't want me to have it at the time but God saw that I got it.

God has something better for me now that they took it. I just have to wait for it, right here in this post. God has already given me another challenge and you have already helped me better understand why."

"She asked me what I meant. I told her when she used the term Willie Lynch to refer to how blacks as a race of people are oppressive to each other I couldn't see it. I couldn't until immigrant children from other countries started coming into our detention center for alleged crimes."

"She asked me again what I meant. I told her that when African immigrant children started to come into detention, they had a difficult time making adjustments. They seemed to always be in trouble especially African children who were Muslim. Many came in on simple charges but due to adjustment difficulties stayed on lockdown from the time they came in until the time they left because of the trouble they seemed to always get into. And after 911 it had become really difficult for them."

"How so?" Elsie asked.

"Sometimes in meetings, they are called dumb, and stupid and even laughed at because they exhibit unusual behavior. One time I had to step in and say I was offended by the comments and laughter of my co-workers especially Black American co-workers laughing at those children. An African staff came up to me afterward and asked why the American blacks laugh and make fun of those kids when they know they don't understand the American system, which is why they are probably in trouble in the first place."

'There is no excuse for the white staff laughing but the blacks whose history came from slavery I just cannot understand.' He told me.

"Thinking about his statement, I could just imagine how it must have been for the poor African slaves. The whites back in the day must have had a field day discussing the unusual behaviors exhibited by the slaves just off the boat as some staff were with the African children in our care."

"I wondered if it took as much as a century for them to learn and whether they were as thoughtless in their treatment to those who came

195

here as slaves long after them. What could I say to that African employee who understood better than those laughing with ancestors brought into this country in slavery, that they too were bound by the Willie Lynch doctrine?"

"Mrs. Johnnie Bea said that she knew some African families and she understood the difficult time some were having trying to keep their children under their control. She also knew they did not understand that once their children were sent to the American public school, their world changed and they faced problems their parents could not conceive of." "While America worked for the parents,' Mrs. Johnnie said she told many African parents who brought their children to 'The Safe Place' they must take note of what it will be like for their children when they are away from them and work on bridging that gap for their children as for themselves."

'It must be hard Susie working in an environment which perpetuates the Willie Lynch behavior,' she said to me. I told her it was not as hard as it was sad. That is why, I told her I intended to sit in that post until the spirit came into my heart with another path to follow."

The room remained for a time silent. After a while, Elsie stood up again placing her slender fingers under Susie's chin saying to her,

"Susie when Teresa and I drove by Jackson and Pine two months ago. There stood a woman standing out on the corner waving a large sign asking voters to vote for white County Executive James Jimmerson over the black County Executive Bill Sanders. I started to get out and ask you what were you thinking but Teresa insisted that something must have you out there."

Everyone looked at Susie.

Chili of course raised her hand "Lord I should have been out there with you." Susie shook her head as if she had been caught in the act of doing something bad.

"You women are something else. But this is what happened girls. When the commissioner ran the first time," Susie said taking the gum out of her mouth she had just placed in there.

"Many of us at work campaigned hopeful that our black candidate would be elected."

"Hold on Susie, work on my neck while you're sharing. I got a serious cramp in it from bending over all those heads all week."

"Here sit over here by the window so I can look out at Mrs. Johnnie Bea's lawn that looks like God came down from heaven and laid it out." The other women came over and joined Chili and Susie all gathering to look out of the window as they listened.

"The last time I saw that lawn it was a serious mess, no one could have guessed the before and after was the same yard," Susie said placing her hands around Chili's neck as she sat in the armchair close to the window.

"Don't forget where you left off Susie," Elsie said reminding Susie she hoped to get an explanation Susie had not finished explaining.

"Elsie many of us loved him. We thought he would always be there for us. We called on him when trouble brewed at the center believing God had sent him to us."

"Little did you know, huh?" Chili said.

"Chili now we know why you have that cramp in your neck."

"Because you don't know how to be quiet and listen. Now go on Susie," Elsie said.

"Amen," the others echoed.

"When he won, we were so happy," Susie said pressing her fingers gently against Chili's neck. "In the past, he'd come down to our department to share his goals with us. And when things went wrong, we went to see him."

"That's it, Susie. That feels so good. Now move to the left."

"Chili let her finish please," Elsie said giving Chili an annoying look. Not seeing her look Chili added, "She should have had a prayer vigil although I doubt prayer would help him."

"Chili if you don't keep quiet Elsie's going to have a fit," Teresa said laughing along with the rest who also noticed Elsie's distress at Chili's interruptions.

"Right after he won the election there was a meeting held for our two departments. I was not at the meeting but a supervisor friend of mine John, told me several employees from upstairs and two from our department blasted him about some promises they felt he had reneged on.

He said they were not just a little cruel in their attack on him. The County Executive and those employees, he said got into a serious argument. It was ugly from there on out.

As a result of that one meeting, he made the statement that 'those people are crazy down there.' Now all of us down there who supported him shook our heads in dismay as we watched him take everything from us. If it was something he thought we wanted we lost it. His revenge never ended." The women shook their heads in silence as they listened to Susie.

"Mind you now, those of us who had campaigned for him counted far more than those five or six people who had angered him. Three of the people did not even work in our department and the two that did was gone long before the impact of his revenge on us was felt."

"How ironic for you that his hatred against your department lasted long after the people he had had it out with had left," Chili said her eyes closed as Susie continued to work on her neck.

"It was told to us that he planned to go out of his way to hurt us. Mind you, many of us who had supported him by then wondered if we had cast the wrong vote as well."

"What did he take from you guys?" Elsie wanted to know.

"Elsie in the early seventies many of the black employees as well as the female employees faced gender and race discrimination. Black staff went to the director at that time and demanded fair treatment in working conditions complaining of always being placed in the worst halls while the female employees complained about having to do selective work. The only way to resolve that problem was to create work assignments according to seniority. That made it fair for everyone."

"I don't mean to interrupt Susie, Elsie," La-Joyce said looking in Elsie's direction "but I need to ask how it made it fair?"

"That was a question I was also about to ask," Elsie said.

"The black staff concerned filed the complaint, but everyone knew that it would not be fair to just make it better for one group and not for everyone so the agreement created stated that according to your seniority bidding would be accomplished. In other words, if you a black employee had ten years of seniority a white employee with less could not come in and take a job slot you wanted. But by the same token if a white person had been on the job ten years you as a black person could not come in and take the job slot he or she wanted or was in. Not only that, female employees could no longer be discriminated against in job placement due to gender. Some people who did not like where they were placed when bidding time came around knew if they worked long enough to become vested, they would be able to move in a desired job slot even if they never got promoted above being a line staff."

"That makes good sense. And if black people fought to make this happen why would a black County Executive take it away? Is that what you are telling us?" Elsie asked

"After that meeting, the newly elected County Executive made it so seniority did not count for nothing much at all. Telling our union officials, that he was taking it back because he could. We were pushed around from pillar to post one might say. He placed us under the umbrella of the adult system and sent in administrators who had never worked in a juvenile system. Not only that, they brought over the mentality of an adult jailer."

"I know that was hell," Chili said as her head bobbed back and forth.

"Yes Chili, it was a tragic event that turned our working conditions hostile because in the first place, they never wanted to come over but were forced by their administrator at the time," Susie said still working on Chili's neck.

"Are you telling us they were forced to come over?" Shenee' asked pointing to the water coming out of the hand of the statue that had turned to face them.

"In the next four years, we knew we were a hated department. When it came time to elect him again, I stood out on that street corner every day I didn't work, rain or shine making my statement."

"But he won anyway," Teresa said.

"It didn't matter because the people who voted him in again had not felt the sting of his betrayal the way we had."

"You are so right Susie like Mrs. Johnnie Bea you took steps to let it be known how that tragic undermining had hurt," Elsie said also turning her attention out to the yard and the children playing.

"A person coming in on probation could be given a slot you had worked years to get into. We cannot use mace or weapons when working with our kids so everything is crisis intervention. The work is taxing to the mind as well as the body because you must act physically in most encounters with out-of-control youth. We had one mental health day every other week so it was unnecessary to call in sick because you always knew every other week you would have a three-day rest before returning to work.

He didn't blink an eye when he took it from us allowing only the older staff to be grandfathered in; talking about how everyone would like a mental health day. Our job is dangerous in that it's both stressful and the realization that you could be hurt or hurt some child was a constant stress factor you have to deal with daily. Adult detention officers are allowed to use mace spray and other devices to disarm their inmates lessening potentially dangerous situations for them. We have too many staff out now from injuries that are in fear of losing their jobs."

"Hey wait a minute Susie, didn't that change split your staff along those lines?" Shenee' asked as the others looked at her as if not understanding what she meant. "What I'm asking is are there some staff who work four days with three days off every other week while others have to work all five days every week? That sounds like a bomber coming in."

"You are right Shenee'. Unlike the adult officers, we had no alternatives to control our youth unless it was to defuse without violence. That did not work on every child so we had to be physical much of the time Sanders didn't bother to talk with us to see what our different problems and concerns were."

"Now that is cold-blooded. It seems to me as a politician he would have expected some such negative reaction and the need to prove the attackers wrong rather than to become what they thought he was in the first place." Rosie said her hand wandering up to her temple as though she was thinking about something.

"To punish innocent employees who had no negative thoughts about him was cruel and against the laws of God Almighty," Elsie said shaking her head as she looked out at the children playing.

"Of course, we all know how some blacks are when they don't feel they need us any longer," Teresa said, her eyes also on the children playing on the lawn. The grass lay like a deep green carpet and the children rolled over it as though it was a blanket.

"As a politician, he should have realized that there were going to be people who thought hard of his politics but not all because the votes he received came from employees who did want him." Shenee' said shaking her head in disgust.

"Look, let Susie finish telling us about Willie Lynch and those immigrant kids. I am sick of talking about the County Executive when we all know he could care less about black voters. He believes it was the white people who put him in office not us." Teresa said.

"No more about me." Susie insisted. "I see La-Joyce is about to deliver over there we need to hear from her before that happens. Not to mention Shenee' has not given up one bit of information about herself," Susie said, looking to see La-Joyce slip back on her glasses and Shenee' smiling as the others looked over at them.

Chapter Thirteen

⊱─┈◈┈◦─◉─◦┈◈┈─⊰

Now that they had all viewed the inside of Mrs. Johnnie Bea's house the ladies went out and seated themselves on Mrs. Johnnie Bea's new screened-in white patio in her backyard. Elizabeth eased into the rocker Rosie had seen and bought just for that purpose.

The new multi-colored lawn furniture matched the white painted wood as did the rosebud archway that stood just below the last step. A winding flagstone pathway led up to the new patio where they sat. There mid-way through the garden, a fat brown statue of a man stood with his hands out as water flowed from them and sprayed the lawn and the garden.

For whatever reason on top of the statue's head Big Tom had taken up residence. From time to time the cat would slowly wander down to where the water came out of the statue's hands and lick some into its tongue, stroll back up to the top of its head to curl up looking out over the rest of the manicured lawn and beyond as though it knew some dark secret it was not about to tell. The children continued to play tug of war and water games in the yard tossing a big beach ball back and forth.

Teresa and Elsie sat beside La-Joyce in Mrs. Johnnie Bea's new swing just like the one on her front patio. Shenee, Chili, Rosie, and Susie took seats in the spacious reclining lounge chairs around her umbrella table.

"Susie, while your work with children brought Mrs. Johnnie Bea into your life. She came into my life quite by accident. I was able to assist her in helping an elderly friend," Shenee' said her blonde hair held tight in her hand to keep the rising breeze from blowing it in her face. The others stopped and became quiet remembering when they had first laid eyes on the woman they had thought was white. Her shoulder-length thick blonde hair and light grey eyes blended with her white skin making her appear to be a white woman. The smile on her face let them know she was accustomed to people thinking of her as a white person. Her slender, neat, and refined appearance confirmed that she was by no means without substantial resources. The jewelry she wore, though simple was in very good taste and quality.

"I'm the daughter of Steven McAfee."

There was a stunned look on the other women's faces when Shenee' revealed the identity of her father.

"At last count, he owns law firms in twenty states. In another country, my father would be considered a white man. Because way down generations ago however it was said that Negro blood tainted his family lineage. In America, he is considered black."

"Tainted!" Chili said in a raised voice.

"Chili, Shenee has the floor now. Let's respect her. It is her story she is sharing, and we must allow her to share it in the way she can best tell it."

"You're right, Elsie. Shenee, tell your story, and I'm listening." Chili said, moving over to where La-Joyce's feet were hanging off the lounge chair. Placed her head next to La-Joyce's right leg and stared up at Shenee'.

"He has always considered himself a black man, though few if any of his professional associates are aware that the blood running through his veins can be traced back to the Negro from which he came.

"I left a package on the counter when I stopped in Nordstrom's to purchase a tube of lipstick," she said to those listening as she leaned back, her eyes on Big Tom and the statue where he sat.

"Just as I was about to enter my car. I heard someone shouting. Turning around I saw this short stout lady waving a bag in the air. She ran up to me and said that I had forgotten my package. I thanked her for returning it. We struck up a conversation surrounding forgetfulness. I gave her my card and told her if she ever needed the expertise of a top-notch attorney, I be happy to see her.

"Months later I received a call from her asking if she could bring someone in to see me. Remembering the forgotten package and her kindness I told her 'Sure.' We sat up a time for her to bring her friend in. The person she brought in was a ninety-year-old white female. Mrs. Johnnie Bea brought with them letters from money beggars I'll call them. I learned from their operation how seedy organizations work on the fear of the elderly for the first time."

"What do you mean," La-Joyce asked

"It seems they are in business to send scare letters to elderly people pretending that their social security is going to be taken away if they don't send contributions to help stop the government from taking this action. In some of the literature, they were asking for as much as two thousand dollars. My client had paid as much as five thousand dollars in money orders while having to have emergency funding to help pay her utility bills."

"Who would take that much money from an old person?" Rosie asked shaking her head in dismay.

"No matter how much my client paid, she received the same letter over and over asking for that much and more. After a while, the letters became personal with her name attached making her believe they knew her and needed her help to fix the social security problem. They must have had a list of the elderly who voted a certain way because they even used the President's name to indicate him as being the person responsible for helping solve the social security problem. Money needed to be sent to him for that purpose.

Thinking if she did not send in the money, she would have no income at all, as soon as her check came my client made most of her money out to those swindlers.

I've seen it all before. The senior woman probably allowed her monthly bills to become delinquent to give to fake organizations that are faceless crooks getting rich from her and others like her making donations that they think are helping them keep money that is being taken from them through a source she thought was helping her," Shenee shared with the women.

"Before I retired, I knew many elderly patients who had been victimized in this manner," Elsie said.

"Someone should tell them better," Chili said closing the patio door to keep out the flying insects.

"Some people are willing to forego paying monthly bills sending large sums of money to these people thinking they are protecting the only income they have. Her friend was persuaded to allow me to take over the task of weeding out those predators. She would send me her bills and any other mail asking for money. In other words, I became her guardian."

"I don't know why anyone would want to take advantage of the elderly?" Elsie said. "But it must be being done legally because it happens all the time. It is a shame there are no laws protecting them from that." "Old people are vulnerable to crooks like that. They know that most old people won't talk about what they are being asked for them to, too many have no one they trust enough to tell what is happening to them," Chili said. It almost happened to my friend Mrs. Jackson. She is seventy-five years old. I saw her at the bank trying to draw out fifteen hundred dollars to pay to get a leaking water faucet fixed. I told her to tell the men she couldn't get the money until the next day and that I would have Tank come over and look at the faucet for her." "I bet it didn't cost nearly that much," Teresa said "Twenty dollars plus tax was all it cost Tank," Chili said.

"Girl, we have to be careful these days. You just never know; I've come across some weird cases," Shenee said.

"Not long after that Mrs. Johnnie Bea came to me again with a problem that needed to be addressed through the legal system. It seemed a Child she was helping had gotten in trouble running with the wrong crowd of boys trying to belong. I looked into the case and got it deferred. My husband at the time kept hounding me about having kids. I needed a diversion so I wouldn't have to deal with problems outside of my practice. I arranged to have my husband Paul mentor the child thinking it would put his mind to rest about having children when I was into my career. Paul became the kid's mentor. They formed a beautiful relationship.

After that Mrs. Johnnie Bea, well she was always telling me when we talked from time to time that she had found in me another Oprah to be proud of. I would smile not understanding what she meant by it but that family was important too. She seemed to be a nice enough person, a bit odd perhaps but I felt a closeness to her as a black woman I had never attempted with other women of my race even women I felt professionally equal to me.

"Although Paul and the kid became close buddies, Paul kept hounding me about children of our own. And like I said I had my career many men said my beauty equals that of the great Lena Horne by far."

"Girl please, you don't look nothing like Lena Horne.

"Lena Horne did not have blonde hair or blue eyes," Rosie said.

"Lena Horne is old Shenee'" Susie said laughing.

"Like wine my dear. And wine is better the older it becomes. You people don't realize it is wisdom that comes with age and years of living." Elizabeth replied getting genuine smiles from the rest of the ladies.

"The women looked at Elizabeth shaking their heads not excusing the wide smile Shenee' gave them.

"Like Rose explained in her early life I too thought I was tight. Maybe in a different way but it was all about me. The waves in my hair lay in the middle of my back and swung just like the white girls' hair swung. Even with a tan, I could have easily passed."

"Girl, you had it going on," Susie said, resting her foot on the white patio stool in front of her. The others sighed, waiting for Shenee' to tell them more.

"One day I came home. There laid a note plastered on the mirror in my dressing room."

"What did it say?" asked La-Joyce moving to relax on the new white lounging lawn chair they had replaced the old one with as she smiled down at Chili who still held fast to that right leg.

Shenee' said nothing.

"Well get on with it, Shenee' La-Joyce has got to tell hers and Mrs. Johnnie Bea will be here before you know it," Elsie said.

"She's right because mine will be coming up next and I want to get it out before my baby is born." Everyone chucked as La-Joyce rubbed her stomach.

"It said, 'Hi Honey I got a baby coming soon so I guess it's time we divorce.'

"You're kidding Shenee', just like that? Rosie asked leaning forward in her seat.

"Just like that," they all said. Their voices rose as though they were in line with each other's thoughts.

"Just like that, he was gone. When we went to court I almost fainted."

"Why? Asked Susie with the others echoing behind her.

"She was the black mother of the child I had him mentoring."

"What do you mean she was black?" Teresa said joining in with the other women who sat staring at Shenee' in shock.

"Do you mean she was black as in color or as in race?" Chili asked.

"Both. She was black, short, and ugly. Her hair looked like...like," Her eyes strayed towards La-Joyce. Their eyes met.

"You are mistaken, sister girl that woman was not ugly she was beautiful with natural hair, because let me update you if you don't already know, black is truly beautiful even black natural hair girlfriend." They all looked at Shenee' waiting for her to comment.

"Yes, you are right. At the time I had not been taught that it was."

"Was it that a white thing? That's what you had going on sister girl," Susie said, "Your momma should have taught you better."

"My mother was raised by her mother my grandmother to believe that if you were white-skinned you had the best of two worlds. White men wanted you because you come from their genes and the black men wanted you because their genes couldn't produce you. If the man was light enough, I was taught to believe his genes produced the most intelligent as well as beautiful children. My mother said not one of her friends was darker than she because if they were she could not bring them home. I am a shade darker than her."

"Well, she must be white," said Chili looking harder at Shenee' saying

"It goes back to what Mrs. Johnnie Bea told Pricilla about color."
"I grew up believing that she was white until I was eight and my grandmother informed me, my mother was black. My grandmother

would never claim to be white. White men used her because of her light skin just as they had used her mother right before her father. It was a tragic part of her life she told me with bitterness. A southern privilege it was, my mother told me, for white men to cheat on their wives with women as light as her mother. They were created for that purpose before and after slavery. Whatever came of it was the problem of the mother."

"What the hell purpose was that?" Chili asked. The other women frowned at Chili. "I know, I know. Mrs. Johnnie Bea even though you are not here I apologize for cursing on your patio. Smiles replaced the frowns and the women once again gave Shenee' their undivided attention.

"It didn't matter how many rapes these white men did they were regarded by the community of whites as most upstanding citizens my grandmother told me. Making mulatto illegitimate babies was the thing to do back then. There was no shame in what he did. It was never thought to be a disgrace to the white man. He had committed no crime no matter how he went about it, my grandmother told me. There was no name for it. It just happened. No one accused them of anything but having their way. The only thing my grandmother and others like her got out of it was the feeling that their offspring were better than children born dark."

"So, they shielded their pain and shame by saying they were better than the darker people of our race." La-Joyce said staring at Shenee' now.

"Of Course, it did not help that darker people of the Negro race helped perpetuate the myth right along with them. And before you tell me you are not Negroes remember during my grandmother's lifetime Negro was the accepted term for the race of black people born after slavery in this country. Am I lying...?" The rest grunted and let her continue.

"It was a messed-up way to think about your race especially when the people who defiled you are the color you want to be."

"Just like Mrs. Johnnie Bea said," Chili reminded them.

"How the hell did you ever get with David? He is as fine as Wesley Snipes but he is also his color." Laugher filled the room at Susie's comment.

"Why didn't you just have kids for Paul? That would have solved your problems," Teresa said waving at the children waving back at her.

"I couldn't. At least at the time, I thought I couldn't."

"What do you mean you couldn't?" Susie asked. "You have two now. So, you can't say you couldn't have children. What's up with that?"

"After we were married Paul took me to St Louis to meet his family?"

"You didn't meet them before. Who's hiding who?" Elsie asked laughing at her joke.

"I'm about to ask the same question," La-Joyce said, "Something is up with that. And with your class come on now."

"We were married in France. He was there doing research with other scientists I was there vacationing. At the time I thought I had better get him before the other women after him stole his heart. Oh, I don't know. He looked white and was my type of man. I knew the other men wanting me were too dark to even consider. He was anxious to give me his name and..."

"I know." Said Rosie. You were anxious to have it."

"Surely that was the way it all happened until..." Everyone moved their chairs closer to Shenee' so as not to miss the bomb they knew was coming.

"We came home because his mother was sick. When we arrived at the hospital and went in it was all I could do to conceal my shock."

"Why?" They all asked in unison.

"Because," she said turning again to look at La-Joyce who was looking directly at her. "She was as dark..."

"As me, oh my God girl you must have done a double take," La-Joyce said as deep dimples settled into her dark cheeks when she smiled. Her glasses settled on her nose.

"There would be no babies for the two of you; I know you made sure of that?" Susie said laughing.

"Girls, that's where Mrs. Johnnie Bea came in. She informed me that she kept asking Paul about me not knowing that we were divorced. I never returned her calls. I left the office not wanting to be there any longer. I wouldn't call her or come by to visit with her like I had been accustomed to doing when I wanted to talk to someone whom I respected as a real friend. Someone you know you can trust. Most of the black women I knew disliked me because of my color and they certainly were not taking me home to meet their husbands or boyfriends. Probably wondering what I had done to lose mine."

"I don't blame them especially before you were safely married again," Susie said as the rest echoed a yes in reply.

"I went into a deep depression. I quit practicing law. I didn't want to go out. I was too embarrassed to tell my family what had happened. After all, being a McAfee woman meant every man wanted you. The kind of rejection I had to face I didn't want anyone to know.

"See, see I knew it was something about you Shenee' that spelled pampered and spoiled," Chili said. The other friends laughed but encouraged Shenee' to tell more.

"How did Mrs. Johnnie Bea introduce you to her Oprah, Shenee'?" La-Joyce asked. "I know she didn't help you without telling you how Oprah would have handled the problem. It's as if she thinks Oprah has the answer to all our problems."

"I wonder if Oprah has problems she can't fix? She seems to know the answer to what everyone else needs to do to fix theirs." Rosie said looking over at the others.

"Let me check on that peach cobbler Mrs. Johnnie Bea will know if I let it cook one minute over," said Elsie getting up to go inside.

"Ain't nobody without problems Rosie," Chili said as Elsie stood up to leave. "Even Oprah with all her money, has problems." Chili went on to say. "Mrs. Johnnie Bea never said Oprah didn't have problems. What Mrs. Johnnie Bea did say was that she handles her problems and keeps on pushing. There is a difference ladies!"

"That's what she forces us to do. Look at a woman who looks like us who is making it. Regardless of how much money you have problems and living goes hand in hand. It is how you handle your problems that makes the difference." Chili's southern accent filled the patio with Mrs. Johnnie Bea's presence. It was something they knew Mrs. Johnnie Bea would be saying.

"You are right because Mrs. Johnnie Bea came right to my house and found me there sulking in my misery. She said she had been knocking at my door for a long time. I thought someone was attempting to burglarize me so finally I went to the door and there she stood with of all things ..."

"Don't say it," they all echoed, "A pot of beans!"

A pot of good old navy beans!" Shenee' answered bringing more laughter. I got my beans too." Said La-Joyce

"We all got our beans because when Mrs. Johnnie Bea, Teresa, and I were coming up in Mississippi beans were the staple that put fullness in your stomach and air out your butt," Elsie said, getting laughter from the rest of the group.

"In she came dressed in a long green smock with a big black pot in her hands." Shenee' said. "The first thing she did was hand me the pot so I couldn't close the door in her face."

"What am I supposed to do with this?" I asked wanting to shove her and her pot back out the door.

'My Oprah girl' she said to me. 'You look like something the cat dragged in. It seems to me you are throwing your life away because some man left you not to mention with the mother of the child he was mentoring.'

"What a blow for you?" Rosie said as the rest echoed her.

"Mrs. Johnnie Bea!" I said,

"I am not going to lie I asked Mrs. Johnnie Bea to leave more than once but she just kept on talking

'My Oprah, what are we going to do with you child? They just don't make our girls like they used to. Back in the day, we were like trees. The winds came sometimes so hard it would bend us backward. Some fell but most of us stood long after the storm was gone.'

"I'm not a tree as you can see," I said to her.

'It's a shame our girls think they can do like the TV girls do and just messed up their lives talking about having sex just for fun and studying about nothing but their looks and their careers. Like that's all life is about. My Oprah Child, there is nothing wrong with two or three babies.'

"Mrs. Johnnie Bea my career was not all I was thinking about. And I don't think Oprah would agree with you. A woman's career is important." I told her.

'Well, daughter I can't say she would but I do know there were times she needed someone older and wiser than herself. A person she could talk to when things got bad for her. No amount of money can make things right always. Sometimes you need a wise voice to listen to.'

"Whose wise voice might that be?" I asked her wanting her to hurry up and finish what she had to say so she could leave."

'Well, if you are willing to eat a bowl of these beans with me, afterward we can take a walk to the park so I can get the exercise My Oprah says will shed some of these pounds off this big butt of mine I would be delighted to give you a bit of an old woman's wisdom.'

"I bet those beans weren't all she brought with her." Teresa said to Shenee' looking over at the children busy now playing in the water the statue sprayed from the garden where it stood.

"She brought a tape of Oprah's" Their voices sounded like echoes as they shouted the answer, they all knew.

"You got that right. After she dished me up a bowl of her famous beans, she put the tape of Brewster Place in the recorder and began to tell me how Oprah had lost her house on account of the boy running out on her.

"Mrs. Johnnie Bea," I told her, "Oprah is playing a role in a movie. Anyway, what has that got to do with me losing Paul to that whore?" I asked her.

'Don't use profanity when you talking about your species honey.' She advised me. 'Only whores in this world are men if there are any because believe you me, they got us outnumbered in the having sex department one hundred to one. Child losing a man ain't no different than losing money. Money can always be replaced. in 'Brewster Place', Oprah started helping other people and used that to help her handle her miseries. You can do that too just think about it like this.' I looked at her seriously wondering what I needed to do to get rid of her. But she just kept right on talking like she didn't see the look I was giving her."

'Every season has a beginning and an ending. Whatever season you are in you are in it to learn something.' "She told me." 'If you let it,' she said. 'That season will teach you about life and living and hopefully, you will become a better person.'

'You see how the character Oprah played looked at her season. She mourned and then looked at the next woman's problems and saw her season was not as bad as she thought. If you close your eyes and refuse to see it, the season will pass away leaving you less aware than when it first comes. Paul was that season, now either you will learn from that season and allow it to pass or you will mourn something forever that will never return at least not in the way you first knew it.'

"Mrs. Johnnie Bea..." I said wondering how rude I would have to be to get her to leave."

'You are the beautiful child. Just like the young girl who lost not only her husband but a child she loved dearly. She drew from the hard lesson she needed to learn from and reached towards the happiness that awaited her elsewhere. Now the character Oprah portrayed was there to help her but she couldn't do it for her. She had to go out and do it for herself. Like I already said you are a beautiful girl. But there is a lesson you don't want to face.' She told me.

"Face! What lesson is there I didn't want to face?"

'You can't use your wants to destroy someone else's happiness. Your husband wanted children and you didn't, not by him anyway, she told me.

"If only I had given Paul the children he wanted. We would still be together.

'My Oprah, no child. There was a lesson in that marriage you had to learn. He just happened to be a part of that lesson. If you were going to have children by that man we wouldn't be sitting here talking now because you would still be with Paul.'

"I looked at Mrs. Johnnie Bea thinking what does she mean? I didn't understand one word she was saying to me until she asked me why I had had no children. I looked at her ashamed to tell her the real reason. It was something I never talked about, something in my past that I never wanted to admit."

Shenee' put her bare feet in between the railing after slipping off her sandals, her mind's eye on the start of a new season. "Mrs. Johnnie Bea made me get out of that house and back into the world. We went walking in the park when she could get over. Every day she came, she'd sing the praises of Oprah and how she was taking care of her business. And I listened wanting to hear good things happening to someone even if it wasn't me.

'Oprah would never throw her hands up and let some man keep her from taking care of her business.' Mrs. Johnnie Bea preached to me every day she came. On and on she'd say 'Oprah knows the ocean is full of men waiting to be caught.' I was just about to tell her I would give up both my hands to have just one of one of Oprah's." The other women laughed while looking at their own hands. I was thinking to myself, Oprah is imperfect the same as me. If not now someday she may fall into a hole money can't dig her out of. It was Mrs. Johnnie Bea who led the way for my recovery. Without her mentoring me. Oprah's life was meaningless to me.

"Suddenly I walked straight into a wall in front of me. At least I thought it was a wall." The looks on the other women's faces made her shake her head, yes.

"His huge body stood like a tree trunk holding me up. When I looked into David's hazel brown eyes Paul's memory melted away like snow falling in the summertime." The radiant glow in Shenee's eyes told the others her heart had been mesmerized. Shenee' looked at the friends Mrs. Johnnie Bea had shared with her saying to them; "Thanks to Mrs. Johnnie Bea, of course, it didn't happen all at once. She had to teach her girlfriend here how it was okay to love a man whose color was black."

"As you know my husband is darker than La-Joyce here and as handsome as she is beautiful. After I met him Mrs. Johnnie Bea always had an excuse to get me to take a walk in the park."

"And of course, you didn't want to go." La-Joyce said waiting as did the others for Shenee' to tell them more.

"I'd be waiting at the door when she got there. The thing is she was missing Oprah."

"She was missing Oprah!" Teresa said, her mouth open.

"I'd ask her what about Oprah I didn't want her to miss her show. I knew it meant a lot to her.

'Don't you worry about that show My Oprah? We got business to take care out in that park honey She'd say to me."

"Mrs. Johnnie Bea ain't missed no Oprah." Chili said shaking her hand."

"You right about that Mrs. Johnnie Bea put her blank tape on and caught Oprah when she returned home," Susie said with a one-two pop, pop as they all laughed.

"Yes," put in Elsie "If Mrs. Johnnie Bea missed Oprah to take you to the park. She was serious about hooking you and that brother up." "Girl Mrs. Johnnie Bea ain't missed no Oprah I'll bet money on that," said Chili. Everyone laughed including Shenee'.

"I'm telling you what she told me." Shenee' insisted.

'Don't you worry about that show me and Oprah got business out here in this park.'

"It didn't take long however for me to move on my own. When he started talking about marriage Mrs. Johnnie Bea insisted, I introduce him to my family."

"Something you didn't want to do because he was black," La-Joyce said.

"Well!"

"Well, what!" they all echoed

"What did you do"? Susie yelled! "You were leading a secret life afraid your folks would see this black man in your life."

"And you ain't even white yourself, girlfriend, you just look white, what's up with that? Were you ashamed of him?" Chili asked standing over Shenee' with her hands on her hips as she eyed her up close. "You were in the same situation you were in with Paul."

"Of course, I'm not ashamed of my husband."

"Let her alone girls she's got two babies by the man. Her son may be her color, but her daughter's picture is the color of her father." Elsie said.

"Did you break it to them before or after the marriage?" Teresa asked taking a seat on one of the recliner lawn chairs as she pulled her apron off.

"No girlfriend, she just walked up to the door knocked, and let her mother and grandmother pass out seeing all that black body staring them in the face standing next to their white-looking daughter and granddaughter right Shenee'?" Susie asked.

"It didn't happen like that. Mrs. Johnnie Bea and I visited my mother together. My introducing Mrs. Johnnie Bea as a friend undid Mother, but it turned out wonderful."

"Are you telling us your mother and grandmother had no problem with your colored friend or your husband as dark as David is?" Susie asked.

"What did you do, pass him off as the gardener?" Teresa asked eyeing the other ladies.

"More like the bouncer from what I saw of him," La-Joyce said putting up both arms.

"My grandmother died never knowing about David, nor did she ever see my children. I explained to David about her prejudice when it came to dark people in our race. Now that I remember, it seemed strange because she hated white men but not white women saying that their white men would come bed a colored woman against her will and still maintain their dignity and respect among their people yet would lynch our colored men for looking at a simple-minded white woman.

Her husband during her marriage was a very dark mild-mannered man as my mother described him. The system at that time, she said let them abuse colored women and their own women folk as well. My mother's brothers could bring home white girls as long as they were not what she called white trash. And believe me, she investigated them to make sure they were from the right families."

"How many children did your grandmother have?" Susie asked. "Sixteen."

"Shenee', come on now, you just said your grandmother's husband was a very dark man, even with a half-white man some of those sixteen children would have come out dark." Shenee stirred uneasily and looked at Susie then away.

"Ten girls and six boys!"

"Not one of them came out black?" Rosie asked.

"Like I said back in that time white men could come to a black woman's house even if she were married and politely ask her husband to leave." It took a minute for her words to soak in but when they did Elizabeth sat up with her mouth open as she and Shenee's eyes locked. Her disclosure took only seconds to soak in for all the women seated there at a loss for words. "The men who came were all white. Her dark black husband soon disallowed himself the privilege of sleeping with his wife."

"That's worse than what Mrs. Johnnie Bea was telling us," La-Joyce said shaking her head along with the rest.

"You must remember my grandmother looked white herself. All her children were light enough to pass if they wanted to. There was nothing my grandmother's husband could do." Shenee' finally said. I learned after bringing David to visit my mother that I have one aunt and uncle I never met before I met David. They both married dark-skinned people. Grandmother never spoke their names. It was forbidden by any of her other children to acknowledge them in her presence."

Your grandmother probably hated the fact that her husband could not protect her but that is how it was back then." Teresa said.

"How many brothers and sisters do you have?" asked Chili getting a questioning nod from the rest of the females present.

"I have no sisters. My brother is an attorney in Hawaii. He is married to an African woman, Nebeena. She's beautiful, but she would never have been accepted by my grandmother."

"When did you find that out" Elsie asked

"It was only after David and I became serious that I shared my secret with him. We exchanged secrets. I have a lot to thank Mrs. Johnnie Bea for. I'm glad she, and as she likes to tell me, Oprah helped me learn from my season."

"Girl that is some life you've got," Chili said, with the rest nodding in agreement.

"Well, it doesn't end quite there."

"Give us the rest," said La-Joyce eyeing the other friends who quickly regained their interest in hearing the rest of her story.

"Mrs. Johnnie Bea insisted I attempt to develop a friendship with Paul and his wife after David and I had our second child because the boy he had mentored knew her well."

"Did you?" asked Teresa.

"My husband and I met and had dinner with his family a year after my daughter was born. After five years my winter was over and as we all know spring brings in a new season."

Chapter Fourteen

>—I—‹♦›—☉—‹♦›—I—<

"What language are they speaking La-Joyce," Elsie asked La-Joyce about the person speaking over the radio Teresa brought outside telling them the weather report for the rest of the week. "German" La-Joyce answered. They were discussing the difficulties they are experiencing traveling in America. There are too many restrictions nowadays. A person would fare better if they traveled by boat they were saying."

"I love to listen to you talk La-Joyce. The way you pronounce your words, well it's like talking to a white foreign person. I mean no disrespect it just does. Don't you think so Susie?" Chili asked.

"She sounds like those educated white folks Mrs. Johnnie Bea spoke of when she was tongue-lashing Pricilla to me," Susie answered.

"You wouldn't believe La-Joyce can speak three foreign languages fluently and seven different dialects." Shenee' said. "She has traveled around the world. And she has lived in countries you, girls, only dream of visiting."

"What are you saying?" Shenee' Chili asked.

"She is about as close to Condoleezza Rice as we ever will get." Shenee' said ignoring Chili's remark. "She truly has lived a privileged life."

"Thank God for small favors," Chili said turning to La-Joyce. "I mean no disrespect but honey you might as well be who you are?"

"Now who is that Chili?" La-Joyce asked.

"You are a Yippee and a nerd. Your parents gave you the type of education most blacks never heard of let alone are privileged to. When you ran away you must have asked yourself if you had lost your mind

Come on girls let's go inside so we can see the car when Mrs. Johnnie Bea gets here. The boys called and said they were on their way home."
"Ran away, La-Joyce you ran away from home? Are you serious? Tell me about it" Susie said to La-Joyce after giving her, her full attention. "For many years I could not discuss that segment of my life," La-Joyce shared. "I had closed that door behind me."

"It couldn't be any harder than mine La-Joyce?" Rosie said I think you need to share also."

"You are going to share aren't you La-Joyce?" The others asked taking seats in the living room that looked directly out on the front lawn.

La-Joyce lowered herself down to sit upon the newly carpeted floor her feet folded under her native style her hands on the sides of her stomach. She looked away from her listeners staring off into space as though entering another world.

"You may not know this but there are people in other countries who, when I told them I was American, truly believed that I was a blessed child. They believe God lives here in America. It is their dream to die and be reincarnated here."

"You are kidding me," Elsie said.

"They honestly believe that everyone is rich in the United States of America," La-Joyce said looking up at the others.

"They believe what?" I hope you told them better." Teresa said shaking her head.

"At the time I knew no better myself. Perhaps I thought it also. I cannot remember it was so long ago, it seems a lifetime ago to tell you the truth. Many, especially in very poor countries believe that there is little or no crime in this country because of the democratic system we have. They believe that injustices that exist in their part of the world do not exist for us. And that everyone is free and is treated equally."

"Lord, help them," Susie said.

"Now ain't that the truth," Chili said.

"They are living in a dream world. Ask the kids down there where I work, they will tell them better than that," Susie added.

"They also believe that there is no hunger or homelessness, no one begging on the streets as it is where they live. Even in many African countries, the belief is the same. Every American, they say, lives with God. If they could die and go to heaven, they believe that this country is where they would come, this is a fact."

"I bet you the foreign kids who come through the juvenile center would tell them differently," Susie said shaking her head as she looked down at La-Joyce. "Your parents should have taught you better than to believe those fairy tales. Did they teach you racism still exists in this country and that there are many homeless people in the United States?" Susie said in stinging words her gum beginning to pop letting the others know she had become irritated.

"No disrespect Elizabeth but white people here in the United States are not hearing that we are all equal stuff no matter what they try to tell us. We know that because every twenty-five years congress had to vote on whether we can vote now you tell me what is up with that equality when white people who also came here from another country have no such restrictions?" Elsie said in agreement with Susie.

"I've learned from Mrs. Johnnie Bea even when the words are somewhat brutal to just listen and learn," Elizabeth said as she listened to their comments concerning the people of her race.

"My parents never taught me that I was different than anyone. They just cuddled me like any parent would their child. We traveled so extensively that it was a must that I be home-schooled. Besides anthropology, my father was fascinated with martial arts. He had me train under a master while living in China. Through this training, I learned how to defend myself and I developed a strong sense of discipline. At the time it never occurred to me my life would depend on those teachings; I simply enjoyed the physical exercise and mental discipline.

While living on the Nile African people saw me as a most beautiful child and thought I was well cared for; in Switzerland, the white children I played with never admonished me because of my race. We skied together and had lots of fun in the wintry weather. I have slept on the ground when my parents were out digging for fossils and artifacts from ancient civilizations.

I never knew bigotry or how vicious and violent racism was until I experienced it here in the States. You women always talk about the racism in the South, well let me tell you I experienced it in New York City in the state where I was born."

"All you have to do child is read Sammy Davis Jr's "Why Me," Elsie said nodding her head in agreement to La-Joyce's statement.

"In our travels, I met many people who looked like me but their attitudes were far different than American black people. Nothing prepared me for the mean vicious attacks of blacks here in this country. I listened quietly as Susie, talked about how Mrs. Johnnie Bea tongue-lashed Pricilla when she made negative remarks concerning Clarence Thomas.

It was once said by a group of my black American classmates after I foolishly insisted that my parents allow me to attend public school, that I reminded them of Clarence Thomas. It took me a while to realize our likeness in their minds was purely physical.

"I hate to admit it but little sister you hit the nail on the head their words were meant to hurt," Susie said putting a stick of gum in her mouth after pulling the first stick out.

"When did you end up in public school?" Rosie asked.

"What do you mean they said you look like Clarence Thomas; you look nothing like Thomas?" Chili said

"Chili, I know you love, me but you are incorrect on that point."

"Come on La-Joyce now what in the world do you and Clarence Thomas have in common really? Those kids just wanted to hurt your feelings?" Susie said.

"We are quite dark in complexion for one thing. When Susie was telling of the incidents occurring with the immigrant African children in her jail I was forced to choke back tears. My flashbacks were so raw, the attacks on my person occurred daily. I recall one particular incident. It happened one day in class."

"Wait a minute, back up. How did you, after being home-schooled, end up in a public school for Christ's sake?" Rosie asked surprising everyone with her participation.

"Didn't you hear me say that I insisted my parents allow me to attend public school where many blacks were attending? I desired to learn about my race of people by personal communication. There was only one television in our home. Aside from public access television, the only films I was allowed to observe were documentaries designed to educate and not entertain."

"I would have been one of those girls laughing at you. Trust me education was not something my friends and I woke up in the morning thinking about." Rosie admitted to La-Joyce.

"What did you think about Rosie?" Elsie asked.

"Boys and beauty Elsie," Rosie said. If you were dressed fine, and were pretty you were in the 'in crowd'. Education was the last item on the agenda. Usually, it was the unpopular kids who were forced to concentrate on school work and most of them were kissing butt to get into our circle. Trust me I know. But look at you La-Joyce versus me. I guarantee you all those students teasing you ended up the same as me if not worse."

"One day during class Rosie, we were lectured on fossils. The instructor seemed limited in his knowledge of this bone he had us view. I kept correcting him. Mylo of course has since informed me I should have waited until after class to correct him concerning the misinformation he was giving the students. At the time it never occurred to me I was embarrassing him in front of them. It became important to me that the correct information be given.

I didn't mind sharing that with my eleventh -grade classmates who, I did not realize at the time, had no interest whatsoever in being educated by me giving them correct information. They laughed at the instructor telling him Ms. Clarence Thomas knew more about bones than he did.

Their cruelties escalated as they began taunting him and me by stating as one girl shouted out,

'La-Joyce needs to be making her way to some hairdresser so she can get that hair of hers done and stop looking like old man Clarence Thomas. Talking about bones. I don't care about no bones I care about what my man is doing!' Her words brought laughter from the rest of the class. My hair was in its natural state my beautician had shaped and conditioned it just the day before I thought to myself 'What is she talking about?'

'Girl where you from talking like white people? Coming in here calling yourself black? You look just like an African for real.'

'The ugly kind.' Someone else said.

'This is not the 70's, get your hair done. Looking like a nigger.' I looked at that girl's hair it had been chemically processed to look like the white girls who were in class."

"They were talking to you like that around white kids?" Chili asked a frown forming on her face.

"The white kids who said nothing at first began to join in on the taunting."

"I don't think I can hear anymore you are making me sick". Chili said shaking her head. "Down in Louisiana where I come from, we called each other niggers in private but never and I mean never in front of white people. How we meant it to each other was a far cry from what white people mean when they said it."

"The word nigger means nothing to me personally," Teresa said.

"But coming up in the South and as an educator I realize the word perpetuated senseless cruelties for not only my ancestors who had no choice in whether or not they wanted to be called nigger. The word was the single most vile force used in the Jim Crow era to excuse what happened to Emmett Till, Medgar Evers, and others who were killed by lynching and other cruel murders during that time.

To the people doing the killing, they felt they were only killing niggers. Have you forgotten what Mrs. Johnnie Bea shared with us?" Everyone even Elizabeth shook her head. For those reasons and out of the respect I have for the suffering of my ancestors victimized by those atrocities I do not use the word ever."

"Willie Lynch is as real as the grave," Elsie said laying down her spoon on the stand beside her.

"My awareness came while examining the appearances of most of the girls. Not one wore their hair in its natural state as I did. I would soon learn it was only fashionable for white girls to do so. I wondered to myself what these girls were mixed with to have hair that lay so straight and long or so curly. A white male student came up to me and told me I needed to get a weave or have my hair permed so that it would look more like the white girls. He assured me no black girls wore their hair in its natural state because it was too rough and ugly looking. I can tell you nothing prepared me for attending public school, not really.

"This is hurting me. I need to go." Chili said starting to rise.

"Girl you are going to sit right here and listen. That is what is wrong now we are in denial and don't want to hear the truth," Elsie said looking down at Chili with her arms folded.

"At that time braids were not even fashionable. My high school classmates did not know who George Washington Carver was, but they made a point of assuring me I was as ugly as Clarence Thomas with my hair in its natural state. Trust me public schooling taught me some real hard lessons in black culture that year."

"What lessons did you learn?" Elsie asked.

"Living in this country as a black American, in the public school, reality sat in quickly.

It was however the harsh dictions of my classmates that made me more observant at home. I came in one day when my favorite aunt, my father's sister was visiting him. They were not at the time aware that I was present. I heard them discussing something of interest and since it was Aunt Mary, I listened in wondering if she was asking Father if she could take me with her to Paris again that summer. I was growing weary of the black public school and the cruelties that existed in its environment.

Aunt Mary was talking to Father about our pet which of course I first thought was Poopie our little cox.

'Where is our little pet?' she was asking Father.

'Poopie is out in the yard running around,' he told her.

'Of course, you know', she tells him, I was not referring to that awful dog but the pet you and Deborah pulled out of the gardener's house.'

"What did she mean by that?" Susie asked popping her gum as fast as she spoke.

"Weren't your parents your biological parents?" Chili asked crossing her legs as she watched the others shake their head as their interest grew.

'Mary,' I heard him say 'I have grown weary of your remarks about La-Joyce!' She threw her head back and laughed asking 'What else would I call the little black thing?' I think when I walked in, I was still too stunned by her words to do anything but react to them.

"The pet would be me I take it or am I the little black thing? My tears were coming so fast I could barely see," La-Joyce said wiping her eyes with the back of her hand until Elsie gave her some tissue. "Which pet do you, Aunt Mary, take me to be, the dog or the cat? Maybe I am the monkey you dragged along to Paris to amuse yourself with all these years!'"

"My God, La-Joyce I didn't realize your parents were not black or I would not have said the things I did," Chili said her hand covering her lips. "I am so sorry."

"No wonder you were always taking up for white people they are your family," Rosie said staring at La-Joyce.

"It must have hurt to hear an aunt you thought loved you refer to you as one of the house pets," Elizabeth said. Her lips set tight as La-Joyce stopped in mid-sentence crying out of control.

"Now La-Joyce, don't leave out the good stuff," Chili said. "You have got to tell us about the look of shock that aunt gave you. I can see her now her eyes had grown enormous, holding her throat appalled that her secret feelings were out of the closet. 'Oh my god I never meant a word of it!'" Laughter filled the room as Chili acted out the role, she felt the aunt had displayed.

"Chili you are a mess girl. Shut up or we will all end up on the floor rolling before she finishes," Shenee said laughing with the others as Chili caught her throat mimicking how she thought the aunt had reacted at being discovered.

"Go on La-Joyce finish. What you are telling us is not funny but it sounds like an ironic, tragic satire; One we are familiar with. Please finish." Susie said as she popped her gum twice then placed it in a tissue after licking her tongue out at Chili.

"She tried to console me and pretend she was only joking but my season with my race of people allowed me knowledge and an awareness I had not before been privileged to. My classmates may not have been able to teach me about bones but they were upfront about jokes meant to hurt when it came to telling you how you looked to them." La-Joyce said drying her eyes. "I knew when someone was being nasty and I had already looked into the raw face of racism so I knew what it looked like even when uttered from white lips."

"Your father must have been devastated," Elizabeth said shaking her head.

'La-Joyce', Father said 'pay no attention to her'

"I must," I told him. "After all she is your sister. You no doubt have known her feelings all these years, yet you allowed me to embrace her as though I were a human person she loved when all the time you knew to her, I was no more than a petted animal tagging along after her."

'It is not as you think' he had said walking towards me.

'No, it's not.' Aunt Mary echoed him.

"Perhaps, I told him as I backed away from him. Mother's feelings are the same as Aunt Mary's." I heard him shouting my name as I escaped from there running not looking back until I ran into Mylo like Shenee' ran into David."

"Did they beat you and yell at you La-Joyce?" Rosie asked.

"No, corporal punishment, my parents were never cruel or physical. I can't remember anything I wanted and was not allowed to have. Under the supervision of my mother, I learned ethics, moral principles, and a need to do the right thing."

"At least they gave you good home training. I cannot tolerate children who are wild and unruly," Elsie said a smile on her face.

"I was punished just like other children I guess though not harshly. Just hearing my father raise his voice was enough to curb my behavior. There was nothing I asked him for he did not provide. I could follow him around even when he was with his friends, who by the way were all white or foreign. They treated me respectfully. I guess one might say I was privileged. Now I realize that privilege put me in a closed box that would cause me many problems once it was opened."

"You never wondered why your skin color was different from your parents?" Rosie asked looking strangely at La-Joyce.

"Of course, as I grew older, I realized I was not their biological child but they had been my parents all my life. I loved them and it never interfered with how they treated me. My running away had nothing to do with how I was treated by my parents."

"Rosie it was her season to awaken to the world and what it was really like. Trust me when she started running, she learned things her parents could have never taught her. Am I right La-Joyce?" Teresa asked turning to La-Joyce as she handed tissues out to everyone including Elizabeth who sat quietly shaking her head as tears slipped from her eyes.

"If there is one thing you want to teach your children early," La-Joyce said after wiping her eyes, "it is not to run away from home. Few survival skills prepare them for the stark reality of life on the streets and you are right Elsie, I wish however, I could have learned them without all the pain and suffering of street life.

While I was out there, reality hit home hard and fast. No one is your friend. It is all about survival. You see life at its worst. Because food is so scarce, drugs take its place even for young children who have no idea how to fend for themselves. All kinds of concoctions were made up to knock the edge off hunger. I witnessed girls no more than twelve sell themselves for a bar of candy without even thinking about it.

"La-Joyce?" Chili said.

"No, I didn't have to because I learned to live close to the land when my parents were out in the wild. Living like that teaches you to recognize ways to replenish your body without having to resort to drugs or prostitution. When I was asked to participate, I refused, telling those around me what properties a particular drug possessed and the resulting harm it would do to their bodies. They of course would laugh and take them anyway. Many young bodies were lying in ditches taken away to the morgue with 'unknown' written on their name tags far more than you can ever imagine. Trust me; it is not a pretty sight."

"How did you protect yourself from physical assault? Chili asked

"As I previously stated my father insisted through my mother's protests that I learn the martial arts. I was taught by a master who demanded discipline of not only your body but also your mental state as well."

"Were you ever attacked?" Rosie asked"

"A few tried but after about three or four of them hobbled off with their manhood severely wounded and the knowledge that I could not be easily beaten, they let me be. I could sense a leaf falling to the ground, so it was difficult for me to be attacked without warning. I have been attacked, but for me, the outcome was always favorable. Unfortunately, this was not so for many others, especially the very young."

"Both boys and girls?" Rosie asked.

"Yes, both especially the very young trust me there were some as young as seven and eight. It sounds unbelievable but quite true."

"My Lord, child you are a rare spirit. I cannot imagine such experiences in my own life; however, I must say I respect how you have handled those experiences," Elizabeth said a freshly made lemonade drink handed to her by Elsie as she handed the rest of the women their drinks as well.

"Elizabeth is right what you have been through and survived reflects your strong self-determination we are proud of you and we know that baby will grow up having the same kind of spirit," Elsie said replacing her frowns with a fresh smile.

"How did Officer Mylo Taylor come to know you?" Susie asked. La-Joyce's face lit up at the mention of her husband's name.

"I think I must have been quite a surprise for Mylo and his buddies. They were doing a street sweep. Mylo didn't know it but I had heard of him before I met him.

Sometimes the police were a welcome sight, especially when there were those on the streets who preyed on the old and weak. When the police did their sweep those were the first to run. They knew the police would be looking for them if someone was mysteriously killed or hurt. Dwayne's name was out there as being a cop who wouldn't hurt us without cause. Lots of people are actually helped by police who catch them.

"Really," Shenee' said.

"Yes, by taking them to jail when they are starving on the streets."

"There are food banks," Chili said.

"You have to be able to reach them Chili. Life on the streets is a far cry from the everyday life you experience, like when you have a car or money for public transportation. I of course respected the law and moved when the officers asked. They began questioning me and I started to run as I did in other cities as I moved from state to state before reaching Washington State. Anyway, they gave chase. I began to fight against their touching me. People gathered around looking because they could not get a handle on me. They had to call for backup. The crowd was yelling, I had done nothing wrong. 'She moved when you asked her to move. Leave her alone.' "I could hear them yelling." 'Racial profiling.'"

"Racial profiling, Mylo is black," Susie said.

"Those of us who lived on the streets are aware more of the actions of the officers we come in contact with. Race is secondary to their actions because it is how they can help or hurt us that is most important to and for us."

"What do you mean?" Teresa asked.

"You first place race in your equation of the person committing the act. When you live on the street you first put a face on the person helping or hurting you then add race to the equation. Anyone can racially profile. Mylo has to stop and make sure he is not stopping people in a car because they are black or because they have committed a crime. He explains that it is in the mindset. You have to be aware that it is happening or you will think like Chili and believe it can happen only under certain circumstances or only by a certain race of people."

"You go, girl. That husband of yours helped you huh?" Chili said.

"Yes, Chili he did, but it took me some years to figure out I had good parents who despite what I thought, had given up having biological children of their own in fear that it might make a difference as to how I felt or was treated.

"No one could have told me a white couple could love a black child. I've seen them love animals in the way you say your parents loved you, I never would have believed it possible. My experience has been so different. You are truly proud of them because you made sure we knew your feelings where they were concerned even before we knew their race," Susie told her."

"Yes, it touched me as well," Elizabeth said.

"Susie is right. You make me have second thoughts about white people because you always refused to speak collectively of them." Chili said.

"No matter what others of my race might have to say about white people, I'll always defend the love my parents have for me. The person I have become is because of that love."

"When did you figure that out?"

Mylo helped me a lot and of course when he shared Mrs. Johnnie Bea with me everything changed. He will not admit it but I think because he and his partner had such a difficult job subduing me, he took an interest in my welfare. He found housing for me. He would come around and ask how I was doing. He'd tell me that I should go back to school."

"For what reasons should I attend school? I asked him. He said to learn. I told him there was nothing schools here could teach me I had already learned.

"He did not believe me until a Chinese woman came up to him and asked him how to get to Logan Street, in Chinese. He looked puzzled, so I answered her question and also told her how to get to the local food bank. Dwayne stood there with his mouth open. When she left, he asked me if I could speak French. I said in French that if I were him, I would go back to school. he did not understand what I was saying and then I said the same thing in German. He told me that I belonged to somebody what the hell was I doing out here on the streets?

"Running away I told him."

"I hope it was in English," Teresa said

"Yes, of course."

"No wonder it was difficult for me to trace your accent, a little New England but more foreign too," Shenee' said.

"When did you meet Mrs. Johnnie Bea?" Shenee' asked.

I was introduced to Mrs. Johnnie Bea by Mylo when he took me down to where they feed the homeless. I have always thought of him as my guardian angel. Posters were posted around the country looking for me. Mylo happened to be a cop in the area where I was living on the streets. He told me there was only one person who could help me get my life back on track. A couple of weeks after he found me housing, he said he had someone he wanted me to meet.

We found Mrs. Johnnie Bea and Elizabeth in the Village distributing food to the homeless people living out there. He walked up to Mrs. Johnnie Bea kissed her on the cheek and said to her.

'You and Oprah still helping those white women.'

She looked up at him with a smile on her face after wiping her brow with a paper towel beside her. She said to him,

'My Oprah and I are helping any woman needing help if you must know. What are you doing with your life that makes sense?' He smiled back at her and said,"

'I brought La-Joyce here to get some of those beans you're famous for.' "She looked at me with a big smile on her face.

'Don't you mind what he says about My Oprah honey' she said handing me a bowl of navy beans. 'He just got that if you ain't helping me syndrome most folks got when they want to talk bad about somebody doing good but it ain't for them. I call it the 'if you ain't helping me you ain't helping nobody syndrome.'

"I looked at her and thought to myself. This woman is one beautiful human being. She speaks out. I wondered how Mylo was going to get her to help me. There was a quiet stillness in the room as La-Joyce told them about her first meeting with Mrs. Johnnie Bea.

'I need you to help this young lady.' He told her. 'She is smart as in intelligent she simply needs someone to guide her.' He said taking the bowl of beans she handed him.

'Looks to me like you doing that quite well boy.' Mrs. Johnnie Bea said still handing out food to those waiting.

'T.' he called her. Her smile got bigger. An old man in baggy clothes way too big for him came up and interrupted their conversation. He carried an awful odor about himself."

"It was Little Willie. I can still smell that vile odor. To this day, I cannot figure out how Mrs. Johnnie Bea got that man to bathe. After he returned from visiting her, he became a different person about everything." Elizabeth said as they all looked out of the patio window at him clothed so nicely working around in the garden he had planted for Mrs. Johnnie Bea.

'Mrs. Johnnie Bea' he said to her when he walked up to get his meal, 'the best thing you did for us is to start the Saturday and Sunday food program. Sometimes I would get up too hungry to start the day now I'm getting up on my way here every Saturday and Sunday morning getting a hot meal. God's gonna' bless you.'

'God's already blessing me. You see this boy standing here he's my hard-headed nephew. I raised him to be somebody. Now he is here helping someone to be somebody. That is the village's way of doing things to help our community grow. You go out now and help someone.'

'Now, Mrs. Johnnie Bea look at me, how can I help someone?' 'You breathing ain't you Little Willie?' 'Yeah, but look at me.'

'I see you and others will see you too. Maybe there is someone under some bridge or lying on some doorstep needing a bit to eat. You go tell them where they can find food so God can bless you some more. My Oprah, some people just don't think.'

'You're right Mrs. Johnnie Bea there is lots of people out there needing your bowl of beans. Let me go right now. I want God to bless me a whole lot more.'

"That soul was lost," Chili said.

"I bet he brought everyone back he found. Probably wasn't enough food to go around many homeless out-of-work people we got in this city." Rosie said.

"She will never finish if you girls keep talking," Teresa said. The living room became quiet again.

"Mrs. Johnnie Bea scared me at first. Her directness intimidated me in the way people say white women are intimidated by strong black women they encounter."

"Those white women..."

"Chili, let her finish please," said Susie

"I promise so long as you promise not to put that gum back in your mouth." Susie smiled sighing as if to say fine.

"Mylo said when he was six years old just starting school Mrs. Johnnie Bea sent him off to school a block away from where they lived.

A car drove up beside him, and inside were several black teenage boys talking to him about using his backpack to take their drugs to distribute similar to what Hot Pepper had Chili doing. At the time he said he did not know how to handle the situation.

'Boys, why are you stopping my nephew.' He said it was Mrs. Johnnie Bea. She walked up to them. 'Look over there.' He said she pointed to the white policemen in the police car across the street watching them. 'They see what you are doing but they don't care. Back in 1954, President Eisenhower had troops come to the South to make sure six black boys and girls got into a white school. Those policemen sitting over there in that police car have the same mindset as those policemen back then. They know what you boys are trying to get my nephew to do. But you notice they are not doing anything to make sure my little six-year-old nephew gets to school safely. They don't care about him or you boys. If they did, they would be making sure you poor rascals were in school getting some learning so you wouldn't end up in prison or dead. I don't understand my people.'

'What don't you understand?' Mylo said one of them asked her.

'Our leaders' she told them should be demanding the same thing now as they demanded back in the 60s.' Mylo said one of the boys asked her what she was talking about. Every colored person in our country,' she told him should be marching demanding that all little children be able to walk to school safely not just white children.'

"He said they never bothered him again but just as Mrs. Johnnie Bea predicted in a few years they were all dead.

"I bet it didn't even make front page news" Elsie said.

"Girl it was probably barely in the obituaries," Susie said.

"Mrs. Johnnie helped Dwayne get my life back on track. A couple of years later he and I married."

"What about your parents? Did you ever see them again?" Shenee' asked

"Mrs. Johnnie Bea would have it no other way. She said you never leave a door closed. I never realized that my running away would affect their lives so drastically. They stopped their work. My father said they had detectives looking for me.

"Even Aunt Mary learned a valuable lesson from it all.

"You have got to be kidding your racist white aunt no longer thought of you as the house pet?" Chili asked causing Elizabeth to rise in her seat and say to her.

"My dear child Auntie Mary could have been black and I don't think she would have thought any different had the child has been white." Chili placed a thoughtful look on her face and said, "You know come to think of it you are probably right Elizabeth after all as Mrs. Johnnie Bea says except for race there is very little difference in our thinking is there?" They both smiled at the other as La-Joyce continued her life story.

"She asked that I forgive her stating she had loved me always, her love was, she admitted 'clouded by her senseless racist attitude.'

"My parents told me my birth certificate first read that I was born La-Joyce Kenny. It was my grandfather's last name. My parents later gave me their last name 'Jordan'. My drug-addicted mother brought me to my grandfather after leaving the hospital with me."

"If the hospital administrators knew your mother was a drug addict, why did they allow her to keep you?"

"Chili!" Teresa said quiet but stern.

"Well, I was just asking."

"My grandfather worked as a gardener for my mother and father.

"You still call them mother and father."

"Chili come on now they are the only parents she has ever known. Why wouldn't she still think of them as her parents?" Susie said an annoyed look on her face.

"I guess you're right. Sorry girlfriend. Like Little old Willie, I wasn't thinking." They all laughed

"He was caring for me in the one-room studio where he lived on their property. My mother told me that she thought she heard a baby crying when their chauffeur drove up to their estate. The studio where my grandfather lived stood near the road where they had to go to get their...".

"My Lord you sound so white."

"Chili that was rude. You know Mrs. Johnnie Bea would not like you saying that to La-Joyce."

"La-Joyce you know I love you baby. You know come to think of it I never thought about how much I sound like poor whites." A weak smile formed on her face as she gave in to the frowns staring back at her.

"La-Joyce we have to love Chili as she too belongs to Jesus Lord help her, please. Continue La-Joyce." Susie said.

"Mother said she drove back along the area where she thought she first heard me crying. When she got closer, she again heard a crying infant. My grandfather explained to her that his daughter had dropped me off. When he produced the drug-addicted baby who could not stop crying my mother said she lifted me from his arms cuddled me a moment and found that I was feverish. I was in the hospital within minutes. My drug addiction was quickly diagnosed.

After months of Mom and Dad traveling down to his cottage to look after me, my grandfather asked if they wanted to keep me for their own. He was getting too old and didn't want to die and leave me without proper handling by someone who had no love for me. My mother after bringing me to my grandfather never returned. He died before I knew him.

My adoptive parents were anthropologists and both were born into privileged and extremely wealthy families. My life started so different from the life of many other people in my race here in America. They say ignorance is bliss. I say that being stripped of one's ignorance can be a horrible nightmare. Up until age sixteen, my life was sheer happiness.

One night shortly after my sixteenth birthday, my father had guests over. It happened while they were discussing some matters my father had to leave the room for whatever reason I cannot remember. I walked into the room to get something I had left there. One of the men began speaking Japanese to the other.

He said 'I see the Jordans still have that black child living with them. I am surprised they have not introduced her to what her world is like in the ghettos of Harlem.'

"The other commented. 'She is a lovely black thing it is a pity her hair is so tight and unbecoming of what the men in her race like. It will be hard for them to find a man who will want her even from her race of men.'

'They are mistaken when they refuse to allow her public schooling at least that way she would learn to understand better the world of her people.'

"What world is this you speak of gentlemen?" I asked startling them with my acknowledgment of the language they spoke."

"Boy you fronted their game," Chili said.

"They apologized to me and father. He asked what had been said. They gestured and left quickly. I was in tears by then.

I couldn't stop crying. When I finally told my parents what had been said they simply thought of me as their black thing. They, of course, said that the men were being cruel and that there were cruel people in the world like them. They had tried to protect me from it. After that, I began insisting they allow me to attend public school in an area that taught children of my race."

"That was a mistake girlfriend," Chili said. Teresa attempted to intercede.

"No Teresa, Chili is right it was the biggest mistake I could have possibly made."

"As dark as she is, with hair tight as hers, and she's acting proud of it, I'm surprised the blacks didn't laugh her out of school."

"Chili!" Susie said.

"No, she is telling you the truth. It was only after I left my parents that I was made aware of my history as a black female in the United States; however, I learned through the harassment and cruel treatment from blacks I came in contact with at school what the men had said in the room that night though harsh, was true. The kids had no understanding for a girl as dark as I am speaking what they called white people's language. Nor...talking white is what they called it.

They had no understanding of my pride in wearing my hair like I was born. It was brushed shampooed, conditioned, and shaped but it was not relaxed with chemicals to look like the white girls and I was much too dark to be thought of as pretty by the black boys attending school there. The only thing I brought into their environment that they envied me for was my intelligence. I was home-taught by my parents. My studies were so advanced that when I entered public school for the first time it was like starting at kindergarten level even some teachers felt intimidated by my advanced knowledge of the school work in their curriculums.

Yet I was a kindergartener when it came to understanding the real American World that exists in this country for the people of the race that I am. People who have a history the same as mine taught me to hate my dark skin and hair texture. It wasn't until I met Mylo that I realized I could love all of me. He made me understand there was something about me that was special when it came to my skin color and hair texture." The women moved in closer and Chili interrupted her asking:

"What did Mylo tell you that made you realize your beauty?"

"I'm not as dark as you and no one has ever told me my color or hair for that matter when it is washed and its natural state is beautiful, especially no black brother," Rosie said agreeing with Chili. "So, I need to hear what he had to say."

"Oh, Rosie let her finish," Elsie said shaking her head.

"Rosie come on you know you are beautiful," said Shenee'. Rosie looked at her and rolled her eyes saying in a not-so-pleasant tone:

"Girlfriend, no disrespect but your hair is what the brothers think our black women's hair should look like not to mention your color."

"Rosie, are you hating on Shenee' or what?" Elsie asked giving her a stern look.

"No, Elsie' I'm not hating I'm just saying that's all."

"Rosie being dark in this country is not beautiful at least it was not for me until Mylo told me that every time he looked at me he saw what he as a black man could produce. His sperm produced dark skin and a natural tight hair texture.

'Your hair and your black skin must be beautiful to me' he said because only from my sperm can the texture of your hair and color of your body be formed, he said touching my face as he moved his hand over my hair that was at that time worn natural.

"If we ever have a daughter, we will teach her love for her black body and make sure she understands that if the person wanting her does not treasure the gifts that produced her, they cannot love her. My son will learn from his father while he may love anyone he chooses to love, his love for himself comes first from the pride of loving what his body produces."

"Not all men in our race think what their bodies produce is unlovable when it comes to a female of their race as dark as me. I believed Mylo when he said that because whether you know it or not even the homeless men out there on the streets with nowhere to lay their heads displayed loving values for their women many professional men with money lack. I listened with happiness in my heart as Mrs. Johnnie Bea told me.

'I knew there was some good in you child for Mylo to take an interest in you. My Oprah and I will take care of you until you can get back to those parents looking for you."

"I don't want them back," I told her at the time I was finally able to discuss them with her. She just smiled and said,

'We'll talk on it. I wouldn't want to send you back to people who would mistreat you child. Some rich people are just as awful to their kids as some poor ones are.' She told me.

"She found out they did love me before she told them where I could be found.

"My parents are just as excited as we are about our coming event," La-Joyce said pointing at her swollen stomach. Mother is at my home doting over me all the time when I'm not visiting with her. It is that way with mother and daughter. It took a lot but I learned that what Mrs. Johnnie Bea said was true."

"What was that? Teresa asked.

"Real parents are about loving what God gives them. It is a man who had to put race in the equation."

"I love that Mrs. Johnnie Bea and her Oprah cause those five children of Rosie is a blessing to me and I am not their biological Aunt. La Joyce loves her parents. They are the only parents she knows. Chili it doesn't matter what color your child is or who it was born to, as Mrs. Johnnie Bea who has no biological children would say. It is who loves them, Teresa said.

La Joyce, it is a blessing that you have white parents who love you and who you love." "Mrs. Johnnie Bea should be arriving soon I want to be outside waiting," Elizabeth said rising from her seat. Everyone agreed as they smiled and nodded their heads her way.

"They are driving up now ladies," Elizabeth said.

"We finished just in time to welcome Mrs. Johnnie Bea home," Teresa said walking towards the door.

Chapter Fifteen

*I*t had been a long day for Mrs. Johnnie Bea. All those tests the doctor insisted that had to be done before releasing her. She suffered through them, leaving no reason for the young doctor to delay her release insisting she stay another day. She did not want to see another hospital for a long time to come, she thought to herself looking around the room that had been her home for the last month. Though she did not want to spend another second there more than was necessary she let tears ease down her cheek.

Her thoughts were on the visitors that had darkened her door warming her heart when they entered her room. Most shared problems she had no way of solving. The advice she gave she had no way of knowing how it would work for them except that it was advice she had given most of her life to those she loved.

More tears fell as Mrs. Johnnie Bea walked around the room with her cane to aid her. She looked at the pink crocheted blanket Elizabeth had made for her she would be taking home with her. In her mind's eye, she could see Elisabeth seated over on the big cushioned lounge chair crocheting some days, embroidering along with her on other days. Many days they hand quilted together on one piece Elizabeth had brought in for her to take a look at.

The talks they had filled hundreds of would-be empty hours when she came to visit bringing news of the Village and 'The Safe Place' and how they had expanded under the care of her ladies as Elizabeth called them and her nephews who came to oversee matters from time to time. Mrs. Johnnie Bea looked at God's miracle and thought what a blessing it had been to learn her lessons in love. It was as if she had fallen into a pit and found gold lying inside. Who would have guessed she and Elizabeth could become close friends? When all the poverty and riches were removed God in his wisdom had allowed them to see inside each other's hearts, Mrs. Johnnie Bea thought to herself.

She thanked God for the treasures she never would have been privileged to have if Big Tom had not scared La-Joyce and she hadn't mistakenly taken him out the front door.

When Dwayne and Mylo walked into her room Mrs. Johnnie Bea was seated in that wheelchair she had hated. The head nurse insisted however that it was their rule. She must use a wheelchair to leave the hospital. Some policies could not be broken. Her nephews kissed her cheeks.

"Let's go Boys I don't want to lose my religion up here with them trying to keep me any longer. I miss my home and I need to see about my cat."

A black Escalade pulled up outside the entrance of the hospital. Mylo placed Mrs. Johnnie Bea's cane inside. Dwayne helped Mrs. Johnnie Bea inside. She scooted over behind the driver's seat. When Mylo pulled off Mrs. Johnnie Bea leaned over looked out the window and spoke.

"Thank the Lord I am finally out of that place."

"I hope you don't fall those steps again," Dwayne said smiling over at his aunt.

"Mylo, I thought I told you and Dwayne to have those steps fixed before I got back home. Are they fixed?" Mrs. Johnnie Bea asked a frown starting on her face."

"I forgot T but I will get on it first thing in the morning after all you've got me and Dwayne to help you inside the house and you won't be coming out for a while," Mylo said smiling in his review mirror they had driven off.

"I don't know what kind of kids folks are raising these days can't remember a thing they're told to do. And what do you mean I won't be coming out for a while? I'm going down to 'The Safe Place' first thing in the morning. You make sure you boys come and pick me up.

"Yes ma'am" they both answered in unison.

241

"What kind of automobile is this, Dwayne?"

"It is an Escalade T," Dwayne answered

"Escalade, it looks more like a house inside here. When did they start making TVs inside cars? Mylo are you sure Dwayne is in a legal business singing is one thing but can it support an automobile like this?"

"T your young rapping nephew is driving a Cadillac SUV Escalade because famous hip-hop singers like him make that kind of money."

"As long as it is legal I'm down with it as my children at The Safe Place say." Mrs. Johnnie Bea said as she looked around in the SUV shaking her head all the while smiling.

"Dwayne, I hope you're not singing songs that smite women folk with degrading names. You know how I feel about white folks hearing our boys singing like that about our women and don't tell me no different that it's about all women because I know better."

"They don't feel their women are in that category. They are on the same pedestal they were on before white men were forced to share them with you black boys Now if you want to degrade your women that is on you. Do you understand what T is telling you?" Mrs. Johnnie Bea asked taping Dwayne on the back of the head with the knuckle of her forefinger.

"I do understand T and I don't do it, not anymore I don't"

"My Oprah I tried my best to raise you boys to have some principles, integrity, and Lord have mercy, some common sense.

"Mylo, La-Joyce is about due to deliver that baby, isn't she?"

"Anytime soon, I should be holding my son in my arms."

"Dwayne we'll have to get you married off soon. It's not good to tie yourself up with loose women too long. You run around having free sex for years and by the time you marry you have used up all your energy. In a year, you can't serve your wife properly." Laughter filled the car.

"T now you know I know better Mylo, how many times did we have to watch Oprah in 'Brewster Street'?"

"I think we watched it and 'The Color Purple' about a hundred times while T explained to us the pain and suffering of black women and the respect they deserve."

"That's right you should treat any woman with respect but most surely your kind boys didn't I teach you anything that stuck."

"White women too T. After all it was a white woman who caused Oprah to have to stay in that prison hole for seven years, I think it was," Mylo said.

"And didn't she take her to visit her family and then make her leave her family and drive back home with her? Oprah looked like hell. Even I felt her pain being a woman of my race done that cruelly. It said a lot about the white people living back then. Nothing was as profound in the telling of our history as her face T." Dwayne said grasping hands with Mylo.

"All those years down in that hole may have ruined her body but God kept her soul as good as it was the day she went in." Mrs. Johnnie Bea said to her nephews right quick.

"It would have helped if God had taken a little mercy on her face T, He allowed us to see the depth of the hell she must have endured," Dwayne said shaking his head as he looked over at Mylo seated beside him looking sadly back as his aunt.

"Hush your mouth boy the movie symbolized more than just looks. Oprah symbolized our women and their tragic past. Any woman should be respected no matter what her race. When you see she doesn't want respect leave her and find one who does. Don't tell me Mylo you have forgotten the five rules I taught you and Dwayne to see if the woman is right for you."

"Yes T!" They echoed to each other.

"Well, what are they?"

"Take her to a daycare and see how she acts around children." They both said in unison. "Take her to a place where they serve food for the homeless and see how she acts around people less fortunate than she is. Take her to a place where men congregate to see how she acts around other men." They said smiling as they looked quickly at each other. Go meet her people to see who brought her up.

"Now what is the most important one I taught you, boys? I see neither of you mentioned that one."

"Which one is that T.?" Mylo asked.

"No sex before Marriage," said Mrs. Johnnie Bea causing her nephews to laugh so hard she had to join their laughter. Saying to them:

"Didn't I just tell you if you use yourselves up on loose women you will soon, and I mean soon be worn out before you are thirty? Now mind what T has told you. I don't know how many women come to me telling me their men can't do a thing. It's because they wore themselves out too early in life." Mylo and Dwayne continued to laugh so hard Mrs. Johnnie Bea had to stop and say, "You better shut up and keep your eyes on this road before you run us into something. You know T is telling you right," She said causing them to laugh even harder.

Dwayne slowed the Escalade down. Mrs. Johnnie Bea looked out at the home she had left. As Dwayne drove them closer, she looked at the small stone structure much like the one in Elizabeth's yard that she had admired. Her lawn had been manicured with flowers blooming around the edge of a circular walkway. Her eyes stretched when she saw Elizabeth standing in the yard wearing her gardening gloves as she called them cutting at some roses that must have been transplanted."

"Boys get T's cane and help me out of this bus so I can see if I'm still in bed at the hospital dreaming."

"You aren't dreaming T," said Mylo echoed by Dawyne who opened the door of his escalade to help her down from it. "We decided to be Oprah and let you know how much we all love you. Both Mylo and Dwayne kissed each side of her cheeks as she descended from the escalade with their help.

"Mrs. Johnnie Bea, we thought we would surprise you." Elizabeth said as Shenee,' Chili, La-Joyce, Susie, Elsie, Rosie, and Teresa hurried out of the front and down the stairs walkway reaching her. Hearing the shouts of kids running from the back of the house Mrs. Johnnie Bea would have fallen over had not her nephews held on to her. The kids were all over her hugging and holding on.

"Let Mrs. Johnnie Bea go so she can come into the house," Rosie said pulling the children from around Mrs. Johnnie Bea's waist.

Mrs. Johnnie Bea stood with the cane and the help of her nephews, looking out at the beautifully manicured lawn with the array of flowers surrounding the winding bluestone pathway to the front door of her brand-new-looking house.

"My Lord it is beautiful. Mr. Taylor would be beside himself with joy at seeing his lawn all pretty like this. I kept saying I was going to do something but it would have never been anything like what I'm looking at. Mrs. Johnnie Bea moved with her cane and the help of her nephews along the walkway to the backyard.

"My Oprah ain't this something. I always wanted a patio like this. I saw it once in a Ladies' Home Journal Magazine, makes a body want to cry. This must be my nephew bringing this fat man in my yard. Mrs. Johnnie Bea said of the statue of the fat man in his work pants standing with his hands held out as water sprouted from them out from the garden onto the lawn when he turned a certain way.

"It was me, Mrs. Johnnie Bea. I talked Elizabeth into getting it. Saw it in the window of one of those antique places."

"You did Little Willie? Lord if this doesn't beat all a garden with collard greens and tomatoes. Hey, what's that on top of that statue's head? I believe that is big Tom," Mrs. Johnnie Bea said hobbling over with the help of her nephews she took the cat in her arms and hugged him. When she released him, he jumped back on the statue meowing.

After circling the house Mrs. Johnnie Bea was led to the front door of her home. A long banner hanging across the living room read "My Oprah, it is good to have you, home."

The very next thing Mrs. Johnnie Bea noticed was the sign that read 'Take Off Your Shoes.'

"Boys you see my white carpet take off my shoes and then you Mylo and Dwayne take off yours. God is so good. He can turn vinegar into wine. Look at this living room right out of the Ladies Home Journal. He may not come when you want him but he is always right on time. Thank you, Lord Jesus." Tears began to fall from Mrs. Johnnie Bea's eyes as she went from room to room looking at her dream home she had tucked away in a drawer.

"What would Mr. Taylor think of this place now? My Oprah" she said grabbing Elsie and hugging her, then Teresa, from Teresa she grabbed Susie, and from Susie to Chili, to Elizabeth, then Shenee' kissed her cheeks as the tears fell hard and fast. Lajoyce smiled as Mrs. Johnnie Bea touched her stomach and then grabbed her into her arms. When

Mrs. Johnnie Bea pulled the last of her girls into her arms Rosie fell in them crying as hard as she was.

"Mrs. Johnnie Bea," said Elsie placing the Ladies' Home Journal in her hands saying "You, Teresa and I love looking through the Ladies' Home Journal, and your eyes have always come back to these pages. Look around you. We did a good job on this place. Now it is what you have always dreamed of having. Mrs. Johnnie Bea pushed passed everyone allowing her cane to step first."

"My Oprah, will you look at this! Lord Jesus. Look at this new kitchen, an island just like the one in my picture. Oh my God, everything came right out of that magazine. I love it. A new stove without a stick, My Oprah, Lord you may not come when I want you but you are right on time again."

"That's how God works children some suffering is for a reason." Mrs. Johnnie Bea said looking from room to room. When she walked into what was once her sewing room, she looked at all the pictures on the wall saying "My Oprah" over and over again as she touched first, the large picture of Oprah, her picture, and that of Mahalia then all of the pictures around the wall Her mouth stood open when she turned seeing the Sixty-inch flat-screen TV.

"Mrs. Johnnie Bea now you can see Oprah just like you are at the movies. Susie said.

"Take a seat on your new couch and see what's playing," Teresa told her.

"Lord, have mercy I know I am going to have to buy some plastic to cover this couch." Tears abated as the ladies looked at Chili and broke out in laughter.

"Mrs. Johnnie Bea. I hope you are enjoying all the fruits of your labor about now." It was Elizabeth on the big screen TV.

"We wanted you to experience the happiness you have given us," Elizabeth said as she stooped over and cut a rose then blew off the petals allowing each to flow in the air. Elizabeth wiped away a tear saying. "We have soared to high places together in one room becoming one in spirit."

You have given me so much Mrs. Johnnie Bea. Money is something I have too much of but like you told me once. It cannot buy the one thing that is free but hard to find. That is a connective relationship with another human being who cares about you just because you are you. A friend who will cry when you cry laugh with you, and be there when you need a friend to call on. Oh, by the way, I did appreciate you telling me I needed to teach my grandson how to love someone other than himself and the toys I can buy him.

I took away that precious Jaguar of his and placed his trip to Europe on hold until he spent a month volunteering at The Safe Place with the children. He eventually began to ask to return. I even made him do a stretch in the Village dishing out food to the homeless something he did not enjoy but he did it. And as you would say my friend, that is what life is all about isn't it? Thank you for teaching me the value of love of true friendship. Ours will last a lifetime." When the scene ended, Mrs. Johnnie Bea reached over and hugged Elizabeth as they prepared to watch what was coming next. Susie flipped to the next scene Mrs. Johnnie Bea stretched her head forward.

"Elisabeth is right Mrs. Johnnie Bea."

"I know that is not little Willie all dressed up." Mrs. Johnnie Bea said looking closer at the TV screen after placing her glasses on.

"I used to dress like this. Years ago, when I owned a chain of Barbecue restaurants. I was a well-to-do man. Because I believed everyone should be taken, I grew to have no feelings at all for anyone. I treated my employees with such disrespect they hated me. They started to undermine all my business deals. One day I just stopped feeling anything. I walked away from the kind of person I had become and life itself.

You made me want to be someone again with your kind and generous ways. I'll never allow myself to get caught up in taking again without giving back. I plan to go find a need and do something about it. I guess that bath up at that hospital helped some too, you know," Little Willie said scratching his head as Mrs. Johnnie Bea shook her head at the new haircut and trimmed beard he was sporting. "You know what I mean." Little Willie said waving from the screen. Willie gladly accepted Mrs. Johnnie Bea's outstretched arms as he smiled walking over to get his hug.

"By now you are here enjoying the gifts from the seeds you have sowed," Susie said speaking from the screen on the TV. "I want to thank you for all the blessings you have caused to come into my life. I don't know whether or not you remember but when I first came to you and told you God had placed in my spirit that I needed to work with the girls I was rebellious having worked with the boys so long. You smiled and told me you didn't want me to be like Jonah and have to be spit out of the belly of the whale. You gave me Yolanda Adam's CD called Victory and told me to begin playing it when I start working with the girls. I told you all the girls were interested in was rap and hip hop. You told me to play it anyway. Mrs. Johnnie Bea not long after I began playing that CD the girls stood in their windows at bedtime and asked me to continue playing Yolanda they loved her songs so much. Each had a different song that soothed them and each would ask if I would play it. Soon my girls became flowers blooming as their behavior improved.

One night while driving with my daughter she turned the radio on. A listener came over the air and made a dedication to the detention staff Mrs. Susie who had helped her while she was in detention. It shocked me so. It was called I Believe I Can Fly. Shaharra kept saying over and over 'Mom, they love you. I can't believe a girl in juvy would be dedicating a song to my mother I am so proud of you.'

Mrs. Johnnie Bea. even though you have had no biological children you have been blessed to parent so many. You have proven that mothering is a genetic part of the female makeup that comes to her at birth not when she gives birth. Thank you for placing who you believe Oprah represents in all of our hearts so that our love can flow out to others." Susie smiled and held up the CD of Yolanda Adams she had played over and over for the girls in the juvenile detention center. Susie fell into Mrs. Johnnie Bea's arms weeping with happiness.

"Mrs. Johnnie Bea," said Shenee' in the next scene as she extended her hand holding a shirt she turned to show the people behind her all wearing purple Tiki torches and white sweats suits designed the same as the one she wore and held. They stood with their back to those watching *"In Recreating the Legacy"* was written on the back of their sweatshirts. When they turned to face the camera *"My Oprah" was printed over the*

*picture of the Tiki torch its flame burning on the front of the sweatshirt.
Each of the forty women held a similar torch as Shenee' El*sie, Susie, Rosie,
La-Joyce, Chili, and Teresa stood waving along with the rest. "We
gave you a promise that we would do something to make a difference,"
Shenee' said turning again to face those behind her. There are forty of
us women from many different races all willing to carry the Torch with
you. We have been working on coming together in a summit where
we spend seven days talking and connecting our views just as you did
with the seven women you brought together to create your village. after
we learned it was not Oprah's life you hoped to change but ours you
wanted to guide so that we could carry the torch for you we are working
to make that happen.

We will not be able to change the entire world. We can, however,
work together creating villages where prejudice, hate, and violence will
not abide. Our goal is to help those less fortunate and of course, those
who have money but pain and suffering that money can't ease. You
taught us well. It is time you enjoy the fruits from the seeds of your
labor." Shenee' smiled and kissed Mrs. Johnnie Bea's cheek as their tears
intermingled.

In the next scene, Mylo and Dwayne stood smiling with similar
sweats on. Behind them were forty smiling men.

"T these are the husbands and boyfriends of the ladies you saw in
the previous scene. We cannot let the women leave us behind." Mylo
said. Both Susie and Shenee' spoke our hearts. You always taught us if
we put a spoon to our mouths and look around and see someone who
is sitting with an empty plate we have to share our blessings. We have
shared the beans we grew up on many times over and as you can see
our bounties have been plentiful. You minimized the pain of losing our
parents with love, kindness, and strict switches that came swiftly if your
rules were not followed."

"And of course, after the switches were thoroughly applied along
hour speech on why they were necessary," Dwayne said. "Then came the
kisses and hugs that made us ashamed of our misdeeds. You never knew
it but Uncle Taylor told us it was he who couldn't give you children but
you loved him anyway just like you loved two little orphan boys. He

said he didn't mind when people called him Mr. Johnnie Bea because you and him were the same, what's in a name anyway?"

"For us," Mylo said, "the most memorable time was when we came home from fishing with Uncle and you made us clean all the fish. For the ones we didn't keep you had us bag them and take them around the neighborhood to elderly people you knew. When they offered us money you allowed us to take it saying that we had a right to pay for our work.

Remember Mrs. Turner would only give a nickel and you smiled and said it was the widow's mite. You were teaching us to help even when the rewards didn't seem what they should be because the need to help was more important. It helped us to learn humility and kindness for those less fortunate and the elderly realizing one day as you always used to tell us old age will either shine or rain down on us. Thank you for being that kind of parent. If you are crying about now don't wipe them away let them flow. To us, they represent the stream of love given and now returned. We love you and respect your father's dream that lives in you as his legacy to the world." The scene ended. Mrs. Johnnie Bea looked down rubbing her fingers on the soft velvet couch saying to no one in particular

"I'm going tomorrow and find me some plastic." Laughter filled the room.

It was time, Elsie told them, for dinner which would be served on the long extended patio where the children and adults could enjoy Mrs. Johnnie Bea's home coming together.

Epilogue

*T*oo much had taken place. Too many blessings had come to Mrs. Johnnie Bea, far outreaching any dreams she was capable of dreaming even though, she had encouraged so many others to dream that seemingly unattainable dream. Now the one thing she had prayed would not happen, happened to her with no way of stopping it. Mrs. Johnnie Bea found herself back in the hospital seated beside a hospital bed about to witness for the first time in her life, childbirth. When La-Joyce who opted to have a natural birth screamed out as her baby slipped from her body. Mrs. Johnnie Bea saw God's creation unfold before her eyes. When they cleaned and gave La-Joyce her son she smiled at her parents and gave their son to his father. Mylo turned and handed the baby to Mrs. Johnnie Bea who looked upon the tiny infant and then at her nephew saying to him,

"It is not the gift of wealth that makes a man immortal but the seed of his groin that leaves its mark upon the earth like an acorn that falls from a tree. If the acorn withers and dies from like of attention and care the man's legacy dies. If, however, the man attends the duties of caring for his seed nourishing it to grow strong and mighty his legacy shall live long after his years upon the earth. Through this baby, your legacy shall follow your lifeline for generations to come." Mrs. Johnnie Bea gave the baby to Lajoyce's mother who gave him to her husband. They all smiled at the little bundle they would all enjoy.

When Mrs. Johnnie Bea finally arrived home from the hospital, she looked out her bedroom window into the starlit night to see her father's

smiling face as his voice whispered, *"Ole Breeze I am not the minority they say I am. I am what I remember I am and that is a descendent of Kings and Queens, and free men as well as slaves. I am part of the universe. Yes, Ole Breeze, remind me I am a part of the wind, the rain, Ole Breeze, I am one of the heavenly bodies that not only shines at night but one of the heavenly bodies that has been shining for an eternity.*

Who I am has never changed. At this moment I am a human on this planet yet my presence is as eternal as yours. Thanks, Ole Breeze, for reminding me that it is only when I forget to remember who I am that I become what others say I am."

Mrs. Johnnie Bea lay under her pink crocheted blanket given to her by Elizabeth and the new beige satin covers of her new bed smiling down at big Tom who lay at her feet, "My Oprah, what a day we've had." She said to Big Tom at the foot of her bed a smile on her face. My loved ones are carrying the torch just as my father would have wanted it to be carried. What a journey this has been for me." Mrs. Johnnie Bea said as her eyes closed. She fell asleep the rest of the night. Thinking of waking up the next day to see Oprah at four O'clock on her brand-new 60-inch flat-screen TV.

When I finished the challenge of writing My Oprah in Creating the Legacy and handed the manuscript to my daughter to review her words were,

"You wrote it not just about Oprah but all of us as humans on this earth showing the good in our flawed selves no matter who we are or what may befall us. In the end, it will be up to each of us to confront the obstacles that may block our path to obtaining our goals. Building better communities for everyone to live safely in was the legacy Mrs. Johnnie Bea's father wanted his daughter to carry on. Mrs. Johnnie Bea used Oprah's life to say though the struggle is hard it can be done.

Helen J. Collier {author}

Printed in the United States
by Baker & Taylor Publisher Services